The Watcher Tower

The Descendants of Light Series

BOOK TWO

TROY HOOKER

COVER DESIGN BY
Diren Yardimli
COVER ILLUSTRATION BY
Rosauro Ugang
ILLUSTRATIONS BY
Stacy Hooker and Emily Anderson
EDITING BY
Jeannie Wilson and Dawn Carter

Descendant Publishing, LLC

The Watcher Tower, The Descendants of Light Series,
or any portion thereof may not be reproduced or used in any
manner whatsoever without the express written permission
of the publisher except for the use of brief quotations in a book review.

Printed in the United States of America.

Cover Design By Diren Yardimli
Cover Illustration By Rosauro Ugang
Interior Design and Illustrations By Stacy Hooker
Map Illustration By Emily Anderson
Editing By Jeannie Wilson and Dawn Carter

First Printing, United States of America, January 2020

Library of Congress Control Number: 2020900719

ISBN 978-1-7344584-0-4 (Softcover)

Descendant Publishing, LLC
PO Box 29
Byron Center, MI 49315

www.descendantpublishing.com

3 5 7 9 10 8 6 4 2

To the staff, colleagues, and administrators, thank you for the years of friendship and guidance you offered during my time at EDCS.

To my students, thank you for making teaching a consuming, yet rewarding occupation. Your candid honesty and wild inspiration will forever leave an imprint on my life.

MEDARAN
CITY
REGION OF TELOK
ANCIENT LAKE
LION PLAINS
MARIPOTH RIVER
REGION OF NAIS
FOREST OF MARIPOTH
SAINIA CITY
DARK
REGION OF THALO
WORM SPRINGS
CLEAR LAKE VILLAGE
CLEAR LAKE
LAND OF GIANTS
LION CITY
NORTHROPI VALLEY
SAND LAKE
AGAM MOUNTAINS
SHIMSHON MOUNTAINS
JESTERS PASS
SEA OF YARFEY
SAND CREEK
MT HALPA
ANORI FOREST
LAZULI POOLS
DEEP CITY
KARIN LAKE
OLDHOR
CEMBRO CITY
HELL MOLOCH
GREAT SWAMP
OUTER DUNES
KARIN RIVER
REGION OF THEMANE
MERKUST HIGHLANDS
OUTER DUNES

SHEBA HALOTH
LAKE
MOUNT TANNIN
SEA OF YAHM
SADAK MOUNTAINS
WATCHER TOWER
MOUNT MORSHIKA
ANEY DESERT
RAUCH LAKE
MAYET SAL
N
W
E
S

Chapter One
Dark Watchers

The summer heat was already winding down in anticipation of an especially long winter in White Pine. Sam stared at the giant marshmallow-like clouds drifting lazily above him, certain they hadn't moved but an inch in the last hour.

It was mid-July, and the sun had given up its angry heat for the day, submitting to a soft cool breeze that rippled through the field next to the abandoned town. The four youths spent the day exploring the ruins of a once thriving copper center turned ghost town, inspecting the remains of storefronts and residences that used to be the pinnacle of town life on the edge of a mining boom in rural northern Michigan.

As the day wound down, however, the four had given up finding any more items of interest, having already collected quite the treasure chest of seventeenth century medicine bottles, copper mugs, and a partially intact map of the town framed and hidden underneath an old potbelly stove.

In the tall grass lay a slender girl with strawberry-red hair, motionless except for the soft rise and fall of her chest in the afternoon sun. In the grass next to her, Sam contemplated for the thousandth time the reasons she would like him.

Only feet away but still out of sight from the two camouflaged in the tall clumps of grass stood two more youths—one thicker boy with glasses and a pale face. The other was a petite Asian girl with shoulder-length silky black hair named Lillia.

Gus planted his feet on the dusty ground in front of the abandoned prospector's office, holding his hands outstretched in front of him. His shadow cast a long dark disfigured outline of himself on the building's rotting exterior. He closed his eyes, stretched his palms toward the building, and waited.

"Seriously Gus, concentrate. Get your head out of the snack cake and focus," Lillia scoffed playfully.

Gus concentrated, trying not to think of the bead of sweat that was trickling lazily down the side of his round cheek. Sam and Emma sat up quietly to watch him through the small opening in the scorched summer grass.

For what seemed an eternity, Gus stared at the wall in front of him, expecting something to happen. At last, a tiny blue spark fizzled from his palms and lit the grass on fire at his feet.

He lowered his arms, still staring at the untouched building. "I just can't seem to get it."

Lillia stomped the fire out in the grass. "Really, Gus, you are hopeless."

Sam laid his head on the grass. Gus had been trying the same thing all summer—to produce a bolt of Light. He hadn't had so much as a hint of success, except for the same sputter of Light that would spit out of his palm for a moment and then disappear. After which, of course, he would mope for the rest of the day.

The summer had been wonderful overall. They had spent the good weather days exploring the better part of the Porcupine Mountains that rose skyward near White Pine, and on the rainy days they spent untold hours in Chivler's Bookstore, riffling through old dusty books

about any subject related to the history of Lior, Julian Lawrence, or the Watchers.

Chivler would often allow them to remain after the store closed to listen to Gus read from by the light of the fireplace in the back of the old building. Sometimes Sam would take notes in his journal if he found the information relevant, but most times he would sink into the old leather chair and allow the words to swim around his head while he listened.

They had learned much, but it hadn't been easy because of the lack of information available on the Creation side. Descendants were truly secretive people, not for their own benefit, but for humankind. After the great Watcher Battle and the migration into Lior, the first Descendants had made a covenant to keep their way of life a secret from the outside. They hid their gifts from the world and kept written documents within the realm of Lior.

It surprised Sam that Mr. Sterling allowed anyone near Chivler's because of the Dark gate. Oddly, Mr. Sterling believed it best not to draw attention to the fact they might know where it was, and therefore encouraged them to be there. As long as they kept a wary eye, of course.

According to Gus, though the Dark creatures could now sense the open gate, its exact location would be difficult to locate for anyone who wasn't privy to the information. Anyone looking for it would need to do some digging, either through research—or extracting the information from someone who knew where it was.

Since the incident with Arazel, all of them were now a target. There was still a question of whether the Dark forces knew they were in White Pine, so they needed to assume the worst. In response, Emma's father, Jack Sterling, and several of the other protectors had taken care to remind them that none of them were ever to be alone, and always be on the lookout. They also encouraged them to stay out of the woods at night, which was agreeable to the youths, anyway.

Short of hiding out in a cave somewhere, they did their best to balance fear with daily life. They had several Descendants watching out for them, and they practiced Light manipulation as often as they could. They were, therefore, as safe as they could be for the time being.

Mr. Sterling prepared them, however, making them practice evasion procedures in case there was an incident. In Chivler's, this involved installing a trapdoor to the right of the fireplace where they did their reading.

They had also practiced sending Light scribes—which were messages written in the air and delivered to another Descendant almost instantly. In addition, the Sterlings, Miss Karpatch, the Farmers, Sam's grandfather Amos, and the Ablesworths had all been assigned to keep watch on the gate more closely, taking turns almost around the clock to report on any suspicious activity.

Chivler refused to abandon the store simply due to the presence of the gate. He admitted that he had known about the gate all along, stubbornly informing them that since he had faced the Metim once before, he wasn't afraid to do it again.

Most of what they dug up from Chivler's extensive collection of books from Creation authors turned out to be only opinion or speculation about spiritual realms and beings. Every once in a while, however, a particular book would mention something that would make them wonder if the author had inside information into the strange world of Watchers and Dark creatures.

One particular book Sam found most interesting was the Creator's own book. Often Emma would request for Gus to read it after a long rainy day of digging though ancient manuscripts and accounts of thousand year old battles. Sam certainly didn't mind.

Although there wasn't anything directly about Lior, it had helped Sam understand who he was and how he fit into the crazy world he lived in. It also seemed to encourage him to deal with his own anger and resentment, of which he had begun to take more notice. The more he learned of the Creator's love for his people—and for him personally—the more he felt he could let go of the hate he carried around.

It was still odd to call himself a Descendant, and even more odd

to know that he was the son of Nuriel, a great Watcher. The Watchers were known around the world as the angels, but to most, they were just a myth or a fantasy. But now, Sam knew it was more than a legend, and Lior was far more than he could have ever imagined. The spiritual world was real, just like the Watchers who had existed since the dawn of time.

Emma and Gus had pestered him about his encounter with his father, Nuriel, ever since arriving back in White Pine. They forced him to recant word for word his meeting in Ayet Sal repeatedly until he felt he was the subject of a very long interrogation. He knew they were only curious, but he honestly couldn't recall all of the details of the meeting. Even though he had replayed it in his mind many times.

He did remember the visions that Nuriel showed him after telling Sam he was his father. He remembered the way he felt when he placed his hand on him. It had calmed him, and caused him to feel safe, and trusting. It was like Nuriel had known Sam his entire life.

It seemed rather nefarious at first that Nuriel would want him to open the gate. It was what the Dark forces wanted—to travel the gates freely, uniting the two worlds for their Dark purposes. It was the reason Arazel had hunted down Sam and the others when leaving the Old City, to use the Watcher Stone to open the gate. And now Sam had done exactly what Arazel and the Dark Lords planned to do with the Stone.

He played the reasons over in his mind, doing his best to keep his doubt at bay. Nuriel had their best interests at heart, even though it appeared his vision lined up with those of the Dark forces. Sam trusted Nuriel, however, as did several of the other Descendants that were close to him. Sam hoped they were right to do so, because the results could be catastrophic if they weren't.

But Nuriel was his father, and had shown him visions, feelings, memories of his childhood—of his mother. Visions only a person who knew him intimately could know. He needed to trust that.

Mr. Sterling had also been keeping them updated on the happenings in Lior. He told them how the regions were beginning to see the true effects of the Darkness since the curse of Kachash had been lifted. With the Dark gate open, the shadow over Lior had lifted, and Lior was recognizing the Darkness again for the first time. It was as though Lior was waking up from a very long nap.

A hand smacked Sam in the stomach, shaking him from his thoughts.

"Come on, butthead. Shall we show him again how it's done?"

Butthead was the playful nickname Emma had called him since the beginning of summer.

He stood to his feet and helped her off the grass. "Sure. But let's not rub it in too much. He seems to get more touchy about it lately."

She pulled him over to where Lillia was helping Gus with his stance.

"Remember, you do not control the Light. It *allows* you to use it," Emma said.

"I know, I just…" Sam stopped, allowing the warmth to creep down his arms and into his outstretched palms.

Emma grabbed his hands.

"You are going too fast!" she whispered harshly. "Just like Chivler showed us, *slowly*…"

Sam cleared his mind, looking only at the run-down building in front of him. He fought back the feeling within him, forcing himself to calm his emotions as the Light surfaced to his palms. Briefly, he looked at Emma, who smiled at him, her perfect lips glistening in the waning sunlight.

She took her place next to him, holding her palms outward in front of her identically to his. Lillia, too, stepped up beside them and positioned herself facing the wall.

"Ready, lovebirds?" she asked.

"One, two…" Emma held her breath as she seemed to pause for a moment in anticipation of what would come next.

"… three."

From the palms of the three youths exploded three brilliant beams of luminescent blue Light directed at the wall, instantly searing three

fist-sized holes in the building's exterior.

As the Light gushed from his body, for a moment Sam worried the Light would waver out of control from its immense power as it had so many times before, but calmly he regained control of the beam as Emma had patiently taught him.

Almost instantly, the three collapsed into the grass following the wielding of such great Lazuli force, exhausted from just seconds of utilizing their gifts. Prepared, they dug into Emma's backpack and opened the root cake and iced tea Mrs. Sterling had made the night before.

Gus sat with them, refusing the cake but accepting the tea, looking slightly thinner than he did only six months prior in Lior.

Emma patted him on the knee. "You'll get it, Gus. It just takes practice."

Gus shook his head. "I know what to do. I just can't seem to get the Light to understand that."

Lillia smacked him in the back of the head, making him scowl even more. "How many times do you need to hear it? The Light doesn't submit to you—moose—it *allows* you to use it."

"Yeah, I know, I know. I guess it just comes easier for some…"

Emma stood slowly, attempting to regain her balance as the strength returned to her body. "When Mentorship starts, you won't need to worry about it then. Everyone figures out how at some point."

Sam accepted Emma's hand to help him stand, which he also did for Lillia. "Speaking of Mentorship, when does it start?"

Gus picked up a rock and tossed it against the building, which was still sizzling from the holes of the Lazuli beams. "The induction commences at the conclusion of the Light Festival. They induct Mentees just after the games. We will leave straight from the stadium to the school."

Sam remembered seeing the hundreds of teens his age filing out of the back of the stadium as the festival concluded. Where they disappeared to, he had no clue, as the only thing resting behind the stadium perched on the side of a cliff was a grand vista of an angry, dark sea below.

As they picked up their backpacks to begin the three-mile journey through the woods home, a small blue orb the size of a baseball came careening out of the trees and stopped dead in front of Emma. She did not flinch as the other three instinctively dove out of the way of the curious blue ball of light.

"Calm down. It's just a message from mom and dad."

She reached out to the small orb in front of her. Promptly, it unfurled in her hand to reveal a message with letters of Light that seemed to burn their imprint into the very air they occupied.

Emma watched the letters fold back into the orb and then disappear. "I was worried about this. They want us back right away."

Lillia dusted herself off angrily. "What's the problem? Miss Karpatch needs to move her classroom for the third time?"

"I don't think so, 'Lil…"

Gus awkwardly tried to help Lillia dust herself off, but then backed away when she just about smacked him in the face. "It's not like we get a Light message every day, especially while here. What's going on?"

"I'm worried. I—well, never mind. I shouldn't even try to guess."

"Seriously 'Em? Why do you even act like you will try to keep it from us? You can't keep secrets to save your life," Lillia said.

Emma pulled her hair back into a ponytail and sighed. "I overheard Dad talking with Chivler and Mayor Phillis last night about the Dark Watchers here in Creation. They're worried they might come out of hiding."

Lillia turned an eyebrow up. "Meaning? We've all known they were here, but what makes it any different now?"

She shrugged as they headed toward the tree line back to town. "Don't know, really. I hear lots of stuff, but this time it sounded a little different, I guess. More *urgent*."

Gus whistled. "No way. The Fallen Watchers in Creation have been silent for thousands of years."

Emma snatched up her backpack hidden in the tall grass. "I—I'm

not sure—and you shouldn't make it more than what it is. I could have heard all wrong."

"That doesn't mean we should *ignore* it." Lillia mumbled.

Gus took the rear as they filed onto the makeshift trail through the pines. "It would be interesting to find out, that's for sure. The Metim have been active here since the pre-diluvian era—"

He paused at the frustrated sound from Lillia in front of him for using such large words. "Pre*flood*, that is. But the Fallen Watchers have largely been silent, or nonexistent." He finished.

Sam ventured a guess. "Maybe the Watchers killed them all off."

Gus hurried up next to Sam, and for the first time, Sam noticed him not huffing as much as he normally did.

"I suppose that's possible," He said. "Between what was recovered in the Lior Library after the fire in the Old City and from what had been passed down verbally, we know the Watchers had been in a battle with the forces of Darkness since the time of Creation. That is—until fifty years ago, when they agreed not to intervene in Lior's affairs."

"And both the Watchers in Lior and Dark Watchers here have been silent ever since," Lillia added from the front of the line. "Creepy, isn't it?"

Neither of the boys answered her. They had heard Lillia's conspiracy theories all summer about what had happened with Arazel and Cooley—how half of Lior's Council was involved in the scheme to hide Lior from the truth about the growing Darkness.

Lior had indeed seen many new spots emerge since Sam opened the gate, but there were no more conspiracies emerging from the grand halls about Lior councilmen setting off Darkness detectors in the City Center Chamber.

It did not ease the Council's fears, however, knowing the Dark gate was open and that the curse had been lifted from Lior. Reports from the regions had included little in the way of activity from the Metim and the Dark forces, but they knew they were out there—and now up to something. And there was the nagging feeling that told them what they had seen thus far was not yet the full truth.

"What do the Dark forces want with Lior and Creation, anyway?" Sam asked as they hustled through the last part of the trees and into the field outside of town. It was a question that had been plaguing him for quite some time.

"To control it," Lillia answered.

"To control Earth is to control the Creator. Well—at least the heart of *the Creator.*" Emma added.

Sam chuckled. "Are you kidding me? Why would the God who created Earth and Lior be weak enough to subject himself to what happens here? Isn't that making himself a little too vulnerable?"

"Perhaps. Yes," Gus answered, chuckling nervously. "But it's not a question of power, but of willing submission. He allows himself to be vulnerable to keep Creation free to choose."

"Sounds dumb," Sam said, the words dribbling out before he could stop them.

The group veered left toward the Sterling household. The first traces of the evening sunset were making their way across the horizon.

Hearing his comment, Emma turned, facing him directly. "Samuel, you should know by now this is how the Creator works."

Chapter Two
Dragon Blood

Deep in the heart of one of the darkest caves on the island, a black icy mass flowed through the depths of the darkness. The cloud moved ever so slowly, making its way like a disease through the temperate air of the cave, forcing itself upon the warmer climate and subduing it into a frigid likeness of itself.

It moved this way and that through the black, as if searching for something. Twisting and turning, the cold mass flowed down the long narrow corridors of the damp cavern in its search, sure to avoid any hint of Light that may poke a subtle finger through an opening from above.

The cloud halted just in front of a small sliver of Light that dimly illuminated the corridor from a crack in the ceiling extending several feet through the rock to the open sky above. Unwilling to pass through its golden glow, it waited.

Silently, the dark cloud pulsed with hollow, unearthly forms occupying its dense exterior. Their faces bubbled to the surface then sank beneath, their mute glassy eyes void of life or substance.

Then, as if enslaved by an unknown force taking hold, the mass was pulled toward the Light forcefully, squirming and writhing in pain as it passed unwillingly into the beam of light. Yet, even through its pain, the dark cloud accepted the torture for the moment, quickly submitting to the unknown force controlling it as a servant would its master.

In the corner of the damp, musty room beside the corridor, a form emerged from the darkest corner and moved weakly toward the mass. He watched it writhe in pain under the illuminating presence of the light in the cavern. Softly, the form passed its hand over the pulsating faces, their former expressionless eyes now showing agony as they inherited the pain of their carrier.

"You have come for me, Sevel," the form spoke, crossing fearlessly into the path of the light from above.

The form was like a taller man, but yet unlike any other human form, featureless in its face and body. The color of its skin was dark and tainted with a deathly tone of grey and black, which crawled fluidly over the body as though it were a liquid.

The light revealed the morbid picture of the form in its entirety—a creature loose in its definition of a person, yet its mouth moved in ripples across its face as it continued to hold the dark cloud before it in captivity.

"Do not resist me, Sevel, for I have made you to be a servant of the true creator, the righteous judge of all things."

The cheerless form lifted an arm toward the cloud. "Submit, oh Darkness, for your true master Nasikh has need of you."

The Darkness twisted in agony once again as the invisible force overcame it and forced it into submission. Suddenly, it was sucked instantly into the form that called itself Nasikh, disappearing beneath the ripples of liquid skin. Nasikh lifted its faceless head and breathed deeply, integrating the Darkness into his own body.

In a display of force, massive billows of black erupted from Nasikh's body, exploding throughout the corridor and extinguishing every crevice of air and light with the choking, acrid Darkness.

Dragon Blood

Nasikh leveled his expressionless face to see the results of his invocation of power. The small burst of Darkness coursed through his form, strengthening him.

Leaving the cool protection of the cave behind, Nasikh stepped into the light, his form transforming into that of a human being. His body, however, retained the elements of his shifting, fluid-like skin. His face was like the face of an old man, deeply wrinkled and weathered, his eyes hollow and vacant. He bore a large scar on either side of his thin, callous lips.

The sun was fading on the island where the cave was located. In the distance, the silhouetted shapes of alien-like Dragon Trees with eerie cauliflower-like canopies stretched into the blood-red sunset. The strange trees seemed to appear out of nothing in the parched landscape, as lone towers in a forest of dust and rocks.

Cursing, the shifting form of the man moved weakly toward one of the closest trees in almost a gliding fashion, weaving in and out of the boulders that appeared to vomit themselves out of the cave entrance.

With the longer of his yellowing fingernails, he gouged through the scale-like bark of the curious tree to the tender wood beneath, twisting and turning the nail until a splintered hole was visible.

Almost immediately, the blood-red sap poured from the trunk and down his malformed hand to the dusty ground, where it coagulated into puffy red clots near the trunk. The dark form allowed the sap to flow down his blackened arms for a moment in gleeful awe, as if enjoying the very nature of the event simply because of its violent symbolism.

He waited until his arm was completely coated in the dark red liquid, then held his arm above him where the sap pooled and dripped into his mouth. It seemed to give him strength, but it was not enough. Bending down to meet the punctured trunk with his lips, he sucked the thick fluid out from the hole for several minutes, paying no mind to the streaks of red trickling down his chin.

Finally, he stood, satisfied with his exploitation of the tree. The branches, once unyielding reservoirs of life-giving liquid, were now beginning to become gnarled and lifeless appendages.

He had no care for the Dragon Tree or its demise. He only thought of the task before him. There was much work to accomplish, many to bring under subjection, and many to determine their loyalty and effectiveness to the cause.

The plan was set into place long before he had been imprisoned in this place. He scratched a message into the air in front of him, the Darkness following his sap-covered hand. His loyal ones would need to account for their time. Had they completed the work he had given them?

First, he had to find the one thing that had resulted in his awakening, the single reason the Darkness sought him out and brought him out of hiding. He had to find the boy called Samael.

****

"Thank you all for being here this beautiful evening, and Cindy and I welcome you to our table once again."

Mr. Sterling took his place at the head of the table under the soft glow of the lights gracing the outdoor overhang of the covered porch. Mrs. Sterling had dozens of unique and interesting hanging plants everywhere surrounding the table, making Sam feel like he was deep in a tropical forest.

It wasn't the first time he had been here. They had dinner nearly every Sunday with the Sterlings and a few others from church, and he always enjoyed coming.

The Sterling's house was known for its immaculate nineteenth century elegance, yet Mrs. Sterling ensured it retained a sort of simple beauty with the style that Sam found intriguing. It reminded him of Emma, in fact.

He and Emma hadn't truly been dating since leaving Lior the previous fall, as Sam would have liked, but he respected her decision

to take on a more "courting" aspect to the relationship. It seemed no different to Sam, in any case, as they still found the time to spend nearly every waking moment together. Much to Lillia's disgust, of course.

Tonight felt different, however, and Sam knew Emma was right about a general feeling of urgency that was circulating around the group. It wasn't their normal jovial conversation ringing out through the late summer evening air tonight. There were, in fact, few that chatted at all as Mrs. Sterling set the last of the piled-high plates of food on the table. Candles flickered softly in the evening breeze.

At the table tonight was the usual group, which made up the entirety of the people that Sam believed had traveled through the gate to Lior. Gus's and Lillia's folks were there, the Abelsworths and the Farmers, Miss Karpatch, Mayor Phillis, Fenton Chivler, and Sam's grandfather Amos. He also had a hunch there were a few others that knew of the group's involvement in the spiritual realm, but were either given limited information or had been sworn to secrecy. Nor they had been given the option to travel to Lior. Pastor Jeffries came to mind, as he seemed to have a unique insight into the group's affairs.

After a prayer from Sam's grandfather, the group passed around the bowls of food, keeping to only cordial conversation. Emma was right, Sam thought. Something big is going to be discussed tonight.

Midway through his second ear of sweet corn, Sam felt Emma's hand on his knee under the table. Startled, he nearly called out as his corn clattered to his plate. Momentarily, the table stopped its conversation to look at the commotion coming from Sam's direction. With his sheepish grin, they returned to their salads and casual discussions.

She held her hand there for a moment, until he felt something soft brush across his knee and then rest there, like a butterfly's wing come to rest. Reaching under the table, he picked up the delicate item. Right away, he could tell it was a flower.

It was a white bloodroot flower, native to the upper peninsula of Michigan. It was a simple flower, but beautiful. Earlier in the day, she had shown him a patch of bloodroot, which had a curious quality in its roots that made it bleed a red, milky sap when it was cut open. It wasn't a rare flower, but it was useful. In fact, at Osanna's natural herb shop in town, there were many items made from the plant, including topical ointments and a tea that turned blood-red when brewed.

He smiled at her, and leaning into him, she put her head on his shoulder for a moment. It felt good to know she still felt the way she did for him, even if they weren't really dating.

Lillia rolled her eyes in disgust at the display for the umpteenth time that day. Sam was used to it by now—in fact, he enjoyed taunting her with it once in a while.

Mr. Sterling cleared his throat. "While everyone is finishing up, Mrs. Sterling would like you to know there is fresh strawberry pie and coffee in the dining room. Once we clear the table and the pie is safely out of my reach, we will get started with a brief item of discussion."

Not wasting time, Gus followed Miss Karpatch into the dining room after the pie. Sam didn't want to miss out on Mrs. Sterling's famous pie either, so he set the flower on the table and snatched up his and Emma's plate. He was very interested to hear what Mr. Sterling had to say, but there was no sense missing out on strawberry pie.

He considered asking Miss Karpatch as she poured him and herself a cup of coffee at the credenza, but he held his tongue. Instead, he resorted to telling her about what he had discovered in a folklore book Chivler had loaned him last week, containing a tower structure that had a striking resemblance to a Lightbase.

"A Lightbase wasn't necessarily the main purpose of the building, although it could have functioned as both, I suppose…"

Miss Karpatch dipped her spoon in her cup to dissolve the sugar she had added. "Interesting that it would speak of a structure that mentions a blue light in the sky. I wonder if the author was perhaps a Liorian and never realized it."

"Could be. But I just wanted to run it past you since you are the expert on ancient buildings in Lior."

She laughed. "Thank you. I suppose that's a compliment. Just think, last year you couldn't stand to even look at me. Now you're asking for my advice about history."

Sam's face reddened. "Don't worry about it."

"But about the building, you may be onto something… we can discuss it another time. Mr. Sterling is gathering the troops back to the table."

"I know all of you have been working tirelessly in these last few months, taking patrols late into the night," Mr. Sterling began. "And you should know that the Council, the Protector's Office, and Cindy and I both are grateful. Even more so, all of Lior in is your debt."

There were nods from everyone at the table, though no one responded. They knew there was something more he was about to tell them. Something significant.

Mr. Sterling lowered his voice.

"Today, I have news regarding the latest investigations into the spread of Darkness in Lior, and of the current strength of the Metim. As most of you know, Kachash's deception has been lifted with the opening of the Sha'ar gate. There have been many areas of Lior that have reported large strongholds of Darkness in each region…

"Following the investigation, it has been determined that the Metim were indeed responsible for the abduction of Chivler, as well as for the exceptional storm that occurred the night we left for Lior—"

"Jack, are you saying that the Storm Lord, Sar Sehrah, could be responsible for the storm?" Lillia's father interrupted. "I thought he's been locked up since the fall of the Old City!"

"We don't speculate. We know it was him." Mr. Sterling said, looking down at his worn leather journal. "He passed through the Peru gate with about forty Metim on orders from Kachash, then made his way up here, where they abducted Chivler."

"We believe Sar Sehrah and the other two lords, Yaren and Taurs, were freed some time ago," Sam's grandfather Amos spoke up. "Their apparent imprisonment was all part of the deception Kachash put in place."

So it was true. The three writhing imprisoned Lords of the Darkness were simply a part of the wool that had been pulled over their eyes.

Mr. Sterling nodded, sighing deeply before continuing.

"There's more, I'm afraid. I just got word this afternoon that there has been a Seer report of disturbing news."

At his words, Mrs. Sterling turned away to hide her obvious concern. No doubt Mr. Sterling had confided in her before dinner.

"One of Lior's Seers believes he has felt the presence of the Dark One, Nasikh, stirring somewhere in Creation."

There were multiple gasps from around the table. Tears flowed quietly down Mrs. Sterling's cheeks. Gus looked like he had just been punched in the gut.

As Mr. Sterling comforted his wife, Amos stood suddenly, coffee cup in hand. "My friends, while this is certainly a cause of concern for us all, I want to remind you of a very relevant truth from our Creator, the Lord of all things, great and small. He is the source of our Light, and of our strength. Without him, we are left to our own devices, serving ourselves, fearing all those who come in our path. It is not our place to fear, but to place our trust in the source of strength, bowing not to a master that seeks only to enslave us."

Sam had seen another side of his grandfather the previous year when he showed up in the Council meeting that was called to determine the fate of Sam's life in Lior. Until now, however, he hadn't truly recognized the powerful wisdom that resided inside of Amos. His wisdom often left Sam in awe of him, as it did now. It was no wonder he had been Chancellor. He acted the part.

Mr. Sterling stood. "Amos is absolutely right. We must not allow this to occupy any space in our emotions. We are warriors of the Light, and in the Light, we will stay," He said. "Which leads us to some new tasks for each of you regarding the gate. We suspect that the Metim have been entering and exiting the gates with the help of the Dark Lords—"

"Mr. Sterling, perhaps, if I may…" the Colonel raised a hand. "I have been wondering how that could be possible, the Dark Lords passing through the gates. Do they not submit to the Darkness?"

Jack nodded to the beefy man sitting across from him. "We aren't

sure how, exactly, but we have a theory. We think somehow the Dark Lords are holding onto the Light just long enough to use it for their advantage. If that's the case, traveling the gates could be possible."

Miss Karpatch cleared her throat. "They are fallen Watchers, and indeed, masters of deception and magic. No doubt they have trained themselves to hide the Darkness within them just as they did with all of Lior."

Mr. Sterling nodded. "Of that, I have no doubt, Sarah. We must be more mindful of our surroundings than we ever have before. That means being extra purposeful at our posts here in White Pine—for we not only service the gate we have been traveling through into Lior, but now the Sha'ar gate falls under our protection."

"Mr. Sterling, should we request additional help from the PO or the Sons of Light?" Gus asked, setting down his fork.

"I don't believe it would be prudent to call extra attention to either gate, and the Council agrees," Mr. Sterling answered. "We don't know how many, if any, that know of their locations. Since it is only a theory, it could disrupt our secrecy if the Dark Lords discover us to be gate protectors. It may only be a matter of time before they find out, but for now, we should operate under the assumption they don't know."

Gus nodded, and Mr. Sterling looked around the table for any more questions or comments. Finding none, he handed each family— Daniel and Katrina Farmer, James (the Colonel) and his wife Violet Abelsworth, his grandfather Amos, Miss Karpatch, the Mayor Robert Phillis, and Chivler—a small piece of rolled parchment. In them, Mr. Sterling explained, were the details of their assignments.

"The Mrs. has informed me that she would be willing to provide dinner starting next week as we will need to meet regularly to further discuss how we will respond to these new events."

There were more nods and chatter about Nasikh around the table as Mrs. Sterling brought out another fresh pot of coffee and the rest of the strawberry pie, which Gus, Lillia, Sam, and Emma quickly dug into.

Mr. Sterling would not let the group become too distracted with conversation, however, and after waving off another cup of coffee from his wife, he held up a hand, as if he was about to put the icing on the cake of an already terrible announcement.

Sam had just stuffed an extra-large bite of pie into his mouth when he suddenly realized he was the only one who hadn't discovered the conversation hadn't finished.

"There is another matter we need to discuss with our youngest members of the table here tonight. Emma, Sam, Gus, Lillia, please listen carefully."

When the clanking of silverware quieted, Mr. Sterling turned to the four youths. "During this most dangerous time, something of grave importance has come to our attention that will be of utmost concern for the four of you."

He paused, and suddenly there was an uneasy silence in the room. Though none of the adults seemed particularly surprised. "Given your most recent confrontation with the Dark lord Arazel on your journey to the Old City, we feel it best that you are given special protection for the time being. You may have already noticed the extra measures taken to ensure your whereabouts in the evenings during these past few months."

Sam hadn't been certain of the extra precautions until hearing Mr. Sterling just now. None of them had been given free rein of White Pine after dark. In addition, there were many occasions they had remembered not being able to even walk to town alone, especially in the late afternoon and into the evening. They had protested about it a time or two, but in the end, they always knew they were only looking out for their wellbeing.

Sam had pinned it on the fact that they were in new territory with the Sha'ar Gate being opened. Everyone was already on edge, but Sam had also noticed the restrictions increasing as summer began. It was annoying, but he tried not to complain.

"Of course, it was perhaps more than necessary, but we had to be sure you were protected."

Amos set his coffee cup on the table. "You should know it was only in your best interest."

There were nods and acknowledgements from the other parents at the table, who obviously had been in on the plan from the beginning.

"What is it, Daddy?" Emma said, concern on her face. Her look resembled much like it did the night they found out they were journeying to the Old City alone months ago.

A few of the others clearing their throats clued Sam that the next part would not be easy to hear. If not just for Sam, Emma, Gus, and Lillia, but for the adult protectors as well.

"We believe you—all of you—could be primary targets of the next Metim attack," Mr. Sterling said quickly.

Emma's eyes widened, but she said nothing. Cindy Sterling, however, struggled to fight back the tears.

"You think because of Sam, they will try to get to him through us," Emma said, a resolute calmness in her voice.

Mr. Sterling nodded to his daughter. "We think that one goal of the Metim will be to persuade Sam to submit to the Darkness so that they can begin the next phase of their plan."

"To destroy the Watchers and all of Lior," Gus said slowly.

"Yes. That is the problem we will eventually face."

"So, what do we do about it? Sam, I mean,"

Lillia picked at a wayward strawberry on her plate. The worry in her voice was subtle, but Sam could hear it. She was excellent at hiding her emotions.

"It's not like we can go into hiding or anything."

Mr. Sterling glanced at his wife. For the moment, she appeared to be holding it together, though barely.

"Actually, Lillia, that's exactly what we are planning for you to do."

Chapter Three
Watchers in White Pine

The next morning, Sam didn't want to get out of bed. The morning was chilly in his room and the sheets were extra comfortable. But with the birds singing to the bright sun outside his window, he knew the day would heat quickly. And now, with the news from last night in the forefront of his mind, there was a lot to do.

He smelled coffee and bacon the moment he lifted his head off the pillow. His grandfather may have been the Chancellor of Lior, but he still knew how to cook breakfast.

"Made a few extra blueberry muffins today."

Amos took two plates off the shelf and set them on the table, where a steaming pile of eggs and bacon and two cups of coffee already sat.

Sam used to decline his grandfather's famous Saturday morning breakfasts when he first arrived in White Pine, but since returning from Lior, he truly looked forward to them.

It started out rather awkwardly with the two, grandfather and grandson, eating silently without so much as a word about the weather.

But now it was different. They chatted about many things—Lior, the Creator, even his relationship with Emma. It wasn't strange anymore.

"Thanks, Grandpa," Sam said as he gulped his coffee a bit too fast, spilling the hot steaming liquid down his tee shirt.

"Today's a pretty big day, isn't it?"

His grandfather handed him one of the cloth napkins from the shelf beside the little table in the kitchen to wipe up the coffee. "I suppose it requires some extra calories."

Sam sipped the hot coffee more gingerly this time, enjoying its strong flavor but mild aftertaste. "Not that I'm complaining about missing school this year, but I guess I can't really understand why sending us through the gate to hide out alone at the cabin on the other side is better. Couldn't any Metim attack us there just as easily? And we would be alone, so you wouldn't be there to help us if we needed it."

Amos stood and walked over to the bookshelf. Pulling one of his leather journals from the shelf, he opened it to a certain page, handing it to Sam.

He pointed at the drawing in the journal. "There is a very good reason I built that cabin where it is now."

Sam looked down at the sketch of the cabin nestled in the trees, as seen from above. All around were towering mountain peaks surrounding the structure, except for the tiny trail that led up to Jester's Pass. It was the only way to Lior City.

His grandfather had built the cabin himself. Sam should have noticed the similarities between the one in Lior and the one here in White Pine. They were almost identical.

"Every time I would come through the gate on my way to the City, I noticed that my Light scribes would often have difficulty reaching the person I was writing to."

Sam scowled. "You think there is something that was interfering with them?"

His grandfather nodded. "One night, while traveling from Creation, I happened to notice a group of Metim waiting to attack me as I came through the gate. Truthfully, there was no way they could have not seen me, but they didn't. As I slipped past them, I heard their muffled voices talking about how their ability to use the Darkness was compromised in that place."

"Like something is blocking the use of our gifts and their conjuring…"

"Exactly. They were given exact instructions by a friend of mine who had turned to the Darkness, and yet they could not see me. After having a few trusted experts from the Office of Research out there, it was determined that the strange force affected the entire area surrounding the cabin."

Sam remembered the very fearful first night entering Lior through the gate. He had let go of Emma's hand and became separated from the group. Alone in the darkness, he had encountered something, or some*one*. Someone, or something, with glowing green eyes.

Perhaps it was because the others came to his rescue at exactly the right moment, or maybe it was because the unknown individual—or creature—never saw him.

"It is the safest place you can go, and while Gus and Lillia's parents were reluctant at first, all agree it is best."

Amos looked briefly out of the window of the cabin as the rays of sunlight suddenly poured through. "The others are needed here to protect the gate. I'm afraid once again you will be on your own."

Sam still couldn't believe it. Yesterday, he and the other youths were counting the last days of summer before the start of the school year, but now they had been given only one day to pack for Lior.

They had instructed them to travel to the cabin just to the other side of the gate, and remain there hidden for three months prior to the Light festival. Late that night, the other protectors would escort them to the gate, hand them some provisions, and give them a blessing before crossing through.

It was a concept that Emma wasn't happy with, but she had accepted it more readily than the journey to Old Lior. Sam was in danger, and she and the others would do pretty much anything to ensure his safety.

"Against my better judgement, Mrs. Sterling has decided that she

will check in with you once more before the Light Festival when we can rejoin you. I'm sure she will plan to replenish your supplies at that time."

No doubt Mrs. Sterling was beside herself, allowing her daughter to once again go off with three inexperienced youths. But times were changing, and no doubt she would spend much of that time busying herself with protecting the gate.

Lillia's folks were stern and unemotional about the situation. They reminded Sam of his foster parents occasionally. The one major difference being that they hadn't abandoned their child.

Gus's father was one of the few who had no reservations about the issue. As a former military man, he believed that all young people should be urged into becoming independent in order to make them stronger. Gus's mother, however, when she heard the news, pleaded with the group to keep her baby boy at home, where she could keep him from starving to death.

After clearing the table and washing the dishes, Sam and his grandfather planned to finish packing, then meet with the others to go over supplies and security details. While the cabin provided everything they needed, including wood-fired heat and recently installed indoor plumbing, they would need to spend a day or two chopping wood and setting up the Lazuli lanterns in specific patterns to ready the cabin once they arrived.

They spent the rest of the morning checking and rechecking the list of items Sam would need for the journey, including books that Mrs. Sterling had given him for studying math, science, Lior history, and the Light gifts. While the math and science books were mostly the same schoolbooks he had always known, they differed because everything in them pointed to the Creator as the source of Light for all, who gave all things a purpose and design.

He had wondered at first what they would tell the school about their absence, though the more he thought about it, the easier an excuse sounded feasible. The connections the protectors seem to have in town afforded them many special privileges.

At noon, his grandfather dug out the old red truck from the barn and they headed into town for a few supplies. The new Iggy's grocery store had opened this year, but Amos still chose to shop at Orvil's Country Store for his groceries. Sam figured he did it because the widowed old Mrs. Orvil needed the income.

They bought canned food, dried meats, cheese, flour, sugar, salt, a few fishing odds and ends, and four boxes of rifle ammunition for hunting rabbits and squirrels. Mrs. Orvil peered at Sam over her spectacles, but said nothing at the purchase. Suddenly, Sam guessed why his grandfather chose to shop there. Mrs. Orvil may have been a gossip, but when it came to the protectors, she knew how to keep a secret.

They stopped in at Carter's for some candles, matches, and an axe sharpener as well, and Amos made sure that Sam had an extra pair of leather gloves and fleece-lined jeans for the chilly mountain nights.

Before heading over to the Sterlings' to meet the others, his grandfather bought Sam a late lunch at the diner and stopped by the tiny post office where he picked up a large canvas sack. Sam recognized it right away.

"Ten pounds coffee beans, unroasted," the postal attendant said, unbothered by the curious cargo.

"We have always roasted our own coffee here, and at the cabin," His grandfather reminded him, smiling. "We People of the Light take our coffee very seriously."

Sam had noticed—and had appreciated the Descendants' exceptional coffee-making skills. While there was a coffee shop in town which he, Gus, Lillia, and Emma did frequent during the cold autumn afternoons after school, it didn't compare with the amazing taste of any one of the protector group's brews.

When they finally arrived at the Sterlings' after dark, Lillia's and Gus's parents were already there. Miss Karpatch was there, along with another man Sam had never met before.

The two were deeply engaged in what seemed to be a debate they had had many times before.

"I know you still believe it can't be recovered, but I just can't help but check out the research if it is handed to me," Henry Bostwick said animatedly, his dusty pants and faded shirt looking out of place in Mrs. Sterling's impeccably clean living room. He looked as though he belonged on an archaeology dig somewhere in the desert.

"Henry, the Tower of Migdal Babel is long gone. Even though it was built after the flood, its location has always been thought to have been between two rivers. Do you know how often rivers change shape? I really don't think you are going to find it buried under six millennia of shifting landscape and river sediment."

Henry's long, wavy, unkempt hair was pulled back into a ponytail. "Yes, but Sarah, what if it *was* accessible? It would truly be the archaeological find of history! Imagine the secrets we could uncover in that place!"

Sarah Karpatch rolled her eyes. "I appreciate your enthusiasm, Henry, but even if we did find it, the tower was never even finished. We only know it may have some resemblance to some of the structures in Lior. The rest is conjecture."

Henry attempted to argue his case, but was waved off by Miss Karpatch. "We can discuss this later. Dinner smells amazing."

She pursed her lips and disappeared down the hallway to the kitchen, and Henry turned his attention to Sam.

"Ah! Here's one with a taste for true history!"

He stuck out his hand to Sam. "Name's Henry, and you must be the one everyone seems to be talking about."

"Nice to meet—"

"As one who appreciates ancient artifacts, perhaps you'd enjoy this," he interrupted, handing Sam a rolled-up paper, which contained a crude sketch of some strange symbols that appeared to be a sort of lettering. To Sam, one of them looked vaguely like the *Irin*, the Watcher wing. Except that it wasn't alone in the image as he had seen it before, but carved inside of a structure that may have been meant to resemble a tower.

"I traced this from a cave in the Amazon," he said almost giddily.

"I am certain it matches the symbol on the first Watcher Tower. You may know it as the Tower of Babel."

Sam knew the name. It was the story of the tower that an ancient civilization attempted to build to reach heaven, but failed. God forced them to scatter all over the world, hence the first known separation of languages. But he had always heard the story as a legend. Now, as a Descendant and follower of the Creator, he thought differently.

"Most of this is pretty new to me. But if you allow me to borrow it, I would like to have Gus—"

"Of course, Of course! Take it! It is a copy and I have more," Henry cut him off again, chuckling loudly. "But be aware, I ran into some pretty wild stuff while searching out its origins. It seems there are some secrets the dead do not easily give up."

Then a thought occurred to Sam. "Sir, why would there be evidence of the tower in the Amazon? Shouldn't it be located somewhere in the Middle East?"

"A wise conclusion, my good man. But now let me ask you a question." He paused, his face creeping into a smile. "What if the tower we all know from the text wasn't the only one? What if there were in fact towers being built all over the earth?"

It was an interesting idea, but one Sam knew nothing about. He had made an attempt to learn more about the history of the Descendants and the Creator with Gus's weekly readings in the summer, but there was still so much to understand. He was intrigued by Henry's conclusions, but right now there were other things to be concerned with. Perhaps it was best at the time being to leave the major archaeological finds to the dirt diggers like Henry Bostwick.

The large group sat down to one more of Mrs. Sterling's famous dinners before they would trek the hour-long path to the hidden arch within the cavern. Then, from there, they would be on their own.

"Dinner was fabulous as always, Cindy," Miss Karpatch said as she excused herself to help with the dishes.

All agreed that it was yet another dinner that would rival the others, as the last of the baked chicken, rolls, and mashed potatoes were

divided among the four youths to take with them. Mr. Sterling stood and patted his stomach, looking out from the porch at the soft wind blowing through the dark silhouette of the pines.

"I believe it is nearly time. The hour is late."

Sam glanced at the clock on the wall just inside the house. It was nearly ten o'clock.

Amos set down his cup and stood suddenly with Mr. Sterling. "Would you all stand with me to wish our brave young people a safe journey?"

As they had done so many times before, Amos led them in prayer to the Creator. "Our dear sovereign Lord, we come to your presence in honor and respect of who you are. We ask of you tonight to grant special mercies upon our sons and daughters of Lior. We pray for understanding, for protection, and for power that you have entrusted us with. We ask—"

Suddenly Amos's prayer was over. Sam looked up just in time to see what had captured his and the others' attention.

Chapter Four
Noise in the Hills

Inside the pines beyond the yard stood a figure. Even in the dim light of the moon, his dark silver robe seemed to glow as if Lazuli Light itself were woven into the fabric. Beside him, he carried a staff with a handle carved into a flame that illuminated the wielder's hand.

Nuriel. Sam leapt from the table, nearly spilling coffee all over the Abelsworths.

Rushing out into the cool night air, Nuriel met Sam partway to scoop him up in his arms. The warm touch of his hands wrapped around him reminded him of their first meeting in the desolate streets of Ayet Sal.

"What—are you doing here?" Sam asked, out of breath.

"I've missed you, Samuel," Nuriel laughed. "Take me to your friends. I would love to make their acquaintance."

Beaming, Sam hurried Nuriel and his glowing staff over to the astonished group half-seated at the table. "Hey—everyone, this is my, uh, father. Nuriel."

No one spoke, only gazed at the man with long dark hair and tanned skin.

"My friends, you do not need to fear me. I am your servant."

Mr. Sterling snapped out of his daze and rushed over to greet the Watcher. "I apologize, good sir. For a moment, I had to collect my thoughts. I am Jack Sterling, and this is—"

"Cindy, so good to meet you." Nuriel stepped quickly to extend his hand. "I can tell by the wonderful smell that you are talented in the kitchen."

Mrs. Sterling blushed and smiled. "We welcome you to our table, Mr. Nuriel."

Nuriel faced the rest of the group, greeting each before turning his attention to the four youths, of whom three had not yet quite been able to comprehend the man standing before them.

"I'm afraid I am not here on cordial terms this evening," he said gravely. "As I am sure you are aware, a dark plot has been uncovered that will affect these four young people."

Mr. Sterling nodded. "We are aware."

Nuriel smiled. "What you do not know, however, is that the attack is to take place this evening, here, in White Pine."

Miss Karpatch gasped. Henry placed a comforting hand on her shoulder.

"Mr. Nuriel, sir, not to question your allegiance, but how do we know this for certain?" Henry asked pointedly.

Nuriel's staff came to life, and a bright blue projection, much like a hologram, appeared above the table.

In the image, a small, simple town was pictured, surrounded by dense pine trees.

Immediately, Sam recognized it as White Pine. He could almost make out his grandfather's cabin to the west of the town. The image reminded Sam of the holobooks in the hidden library of the Old City.

In the outer edges of the projection, faint spots of Darkness could be seen moving ever so slightly. The blots appeared, faded into the trees, then gathered once again in greater concentrations.

Nuriel pointed to the spots, which were growing by the second. "A small force of Metim here in Creation has gathered after many years of hiding in the shadows of our earthly brethren."

An unholy hush came over the group, watching Nuriel and the terrifying images emanating from his staff. Mr. Sterling looked the most disturbed as he attempted to make sense of the dangerous situation.

"If… this is really the case, what can we do?"

Nuriel smiled, as if unaffected by the evil gathered just outside their sleepy town. "I must apologize for the trespass, but the Watchers have been acting outside the agreement with Lior for some time now."

He glanced at his staff, and the image faded, and a new one was present. Twenty warriors wearing similar dark silver robes with glowing edges like Nuriel's appeared in the projection. Some carried staffs, and others gleaming swords. Each was gazing into the trees just beyond where they stood, as if waiting for someone to make the first move.

Sam remembered the night in the woods with Arazel and how the Sons of Light bravely fought the Dark Watcher without concern for their lives.

Gus peered over the top of his glasses. "Incredible. Watchers here in White Pine…"

"We believe soon is the time that we reunite for the sake of humankind, Watcher and Descendant alike," he said softly. "But now, we fight for the Light in secrecy."

Miss Karpatch stood to her feet. "We will fight with you. Now, *and* then."

"As will I," Mr. Sterling nodded. "And I am certain the others will feel the same."

Again, Nuriel smiled genuinely. "I am grateful. Our numbers are small, and we cannot withstand the Darkness in every attack. You will be called upon—if not tonight, another."

Mrs. Sterling stood halfway in her chair, a look of panic on her face. "What do we do about the kids?" she said, taking her daughter's hand in her own. "Should we still take them to the cabin?"

Nuriel extended his hand and placed it on her head, and she was

instantly calmed by the touch. "Be still, my sister," he whispered, looking into her eyes, then around the room. "Your plan is a good one. The young people would be safest in the cabin alone."

"Are you certain? I mean—" Jack said, looking in the direction of Cindy Sterling, who suddenly seemed at peace with Nuriel's words.

"Unfortunately, in these dark times, no one can be certain," he said. "Until the day of the Creator, you will have to place your trust in Him—and in yourselves to make the best decisions. But now… my time has expired. Some brethren have cleared the path to the arch for you, but it will not hold forever. Please go soon."

But before anyone could respond, Nuriel was gone again, just like the first time they met in Ayet Sal. It was almost as if he was bound by the rules or wishes of something or someone else. Perhaps he answered to the Creator himself.

One thing was certain—in Nuriel's presence, there was something that made you feel calm, at peace, protected. Sam, however, wished he could see his father for more than a few moments at a time.

They heeded Nuriel's warning and departed immediately for the arch. Henry, Mr. and Mrs. Sterling, Miss Karpatch, and the four still awestruck youths each carried part of the large collection of sacks that would become the entirety of their food, clothes, and other items needed for the three-month stay at the cabin.

At Mr. Sterling's request, only a small group would accompany them to the gate, so Mr. and Mrs. Abelsworth, the Farmer's, as well as the Mayor, who had stopped by, wished them farewell and sent them off.

"Just around the rise," Mrs. Sterling said in a hushed tone while glancing behind her, as if expecting a heavy cloud of Darkness to descend on them as they walked through the forest.

Sam understood her concern, as his own nerves were heightened. Though they had all felt the strange sense of comfort with Nuriel's arrival, the sudden gravity of the situation had left them stunned. He stole a glance back at Emma, who seemed focused on the path in front of her, doing her best to keep her emotions submerged.

They had experienced more than most at age fifteen, but there was no reason to succumb to the fear now.

Mr. Sterling hurried them through the invisible opening of the rock wall. "Quickly now, get the supplies inside and put them in the center of the arch…"

The opening led into the cavern where the arch stood glowing and pulsing a soft blue from the Lazuli flowing beneath its surface. "Unfortunately, we do not have time for a lengthy goodbye, so we will get to it and get you on your way," he told them.

Mrs. Sterling cleared her throat and held out her hands to both sides of her, taking hold of Emma's and Lillia's hands as they bowed one last time in prayer to the Creator for protection.

Tears poured down Emma's face as her mother embraced her, urging her to take hold of the arch leg. Henry and Miss Karpatch did the same, instructing Sam, Lillia, and Gus to follow Cindy Sterling's lead.

Mr. Sterling was the last to place his hands on the arch leg. It brightened as the Lazuli Light made its way up the exterior of the beautiful structure. "We will activate the arch, but only you four will walk through. May the Creator be with you in spirit and with truth," he told them.

The room filled with blinding Light, and suddenly the cavern disappeared. In front of him, Emma held out her hand, beckoning to Sam to join her in the center of the arch. Gus and Lillia were already with her.

Together they walked toward the outer edge of the arch, the faint form of Henry and Miss Karpatch in front of them.

The intense Light enveloped them, bathing them in the warm glow of the Lazuli. The arch, Henry, Miss Karpatch, and the cavern disappeared.

Sam wanted to stay in the warm glow forever, as the incredible feeling of peace once again overcame him. It drew him into its gentle arms, comforting his worry, and calming the fear he had been carrying. It was almost like being with Nuriel.

The hand he held pulled him along until the Light faded behind him. Blinking, he felt the biting cold licking at the exposed skin of his arms and face. The late summer heat had disappeared, and the icy mountain air of Lior now reminded him he had forgotten to dress accordingly.

Emma slung her coat over his shoulders. "You bonehead, you forgot your sweatshirt again, didn't you?"

"It's in one of these canvas bags."

"Well, let's not just stand around and freeze. The cabin is that way."

It was especially cold in the valley as the winter season of Lior was just ending. Snow had drifted heavily against any solid object it could. While the pines afforded some protection from the snow that was still falling, they still had a foot or more to trudge through to get to the cabin.

The cabin was dark as they emerged into the clearing from the pines. The river that flowed from one edge of the clearing to the other sparkled like diamonds in the light of the full moon, and it flowed freely even though it was well below freezing. It was a majestic scene, perhaps even more beautiful than the first time he had seen it less than a year ago.

Like Mr. Sterling taught them, Gus dug into his pocket for the small white device made by Bogglenose and pressed the small button in the center as he waved it over his head.

The dark windows of the cabin illuminated a curious blue. They waited, like Mr. Sterling warned them, for the Lazuli lamps inside to come to full strength. If they didn't, he told them, the Light could not expel the Darkness inside, if there were any.

"There has never been an intrusion into the cabin the forty years of its existence," Gus said.

"Doesn't mean it couldn't today," Lillia retorted.

They approached the cabin cautiously, keeping their eyes on the windows for signs of movement or the slightest hint of Darkness prowling inside. Finding none, Gus handed the Light key to Sam to open the door.

It was cold and dark as they entered, but for the most part, the cabin looked untouched from their last visit. It was a medium-sized cabin, not quite the size of his grandfather's back in White Pine or the one from the Circle in Lior, but it was cozy. There were two small bedrooms on the main floor, and a loft with four bunks upstairs that overlooked the living room below.

The two girls shared one bedroom on the main floor, while Sam told Gus he could have the other. Sam would be perfectly happy upstairs by himself, though part of him wished they could all sleep in the same room for the time being.

When they had sorted their personal items into their separate bedrooms, Gus got to work on a fire while Sam braved the weather to find more wood from the shed. Lillia and Emma dug out the coffeepot to get a pot started before they unpacked the supplies for the little kitchen.

Sam snatched up one of the Lazuli lanterns to take with him to the shed. He paused, returning upstairs to grab for his boots from his pack, remembering that he had foolishly worn his tennis shoes through the arch into the snow.

The moon gleamed in the silence of the frosty night as he stepped onto the porch of the cabin. He shut the door behind him. He held the Lazuli lantern close to him, which cast a delicate blue hue to the pure white drifts banked against the cabin's exterior.

As Sam walked to the shed, the only sound he heard was the faint rush of the river as it bubbled around the ice near the banks, and his own footsteps as they crunched through the powdery snow beneath him.

It was an eerie feeling, and he fought the urge to turn and run back inside. But the fire would not last long without more wood, and he refused to let fear dominate him.

The mountains surrounding the cabin towered breathlessly around him, their peaks seen easily with the light of the full moon. Thousands of feet into the air they rose, silent, as though stone giants of the splendor of another time and place, now frozen in time as visual

testaments of what they once were. Sam marveled, wondering what it would take to summit any one of their rocky faces. No doubt it would take plenty of climbing equipment, a hearty dose of courage, and every ounce of physical strength one could muster.

As he returned from the shed with an armful of wood, however, something made him pause and turn behind him. A sound, like a soft hum riding a wave, pulsed ever so slightly from somewhere in the mountains.

He turned to search for the source of the hum, but there were only trees to block his view. He attempted to pinpoint which direction it came from, but the acoustics of the mountains prevented him from doing so.

Then, the tiniest flicker of light caught his eye high up the mountain to the left of the cabin.

Setting the wood on the front porch, he made his way across the small wooden bridge over the river to the edge of the clearing, where the trees stood like a wall between him and the mountains. Choosing the tallest one he could find with the clearest view of the valley, he began picking his way up the dense branches of the pine.

As he climbed higher, the top of the tree swayed under his weight. Deciding not to go higher, Sam peered out from the branches of the tree in the direction where he had seen the Light.

Shimmying himself onto the branch further out from the trunk, he did his best to concentrate on the mountain to see if the light would once again present itself, but there was only darkness. A small path up the mountain, however, became visible in the moonlight just below where he believed he had seen it. If only he were closer…

"What on earth are you doing up there, Samuel Forrester?" Emma called from below. The sudden noise nearly caused Sam to lose his balance.

"How—did you find me?" he called back from his perch.

"Your tracks in the snow, you dope. Now get down here. The fire is almost out."

Sam picked his way back down the pine tree but noted the direction from which he had seen the Light and believed he had heard the sound.

Emma wrapped her coat on his shoulders yet again as they headed back to the cabin. "You're not very bright, you know. That's twice you've gone out into this weather without proper clothing."

With the fire once again roaring, the four could get some much-needed rest. With the pot of coffee gone, and with a good dent in the root cake Mrs. Sterling sent with them, they curled up on the floor beside the fire for the night. That night, Sam got his wish as Emma suggested they camp out in the living room instead of being apart. None of them objected.

As they drifted to sleep next to the fire, Sam told the others what he had seen and heard in the mountains. He was careful, however, not to give the impression that it was yet another thing to worry about. They had plenty of other things to concern themselves with, not some random noise in the hills.

Chapter Five
Snowed In

The next morning, Sam awoke to the smell of coffee. Before heading to the kitchen, he slipped out to the porch to see if he could view the mountain, but he could only see white as the snow whipped around the yard.

Already a foot had fallen, and the skies showed little sign of letting up.

Emma joined him, holding a steaming cup of coffee. "Mom told me the storms up here in the mountains can last for days. Better get some more wood. The fire's out."

After breakfast, they all got to work putting the rest of the supplies away and cleaning up the cabin from the months of collected dust. Emma and Lillia shooed the boys out of the kitchen while they got to work cleaning out cabinets and sweeping the floors. Sam and Gus were given the job of cleaning the chimney and bringing in as much wood as they could before the snow got too deep, as well as making sure the toilet and running water were in proper working order.

After lunch, they had the entire cabin cleaned, all the linens washed and placed on the beds, and dinner cooking in the pot over the fire. They spent the rest of the day reading and playing board games. The one they liked the most was called *Stump the Golem*, where one player was made the mud monster and attempted to capture the others.

It was three days before the storm let up. The snow was waist deep, and the four friends were sick of being indoors. The morning of the fourth day, when the sun finally poked its head above the trees, Gus promised to take them to a place that he assured would be a surprise for all of them.

"I'm not sure why on earth you would have us bring shorts when it's freezing outside," Lillia said as they slipped on their boots and cinched up their backpacks. "How far is this place, anyway?"

"Really, Gus, I wish you would just tell us where we are going on such a frigid day," Emma agreed.

Gus smiled as he opened the door. "You are just going to have to wait. Remember, it was you that said you wanted out of the cabin."

The day was overcast and slightly warmer, although it had no effect melting the mounds of snow they had gotten from the storm. As they headed behind the cabin into the trees, Sam strained to listen for the hum he had heard several nights ago while in the tree. While it may have been only his mind, he thought he caught the faint noise once more.

The path behind the cabin wound swiftly upward as it approached the rocky mountain face, which was only a few hundred feet from the cabin's back door. Then, it jogged abruptly to the right and climbed at an even steeper angle.

It didn't take long before they needed a break. Gus had warned them the altitude was significantly different at the cabin than in White Pine, and they would likely be out of breath as they climbed. After a few moments' rest, Gus prodded them on once again. Before long, they were far above the treetops, where the smoke from the chimney lazily ascended into the thin air.

Around the corner of an especially large ledge jutting out from the mountain face, the path descended into what looked like a tiny clearing

nestled in a tight cluster of pines butted up against the mountain. In the middle of the clearing was a medium-sized pool of water, steam rising from its surface. The steam rose and settled over the pool, looking much like a solitary cloud that had descended to enjoy the warmth.

"It's a hot spring. Miss Karpatch told me about it," Gus beamed as icicles began forming on his eyebrows. "There is Lazuli in the stream, too, so it glows at night."

Sam couldn't believe Lior could be any more beautiful, but here it was. An oasis of blue in a sea of pure white snow next to some of the most majestic mountains he had ever seen. Truly, in his life, he never could have expected to experience a place like this. And yet, here he was.

They trudged the last few hundred feet through the snow as the path descended to the curious hot spring. Sam was the first to strip down behind a boulder nearby and get into his shorts, the cold instantly nipping at his skin. He managed to slip into the warm water just as the girls found a spot to change in a crevasse where the steaming stream emerging from the mountain.

Gus and the girls soon tiptoed into the water, about the time that Sam found a spot in the shallow pool where the warm water came right up to his neck. The temperature was perfect—though if they wanted warmer water, they scooted closest to where the stream emptied into the pool.

They spent most of the day in and out of the hot spring, enjoying the contrast of the cold air and the warm water on their skin. Mid afternoon, they dressed and explored the crevasse where Emma and Lillia had changed their clothes. Quickly they discovered it was much more than a crevasse, as the wide opening followed the stream further into the mountain, leading to a wide cavern.

Not far inside, the air became unbearably humid because of the heat rising off the hot spring, so they abandoned their expedition into the mountain. Instead, they found a spot near the crevasse opening to eat the lunch they had packed.

"This was an amazing place to come to, Gus," Emma said, the humidity in the air causing her strawberry hair to coil like hairy snakes on her head.

Lillia smacked him on the back playfully. "Yes, Gus, thanks a lot."

"It's really nothing," He said. "I was planning to come here, anyway. But thank Miss Karpatch. She told me where to find it."

It was strange. While Sam listened to them talk, an ambient noise passed by him. Straining, he listened above their conversation. There it was. The humming noise again.

He put his ear up to the crevasse wall. Louder, it pulsed. Hummmm… thump. Hummmm… thump. What was it? Could the others not hear it?

Maybe only he could. Or, perhaps, it was amplified for him. Like the way he heard everything so much clearer while they were on the beach beside the Lazuli pool near the Old City. The insects, the scurrying of little animal feet—it was as though it had been inside his head.

Or maybe he was just going crazy…

Lillia finally noticed him. "Newb, what are you doing?"

Sam motioned them to come listen to the crevasse wall with him.

"I don't hear anything. Except maybe Gus's heavy breathing," Lillia said.

"Me either. Sorry Sam," Gus agreed.

Emma listened a bit longer, her eyes closed, both palms to the wall. After a few moments, however, she agreed she heard nothing.

"Was it the same sound from the other night?" Gus questioned as they made their way out of the crevasse toward the hot spring.

Sam tried to remember. The first night he heard it, the sound was so far away. "Yeah, it was. I mean, I think so."

"Are you sure you are hearing… anything?" Lillia said, not wanting to sound disbelieving. She chose her words carefully, recalling that his senses had proven effective in helping them during their journey to the Old City.

"I don't know, maybe," he said, scowling.

Maybe Lillia was right. He was hearing things. His nerves from the

past week had been put to the test. Besides, the last thing he wanted to do was spoil a day of relaxing.

"I'm getting back in the pool," he said, changing the subject. "I'm sure it's nothing."

Back in the warm pool, they talked about anything and everything, enjoying each other's company and a break from the biting cold. As the day progressed into late afternoon, they packed up to head back to the cabin for dinner. Pausing, they marveled at the Lazuli Light that glowed in the spring as it flowed from the mountain face in the waning sunlight. It gave an almost unearthly fantastical feel to the hidden pool, a picture that only belonged in dreams.

They didn't want to leave, but knew the stew they had left cooking was certainly cold by now. If they had any chance of staying warm in the cabin overnight, the fire had to be revived.

Changing in the warm air of the cavern, they trudged their way through the snow back to the cabin, taking care to not misstep in the quickly advancing darkness.

About halfway home, it began to snow once again, some of the enormous flakes making their way through the dense branches of the pines above. Concerned that they may have another storm rolling in, they made sure to each grab an armful of wood from the shed as they passed by.

With the fire roaring once again and dinner safely in their bellies, they sat down to enjoy a cup of coffee before crashing into bed. Just before retiring, however, they made a collective decision that they would at least consider investigating the source of the noise Sam had heard the night they arrived, and while in the crevasse at the Lazuli hot spring that day.

The last thing Sam remembered was the wind picking up outside the cabin as Gus tossed another few logs on the fire before the four stumbled off to their beds.

****

It snowed for another four days after their trip to the hot spring. They were now used to being trapped inside, so they found ways to keep themselves busy. Gus reread every book and journal in the cabin, just in case there was a mention of something in the woods that may clue them in to what the hum might be. Emma took up knitting, and Lillia taught Sam how to whittle wood. In the evenings, they would play board games or read, drink coffee and tell stories, or take turns at the coffee roaster in the pantry. On frigid nights, they would sleep by the fire and Gus would tell them more about the Watchers and stories of ancient battles with the fallen.

On the morning of the sixth day of the storm, while out getting more of the dwindling wood pile, Gus and Sam noticed that the top of the snow drifts glistened, a sign of a break in the below-freezing temperatures.

One more week brought a radical change in the weather, and though still cold, quickly the days became sunny and above freezing. The piles of snow against the cabin and the boathouse began to diminish.

Emma took Sam outside on one such morning to teach him how to tap birch trees for making syrup. After collecting three days' worth of sap, they boiled it down to make enough syrup for several mornings' worth of pancakes.

As the sun shone brighter and the days warmed enough to see the mountain trails open, they began to plot how they would get to the location where they believed Sam had heard the strange noise.

One night, while they were going over the equipment and maps for the hike up the mountain, there was a sharp knock at the door. Stunned, they froze. Sam's heart skipped a beat.

"Hallo there!" came the muffled voice of a middle-aged man on the porch.

Emma sprung up, flinging open the door. "Daddy!"

She was met with a scowling Mr. Sterling. "Emma! You *must* respond when someone knocks on the door! Don't you remember how we showed you?"

He then snatched his daughter up in an embrace. "It's dangerous, even out here."

"I'm sorry, Dad. I will do better next time. Where's mom?"

"Well, let's get inside. There's much to discuss, and I could use a cup of coffee."

Once the pot was on the stove, Mr. Sterling laid out all that was happening in Lior and White Pine. Sam wasn't sure how they were able to communicate between the two worlds, but he figured it was necessary for them to keep up to date.

Emma handed him a large mug. He gingerly took a sip. "The Metim attack was put down for the time being, but we are certain they will return. The location of the Sha'ar gate cannot be kept a secret forever."

"Do you think they know where it is?" Gus asked.

"No. Not yet. I think they know the general area, but not the exact location. When they are certain, they won't be attacking with such small numbers."

Lillia plopped next to the fire with another cup of coffee and a leftover blueberry muffin they had made the previous morning. "What about Nasikh? Any more about the Dark One?"

"It seems that some of the Dark Watchers living in Creation are much more active. Gatherings are occurring all over the world according to the Lior regions…" he said, pausing, as if exhaustion was catching up with him. "But I would not like to burden you with this now. We must instead discuss when and how you will get to the city for Mentorship."

Emma frowned. "What do you mean? You're not coming with us?"

"No, I'm afraid not. We have decided that too much arch travel is creating unnecessary risks. Which… is why your mother did not come," he said sadly. "I came here tonight to tell you that you must go to Mentorship—and the Light Festival—alone."

"No…" Emma pleaded.

He reached over and brushed the hair out of her eyes. "Emma, I know it's difficult, but for the safety of all, we must do this. I took a risk in coming here tonight to tell you this. In fact, we are concerned that some of us are even being watched."

From the demeanor of the others, Sam knew that this was not normal behavior for the Descendants. They had always traveled the arches freely, and now, they were limiting their access to and from Lior. Mr. Sterling and the others must have been truly worried if they would miss out on their own daughter's Mentorship ceremony.

"I can promise you that as soon as it is possible, we will meet up with you after Mentorship."

She fought back the tears. "But that's another three months!"

"My darling daughter, you knew you would be gone for Mentorship, but now it will be just a few more months without us. Creator willing, we will be there when you arrive back in the city after you have passed your tests."

Emma said nothing more. Scooting closer to her father, she put her head on his shoulder, nearly spilling his coffee.

He retrieved a curious-looking key from his pocket and handed it to Gus. "This key will activate the Lightway here on the mountain. It is located on the peak called Thea, directly to the right when you are looking out of the cabin."

"Wait—wasn't the Lightway here disabled?" Sam asked, remembering the long trek they took to get to the city the last time.

Mr. Sterling grinned. "No, it wasn't, but we felt it best to make it seem that way with the Dark spies we had hiding in the city."

Sam remembered Cooley, and how he had been working for the Darkness inside Lior City. He wondered how many more they had caught now with Kachash's curse lifted.

"How hard is it to get to the top of the mountain where the Lightway tower is?" Gus asked, no doubt thinking of the snow and rock that surrounded the dangerous peaks of the valley.

Mr. Sterling grinned again. "Not hard at all, actually. There is a secret tunnel at the base that will get you there in a jiffy. I wouldn't go eating too big of a breakfast before traveling, however."

No one knew what he meant by that, but they nodded in acceptance. Meanwhile, Gus wrote Mr. Sterling's directions in his journal.

"Since Lior City requires a special code from the Lightway, I have stored it here in this box, which will keep it contained until you need it. Only open it when you are safely inside the tower and do not write it down. While we have never had an incident through the Lightway as of yet, we want to make absolutely certain we are maintaining secrecy. Understand?"

They nodded, accepting the tiny wooden box that Mr. Sterling removed from his bag.

"Now, I would plan on leaving for Mentorship the day before the Light Festival," he said, yawning rather loudly. "The Helel Malach for new students doesn't start until the closing ceremony, but you will need to make sure you have everything you need to take with you. Cindy has sent a list and some money with me for you all to purchase needed supplies."

Lillia accepted the pouch and list with the supplies and immediately disappeared to stash it. Gus stood to get an extra bowl of vegetable soup for Mr. Sterling, while Emma stayed close to her father. Sam did his best not to envy her, thinking of his own fleeting time with Nuriel. Part of him wanted to be angry he couldn't spend more time with him.

When the others returned, Mr. Sterling asked them to tell him what had transpired while they had been away. Other than the storm and the visit to the Lazuli hot spring, the only information they had to offer was the flash of light in the hills and the sound Sam had heard. They recounted everything they could to him while he ate, doing their best to reassure him that other than that, nothing out of the ordinary had happened.

Finishing his bowl of soup, Mr. Sterling agreed that they should go and check out the location where Sam believed the light had come from. He warned them that straying too far from the valley, however, would put them in danger of being spotted by Metim. He also warned them that being caught in the mountains during a storm, no matter the season, was a recipe for disaster.

# Chapter Five

When it was time to call it a night, Gus moved upstairs with Sam to allow Mr. Sterling to stay with his daughter before he had to leave the next morning.

In the loft, Sam asked Gus if he thought Mr. Sterling may have been holding back some details about what was happening in White Pine from them.

Gus chose not to speculate. "There's no way of knowing," He said, blowing out the small candle on the nightstand. "But at this point, I have learned to trust the Sterlings' decisions, even if they don't make sense at the time."

Sam sighed as he pulled the covers up to his chin to keep out the cold air.

"I know," Sam said. "I just have a bad feeling about it."

Chapter Six
The Watcher Device

Mr. Sterling was gone the next morning before the sun had fully crested above the mountaintops. Before leaving, however, he had set out a napkin with a stack of root cakes and a note from each of their parents.

As Sam made coffee, he noticed one of them had his name on it. So when the coffee was finished brewing, he sat in one of the armchairs and opened it.

Dear Sam,
Please do not think I am silly for writing, but you must know that
while you are gone, we do think often of you. Since you have come into
our lives, we have thought of you as one of our own. Please take care of
yourself and come back home to us.

With love,
Mom Sterling

Sam couldn't help it—the tears just flowed. No one had ever written him a note like that, especially any of his foster parents. He knew Mrs. Sterling wasn't his actual mother, but she made him feel as though she cared for him as one.

Not that Amos didn't care, but there was a difference between a mother and a father in the kind of love they gave. He wouldn't have ever admitted it before, but perhaps for the first time in his life, he did look at Mrs. Sterling as the mother he never had.

After Sam became a Descendant, Amos promised he would tell him about his mother. All that he knew, anyway. But Winter and Spring came and went, and Sam didn't have the guts to ask him again. He wasn't sure he wanted to hear what happened to her, anyway.

When the others awoke and they had devoured every bit of root cake left for them, they made a plan to hike the next morning to wherever the humming sound had come from. Mr. Sterling had guessed it would take nearly half the day to reach, given the altitude and terrain up the mountainside. If they were to make it back to the cabin by nightfall, they would have to hurry.

They spent the day checking their equipment, preparing food and other supplies to take with them, taking naps, and practicing mountaineering techniques with ropes and knots in daisy chains to prevent falls. While it wouldn't be like actual climbing, they believed there could be parts of the trail that would require more than just a steady footing.

When they awoke the next morning, the weather was nearly perfect. The sun had not yet risen over the peaks, but it was clear the day was going to be warmer than usual. They made sure to pause for a few muffins, boiled eggs and coffee before they got started, and went over the map one last time to pick out the potential hazards along the way. Emma forced them all last minute to pack a sleeping sack just in case they were stuck on the mountain overnight, which they hoped wouldn't happen.

They crossed the stream and found their way through the woods

in the direction where Sam and Gus believed they spotted a weak path high up the mountain.

As luck would have it, only a half hour into their journey, Lillia stumbled across what looked like a faint animal trail leading in the direction they were traveling. They followed it, quickly discovering that someone had purposefully placed stones in spots to create makeshift steps up the more difficult terrain.

Gus's first thought was that it was Sam's grandfather who created the trail. As the overgrowth thickened, however, he changed his mind, concluding that it had to be much older.

They continued on the trail until reaching the convergence of two sheer rock faces to either side. They created a magnificent passageway between them, only wide enough for two people to fit side by side if they were rather thin.

Carefully, they wound their way through the tight gap, trying not to think about what would happen if the walls were to collapse.

"Look at it this way," Lillia said, attempting to ease the tension as they squeezed through a particularly thin part of the passageway. "If it does collapse, we will all die quickly."

A few hundred meters inside the passageway, the path opened up to a small canyon only a few meters wide. Blue sky poured in from above. To the left of the path was another opening in the rock face, where a crude set of thin stairs led upward into the mountainside at a sharp ascent.

They paused, nibbling on some homemade grain bars and drinking deeply of their canteens. Then they proceeded up the stairwell cautiously, noting that the years had not been kind to it.

The stairwell abruptly disappeared as the four reached the top of the rock face, having climbed some forty meters according to Gus's altimeter.

After another brief break, they assessed the way that lay before them. It would not be an easy trek. Several large boulders had fallen from the mountain face, many landing on the thin ledge that was to be their path. Finding a viable way through was going to be treacherous work.

Fortunately, the ledge widened on the other side as they passed the fallen boulders from the rockslide. The path turned sharply into the mountain once again, where they used the ropes to scramble up the steep pathway that led toward the summit.

They were still many meters beneath the summit, but the path ended at a broad ledge that overlooked the valley below. A solid rock wall rose skyward at the back of the ledge.

Lillia plopped down on the ledge precariously and dug through her pack to find her water bottle. Emma scolded her for not thinking about the consequences if the ledge suddenly gave way, but she ignored her. Tipping back the bottle, she drank deeply, admiring the valley below.

"Guess that ends that." Gus said, setting his pack against the wall and digging out his map. "According to my drawings and this map, we are at nearly the exact spot where Sam would have seen the flash of light."

"There's nothing here." Emma circled the ledge, kicking at the loose rocks scattered on the ground. She glared at them as they tumbled away, as if one of them might tell them what to do next.

Tired from the climb, Sam wandered over to where Lillia sat. He stared at the tiny cabin below them, watching the early afternoon fog hang just above the treetops. Through peeks in the fog, they could see the little river sparkle as the sun danced across its surface.

The chilly wind forced them to dig out extra layers. Not far above the ledge was the peak of the mountain, where mounds of snow still wrapped the summit. No doubt, on the cold winter nights, the mountain was truly a brutal place to be.

It wouldn't be long before they would have to head back. And given the terrain they had encountered on the way up, they would have to hurry or get caught in the dark.

Sam stood to join Emma in circling the ledge, looking for answers. It didn't make sense. Why would the path end here?

Both Gus and Lillia chose to let them search without them. They

were exhausted from the altitude, and the disappointment of finding nothing seemed to discourage them.

Emma paced back and forth on the ledge, then stared at the rock wall where Gus sat, chewing on a piece of dried meat. "I just don't understand this place," she said, frustrated. "It's almost as if something was once here, or it was—"

"Hidden." Sam thought of the arch in the cavern near White Pine. The opening contained a strange optical illusion that hid the opening for the unwary passerby.

Both Sam and Emma hurried to the wall, feeling along its surface for any sign of an opening. Hearing the conversation, Lillia and Gus joined in, hoping to aid the effort.

"Wait," Sam said, stepping back from the wall. "Come look at this."

The others stepped back with him, gazing at the wall.

"See it?" He said, pointing to the wall on the right of the ledge.

"No, Newb. What are we looking at?" Lillia said.

"There. Look carefully, just to the left of the pathway back down the mountain."

"An opening! How did we not see it?" Emma exclaimed, rushing to the masterfully hidden entrance. Still, as she drew close, she had difficulty spotting it.

"It's an opening to another cave, which means it will take time to explore," Lillia said.

"I agree," Gus said, picking up his pack. "The sun's going down fast. If we are going to spend any time inside, we better get a move on."

Then he shuffled over to the others, who were examining the exterior of the entrance.

Sam slipped into the opening first. Remembering his lantern, he pulled it from his pack. It glowed immediately in the darkness.

Lillia followed, then Emma and Gus. The entrance opened up slightly into a long tunnel that led straight into the heart of the mountain. Almost immediately, Sam began to hear the humming noise he heard while at the cabin, and again at the hot spring crevasse. As they ventured further, the sound grew louder, like a pulsing hum of a strange machine hard at work.

They had barely noticed the temperature change at first, but the deeper they went, the warmer it became. Eventually, Gus began shedding his overcoat and removing his winter hat and gloves.

He wiped his forehead from the beads of sweat that had built up on his skin. "I've heard that most caves stay right around sixty degrees, but I daresay this one is an exception."

Sam, too, realized it was a little too warm for outerwear and slipped off his jacket and the leather gloves his grandfather had bought him before they left.

"Strange. I feel like this could be as warm or warmer than the crevasse at the hot spring…" he said.

Quickly, he realized the potential connection. "Could these two tunnels be part of the same cave?"

Gus tossed his coat to the side of the tunnel, no doubt hoping to pick it back up on the way out instead of carrying it. "Could be the same network of caves, I suppose. We are a bit higher in elevation than the hot spring, but I guess they *could* be coming from the same source."

Before they went any deeper, however, their questions were answered. As they turned the corner of the long tunnel, a massive pit of molten Lazuli stood suddenly before them.

Deep in the center of the mountain was a monstrous pool, heated by a deep pocket of super-heated gas and lava. Strangely, the molten pit took on an almost purple glow as it mixed the two elements.

They stood on the edge of the pool, in awe of what lay before them. Sam remembered the large pool below the City Center when Sayvon led him on a tour, but this was so much more.

The molten goo bubbled and oozed far below the massive cavern, partially taking on the properties of Lazuli as wisps of blue lazily rose above the surface and up the walls of the pit. The heat from the pool made Sam wonder how any snow rested on the mountain peak at all. Considering it, he recalled noticing that this peak contained far less

snow than the others, though it was still covered. They had just failed to put the pieces together.

"I can feel the Lazuli here. It is so strong," Emma said, holding her hands out in front of her toward the pit.

"Yeah, wow, I feel it for sure," Gus said, wiping the sweat from his brow. "I wonder if this is what could be causing the disturbances in the valley, like what Mr. Sterling told us about."

The others eyed him. It wasn't normally the case that large concentrations of Lazuli would cause problems with the gifts. Instead, they would enhance them. Perhaps something else was going on here.

"Do you still hear the hum?" Emma asked.

Sam glanced around the cavern, where the pathway veered off to the left of the pit. There was an opening in the wall not far down the path, where there appeared to be a smaller room carved out of the rock. Sam pointed in the room's direction.

"Over there," He told them.

Immediately upon entering the small room, they noticed the ring-like structure in the center. It resembled a large brick fire pit. Upon closer examination, however, they realized that the material that made up the ring was not typical brick material, but of Lazuli rock that had cooled and carved into the shape of bricks.

"Hey, look at this." Lillia said, standing next to the ring. Rising up from the ground at her feet was a pedestal, slowly making its way to waist-level.

"Come closer," she motioned.

Sam and Gus both stepped up to the ring and two more pedestals of Lazuli stone rose up near their feet. Another arose for Emma, too, as she drew closer.

"What do we do?" Emma whispered.

Sam heard the hum deep within the ring clearly now. Whatever it was that was making the sound, it was here.

"Do you hear it?" he pointed. "It's coming from here, I am sure."

"Hear what? The hum?" Lillia smirked. "Nope. Still just you, nerdboy."

The others shook their heads as well. Why could he hear it, but they couldn't?

Hummmm… thump. Hummmm… thump.

Something inside him urged him to reach out and touch the pedestal in front of him. Instinctively, he raised his hands above the stone platform.

"Sam! Don't touch it! Are you crazy?" Emma yelled from across the ring. "We don't know what this thing does! It could be a weapon, or a trap, or a Dark monument of some sort!"

"It's not," he said suddenly, surprised at his own words. "I'm not sure how I know, but I just do."

Lillia snorted. "Seriously? How could you know that… unless you're a magician or something?"

"Or a prophet," Emma said quietly.

Lillia threw her hands up. "And now he's a prophet? So we should just follow him around like he's the Creator or something? For all we know, this thing could be built by the Dark forces."

"No, Lillia. There wouldn't be Lazuli here if that were true. I think—"

"Not true. Didn't Nuriel tell us the Dark Lords were traveling the gates? Why couldn't they do something like this?"

Emma scowled at Lillia. "And what would be the purpose of that?"

"I don't know, disrupt gate travel. Maybe it's what they are using to help them travel the gates." Lillia retorted.

"No way. The protectors would have noticed it by now. And does this look like it was built only a few years ago? I wouldn't put a lot of stock in that theory—"

"Wait. Both of you," Gus stopped them mid-argument. He turned to Sam. "How did you know about this place? It's obvious that it is not here by mistake, yet somehow you heard and saw *something* here."

Sam had considered that, as well as Lillia and Emma's arguments, too. If there was something here, he had seen it, but none of the others had. Could this be the connection to the Darkness he was so worried about?

It was a stretch, but he hadn't had much faith in himself after hearing he could end up becoming a slave of the Dark One. Sure, the Legend said he would be second to him, but what did that really mean? Servanthood. Doing as the Dark One wished. Carrying out his plans.

They were dark thoughts, but he wasn't going to leave anything out in his quest for truth.

"There's only one way to find out," Lillia shrugged. Then, much to the others' surprise, she stuck her hands on the pedestal in front of her.

Lazuli Light crept up the sides of the stone pedestal and met her hands. Instead of removing them, she allowed her own warmth to meet the Light as it crawled up her arms. She closed her eyes, then nodded and smiled.

The others did the same. The Light crept up each pedestal to meet each of their hands, as it had Lillia's. Sam felt the warmth of the Light flow through him, and he allowed it, basking in the feeling it provided. Even in the warmth of the cavern, the warmth the Light provided was still soothing.

He opened his eyes, seeing the others doing the same. The humming grew louder, more intense. Suddenly, there was a pulsing blue orb of light in the center of the ring.

The orb grew steadily brighter until they had to shield their eyes from it, and forcing all of them to step back from their pedestals as it continued to grow.

Then the orb disappeared. Left in its place was a large holographic projection of a globe at eye level in the dead center of the Lazuli stone ring.

It held stunning detail, with mountains rising in three dimensions, valleys and rivers flowing animated in full color, and cities complete with tiny buildings. Some pulsed blue as if alive, but others were dark and lifeless.

Gus stepped up to the holographic map after a few moments, walking around the ring as he studied every side carefully. Sam and the two girls watched him work, careful not to disturb him. This was most certainly his area of expertise.

On his fourth turn around the holographic image, the pedestals sank back into the floor until they were once again flush with the stone and unnoticeable from a casual glance. Upon closer inspection, Sam saw that there were, in fact, pedestals spaced evenly around the entire outer ring. No matter where they would have stood, a pedestal would have been in front of them.

"They knew where we were standing," Emma said, relaxing. "That's not like Boggle's inventions."

"It didn't feel like the Darkness, either," Lillia admitted.

Sam remembered the old inventor they met the previous year in Lior. He was eccentric, almost perfectly defined. A genius inventor, but would lose his shoes even if they were on his feet.

He had invented the Lightway and the hololibrary at the Old City, and numerous other amazing things that used Lazuli Light to make them work. Some of which, like the Lightboards, had allowed Sam and the others to evade the Dark Lord Arazel at the outer dunes Light tower.

But the holographic map in front of them was different, not like Boggle's. Not that Boggle's stuff wasn't amazing, it was. But this was truly extraordinary in its design.

"It's Lior," Gus finally said, staring at one particularly bright city. "Look, Lior City… right there."

He pointed at the unmistakable shape of the city walls perched on the Yarey Sea coastline, and the forest where Sam had met the old lady Wrenge.

"How old is this place and this device?" Lillia asked, putting her hand out to touch one of the mountain peaks flanking the coastline. As she touched it, the map exploded at the very place she had touched, revealing a much larger version of the mountain close-up for all of them to see.

As they all marveled at the detail of the new image, Sam realized something very peculiar about four tiny dots deep within the mountain.

He ran to the other side of the room near the entrance, then out to the edge of the large Lazuli pit, and then back again. The entire time, he watched the tiny dots in the center of the mountain. The others watched with interest.

Unbelievable, he thought. *How could this be?* He glanced around the room, looking for something—a camera, a device—something that would give him a clue how the map knew they were here.

"Mind telling us what you're doing?" Emma scowled at him as he ran back to the globe.

He pointed at the four tiny dots on the image. "The map. Those dots. It's us. It must be real time, but I can't find where a camera or anything might be—"

Gus had been ignoring Sam during the entire ordeal, but now had his journal in his hand and was thumbing through the pages. "That's because there isn't one. There's something I read a long time ago about ancient Watcher devices that were used. I think this is one of them."

Emma turned her attention on him. "Watcher device? Like the arches? Really Gus, that was all just scholars talking."

Gus ignored the statement. Instead, he read from his journal aloud. "According to *Ancient Watcher History* by Choam Biltan, the arches were 'only one of many artifacts built by the Watchers, but many may have been lost over time to war or sabotage. Some were dismantled by the Watchers themselves. They built devices that would keep records of events, monitor communication between the expanse of Lior and Creation, and contain weapons of great power.'"

Lillia stepped back up to the giant holographic map, which had returned to its normal image of all of Lior. "Boggle talked a lot about that. He said there was some pretty crazy stuff. Both from the Watchers of Light, and on the Darkness side."

Emma blinked. "Gus, how do you know it's something built by the Watchers?"

Gus ignored her once again, much to her disapproval. But then he held up his journal for all to see. On the page, he showed them a carefully drawn image of the Irin. It was the symbol etched on every arch and displayed in thousands of other places by Descendants of Lior. "I am not positive, but I know that this is the symbol for the Watcher wing, the symbol of a connection with the Watchers."

"We know that, Gus," Lillia said. "And so does the rest of Lior. The Watchers showed the Descendants lots of things."

Gus held up a finger. "Yes. But what if some devices weren't meant to be found?"

They looked strangely at him, like he had just learned a completely new language without their knowing. But then they understood, for as he turned and pointed at the cavern wall behind him, a very old carving of the same symbol drawn in his book became apparent where they had not seen it before.

Perhaps Gus was right. If no other Descendant knew of the map, maybe it was because the Watchers had intended them not to.

Chapter Seven
Tower of the Gods

Time was slipping away for them to get back down the mountain before night would descend on them. Gus, Sam, Lillia, and Emma circled the map image, pointing out various parts of Lior, even zooming in on Lior City to see the tiny ant-sized people moving about and even the great dragon Orono inside his stone house.

It was Emma who discovered the fact that given the right motion of the waving of one's hands over the image, the map seemed to race backward in time nearly a thousand years, as though every day's events had been recorded and were available for them to see.

"This is unbelievable!" Gus said upon learning of the discovery. "This would be invaluable to the PO Office and the Sons of Light! Not to mention the Office of Records and Research! Just think of the possibilities in the fight with the Darkness!"

"I think it's creepy," Emma said. "And dangerous. Someone could have literally been watching us—and everyone else this whole time. Think if the Dark forces got a hold of this contraption. We wouldn't stand a chance."

Gus nodded, with Sam and Lillia following suit. "It would be bad to end up on the wrong side. We'd better report this as soon as we get to the city. I'm sure they would send someone out to retrieve it."

As they were talking, a particular spot on the map caught Sam's attention as it would pulse with light ever so slightly, then it would disappear for several moments before returning once again. The area where it lay was on the far right of the holomap (as they had come to name it), to the edge of the image where the details seemed to blur into indistinguishable nothingness. The Divide.

At first, Sam believed he was seeing something on the map that wasn't there. After watching it for several moments, however, he became convinced his eyes weren't deceiving him.

It was strange too, as his gaze was naturally drawn to that one section of the map and nowhere else. Like the map was trying to show him something. The humming that had subsided for the most part was back in full force, so much so that Sam wondered if it had a direct connection to his brain.

He reached out and touched the spot on the map, which exploded into life size for all of them to see. It was a tower, of sorts, not star-shaped like the Light towers used for the Lightway, but wide at the base and sloping inward as it reached the top. It was dark, almost black, and was rippled throughout with what looked to Sam like Lazuli.

High up the face of the tower was a large symbol carved into the stone that startled Sam for a moment. *The drawing.* His mind went to Henry Bostwick and the sketch he had shown Sam the same day they left for Lior. It was the symbol of the Watcher wing inside the tower.

"What is it?" Emma asked, handing him a piece of dried fruit.

Sam turned the holomap around to see every angle of the tower. Strangely, it was the only place they had looked at on the holomap that would not show them the inside.

"I'm not sure, actually. I just saw Mr. Bostwick had a drawing that was similar to this."

He pointed at the Irin symbol on the tower. "It looked like this

tower. The sketch he showed me had the wing on the tower just like this one.”

Gus peered at the closeup of the image. “You’re talking about the Migdal Babel. The Tower of the Gods. Henry’s been looking for it for years.”

“And the crazy bat’s never found anything, except a few old symbols. And maybe a few new rainforest diseases along the way…” Lillia said, plopping down on the sandy floor.

“Well, maybe he hasn’t, but the Tower of the Gods is *real*. Although it’s never been found, there are records of it having been constructed somewhere in Creation by fallen Watchers,” Gus told them.

“So it was an evil place…” Emma said, peering at the image. “But this one is in Lior. It can’t be the same thing, right?”

Gus shrugged. “Probably not. It must be something else.”

Suddenly, Sam didn’t feel so good. He wasn’t sure if it was the heat of the cavern, the constant droning hum of the machine, or staring intently at the holomap for so long. Whatever it was, it made him want to throw up.

“Sam, you’re white as a ghost.” Emma said, feeling his forehead. She peered into his eyes. “I think it’s time we pack up and get out of here.”

“Oh, wow!” Gus exclaimed, looking at his watch. “It’s nearly dusk! If we’re going to make it down, we have to leave *now*!”

For a moment, they considered sleeping in the cavern for the night, but given Sam’s sudden condition and the fact that they were running out of water, it was best they risk the trip back to the cabin. Seizing up their packs, they helped Sam into his own pack and made for the entrance.

Past the super-heated pool of Lazuli they went, at which point sweat poured down Sam’s face, soaking his tee shirt.

They slipped out of the hidden entrance to catch the last of the sun making its way below the mountain peaks. The temperature had dropped since when they had first arrived, feeling good on his skin.

Sam drew in deep breaths of the sweet cool breezes drifting down from the summit above.

If they were lucky, they could hurry down the most treacherous portion of the path before the last of the light.

The cool air did not sustain Sam for long. Soon he began to sweat again, and as they started down the mountain, it was all they could do to keep him from discarding every layer he had on.

The sun submerged below the peaks. With the lack of ample light, Sam was certain that either Gus or Emma would stumble as they aided him past the dangerous rockslide. Fortunately, they did not.

While petite, Emma had a sort of strength to her that surprised Sam. At the moment, however, she could have been a superhero and he would not care. His head was swimming, and his legs and torso ached as if he had just run a marathon. Certain he would not make it, he pleaded groggily with them to stop and come back for him in the morning. Of course, they refused.

About the time they reached the crevasse, Sam had lost consciousness. The rest of the journey back to the cabin was spent taking turns carrying him the best they could. Two of them would link arms as they propped him up, while the other was tasked with finding traces of their previous trail in the hazy light of the moon. It was slow going and tedious, but at least they were making headway.

When they stumbled up the cabin steps, Sam had regained consciousness, which put Emma's mind at ease. She had made it a point to check his breathing every few minutes just to make sure they hadn't lost him.

Sam was present but not, and although he knew they were in the cabin, he could not remember any of the journey home. His head and body ached, and all he wanted to do was sleep. Frustratingly, Emma and the others would not let him. They were constantly forcing him awake to drink several glasses of water, all the while exchanging the damp rags on his forehead with colder ones dipped in the stream.

Emma dug into the herb drawer in the kitchen for the dandelion and Liorian Kararah root tea her mother had prepared before they left,

which promised to alleviate symptoms of flu and fever. She quickly prepared a pot while Gus dug through some of Mrs. Sterling's herb books on the shelf for any additional remedy suggestions.

Sam drifted in and out of sleep, doing his best to comply with the others that were trying to help, but he found it impossible. All he wanted was to sleep, to rid himself of the pounding headache that only seemed to grow worse.

All the while, his mind shifted from the present reality of the cabin to the cavern where the ancient Watcher device lay, which still hummed in his head. The image was always the same—the structure that stood high on the mountain near the boundary of the Divide. A dark tower with the blue Lazuli Light that crept up the side and concentrated brilliantly at the top. It was the only place on the holomap that would not allow them to see inside.

But there was something else he was seeing. Something Dark, a creature of sorts, that would flash in his mind between the shifts from the cabin to the cavern. Briefly it would show itself—a form of a dragon, but not quite, as its stature seemed to change into that of a man of sorts. Its skin was almost fluid in its design, so much so that he couldn't quite make out its features.

But he was too tired to dwell on any of it. His temples still throbbed, and his body ached fiercely. Finally, whatever Emma had put into the tea began to work its way through him, long enough to ease the pain for a few moments. Long enough for a brief rest…

✳✳✳✳✳✳✳✳✳✳✳✳✳✳✳✳✳✳✳✳✳✳✳✳✳✳✳✳✳✳✳✳

"Sam, wake up."

It was Emma's voice. She was at his side. The light in the window had just begun to spill into the tiny living room. "You were talking in your sleep again," she whispered, attempting to keep the snoring Gus from stirring beside them.

"It can't be morning already," Gus said groggily as he woke with a loud snort. The sound woke Lillia, who had curled up in the chair beside the three laying on the hard pine floor in front of the fire.

"I will tell you what…" Lillia yawned. "Between Gus's snoring and Sam's talking, it's lucky we got any sleep at all."

"What was I talking about?"

Sam looked around the room at each of their faces. They exchanged puzzled glances, unable to tell him any of what he muttered with any clarity.

"Destruction…" Gus said, yawning again. "I heard you say the word destruction over and over."

Lillia shook her head and turned back over in her chair. "Sounds exciting."

Emma tapped Sam on the shoulder. "How are you feeling?"

Strangely, he had remembered nothing of the sickness the night before.

"Good, I guess. Just a little sore," he said, sitting up. "I don't know what happened. I just blacked out, I think."

"I'll agree with that for sure," Gus said, rubbing his shoulders and smiling. "You aren't easy to carry."

Emma stood and walked toward the kitchen. "Well, it had to have been something. A bug or something. Coffee, anyone?"

It was a silly question, especially after the night they had descending the mountain. They nodded anyway.

After polishing off a few pancakes and birch syrup, they got to work, unloading their packs and doing chores for the day. It seemed almost meaningless to worry about those things after their discovery, but they knew nothing was going to be done about it until they were able to get to Lior City. And that was only going to be possible one day before the start of the annual Lior Light Festival, as Mr. Sterling had told them.

Since the Light Festival always began the first day of the seventh month of the fall season (which was October in Creation), they still had a full two months before they could get the information to the Council in the city. Since Mr. Sterling had informed them that the situation was much more perilous than they had anticipated, they were unlikely to

receive another visit from anyone for the remainder of their stay.

Sam racked his brain to think of a way they could get the information about the strange Watcher device to Mr. Sterling or Sam's uncle Talister, who sat on the High Council, but nothing feasible presented itself. They knew communication was dangerous, and only the most skilled Protectors, such as Mr. Sterling, could send out Lightscribes from the valley.

The only option they considered was to leave the valley temporarily to send out a scribe, but there was a danger that someone of the Darkness could detect it as well. Aside from those options, there was really nothing they could do. Nothing, that was, but wait.

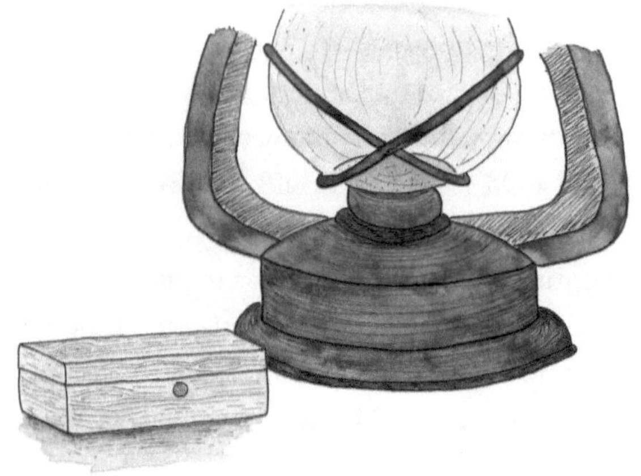

Chapter Eight
The Great Dragon

Around the third night after the discovery of the device and Sam's fateful journey down the mountain, his nightmares began again. Waking suddenly, he caught the glimpse of a person next to his bunk. It was Emma.

"What is it?" She asked. "What do you see?"

Sam squinted to see her delicate form sitting on the bed next to him. "I—I'm not sure…"

He struggled to remember the vivid images. Then, one of them flooded back.

"I think I keep seeing that tower from the holomap."

"The one near the Divide? I don't think an old tower would make anyone want to scream in their sleep."

"I wasn't screaming," Sam argued.

She put a hand on his arm, which had been contorted under his body and was numb from the constriction. Her touch felt like a million needles going up his arm. Yet it warmed him. He sunk into her presence, silently watching her outline as she leaned toward him.

Then she smacked him across the face.

"Why did you do that?!"

Sam jumped out of the bed, twisting his ankle on his slipper and crashing awkwardly to the floor. This, in turn, sent Lillia and Gus rolling out of bed to see what the commotion was.

"Sam's dreaming again." Emma said, unapologetic. She didn't move a muscle to help Sam off the floor.

Lillia rolled her eyes. "Well, thanks for that. So was I." Even in the dark, her hair was immaculately straight.

"What was it about?" Gus mumbled, yawning. He didn't sound quite awake enough to be fully aware of what had transpired. His face looked like a blueberry in the soft blue light of the lantern he held. He blushed when Lillia frowned at him.

"Sam's dream, I mean."

Emma rolled her eyes skeptically. "He says he is seeing the tower from the map in the cave we saw. Because a tower would make anyone scream in their sleep."

He was immediately irritated at her. "I'm not sure what it was that I saw. It could have been the tower, or a giant spider. I'm not sure, really," He lied.

Truthfully, the tower was the only image that he could recall clearly. But there had been something else. Something horrifying in the back of his mind. What had it been?

"I see the tower, and…" he continued, struggling to recall the image of the thing—or a person—who had invaded his mind. As he strained to remember, the blurred image of a gruesome beast blinked, and was gone. "… a dragon. Or… a dragon that's a man, or—the other way around maybe? I don't know…"

Lillia flopped down on the floor of the little loft, trying to hide her interest. "A Dragon-man."

"That doesn't even—" Emma began.

"Exist. Yeah Em', I know," Sam interrupted.

Gus, too, rolled out of bed and took a seat near the foot of the bed next to Lillia. "How vivid was the dream? Like last time?"

"Yeah. I suppose," He answered, still on edge from Emma's smack in the face. He still didn't see the reason for it.

Truthfully, the dream was the same as before. The same vivid energy, dark and mesmerizing, capturing his mind for what seemed like hours on end. Maybe hours, or maybe only a few minutes.

There was something new about this dream, however. Something he was reluctant to share with the others, though he knew he had to. This dream had been *more* vivid than the last one. More real, it seemed. That meant the dreams were getting stronger.

They were silent, working through their thoughts. Perhaps they were simply frustrated and didn't know what to say, or didn't know how to help him. He wondered why they had chosen to sleep near him again. All he did was wake them up with nightmares, regularly interrupting them from getting a full night's sleep.

"It's fine guys, rea—" he began, but stopped abruptly when he heard a soft crackling sound coming from the kitchen below them. It sounded like static.

At first, he wasn't sure the others had heard it. But then they all turned in the direction of the kitchen.

Freezing, they listened, hearts pounding. This time, it sounded like there was a raspy voice emerging from out of the static.

"Why is the radio on?!" Emma whispered, a look of fear in her eyes.

Hunched over as quietly as they could muster, four heads poked out of the loft to the cool, dark air in the cabin below. They strained to hear or see what had invaded their living quarters in the dead of night.

In the dining room attached to the kitchen, a simple wooden box lay on the roll-top desk. It was the box that Mr. Sterling had given them to keep the coordinates of the Lightway to Lior City safe until the day they would use them. The box now glowed blue, something it had not previously done since they received it.

"Place th—box—the lanter—" the voice sputtered through the box's glowing exterior.

"It's Mr. Sterling!"

Lillia hurried down the stairs. She snatched up the small box. "I think he wants us to put it near the lantern to make the connection stronger."

Emma nearly tripped over her feet as she too realized the voice of her father and bounded down the stairs two at a time. "Well, do it already, 'Lil!"

Lillia shook her head. "Chill, ginger. You'll hurt yourself."

The tiny box crackled once again as Lillia set it closer to the lantern as Emma instructed. "Emma, Gus, Lillia, Sam, can any of you hear me?"

While the communication wasn't perfectly clear, Mr. Sterling's voice could now be understood more easily through the soft static in the background.

"We're here, Dad!"

The rest joined in, letting him know they heard him.

There was a moment where only static came through, then Mr. Sterling spoke once again. "I hear you, daughter! Why, you are all up very late, aren't you?" he chuckled. "Your mother is in bed, I am afraid."

Emma smiled, but then her expression faded to disappointment. She might have been a daddy's girl, but no doubt she missed her mom, too.

Gus, being the technical one, wanted to know how the box worked. "Mr. Sterling, what is this device we are communicating through?"

The box faded momentarily, but then the static returned. "It is called a *Tual*. A device we have used in the past to communicate from Creation to Lior. We sent it with you in case there were emergencies. I apologize for not alerting you all to the fact, but again, we had to maintain secrecy."

So Lior had found a way to communicate between the two worlds. Sam wondered how many Tuals were in existence. Judging from Gus's piqued curiosity, no doubt they weren't that common.

"What's the problem?" Lillia said, catching on to Mr. Sterling's previous statement about using the box in emergencies.

"Oh, forgive me again, there is no immediate concern, praise be the Creator," he told them. "I wanted to hear what you found on top of the mountain. The noises Sam was hearing."

Gus took it upon himself to relay the events of the journey into the cave and the discovery of the Watcher device. He was thorough, giving every detail that may have been of importance to Mr. Sterling or the Protectors on the other side. It was only when Emma had enough and interrupted him that he stopped talking.

"And now Sam is having dreams again," she said quickly.

Sam scowled from his perch next to the fire. His silent protest did no good, however, as Emma usually expressed what was on her mind, even if the person she discussed hadn't given her permission to do so.

The box crackled. "That's interesting… Sam, are you having trouble sleeping again? Night sweats?"

Sam shot Emma a sour look, but then answered him. "Just a few dreams, Mr. Sterling."

There was more static.

"You must let us know if it continues. Or, if they become more frequent. Can you do that, Sam, my boy?"

"Yes, Mr. Sterling. I will let you know."

"Good, good. It is very important that you keep these things a secret. All of them, especially Sam's connection to this mysterious tower you speak of. Unfortunately, we are still restricted in our travels or I would come to discuss it further with you. Which—brings me to the reason I am calling at such a late hour."

He always knows how to wrap little bombs up in such neat packages, Sam thought. *Here it comes.*

"We have confirmed that the Dark One, Nasikh, has in fact come out of hiding," he said, the little box crackling.

Static followed his statement. But this time, the silence was on both ends.

"What do we do, Daddy?" Emma said finally. Her voice was resolute and calm. On the outside, anyway.

"Nothing. And I had difficulty even telling you this much. But you should be aware… things will likely be changing in Lior. Security

will be tight. Once you are safely inside the city, you will not want to stray outside the walls or do anything that would call attention to you unnecessarily."

"What about you and the rest of the White Pine group? Are you going to be alright?" Gus asked, posing the question before Emma could.

"We will manage. But I will be truthful, times are going to get more difficult. The Metim are getting bolder."

Emma continued to portray calm, burying her stray emotions. "Please be safe, Daddy."

Mr. Sterling bade them goodnight, and then the static faded, then cut out completely. The box stopped glowing. Emma leaned back against a pillow, her face sullen as she stared at the flames. No doubt she was worried, as they all were.

It was impossible to sleep then, so Lillia retrieved some Fuzer nuts and heated water for tea while they settled in next to the fire.

"Why is everyone so afraid of this Nasikh person?" Sam asked.

He felt as though he already knew, but wanted to hear the story from the others.

"He's only the worst Dark Lord that has ever existed." Lillia said, blinking, as though she couldn't understand such ignorance.

Sam expected more from Gus, but he was curiously silent following the call from Mr. Sterling. Instead, he buried his nose in his journal, a scowl growing on his face.

"He was the first Watcher created, and the first to fall," Lillia continued, using a tone that almost sounded story-like. "He was the highest of the Watchers to the Creator, the greatest of those created beings made to oversee all other Watchers in the universe. His job was to protect the Light that surrounded Creation. And most of all, he protected the Light that lived in the gullas ..." She paused, catching herself. "Sorry, I mean *humans*."

"But he turned to the Darkness," Sam said.

"Yes. And if I do say, it was a bit pathetic that the Watchers were required to protect those idiot sheep when all they did was choose to follow the Darkness, anyway."

Emma frowned. "Lillia… Not all of them follow the Darkness."

"Yeah, but a lot do."

Sam was confused. "Don't some Liorians follow the Darkness?"

Lillia frowned, knowing she was beaten. Still, she continued her story. "So he grew bitter of the Creator's love for the *humans* and eventually turned against him. It was then that he caused the first humans to dishonor the bond that the Creator had placed between them. He caused them to question the Creator's motives, which they did. They eventually brought the first evil into the world."

Sam pursed his lips. "So he was in charge of protecting the world, but instead he turned it against the Creator?"

Lillia nodded. "He became the same monster he was protecting humans against. His job was to stop evil, but he ended up causing it."

Sam had heard the story before, only slightly different. It was the story of Adam and Eve and their fall in the garden when the serpent talked them into eating from the forbidden tree. A story he had always believed was a legend until he had become a follower of the Light.

Gus looked up from his journal, his eyes sullen and his tone grave. "Evil, in its many forms, will always be possible as long as there is the freedom to choose it. The Dark One is known now by those who serve him as the Great Dragon."

Sam nodded, understanding. *This is why Liorians have such trouble with the dragons. They don't trust them because of the significance it carried.* If one dragon turned bad, all of them could.

Suddenly, Sam knew exactly why Gus mentioned a dragon. Only a few minutes prior, Sam had been reluctant to tell them about his dream. In it, there had been a dragon.

"We all need to get a bit of sleep—" Emma began, but then glanced over at Gus. He seemed really troubled by something he read. "What is it, Gus?"

Gus looked up from his journal, his face glowing eerily in the light of the flames.

"I know that not all the Watchers were privy to the inner workings of the gates and devices that were built," he said, pausing. Then he sighed heavily. "But I know the most important of them knew."

The other three's eyes widened at the prospect of what Gus was about to tell them.

"Gus!" Lillia prodded him. "So?"

Gus nodded at Sam. "I can only conclude that the Dark One must have known about the holomap."

Chapter Nine
Warm Springs

After the call from Mr. Sterling, no one wanted to admit it, but the conversation had concerned them. Sam was on edge too, not so much because the Dark One had been freed, but because of his own connection to the Darkness. The Legend spoke of it. Nuriel and Gus knew of it, and Arazel counted on it.

Since revealing to him that Sam was, in fact, the Irin, the third prophet, its implications had plagued him. What it meant, exactly, was unclear. He would be *conflicted*, Gus had said. Conflicted how? Did that mean that he was destined to the Darkness like Arazel said?

He remembered the Dark conjurer calling him *second to the Dark One*. *There was no mistaking that.*

The words had played over and over since their meeting.

Yet, Nuriel didn't seem concerned about him. If he was, he didn't show it. And—of anyone, he seemed to have the most insight into the events following the legend.

It didn't make him feel any better about the situation. Nor did it console Emma, the worrier of the group. She had pestered him

nonstop about his feelings. Did he feel any Darkness in him? She would ask. Was he worried about giving in to the Darkness? If not, why wasn't he worried?

Meanwhile, Lillia shrugged the whole thing off and attempted to teach Emma to do the same—without luck. Gus, the pragmatist, did his best to diffuse the tension by throwing out useless facts about the misinformation campaigns by the Dark One's servants.

But nothing was going to change what had already happened, or what was written or spoken about. He had to learn to live with the unknown for now.

As the days lumbered on toward spring and the promise of warmer weather neared, they relaxed some, enjoying the time outdoors when they could. The cabin was a wealth of natural resources, such as fresh mushrooms, saps, and fish from the river. They busied themselves with various tasks, enjoying their simple accommodations and the chance to attempt surviving on their own.

Some time after their trip up the mountain, however, Gus began to act a bit strangely. Not that he wasn't strange before, he certainly was. He made odd noises when he read something interesting. He wouldn't finish sentences completely, and (the most annoying one to Lillia) he was constantly re-situating his glasses on his nose.

But this time was different. On several occasions, they would catch him walking around the cabin with his eyes closed, turning circles in the living room with his hands outstretched in front of him.

Lillia finally confronted him when she caught him one morning. He had done his best to hide the behavior, but all of them had noticed it.

"Gus, what in the name of the Light are you doing? You look like you're trying to do blind yoga or something. Mind cluing us in?" She asked as she stepped into her slippers at the bottom of the stairs.

Startled, Gus opened his eyes and stared blankly at her. Sam and Emma padded down the stairs behind Lillia.

"I-I well..." He stammered. "I guess I can tell you now."

He motioned for them to come closer to him. "Look."

Gus lifted his fingers in the air and closed his eyes. Suddenly, a subtle but visible blue flame shot from his fingertips.

The others watched in amazement as the flame began to take on a shape—a circle. Inside, the makings of landmasses appeared. Right away, the three others could tell that it was a map.

In fact, it looked curiously familiar. Exactly like the same map from the Watcher device in the cavern.

"Is that what I think it is?" Sam said, already knowing the answer.

"I think…" Gus smirked, "… that the holomap left an imprint on me. If I close my eyes, I can see the whole thing."

Emma frowned. "Watcher devices don't do that, Gus."

The map continued to fill in more detail as they spoke. "Actually, you said we really don't know what they do," Sam defended him.

Gus nodded. "They have always been a mystery to Lior researchers. Some of them that have been collected show signs of having strange properties like the holomap, but most are just simple markers or cultural items."

Lillia was astounded. "So, are you saying that it downloaded part of itself into your head? Are you sure you don't just have such an incredibly brilliant—but stupid—mind that you memorized it all?"

Gus smiled at the offhanded compliment. "I may be intelligent, but not like this. *This* is something greater than I could ever come up with. I have the entire map, it seems, from all eras of Descendant history. From every day in the past to the present. Some of it is still a bit foggy, but it's becoming clearer every time I try it."

Emma examined the smaller version of the map. "That's really cool, Gus. Wow. You may have found your gift as a Seer."

It was impressive. Gus hadn't been able to work up so much as a tiny spark of Lazuli since he started practicing a year ago. Needless to say, it frustrated him. Having the head knowledge to call on the gifts but not being able to manifest it into something physical.

"Do you think that maybe this could be just coincidence?" Lillia said, watching as Gus allowed the holomap to dissipate. "I mean, isn't

Newb dreaming about some tower that was on the map? Maybe the device imprinted something onto him too."

Gus nodded. "I thought of that. Although Sam had dreams prior to coming in contact with the device, so we can't be sure."

Lillia scowled. "But he only started having them again after using the holomap. And—wasn't he the only one to hear the hum of the device? Couldn't that mean something?"

Gus sighed and plopped down on the couch, fiddling with a small blue quilted pillow. "Yes, to… all of those things. But again, we can't be sure. There just isn't enough information on the device. If only your father, Nuriel, were here, Sam."

The mention of Nuriel pained him. He did wish Nuriel was here. All of this was complex, and so frustrating. If Nuriel didn't have the answers, he could at least comfort them.

As the conversation lulled, Lillia used the opportunity to go start breakfast and make coffee. Emma headed to her room to get ready for the day.

Their goal for the day was simple—to check the water-worthiness of the boats stashed in the small boathouse out back. But it was Lillia at breakfast who came up with the plan to go to Warm Springs.

"I remembered Boggle mentioning people there that would know more about the Watcher devices. They wouldn't know everything, but they might be able to point us in the right direction. Plus, Warm Springs is a stellar town," she told them.

Emma dropped her fork. "It's an Outsider's village, Lillia! There's no telling what we might run into. Mystics, Runessoothers… I've even heard there are some areas of town that dabble with Dark magic."

Lillia snorted. "Just because the Outsiders aren't like us doesn't mean they don't deserve the same respect—"

Emma interrupted her. "That's not what I meant. I love Outsiders. I just meant they don't have the same rules as other Lior towns…"

"Okay, you're just arrogant then."

Emma's face reddened. "There are *Metim* that frequent there."

"And scary Outsiders, too," Lillia said, smirking.

Emma's fist hit the table, but she said nothing. Sam raised his eyebrows at her outburst.

"Emma, I thought last year you really wanted to go?" Gus said, trying not to stir up more trouble.

Emma scowled. She had, in fact, said that very thing.

"That was with Mom and Dad and the others," she said through pursed lips. "There's safety in numbers."

"Sure thing, princess," Lillia grinned. Then she punched Gus in the arm. "I heard they make killer giant doughnuts."

Emma said no more, but Sam knew she was angry. She was the type to give anyone her lunch if they needed it, including the Outsiders, but now her generosity was colliding with her faith in them, as well as her fear. Lillia was using that against her.

"It may be our only chance for answers, Em'," Gus said carefully.

Emma looked from Lillia to Gus, to Sam. Then she turned and stared at the dying flames as they licked at the last bit of unburnt log.

"Fine. I will go," she said at last. "But *you* have to tell my father."

****

It was settled. At least until they heard from Mr. Sterling and were given permission or not. Gus agreed that he would be the one to talk with him, since he was the likely candidate with the best reasoning skills.

It took three days to reach Mr. Sterling on the communication device. When they did, it was late at night again like the previous time. He sounded tired and spoke little. When they told him of their plan, however, he seemed oddly compliant to let them go to Warm Springs.

Again, Emma was mystified why her father would agree, but she said nothing. Following the conversation, however, Emma's mood had changed, and she seemed distant. It was likely she had heard the same tone in Mr. Sterling's voice as the others did. It was a concerned one. Not for the four of them, but for something going on in White Pine.

With Mr. Sterling's permission, they planned to mount their

excursion for two days from then, giving them plenty of time to pack what they needed and close up the cabin until they returned.

On a rather cloudy spring day in the mountains, as the cabin thawed from a heavy winter, they checked their gear one last time and set off out of the valley for Warm Springs.

By noon, they crossed Jester's Pass, where the long descent into the valley brought about a vegetation change from high-altitude alpine pines to vast deciduous forests with breathtaking canopies. The Northropi lazily drifted above them in silence as they made their way down the path that hugged the canyon wall. About mid-afternoon, they finally reached the shaded understory of the valley floor.

Humidity licked at their skin as the climate changed. According to Gus, the path to Warm Springs was only a few hours' walk from the bottom of Jester's Pass. Setting off, they made good time on the wide path that wound lazily around scenic bubbling sulfur pools and misty falls.

Gus slid into his role as guide once again. He explained how the site had once been an active volcano thousands of years ago during the creation of Lior. He told them that if they were to explore the area, they would find buried lava pools still simmering with the heat of the past.

They walked on as images of the tower and the dragon-man flashed through Sam's mind. For days, he had wanted nothing more than to forget them, but now he allowed them to roll through his mind, like the last pictures of an old slide reel playing over and over again.

At last, the shadow of a mountain loomed before them, and with Gus's careful guiding, they spotted the faint outline of the arched entrance that would take them up the mountain into Warm Springs.

The entrance was well hidden—concealed behind a waterfall. Had they not been paying attention, they would have missed it.

"Warm Springs was once used as a hideout for the Sons of Light," Gus hollered as the thundering falls drowned out his voice. According to Gus, there were only two entrances, both hidden, and both easily defended. The Sons couldn't have chosen a better spot.

Emma helped Sam re-cinch his pack after donning his poncho. "We've only been here once, but through the Lightway. First time through the waterfall, though," she said.

Gus pulled the hood of his poncho over his head. "Ready?"

With the weight he had been losing, he looked like an overgrown child wearing his mother's dress. Sam stifled a chuckle and noticed that both Lillia and Emma were doing the same.

They passed through the falls together. The water pounded his poncho so badly that he thought for a moment they might be dragged down in the river's current. He held tightly to Emma's hand as they pulled each other along.

Torches lined the walls of the tunnel on the other side, casting curious flickering shadows on the moss coated stairwell in front of them.

Lillia slid out of her poncho and tossed it at the foot of the stairs. "Five hundred sixty-four steps. Here we come."

"You've got to be kidding." Sam said, wiping off his face with the towel Emma handed to him.

Emma ventured up the first few stairs, her hair purple in the torchlight. "We have to remember why we are here. It is important we see who we need to see and get out. I don't want to be here any longer than we have to."

"And we don't even know who—or what—that is," Lillia grumbled.

They climbed in silence. About fifty steps up, the tunnel disappeared. The stairway remained, however, buried in the trees as it continued the ascent next to the mountain. The air became cooler the higher they went, and every so often they would cross a steaming creek that tumbled past. There was no doubt this was the reason for the town's name.

The way up was harsh, and Sam wondered how many had made the climb regularly. Maybe this town was one of the reasons they created the Lightway.

The path ended at the lower street of Warm Springs. A great arched entry stood there as well, looming over a shadowed part of the street.

This entry, however, was guarded by two broad men wearing cloaks of grey. As Sam and the others neared, the guards pointed to their packs.

"They want to search our packs," Gus whispered.

Complying, the four friends took off their packs and handed them to the guards. After a hasty search, they let them through.

"They are part of the *Unburdened*," *Lillia told them.* "They believe they are the defenders of the marginal arts."

Sam smirked, putting his pack back on. "Like the kind that not everyone agrees with, right?"

Gus led them through the entryway to the cobble street. There was a madhouse of vendors hawking their wares, and a myriad of smells from the food carts lining the sidewalk.

"Pretty much," Gus said, his eyes straying toward the food vendors. "They use the 'gifts' that are not necessarily approved by the *Council*."

Emma pulled her robe around her to keep the chilly mountain air out. "There's a reason it's shunned by most of Lior. Miss Karpatch says they do some really sinister things."

"Like skin people alive and eat their eyeballs." Lillia said, acting like she was popping an eyeball in her mouth. "Tasty, but needs salt."

"Classy, 'Lil,'" Emma mumbled, then pushed ahead of the group as they made their way toward the vendors.

As she brushed by, Sam thought he caught her saying, "Because this is where you belong" in Lillia's general direction.

Sam let the smells from the food carts drift past his nose as they walked by the many vendors hawking their wares. He turned to Gus.

"I don't understand why it would exist then. If it's bad to the Light, why does the Creator allow it?"

The question seemed to stump him, who began into a perplexing explanation, but then quickly gave up. Much like Earth, it seemed not everything in Lior had a simple answer.

They had no clue where to begin looking for information about the Watcher device, but they knew they were hungry. Gus chose the closest food cart that offered meat sticks and potato shoots, but before he could give the vendor his order, Emma snatched his arm and motioned for the others to follow her up the adjacent street.

"We're getting settled first, *then* dinner," she announced.

She led them up two streets and marched the group toward the small wooded sign that said *Warm Springs Inn*. It wasn't fancy, but from the looks of it, there weren't many options to choose from. Tiny and stone-faced, the inn perched on the mountainside, allowing Sam the first view of the town and the valley below.

Warm Springs was like a scene from medieval Europe. Cobble streets checkered the sloped village, each lined with quaint stone shops of various sorts. Behind the inn, homes curled upward around the sides of the mountain, lining paths that must have been brutal to travel.

Emma disappeared with Lillia into the inn's office, leaving Gus and Sam to watch the interesting villagers meander by. "We'll get a couple of rooms for the night," she told them.

The villagers dressed simply but colorfully, and none of them seemed in any hurry to go anywhere. Not that they would have anywhere to go, being so secluded, but it appeared that they were content right where they were, anyway. Some wore robes over their colorful outfits and others chose not to, but appearance didn't seem to matter much to anyone, anyhow. Those that passed said hello, smiling. Others stopped and talk to fellow townspeople for several minutes at a time, seeming to care little of the passing time.

Soon, the girls emerged, announcing excitedly that they had secured suites with access to the Lazuli Spa for the night. Sam and Gus shrugged, following them toward the building.

Room four, where Gus and Sam were to stay, was up a flight of stone steps and to the right, while Emma and Lillia had the room two doors down from them.

The suite was small but had the necessities—a small bathroom and two modest but colorful beds against the rainbow-colored wall. On the tiny wood table, a bowl of spiny pink fruit looked perfectly placed against the pinks and blues of the shag rug on the floor. A stained-glass lamp in the corner lit the room softly, providing an airy feel to the

space. If Sam didn't know better, he would have thought he had just stepped into a gypsy's home.

Grabbing the bar of soap, toothpaste, and towel, Sam headed in for a shower to wash the day's grime off. Letting the hot sulfuric water sanitize his body, he thought about what they might find in the depths of Warm Springs, in the outer reaches of what the Light found permissible. He considered the type of people that lived where he grew up in Grand Rapids, in those areas where most of society's norms didn't frequent. Those places where the law was street law, where the economy was survival. Where good motives got you nowhere.

He might not have been one of those people, but that didn't mean he was any different, or any better, than them. Sure, some of them may not have had the best intentions, but that didn't mean all of them did. Here was no different. There were some good people in some very bad places. You just had to look a little harder.

"I must smell like righteous booty about now," Gus said, lifting up his arm and smelling underneath. Disgusted with his own smell, he gagged and plugged his nose.

The interaction was so unusual from Gus's normal behavior that it caused both of them to burst out laughing.

They were both close to tears when there was a sudden knock at the door, which sent Gus running for the bathroom and Sam crashing to the floor beside the bed, half-dressed.

The door flung open to reveal Emma, and Lillia, both showered and ready to go. Gus watched as Sam struggled to unwrap himself from the bedsheets, belly laughing from the bathroom. Finally ripping the sheets from his damp body, Sam managed to hike his jeans up just as the two girls stepped into the room.

"Seriously, you two are incapable of anything," Emma said, shaking her head.

Lillia smirked, enjoying Sam's embarrassing predicament. Then she, too, couldn't help laughing as Gus peeked out from the corner of the bathroom in his towel, laughing hysterically like a wheezing elephant.

 Chapter Nine

"Get in the shower, Gus. Please," Emma said, sighing.

Sam stood and sat on the edge of the bed to slip his shoes on. His hair still smelled like sulfur, but it wasn't overwhelming. It reminded him of visiting his foster mother, Sylvia's brother Richard, on the east side of the state. There, the water always smelled like sulfur, but he had learned to like it because he liked his uncle Richard. He seemed like the only one who really understood Sam. He was always straightforward and truthful with Sam about everything, and Sam appreciated it.

Emma was wearing a green and white summer dress, her hair still wet from the shower. It reflected a burnt orange sheen in the light of the stained-glass lamp. She was still beautiful, even when she was mad. And right now, she was just that.

He knew why—she was afraid. Out of fear, she would show her anger, which was so unlike her normal personality. But this was Warm Springs, an Outsider's village. There was the potential that Metim could be hanging about, and she didn't have her parents around to protect her.

They had dinner two streets over from the inn. The restaurant Emma chose was a cozy place on top of a small tavern with a large stone porch overlooking the lazy streets of Warm Springs. Behind their table was a stone hearth where a fire danced happily, and the ivy-entwined lattice overhead made them feel like they were in a small café in Italy.

Emma's hair glimmered deep reds from the dripping orange of the sunset in front of them. Even Lillia had dressed for the occasion, wearing a small white dress that was very much unlike her normal attire. For the first time, Sam noticed her beauty as she laughed with Gus about the ordeal in the room earlier.

Dinner was home-style and not as abnormal as one would expect. Mashed purple potatoes and thin green beans were piled high on the platter among the plates of freshly baked bread. Roasted chicken came last, seasoned with a sweet-smelling red spice.

Gus poured the group glasses of the Jurana herbal tea that the cheerfully dressed waiter brought to them.

"My thought was to visit Brahm Street after dinner," Gus told them.

Emma threw her hands up. "Great, the absolute worst place to be in Warm Springs after dark. Why don't we just hand ourselves over to Nasikh right now?"

"Brahm Street is where we are going to find answers, if there are any," he said without missing a beat. "It may be the darkest corner of Warm Springs, but it's also the place where information flows freely. Legal or not."

Chapter Ten
Brahm Street

Lillia paid for dinner using the money the Sterlings had left with them. Then they stopped back at the inn to change before heading over to Brahm Street, deciding that it was better not to stick out too badly.

Gus attempted to make sense of his plan as they walked, but he had to admit that ultimately, it was his gut that made him decide. "I just have a feeling about it, okay?" He had told them.

The air had cooled, so they changed into sweatshirts, slipping them on as they crossed the street. Four blocks up the steep cobble street and six blocks west toward the far side of town, they found Brahm Street.

It was the mecca of Warm Springs' nightlife, curled up against the face of the mountain. It was dimly lit and reeked of a mixture of food and poor sanitation. Judging from the difficulty the four had as they maneuvered through the crowds, however, the city was certainly not lacking people willing to participate in the peculiar activities Brahm Street had to offer.

As in all of Lior, there was no electricity or neon signs, but there was plenty of light from the numerous vendors stoking the fires in their grills and adjusting their oil lamps. Some of the more recluse vendors hawked their wares in the dark, however.

One thing Sam noticed as they passed the many dark souvenir shops and dingy clothing boutiques was that Lazuli was scarce. Occasionally, the soft blue glow of the Eben stone on a leather bracelet could be seen as its owner attempted to conceal it under a robe, but for the most part, it was nonexistent. There was no doubt the Light wasn't as welcome here as it was in Lior City.

It was Lillia who led them into the shop with the swinging wooden sign where the fading name *Collectibles* was printed in red and barely legible.

The interior was as dimly lit as the street outside. Along the walls was every sort of curious item one could think of, in all shapes and ages. There were necklaces, crudely crafted talismans, lamps adorned with strange creatures, and countless dragon figurines—each unique in their own way. Some of the artifacts glowed the soft blue of Lazuli while others were dim or held the slightest tint of another color.

Sam scanned the store as Gus and the others browsed the tables full of the unique wares. He hadn't told the others yet that upon entering the shop, something there seemed to tug at him. He hadn't isolated the feeling yet, but it seemed familiar. And it was attached to something tangible. A thing.

He walked purposefully to the table where a book lay with an herb imprinted on its spine. Putting it aside, he gazed at the round object underneath.

A clear, round orb lay on the table in front of him. Reaching out, he picked it up, examining it. He let the silver chain latched to the orb slink down onto the old book.

It was glass-like material, but not quite. He could tell that it wasn't quite as fragile as normal glass, but held a somewhat metallic quality to its thick shell. Holding it closer, he could not see its interior. It had appeared that the artifact was clear through to the core, when in fact it wasn't. The closer he looked, the more he noticed it to be mirror-like.

He studied the object, looking for any Lazuli life in it, but it gave no indication it had any.

He let the object pull at him a moment, trying to discern the feeling it brought. It was steady, but not strong. It felt like a balloon that was pulled along by static electricity.

"Ten Luz, and it's yours for the taking," said the short old woman next to him. She had long, grey hair and dim olive-green eyes.

"What is it?" Sam asked the woman, not looking up from the metallic glass.

The woman swung her cane up. Using its curved shaft, she snatched the necklace from Sam in one motion, bringing it to meet her oversized spectacles that dangled on her nose. "Not much of anything, I suppose," she sniffed. "Some of these items here are of much more value than this old thing."

She peered at the necklace, "Some things of the Light, and some of the Dark, if that's what you're in to."

"And this one?"

"Don't know, boy. This artifact doesn't do anything, from what I can tell. I was about to toss it if it hadn't sold in another day or two."

"I will give you two Luz for it." Sam told her. He knew he only had five in his pocket right then, remembering that he had foolishly left the rest back at the inn.

"Three."

Sam dug in his pocket for some of the Lior money his grandfather had given him. "I'll take it."

The old woman looked down her spectacles at him, as though trying to decide what his motives were. Then she looked at the artifact, and back at Sam, opening her mouth as if to say something. Then she thought better of it.

"Better your junk than mine," she mumbled as she turned toward the dusty countertop where the old register sat. "No returns, no exchanges. And don't even think about coming back if you break it."

Sam nodded and found the others still browsing among the throngs

of artifacts. Emma and Lillia didn't look particularly interested in any of it, but Gus was enjoying every minute, peering at each artifact and then quickly thumbing through his journal to see if he could find any information about its background.

After a while, however, they convinced Gus that they weren't going to find what—or who—they were looking for in the shop, so they ventured back out into the pungent air of Brahm Street.

There were even more people wandering through the smoke-filled vendor booths now as the night settled in. The smells of meat and fermented liquids were everywhere as they as they continued down the street, while intoxicated walkers laughed and carried on around them. Quickly, it became clear that some of the more questionable patrons were peering at the four youths that were so obviously out of place.

Gus steered them into *Argus's Famous Things*, another dimly lit shop that seemed to specialize mostly in books, judging from the many dusty shelves lining the walls.

When they entered, however, they found more than just books. The shop contained all sorts of artifacts from famous people in Lior, some from Descendants and others not.

Most of it was military—swords, armor, and the like. But there were other things like necklaces, Eben stones, and cloaks that according to the tags claimed to be from former council members and chancellors, supposed staffs from former Watchers-turned-Dark lord, and even a claw from a dragon.

Most of it collected dust and had become a makeshift museum. One look at the price tag, however, told Sam that they weren't just looking to show it off.

Sam believed Gus's logic was sound for visiting the bookstore, as they were more likely to find someone knowledgeable about ancient Watcher devices if they knew books. And Emma wasn't going to argue with him if it meant getting out of the prying eyes of shoppers from the street.

Inside, there was a small elderly man tending to the register. Beside him was a much younger girl with unkempt hair and dirt spotting her olive skin. She looked to be only about thirteen years old, though judging from her sullen eyes and appearance, she had seen more than her share of sadness in her lifetime.

They meandered through the store for only a minute or two before Gus glanced at them as if to say, "Wish me luck." Then he headed up to the old man and the young girl to ask them some questions.

As Gus talked with the shopkeeper and the girl, Sam stared at the robe of Festus Gracher, considered one of the greatest Descendant wielders of the Light. He was known for his heroic acts of bravery during the war with the Giants. Festus had passed on years ago, according to the inscription below the robe. He died from old age.

Whether the robe was authentic was unknown, but it struck Sam as odd. The Descendants, with all of their amazing abilities and celestial blood, still could not overcome the ravages of war, nor the inescapable march of time toward old age. No one could escape death forever, not even here. In many ways, they weren't that much different from the humans they criticized.

On the other hand, Watchers were immortal, their bodies not tainted by the frailties of human blood. Formed by the Creator without a destiny with death. The ideal, perfect form, designed to live and serve the Creator forever.

But the Darkness had been strong enough to lure even them, drawing them away from their service in search of an even greater power. That quest for power was led by a Watcher, Nasikh, who was second only to the Creator. His lust for power would not allow him the ability to be satisfied where he was. Eventually, that lust took him down the path of becoming the Dark One.

What about the Dark One? Could he even be killed? And what about Nuriel? Was he in danger of the Dark One?

Sam knew from Gus's discussions over the summer that Watchers could, in fact, die. His grandfather Amos had told him about the many who gave their lives the last time the Descendants and Watchers fought together—in the attack on the old Lior City.

Would the Watchers one day fight alongside Descendants? What

would it take for the Descendants to trust them again?

Perhaps Festus fought alongside them.

Sam turned around to see how things were going just as the old man handed Gus a book with a faded gold embossed star on the front.

For a moment, the young girl next to the old man locked eyes with Sam and refused to turn away.

Sam stared at her facial features, drawn conflicted eyes and thin lips, pursed into a stern resolve of a life too difficult to talk about.

But the look she gave Sam was more. In her eyes was a story she wanted to tell, a pleading of hope she wished someone would see and could do something about. The look was enough that emotion began to well up within him, though knowing nothing of her. Somehow, he still felt her pain.

Heroes and the forgotten. Sam thought. Some were remembered, like Festus, and others wasted away in the bowels of the shady part of an Outsider's town.

The older man slipped from behind the counter at that moment, shuffling over to one of the dustier bookshelves, and slid a small hardcover book from the shelf, handing it to Gus without so much as a glance upward from his shaking hands.

"Thank you, sir. I—" Gus began, but the man waved him off.

"Please, just take it and go," he said feebly.

"Did we do something wrong?" Sam asked him suddenly, not wanting to offend the old man.

The man shook his head. "There are many Ceevers here tonight. We are closing up early. Please, go."

The man walked to the door and opened it for them to leave, and upon a quick glance outside, showed his dismay as the street had grown even more crowded with visitors.

At his urging, Emma snatched Sam's hand and motioned for the other two to follow. Gus tucked the book in his pack and the four stepped back out onto the street once again. The old storekeeper quickly locked the door behind them and flipped the OPEN sign over to CLOSED.

Indeed, the crowd had grown, and an increasing number of the people meandering the streets looked to be the type that had dabbled in the Darkness a time or two.

Since most were hooded, it was difficult to see what they truly looked like. Once or twice, Sam caught a glimpse of a few that would turn their way as they passed, and the hollow eyes and haunting features were enough to make him shudder and turn away.

It wasn't just the people walking past them, however. There were some that were gathering in groups in the darker corners of the street, chanting softly as though in trances. Others heckled street vendors who were franticly trying to pack up their mobile shop for the night.

As they passed some groups, Sam caught the faintest wisp of green electricity from one of the hecklers. Behind it was the unmistakable trail of Darkness following.

"I want to leave, now," Emma whispered urgently, her eyes glistening with fear.

"I agree," Lillia whispered, also having been shaken by the surrounding sights. "Let's move it, slugs."

Emma, still holding Sam's hand, jerked him off the sidewalk and made a beeline to the place where they had originally entered the street earlier in the evening. Gus and Lillia followed quickly behind.

"I think since the Light Festival is so close, those who are followers of the Darkness are getting a little more agitated," Lillia said, keeping her voice low.

Sam huffed to keep up with Emma, who dragged him down the cobble streets toward their rooms at the inn. "What were they? Metim?"

"Some, maybe. But others, not quite." Gus said, glancing behind them as they hurried toward the more lighted streets.

When they had made it back to safer territory, Gus continued. "Some of them could be Metim, I suppose, but most who follow the Darkness are just people, 'Ceevers' as the storekeeper called them. Many would love nothing more than to become Metim, and some might if they make the full transition. Metim are selective who they

recruit, and they are trained wielders of Darkness. They are much more proficient with the ways of the Dark One."

"Creepy, that's what I would call them," Lillia said. For once, no one argued with her.

Back in the confines of their rooms, they eased the tension by soaking in one of the warm Lazuli pools behind the inn. Afterward, back in Lillia and Emma's room, Gus slipped the old book out of his pack and dug into its contents.

"*Ansher P. Salus's Commentary on Celestial Devices*," Emma read aloud. She turned the book over, examining the back. "Do you think something on the holomap Watcher device could be in here?"

Gus picked up the book gingerly, opening the fragile pages until he found the Table of Contents. "Watcher Devices, page one hundred twenty-four."

He turned there, scanning the pages. There were sketches and descriptions of various devices that Ansher Salus claimed were artifacts created by the Watchers. Each was intricately drawn to include every detail, as though the artist had actually seen each device and sketched them at his leisure.

To their surprise, on one such page of the chapter, the unmistakable drawing of the holomap suddenly presented itself.

Gus squinted to read the inscription from the fading ink on the page. "It's called a 'talisgem,' or—a 'reflector.' Ansher believed that it was built around the time of the first Descendants into Lior… and that it was used to monitor the travel of the gates to and from Creation."

"The great Seer of all things," Lillia said, chuckling.

Gus peered down his glasses at Lillia, looking very much like Chivler, when they came to him with another discovery in one of the books from his dusty shop.

"Yes, actually. Just like that," Gus answered, scanning the writing in the margin of the page next to the drawing. "Ansher says exactly that. He says right here, 'While the due course and purpose of the device has yet to be fully realized, it is becoming increasingly obvious that there was intent on the part of the Watchers to observe all activities inside Lior, and to perhaps keep record of all events occurring within its boundaries.'"

"It doesn't sound like Ansher was a fan of the Watchers," Sam said.

Gus ignored him, continuing to search each page as if looking for additional clues. Stopping suddenly on one of them, his eyes lit up.

"Ah," he nodded. "It makes a bit more sense now."

"What does?" Emma kicked her shoes off and snatched a pillow from the bed to curl up with.

"I had been wondering why a Descendant would have had such detailed drawings of the Watcher devices, and how he may have come by some of this information. Especially since the device we just discovered looked like it hadn't been disturbed in years."

"Well, he probably spent his whole life researching them. Why's that so strange?" Emma asked.

Gus flipped back a few pages in the book, then held it up for the others to see. He pointed at the sketched silhouette of a hooded man on the page. "This man, whoever he is, seemed to know about every device that ever existed."

Emma leaned in for a closer look. "The Shadow," she said slowly. "Who's that?"

Sam and Lillia stared wide-eyed at Emma.

"Shadow?" Lillia exclaimed loudly. "As in 'shadow' like the prophecy?"

Sam picked at the flesh of a pink piece of fruit he had gotten from the basket on the table in their room. The words from the prophecy had not let him forget.

He will call unto himself the Shadow... it had said.

Originally, they knew these words as part of a Dark legend, which was in fact a twist on the real prophecy, as Nuriel had revealed to him when they first met. It was, Nuriel told him, originally a promise of the Creator to mankind.

But the phrase didn't sound like a promise. It sounded more like a curse.

Many in Lior had believed that whomever the third prophet was,

he would ultimately submit to the Darkness. Because of this phrase, specifically.

Sam had mulled over every possible scenario, but it still didn't make sense. Gus, Lillia, and Emma had all taken part in discussions about what it could mean, and they had even involved Miss Karpatch on occasion, but no one seemed to have any insight.

As he had so often before, Sam wished Nuriel could explain more to him. More about the prophecy and Sam being the third prophet, more about his mother, more about himself and why he had been sent to Creation without so much as a clue of his ancestry until now.

"We can't be sure there is any connection with this Shadow individual and Sam," Gus said quickly, no doubt attempting to derail Lillia's conspiracy ideas before they even hatched.

Lillia rolled her eyes and flopped back on the pillow beside Emma. "Not like Newb has had the benefit of the doubt before," she said. Look, I agree, there probably isn't a connection. Maybe it doesn't even exist at all. But all I'm saying is, this is all we have to go on at this point."

Emma glared at Lillia, "There's *not* a connection. Sam isn't going to turn to the Darkness. We've talked about this."

Gus quickly changed the subject as Emma continued to glare down Lillia. "I mean, we know there was animosity between the Watchers and Descendants, but what this book sounds like is an exposé. I am going to go out on a limb and theorize that Ansher Salus did not have exclusive access to these Watcher devices."

"You think that Ansher was given the drawings by the Shadow guy?" Emma asked.

Suddenly, Emma's question reminded Sam of the tower from the holomap. The tower was the only device that wouldn't reveal its insides. Was it in Ansher's book?

Sam picked up the weathered text.

He scanned every page, looking for clues to the tower, but found nothing.

When Emma discovered what he was doing, he gave the book to

her to see if she could find something, but she came up empty-handed as well.

After a third attempt from Gus, they put the book down. Without any knowledge of who the Shadow was, or any more information on the tower, they could go no further. Gus promised them he would continue to search through Ansher's work, but even he was discouraged. Perhaps the book would prove to be a dead end.

Gus stuffed it back into his pack and the two boys said goodnight to Emma and Lillia and headed back to their room. It would be a long walk back to the cabin the next day, and they needed to get some sleep if they were to make the climb back up Jester's pass.

That night, as Sam pulled the sheets up to keep out the chilly mountain air, he allowed the images from the mysterious tower in the holomap to creep back into his mind.

They weren't like the Sha'ar Gate visions from the previous year, but they still pressed at his mind. Fortunately, he was learning how to force them back when he didn't need them.

But now, in the darkness with Gus snoring happily beside him, he opened his mind to them.

The hum was there as it had always been since encountering the holomap, but now it felt different. Like it had faded into the background of his mind, slow and steady, like his own heartbeat within him.

His visions took him to the tower, where it hid behind the looming trees that hovered over a pathway in front of where he stood.

In the background, a luminescent red pierced the night, its brilliant hue gleaming from the top of the tower through the trees. The rest of the tower was dark otherwise. Shadows of the leafless trees cast their boughs of black against the tower's light like a web in front of him.

He walked forward toward the gleaming spindles of blue rising high into the night, but every step he took seemed like it got him nowhere. He only wanted to see inside the tower—what the holomap would not show him. But the shadows of the trees would not allow it. Their tendril arms held him fast, refusing to relinquish control.

What was inside that the tower refused to let him see?

Brahm Street

He opened his eyes to the darkness of the room, frustrated that his vision of the tower would not let him go any further.

The room was quiet. An unwelcoming, almost stifling, silence filled the air.

He recalled the people they saw on Brahm Street. Those of them that may have chosen to test the limits of good and evil, or who may have been dabbling in the darker reaches of society to find fulfillment.

While standing on the sidewalk of the old shopkeeper's store, Sam had caught a glimpse of a few of them as they looked toward him. Haunting faces, hollow expressions, their eyes showing a deep pain that wore within, void of life.

Then there were others, like the girl in the shop, that seemed to want nothing more than to get away from anything the Darkness offered.

To anyone on the outside, it looked like a life that they would do anything to avoid. Why would anyone want to experience the pain and emptiness they had? Perhaps it had been a fleeting desire to explore the Darkness that drew them in, or perhaps it was deeper—an anger that wouldn't subside, or a hurt that was simply too much.

Either way, once the Darkness had you, there was no letting go.

Sam had felt it when he saw the Darkness for the first time. Standing on the edge of the field near Old Lior City, he had sensed its power. Subtly, it called out to him.

Was it possible that he too could give in to the Darkness like the Dark lord Arazel said he would?

He will call unto himself the Shadow…

Perhaps it was inevitable that he would struggle to overcome the Darkness but would fail. Maybe he would give in to the Dark One, ultimately. Maybe he had no choice.

He, Samuel Forrester, the Irin, third prophet and revealer of the Darkness, could become a weapon of the Darkness.

No. He would not let it. For his father Nuriel's sake, He could not.

Chapter Eleven
Return to Lior City

While Warm Springs was still stirring, they awoke early and made their way toward the same entrance they had used to come into town.

Before leaving, however, Lillia convinced them to stop by the giant doughnut vendor who had just set up shop for the day. They knew they would pay for the extra helping of sugar later on the pass, but they couldn't leave without one of the famed pastries Gus was so fond of.

With the coffee and giant doughnuts safely in their stomachs, and after taking one last peaceful glance into the valley below where the yellow hues of daylight were only beginning to paint themselves across the sky, they set off for their journey back to the cabin.

Winter in the valley was quickly fading, and the four were able to traverse the path back up Jester's Pass easily. They did make it a point to stop several times to admire the budding birch trees and squirrels as they emerged from their winter holds along the way.

The cabin was a welcome sight after hours on the trail, and they

wasted no time putting stew on to cook and hunkering down in their pajamas next to the fire.

The next few days would be spent preparing for their trip to Lior City and Mentorship, packing and cleaning the cabin for the next time it was needed. The nerves grew as they completed their tasks, thinking of what Mentorship would be like. None of them had ever gone through it, and had no idea what to expect.

Soon the day came to leave. They were ready to go, too. The cabin had been a wonderful place to stay, and they had enjoyed their time getting to know one another. But the lack of news and the feeling of being cut off from the world was setting in. Not to mention the Light Festival in Lior would begin the following day, and they had been looking forward to it for months.

The morning of their departure, they doused the fire in the fireplace and cinched up their stuffed packs. Lillia divided up the rest of the biscuits Emma had made the night before, handing each several.

Gus stowed the tiny box Mr. Sterling had given them containing the coordinates of the Lightway to Lior City into his pack. Sam, who was busy stuffing biscuits into his mouth, checked his pack one more time to make sure he hadn't left anything behind.

"Could you two move any more slowly?" Emma scowled. "We should have left an hour ago."

Lillia nearly spit her remaining biscuit out of her mouth, laughing. "I wasn't going to say it, but Princess is right. The way you two move is painful."

Gus looked confused, but Sam understood exactly what they were saying. They *did* seem to be the last ones ready everywhere they went.

Sam looked forward to seeing Talister and the others from the cabin circle and attending the Light Festival. It had been a year since they been to the city, and he missed it. He was a bit nervous, however, about how everyone from the city would receive him. Much of the city was divided as to the validity of the Dark Legend and Sam's connection to the Darkness, so there was little doubt some would appreciate if Sam never stepped foot in the city again.

The Chancellor and Talister had formally welcomed Sam into their city—in front of everyone. And they had made a point to reassure the city and regions that Sam was not a threat. According to Mr. Sterling, it had worked, too. Most didn't see him as such.

But Sam could not get out of his mind the shouting match that occurred between the representatives of the regions while he stood before the Council. Some of them, especially those from the Telok region, refused to believe there was no connection to the Dark prophecy.

Sam's trip to Ayet Sal on the back of the dragon Orono had helped to persuade some of the Council. But some didn't believe he would be anything other than what the prophecy said.

They closed the door to the cabin for the last time and headed toward the mountain where the Lightway was hidden. In their time at the cabin, none of them had seen any trace of it, nor could they guess how it could be hidden so well in the mountains. But Mr. Sterling had said it was there, so they believed him.

It wasn't long before they reached the sheer mountain face on the far side of the valley.

Much like the arches and now the Watcher devices, this entrance was hidden as well. Since they knew the general location, it didn't take them long to find it. Soon they slipped into the tight tunnel, feeling the cool breezes and damp air of the cavern ahead.

Another of Boggle's inventions stood prominently in the center of the tall cavern space. By the looks of it, it was one of his first. The large copper-colored contraption resembled a giant robot trapped inside the mountain, its metal arms extending out in all directions from its bloated torso.

Near its base, they saw a small door with a lighted blue keypad mounted on the metal. Beams of light from cheese-like holes in the ceiling rained down on the metal structure from above, giving the four friends just enough light to cross the rocky floor to where it stood.

Gus placed his hand on the shell of the device, feeling its smooth, cold surface. Then he circled it, examining it from all directions.

"It's one of the first Lightways Boggle ever created," Gus said, beaming. He snatched out the journal from his pack and flipped through the pages. "Boggle tried for years before he was successful. His first prototypes that succeeded were the larger models."

Sam reached out and touched the surface. He imagined it took quite a bit of effort to coax the first individual into becoming the first test subject. Being shot out of a cannon on a light wave didn't sound like the safest thing in the world to try.

But this Light device was unique, according to Gus, still reading from his journal. This machine sent you upward, rocketing out of the tube at the top of the structure to somewhere in the darkness above.

"Seriously Gus. How are we supposed to stop once we reach the top?" Emma said, refusing to stand too close to the contraption.

Sam had no doubt she was recalling their trip to the old city when they had to skim into the Lazuli pool.

Gus paused a moment while he searched the page. "Well, I'm not sure."

Emma shook her head. "First, we skim a wave last year with *no* training, and now we have to jump into this metal death trap?"

"This was your dad's idea, there, princess, so don't blow your top," Lillia said, shaking her finger at Emma. "Plus, I trust Boggle. He wouldn't make anything that would harm anyone. I'm sure there are—uh, safety features."

Lillia was right, even though she hadn't sounded too confident about it. Emma's dad had planned this, and he would do what was best for his daughter. And Boggle, despite having a few loose screws, was a brilliant inventor.

Sam stepped up to the machine and pressed the large "Door" button on the keypad, which instantly triggered the old machine into action.

The metal giant whirred and ground within its bowels, and soon the small metal and glass door opened with a hiss. Sam stepped inside of it, glancing back at the surprised looks from the other three.

"Well, someone has to be the first," he called from the dark interior of the Lightway. "Gus, mind getting the button?"

Closing the door behind him, Sam sat down on the smooth, curved surface below him. The tube was large enough to fit a few people at a time, but Sam hadn't thought about that. He was tired of being afraid of everything all the time. Fear of the Darkness. Fear of Arazel and the prophecy. Fear of what people thought about him. Today, he was not going to let fear get the best of him. He would be the first to try the machine.

Gus pressed a button on the keypad and again the machine whirred. Sam's heart thumped as he looked up and saw the tiny circle of light far above him. It had to be the opening in the tube where the peak of the mountain met the sky above.

Suddenly the Lazuli Light filled the chamber, the brilliant flood of blue surrounding him, warming him to the bone. He soaked in the feeling, attempting to relax his mind.

The whirring increased in intensity, and Sam felt himself lifting off of the chamber floor. The light naturally curved around his body as he slowly rose higher in the chamber. It was a peaceful feeling, floating through the air calmly toward the opening of the mountain above.

The light disappeared, and the tube went black. The force keeping Sam suspended in the air was now gone.

He felt the horrible sensation of falling as he careened back down the tube. His lungs would not let him yell or call out as his body plummeted toward the ground.

Before he hit, however, another blast of light infiltrated the chamber, jerking him upright and sending him back up the tube at breakneck speed.

Then, as quickly as it began, the powerful light below him slowed, then blinked out, not before depositing him onto a cold stone surface of a Light Tower.

For a few moments, he refused to move, fighting down the urge to spew his breakfast everywhere.

He knew the feeling would pass if he just lay where he was, then he could have a look around. But he just needed a moment to rest while

his stomach and head did cartwheels.

Forcing himself to move, he sat upright, enjoying the icy breezes rushing in from the tower's windows on his skin.

Crawling over to the nearest window, Sam peeked out. Snowy mountains surrounded the tower. Judging from the height, he was now thousands of feet up. The metal beast that had brought him here had shot him up the mountain like a bullet from a gun.

Another device was present in the Light Tower, but this one looked more like the Lightbase he had used in Lior last year. Not only was it an eighth of the size, but it looked much newer and safer than Boggle's ancient contraption buried in the mountain below.

He shuddered to think what Gus would do when he arrived. He had eaten nearly as much that morning as Sam had. And his stomach was much more sensitive than Sam's.

This must have been what Mr. Sterling meant about not eating too much before going, he thought, gingerly situating himself against the stone wall near a window.

It wasn't but just another moment or two when the blast of light shot up the tube and past him, carrying Lillia with it.

The Light rolled her onto the dusty stone, face down. She tried to sit up, but collapsed again, the sick feeling overtaking her.

Sam crawled over to her and picked her up in his arms. She grunted and groaned in protest, eyes still closed.

"What in the name of the Light just happened?" she said, moaning as she leaned into Sam's chest.

"You've been Boggled, I believe," Sam said, swallowing a burp that was crawling up his throat.

Next was Emma, who seemed strangely unaffected by the sickening ride up the tube. Then Gus, who promptly winged his breakfast over the side of the window of the Light Tower.

"How are you not sick right now, Em'?" the green-faced Gus asked her.

"Didn't you guys see the sign on the inside door of the tube?" she said, scooped her hair into a bun. "It said to stand."

None of them had even bothered to read the sign on the door. Obviously, it had been important.

It was almost an hour before the group was ready to attempt the wave to Lior City. Every time they were ready to leave, Gus would turn a pale green and back out.

Finally, after a few more upchucks, he was ready. This time, it was Emma who chose to go first.

Gus removed the tiny box from his pack and pressed the small blue button that was now illuminated where it previously had not been. The box opened, and Gus removed a tiny folded up piece of paper containing the coordinates to the Lior City Lightbase.

With Emma inside the cannon-shaped device, Gus dialed in the coordinates. The blue wave of Lazuli Light burst from the Lightbase, sending Emma out into the cloudless sky.

Sam stood by the window to watch the Lightbase send its traveler, but he couldn't make out Emma's form as the beam streaked across the sky over the mountain tops.

Even though he had ridden in one, the concept of riding a wave of Light still amazed him. Sending a person hundreds of miles from one place to another almost instantly was truly an unbelievable achievement.

Lillia was next, and then Gus, who took some convincing that Sam was able to work the Lightbase without his assistance. Gus finally gave in, and soon he was careening out into the chilly air.

Sam was last, and for a moment, he relished the silence. From the window of the Lightbase, he gazed at the snowy peaks around him. It was incredibly peaceful. The only noise he heard was the deep whistle of the mountain air as it passed through the window's arched frame.

He was still apprehensive about how people would receive him, but part of him didn't care. There were people in his life now, people that already received him for who he was. And that was enough to give him the courage to do just about anything.

Sam dialed in the coordinates and stepped into the Lightbase, leaning back slightly as the machine began to hum. Soon he would be back in Lior. Back in the circle of cabins, where it felt like home.

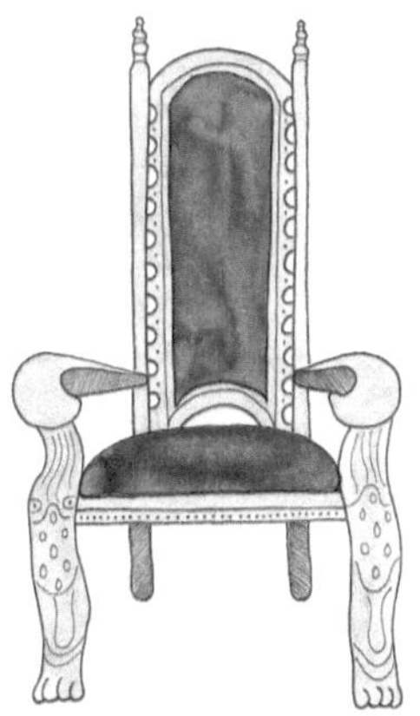

Chapter Twelve
The Darkness Unleashed

Send for Arazel," Kachash hissed to the guard standing before him. The guard's golden helmet cast beams of light throughout the hall. "I need him *now*."

The guard bowed, his sword clattering on the perfect stone floor of the White Palace. Kachash cringed at the sound, balling up his hands in a tight fist and clenching his teeth.

As the guard spun and retreated from the hall with two others, Kachash flopped down on the elaborate throne behind him, staring blankly at the ornate ceiling above.

Soon, the Dark One would request his throne once again in the White Palace. The throne that Kachash ruled from for so long would finally be handed over to the Prince of the Darkness.

He was not jealous, but rather in awe, for he had never actually met the Dark One. The Dark Watchers of old had been gone for years, defeated and dispersed throughout Creation.

He clenched his fist again. Kachash had been only a small boy when his father was killed by the Watchers who followed the Creator.

In his dying breath, he spoke the only words that Kachash now lived by.

Avenge me. Destroy the Watchers.

Kachash had done all he could to seek his father's revenge—and to follow in the service of the Dark One, the real Prince of the Light.

He was certain that he could accomplish both tasks, and he had already succeeded at some level. While he hadn't destroyed the Watchers, he had indeed driven them out of Lior and back to the Divide. Simply by turning the Descendants against them.

He thought gleefully about the attack on the Old City of Lior and the warriors slain by the Dark Forces. The Light followers had not been prepared, stupidly, and it had been their undoing.

The Dark One would be proud. He had killed many—Descendants, and Watchers. The stench of their Light still carried across his nostrils every so often. He remembered their screams, the agony of those who begged him to spare them, swearing to denounce the Light and embrace the Darkness. So long as they were spared.

And the foolish young Watchers who so brazenly believed they could take down the glorious Kachash—they had fought valiantly and died swiftly.

Kachash scoffed. He had been trained by the last of the old Watchers, descended from the lineage of the original Dark Lords. The ancient Fallen ones. They had been the first to follow the Darkness, and the Dark One.

It had taken eight Watchers to kill his father. He was a true warrior, slaying thousands before they betrayed him.

Kachash was one of the last four Dark lords now in Lior. The rest of the lineage had either been killed or banished to Creation.

Their plight had been an unfair move, a sinister act even for the Darkness. The Lords had been extinguished, cut down when they were most vulnerable, trapped in the insufferable mud-hole called Creation. There, an unknown force had weakened or destroyed many of them, instantly turning their celestial forms to nothing more than ash and dust.

The unknown force had been a mystery to Kachash, a silent monster residing in Creation. It had threatened his plans for the future return and rule of the Dark One upon the throne of both worlds.

But now the tides had turned, for the Watchers had cowardly retreated to somewhere beyond the Divide, leaving Kachash alone to rebuild his great army of Metim. Soon, he would begin his assault upon the last vestiges of the Light residing inside of any being that resisted him.

And now, he had discovered the source of the destruction of the Lords in Creation. The force that had driven the Dark forces underground. He knew the secret, and he would use it to his advantage.

The Dark One would certainly receive him as his own, now that he had arisen from his hiding place. Now was the time that all those serving the Darkness had been waiting for, the return of the Dark One to Lior, where he would lead them to destroy Creation and finally conquer the Light.

And in one marvelous act, with Kachash and the other three Lords beside him, the Dark One would slay the one from whom the vile Light began. The Creator himself.

He would make the boy his second, sure, but then Kachash would be next. He was the Lord of Deception, after all, and he deserved the glory from the deed he was about to perform.

"Sar Kachash, Lord of Deception, I am at your service," Arazel spoke, his green eyes blazing in the pure white halls of the palace.

Kachash flagrantly stood from his throne, sweeping down the steps to greet him. "Ah, my servant Arazel. It is good to have you here," he said dreamily. "Please, sit." Kachash motioned to a large table to the side of the throne, where ornate golden candelabras instantly lit at Kachash's glance.

Arazel took his place at the delicately decorated table, the brilliant gold silverware and embellished dinnerware reflecting off the hall's interior.

Another demanding glance toward the edges of the hall brought silver platters of food and wine of all sorts from the servants. The sheer gowns they wore showed their underfed forms. Kachash paid them no mind as they gingerly set the platters on the table, bowing low. Then they slunk back into the corners of the hall.

Kachash snatched up the wine in front of him and took a large drink, some of the red liquid spilling down his chin and onto his robe. "Eat, Lord Arazel. I know you have been hard at work."

Arazel stared at the beautiful form of his lord before him. Kachash, one of the four remaining Dark lords of old, truly believed the calling of the Dark One was for the betterment of both Lior and Creation. That once the Descendants were dead, the weak minds of the created ones on Earth would follow the Darkness. Then, the Dark One would have everything he needed to destroy the Creator once and for all.

Arazel, however, had always been one to question everything. Challenge every belief and cause. It had served him well, and when he made the choice to follow Kachash in his quest to serve the Dark One.

Far beneath the pages of history, too many wars had been fought and heroes fallen, leaving now only a handful of the great armies of the past to push forward into a new future. That future was now primed for the Darkness, and for all those who served it. Since pledging his devotion, he believed he wanted to be a part of that future. Yet, something within him yearned for truth. Truth about who he was, and to uncover the blurred images of the past.

He had given Kachash his devotion, and he had been rewarded with status and power. But now, he questioned Kachash's idealist pursuits. He was strong with the Darkness and formidable in battle, but was he certain that this was the plan of the Dark One? Would he truly be one of the most trusted lords in the Dark One's service?

Kachash drank deeply of his wine once again. "You are quiet, Lord Arazel. Have you not been enjoying your post as my second?"

Arazel nodded. "Sar, lord, I could ask for nothing more."

Kachash's eyes blazed suddenly, as though he suspected treachery in his servant. "Then what ails you, amanah, Arazel?"

Arazel chose his next words carefully. "Sar, I don't mean to question

your orders, but are you certain this is the path the Dark One would have us tread?"

Kachash glared dangerously at Arazel for a moment, but then his eyes softened into a look of sympathy. As though Arazel didn't know better.

He smiled warmly. "My servant Arazel, it is refreshing to hear one such as yourself curious about the Dark One, as his return is so close! I, too, have had my doubts throughout the years in the service of the Darkness. But there was always one that would be there to help me understand once again. One that reminded me of why we serve the Darkness, and not the Light."

Arazel was silent, waiting for Kachash to continue.

"It was I that was there for you in your time of need, Arazel," he said softly. "Do you remember where you were when I found you? Lost, with no place to go, swearing allegiance to nothing?"

Arazel nodded.

"Pathetically weak, in need of a master," Kachash said. "Do you remember?"

Again, Arazel nodded.

He lifted his arms up to his sides, the sheer robe allowing for his perfectly toned arms to be exposed. "When the others chose me, it was because I had a unique connection with the Darkness, as though I was one with its power. That connection is what the Dark One has given me, along with his purpose."

"Yes, Sar, lord."

Kachash's eyes caught Arazel's once more. "You were a follower of the Light. Do you remember?"

"I remember, lord. I was confused, in need of direction. You… and the Darkness… have provided me with more than I could ever ask."

"Yes, yes," Kachash hissed, his eyes gleaming. "I would think a former *Descendant* who had seen the lies of the Light would know that by now."

Arazel glanced down at the uneaten food in front of him. He

remembered only vaguely now the time he had spent in Lior. Even though it was only fifteen years ago, it seemed like a lifetime. He had been a resident of Themane, the forest region in the south of Lior. A fisherman, with a simple life and a simple purpose.

But a follower of the Light, a Descendant, he had also been. Vowing to serve a Creator he had never seen.

Until the morning he returned home to his little river cabin to find his wife gone, and his home ransacked. The only clues he had were the scratch marks on the floor and traces of blood on the door.

Arazel had searched for her for years, believing that she was still alive. But he had found nothing.

The years on the road had changed him after that. It had been hard on him, leaving him exhausted and alone.

When Kachash found him, he had been lying in a pool of his own blood, beaten nearly to death by a group of Outsiders who mistook him for a Metim. Kachash took him in, cared for his wounds, and gave him the name he carried today. He was no longer Maayan, follower of Light. He was Arazel, servant of the Darkness, the first servant of Lord Kachash.

Kachash had taught Arazel to embrace the anger he had been holding within and use it for a greater purpose.

Power.

Because with power, no one can take anything from you.

"I will remember, lord."

Kachash picked up his fork, motioning for Arazel to do the same. "Now eat, Arazel, my servant. You have a great task before you."

Chapter Thirteen
A Light Star

Sam stepped out of the Lightbase to find his friends were gone. In their places stood two Lior guards dressed in long red robes with silver collars. Their statures were very much like Achiam's, the guard of the entrance into Thalo's hall of the City Center. Both sported long gleaming swords, sheathed but with their hands on the hilt.

Blinking, Sam stood before them, searching for his friends.

The taller guard with the thin face motioned to him. "The Chancellor requires your presence."

Sam stood, unmoving. "Where are my friends?"

Both guards said nothing.

He rubbed his eyes as they adjusted from the intense light of the Lightwave. Obviously, he would just have to follow them and hope the others were waiting.

They led Sam down the steps of the tower and to a familiar hallway that held the office of the Chancellor. Two more guards stood at the archway with staffs beside them, both of whom Sam did not recognize the last time he had been to the Chancellor's office.

Their staffs shone blue as the two guards and Sam approached. Immediately, the door to the office opened.

Sam was relieved to see his friends inside the office as the guards closed the door behind him.

The familiar blue wisps of Lazuli Light snaked up the curved arch above the Chancellor's desk, making their way to the top and disappearing somewhere into the ceiling above.

The sun glared on the dome of the rotunda outside the window in front of him. He had forgotten how beautiful the City Center was.

The Chancellor stood from his desk, his silver robe gleaming in the sunlight that poured through the window. "Samuel, my dear boy, how are you?"

Sam looked warily at his friends. They shrugged in return as they sat in the large ornate wooden chairs, holding ceramic mugs with steam rising from their rims.

"I'm good, sir."

The Chancellor motioned toward a buffet table in the corner of the office. "Would you like some coffee? I'm told it's only the best brew in all of Lior, straight from the Nais highlands."

Sam wanted to accept the cup but was more interested to hear the point of why they were there.

"Thank you, but no."

The Chancellor nodded and offered him a seat. His eyes looked even more tired and drawn than Sam remembered. Then he turned to the others and addressed them all together.

"Considering what you all went through last year, I suppose there is no sense wrapping this news up in something more cheerful," he said, sighing. "The truth is, simply, that we have lost contact with the fourth gate to Creation."

Emma gasped.

The fourth gate led to White Pine. The same gate found by Julian Lawrence, the town's founder, and protected by their parents.

Gus put his coffee down and sat upright. "Sir, what does that mean? Lost contact?"

The Chancellor turned and faced the window. "We have been keeping close watch on the gate, without arousing too much suspicion, of course. But as of late, we haven't been getting regular reports of Dark activity from…"

"From our families, Chancellor, just say it," Lillia said with an edge to her voice.

"Please, call me Almeous," he said. "While you are here in my office, I am your friend."

Lillia rolled her eyes.

"That is yet to be determined," she said under her breath.

"Lillia!" Emma swatted her shoulder. "Stop it for once! I want to hear what he is saying!"

The Chancellor sat down. "She is right to question me, dear Emma. I do not deny I have been less than forthright with you in past events."

"Then *please* tell us what you know," Emma said quietly.

Chancellor Almeous stood, walking over to a bookshelf on the wall. He picked up a small object that looked like a bookend. As he brought the object closer to the four seated, Sam observed it as a dragon carved intricately into a block of stone. Indeed, it was a bookend, but elegant all the same.

He set it on the table opposite them. "This is called a—"
Gus's eyes lit up. "A *Tual*," *He interrupted.*
The Chancellor nodded. "Yes. It is one of a few ancient devices we were given by the Watchers a very long time ago."

Gus's excitement faded as he remembered the gravity of the situation.

"It's a communication portal between Lior and Creation. That must be what's inside the radio at the cabin," Gus said.

The Chancellor glanced at Gus and nodded. "There are others. One of which is kept at your home in Creation."

Emma shut her eyes, inhaling deeply. She had taken to doing breathing exercises after their encounter with Arazel the previous year. It seemed to be helping. "You've lost contact with them—what does that mean?"

"It means simply that. We cannot reach them through the Tual."

"What about the gate? Can't someone go through and check on them?" Emma was losing her nerve quicker than she could compose it.

Almeous shook his head. "We have tried. Unfortunately, the gate has been disabled, and we are unsure why. The Sons are entering through the southern gate this very evening to make their way to White Pine to find out why there has been no answer."

Sam looked at Emma, who was doing her best to fight back the tears. "What then?" Sam asked the Chancellor. "Can we go with them?"

He shook his head. "I am afraid they have already gone. But I admire your bravery."

Then the Chancellor reached out and took Emma's shaking hands in his. "It is best that we leave these things to those who know how to handle it, anyhow."

Gus, who seemed to never let the emotions get the best of him, stood suddenly and walked toward the brightly lit window. He stood with his back to them, breathing heavily as he gazed out of the glass.

He said nothing, but Sam knew what this meant. He was afraid. And if Gus had a reason to fear, so should the rest of them.

For several minutes, they sat in silence, contemplating the Chancellor's news. Sam put his hand on Emma, but she shrugged him off, standing to join Gus at the window. Lillia and Sam sat alone, facing the Chancellor.

Sam broke the silence. "What can we do?"

Lillia folded her arms and sat back in her chair. "Nothing. Why do you think guards walked us here? They want to make sure we don't bolt."

The Chancellor didn't reply to Lillia's comment.

Sam leveled his eyes and met the Chancellor's. "Sir, what about the Sha'ar Gate? Has it been tampered with?"

Almeous shook his head. "The Seers have been concentrating their efforts on the gate and have reported nothing."

"Then what do we do?"

He sighed, his eyes showing empathy. "You must go to Mentorship,

just as planned. It is the… *safest* place at the moment."

Sam watched Emma sit down next to them once again. She seemed to regain her composure. "Before we left, there was an attack—" she began.

Gus spun and held his finger to his lips, stopping Emma from saying any more.

Almeous nodded. "We are aware. The Metim had found a way to manipulate the Light to use the arches. They called off the attack when they saw our forces arrive in White Pine. That is when you came to stay in the cabin."

How did the Chancellor know all of this? Sam thought. Obviously, he had been talking with Mr. Sterling. But what else did he know? Did he know about Nuriel, too? And the Watchers that had been intervening without the Descendants' knowledge?

Emma didn't seem to want to drop her previous statement. "So there could have been another attack. After we left."

It must have been only days ago that it had occurred. Sam thought. After they had talked with Mr. Sterling.

"Yes," he told them. "But with the Creator's graces, I pray that isn't the case. I have arranged for you four to travel to Mentorship separately from the rest of the inductees—"

"No," Emma interrupted him. "My father never said anything about that, and I'm sorry sir, I know you are the Chancellor and he respects you, but I won't do that without hearing from him first."

Almeous looked taken aback at first, then grinned Emma's sudden defiance. "Talister said you would say that," he told her. "Then I will defer to your judgement, Emma Sterling."

Then he turned to the rest of them, his smile fading into a look of profound uneasiness. "But I must warn the four of you. Do not stray from the city on your own. Times are uncertain, especially now."

****

"What do you think that was about?" Lillia said quietly as she flopped into the chair once they had finally made it to the cabin circle.

Emma was busying herself in the kitchen, putting away the groceries that had been left by Mrs. Mirke. Sam thought it wise that Lillia had chosen not to involve Emma in the discussion.

The sun had just dropped behind the pines near the cliff's edge overlooking the Yarey Sea. There was a chill in the evening air, so Gus was carefully arranging kindling into the fireplace.

He lit the paper underneath the wood. "I think there is more that isn't being said," He said, keeping his voice low. "Something significant that they know, but won't let on they know it."

"Stop talking in riddles, *Gustav*," Lillia hissed, the sarcasm thick as she purposefully used his full first name. "You know princess is going to lose it if we don't figure out what is happening in White Pine."

Gus turned angrily from the fireplace to wave a thick finger at Lillia. "It's not just her that's worried, you know," he spat.

It was out of character for Gus to get angry so quickly, but Sam believed it was called for. Sometimes Lillia didn't seem to care enough about others's feelings, even when she was experiencing the same pain herself.

"I don't think there's much we can do at this point, but wait, Gus," Sam said. "We are all worried, but we have to trust the Creator to look after them."

Gus and Lillia shot surprised glances at Sam. He knew what they were thinking. It had only been last year that he had chosen to follow the Creator. Now, he was reassuring them of their own faith.

Gus slunk down next to the growing fire, somewhat feeing embarrassed.

"He's right, you know." Emma said, appearing the kitchen doorway. She was smiling. "Yes, I was listening."

"I—" Gus began.

"We will go to Mentorship, and we will remember that our families are trained Protectors of the arch. They know what they are doing," Emma continued. "But… that doesn't mean we should sit by and do *nothing.*"

Gus nodded, agreeing.

"What do you think we should do?" Lillia asked.

She furrowed her eyebrows. "We have a lead. Well, sort of. The tower, and the man called the Shadow. I don't have a clue how any of them are connected, but something tells me they are."

"That's not really a lead, Emma," Lillia scoffed. "We have an old book and some fantasy tower here in boy wonder's brain. That's not much to go on."

Sam wasn't offended. He had gotten used to Lillia's comments. But she was right. They had nothing to go on, and none of it seemed to relate to each other.

But what happened to Sam in the cave was real. And the encounter with Arazel had been real. And the fact that they couldn't contact their families in White Pine was real.

And, of course, the fact that everyone believed the Dark One had awoken seemed real enough.

He had learned to trust Emma's instincts about many things. This time would be no different.

"I know what to do," Gus declared.

Lillia sat up, smiling. "Boggle? You want to go see Boggle!"

Gus smiled back. "Boggle," he repeated.

✶✶✶✶✶✶✶✶✶✶✶✶✶✶✶✶✶✶✶✶✶✶✶✶✶✶✶✶✶✶

The next morning, with some flapjacks and birch syrup safely in their bellies, the four headed out for Boggle's. Talister had been busy with council duties in the North but promised to return as soon as he could, so that gave them all day to visit with Boggle. Later, they would catch some of the Light parade that kicked off the feast and the start of the Light Festival.

A knock on the old wooden door of the inventor's home produced a very tired-looking man in a hastily drawn up robe.

Emma looked peculiarly at him. "Boggle? Are you—okay?"

"Who's asking?" the inventor said, unwilling to open the door completely.

Emma stepped up closer to the half-opened door. "Boggle, it's us, Emma, Lillia, Gus, and Sam."

He peered at them through his fogged spectacles. "Emma?" he said, repeating the name. "You four? What are you all doing here?"

The old inventor backed away from the door to let it open. He gestured for them to enter quickly.

They followed him up the stairs to the workshop. It looked as though it hadn't been touched in weeks, perhaps months.

He sat hesitantly at his workbench with a cup of coffee, eyeing the teenagers. All around them were thousands of Boggle's inventions, once whirring with life but now suspended in a frozen state. Several layers of dust had settled upon them.

Lillia picked up a carved wooden bird that glowed faintly when she touched it. "Boggle, what happened to your shop? It seems… well, *dead.*"

Boggle sighed and rubbed his eyes where the spectacles had left a dent on his upper nose. "It's hopeless, it is. Hopeless," he mumbled, as though he was talking to himself. "I had hoped it wasn't the case, but there really is no denying it now…"

Lillia shook her head. "What's hopeless, Boggle? You're not making any sense."

Boggle looked up as though he just noticed they were there. "What can I help you kids with?" he said oddly.

"Don't act like we aren't old enough to know something's wrong, Boggle," Lillia said.

He frowned, shaking his head. "This isn't something you kids should be a part of. It's probably best you all get back before—"

"No, Boggle, we aren't going anywhere. And anyway, we have something we need *your* help with," Lillia said forcefully.

He squinted at her with his spectacles in hand. "Lillia, when did you grow up so much? It was just yesterday in my shop you were helping me with the Lazuli Poppers…"

Lillia turned red. It was one of the few times Sam had seen her do so. "Boggle, I know a trip down memory lane would be fabulous, but we are here about something very important."

He lifted his head, looking at each of them.

"What did you say you wanted help with?"

Lillia nodded to Gus as if to say, *It's your turn.*

Gus then proceeded to tell Boggle the story about their past few months at the cabin, the Watcher device, the trip to Warm Springs, the holomap, and even the meeting with the Chancellor. Sam and the others were perfectly fine with him doing so, as Boggle had always proved to be trustworthy. He was, in fact, one of the few they felt they could reveal anything to.

Boggle's eyes were wide as he listened intently to Gus's story. When Gus finished, he said nothing, only stood and ambled over to a dusty wardrobe in the back of the spacious shop. He returned with a small box, setting it down on the table in front of them.

They at once jumped to their feet and stood over the box Boggle set down, peering at its worn, exceptionally bland exterior. Lillia wasted no time opening it, and they all examined the contents.

Sam was stunned to see a small metallic, clear orb, identical to the one he had purchased from the old lady from Braham Street. Except for one minor difference… Boggle's glimmered a subdued blue.

Emma reached out to touch it. "What is it, Boggle?"

Gus placed a hand over Emma's hand. "Best not to do that, 'Em," he told her.

Boggle glanced at Gus. "You know what it is?"

Gus looked closely at the artifact, examining it as best as he could without removing it from its wooden box. "I think so, but I can't be sure."

He adjusted his glasses, then pulled out his journal and thumbed the pages, stopping on one. He held up the page and pointed at a drawing of a man dressed in a long robe. Around his neck hung a circular object that shone brightly. "It's a Kochan. A Light Star," He answered. "The existence of this object is supposed to be only speculation."

Gus fidgeted with his glasses once more. "But when I drew this, I was studying the ancient wars. Each time I saw a Watcher in one of the old texts, they were wearing it."

Boggle nodded. "I had come to the same conclusion before this one was given to me."

"It's considered to be one of the most dangerous artifacts in existence," Gus said in a near whisper.

Emma's face flushed. "Boggle... Then why do you have it?"

Boggle's eyes lit up for the first time since the four had arrived at his workshop. "Oh! It was given to me a long time ago by a man in Sainia City in the mountains..."

He paused, as if trying to remember the event. "He told me to keep it safe for him, and that he would return someday to retrieve it. Strange... very strange it was."

Emma was astonished. "And you've not heard from him since? He told you it was dangerous, and you still kept it?"

Boggle's lips widened into a smile. "No way! I did the research on my own about that there little beauty. It may be dangerous, yes, yes, but if I were to abandon every dangerous item that crossed my path, well... well... you can't stop science, no!"

"I'm almost certain the thing is harmless, anyhow."

"Who was it, Boggle?" Lillia pressed. "The man that gave it to you?"

Boggle frowned. "I don't know, honestly. I was just enamored with any Watcher device at that time. I was so young then..." He faded off into thought.

Sam had been silent about the fact that he had something that looked very similar to the Star until then, but now he dug it out of his backpack and set it on the table next to the box containing the other. The two pieces were identical. Without close inspection, one would not be able to tell the two apart.

With one exception, perhaps. Boggle's Star emitted the soft glow of Lazuli. Sam's did not.

Chapter Fourteen
Darkness Detected

What is *that*?!" Lillia pointed at the two artifacts next to each other. All of them were stunned, including Boggle, who looked from the Star to Sam, and back again.

Emma's eyes blazed, piercing Sam's skull as he did his best not to look at her. "Where did you get that?!"

He knew she would be angry, because that was how she reacted when she was confused or afraid.

"I bought it in Warm Springs," he told them.

Truthfully, he had all but forgotten about it until then. "I don't know why. I just thought it was interesting."

Boggle whistled. "This is unexpected. It is."

Emma backed away, having just noticed the difference between the two. "Why is Boggle's glowing?"

Boggle squinted, even with his spectacles high on his nose. "Yes, yes, it is. I hadn't noticed that before. It must have only recently happened."

"What does that mean?" Lillia asked.

"I—I'm not certain…" Boggle answered.

Lillia drew in a breath. "But you know something."

Boggle wouldn't answer, so Emma turned to Gus.

He shrugged his shoulders. "I only know they were worn by Watchers. They thought it might have been an activation device for one of the other artifacts."

"Another key to something," Sam whispered.

Gus shook his head. "But I can't be sure. I only speculate based on what previous scholars have suggested."

"Boggle. What *are* these things?" Emma pleaded with the old inventor.

He pointed a bony finger at the drawing in Gus's open journal. "I've seen that drawing before. I'm fairly positive that Watcher is the Creator."

Gus scowled at his journal. "As in the Creator?"

"The one and only."

Gasps circulated the group.

Lillia leaned over to examine the artifacts. "You mean that these things could be the *Creator's*?"

The others moved closer as well. For a few moments, they all peered dumbfounded at the Stars. Boggle's continued to glow, which was now casting its Lazuli Light onto the Star next to it.

Again, Emma backed away from the table. "If one of them is the Creator's, why are there two?"

"Maybe he has another… you know, for backup?" Lillia suggested.

Boggle cleared his throat. "Now, you mentioned something about the tower earlier, which is why I retrieved the Star for you all to see. There is a tower I know of, believed to have been built by the ancient Watchers. It's thought to be located somewhere near the Divide."

The four friends pondered this. Was Boggle implying the tower was *real?*

"There's very little information about it—especially its exact whereabouts. But I think… it may have been built to prevent any of

the celestial beings from becoming too powerful. According to legend, anyway."

"A weapon?" Sam suggested.

Boggle nodded. "A weapon to remove the power from any celestial being, Light or Dark, in case they got out of hand, so to speak."

"And the Creator had the key to use the tower if need be," Gus offered, which caused everyone to gaze at the Stars once more.

First, the Sha'ar Gate, now a key to an ancient weapon, Sam thought. *A weapon controlled by the Creator himself.*

"But two were made," Lillia said, looking perplexed.

"Maybe one is a fake," Sam thought aloud. "It has to be mine. It's the only one that doesn't glow."

Boggle circled the table to get a closer look at Sam's Star, his robe flapping as he moved. "Yes, yes! That could be it," he said, chuckling heartily. "A fake. Made by the Metim to try to activate the tower. But they failed, so the imposter ends up in some chalky shop in Warm Springs. And here I was thinking there could have been another key holder. Silly me!"

His eagerness vanished, replaced suddenly by the deep sadness they saw in his demeanor upon entering earlier.

"What is it, Boggle? Seriously. We want to help with whatever is wrong," Lillia pleaded.

Boggle sighed sadly. "I hadn't told anyone I had the Star until now. I didn't want to drag you four into this, but Light-help-us I had been talking to the Creator—you know, while I was alone—and I asked Him to send me someone that could help…"

He paused, his eyes distant. "And now, here you are."

Lillia patted him on the arm. "We would always help you, Boggle. You know that."

"Thank you, Lillia, I know you would," he smiled, patting her hand.

Then he turned away from the table, taking his place once again at the window overlooking the Yarey Sea. It was calm and exceptionally green in the sun that glistened off the surface.

"It's no use either way," he muttered.

Emma was noticeably losing her patience, as if Boggle was a toddler who was throwing a fit. "We can handle it, Boggle. Please, just tell us."

Boggle's shoulders slumped for a moment, then he turned and strode over to what looked like another table. He motioned for the others to follow.

"Please don't hold this against me," he said.

He removed the canvas tarp covering, and with a wave of his hand, the table sprang to life. Designs painted onto the table's surface rearranged themselves, moving about like ink poured into a glass of water. Before long, the designs had transformed into a map, recognized as Lior.

Another wave of Boggle's hand brought about blue blotches of Lazuli concentrated in various regions of the land. "This is the Descendant population of Lior," he said.

He waved his hand once more, and blotches of green emerged from outside the Descendant regions. There were concentrations of green, though not as numerous as the blue. "And this is the Metim population, which as of recently has just become more visible. Thanks to the opening of the Sha'ar Gate," he said, winking at Sam.

Lillia was not surprised. "This is not news, Boggle. The PO is already keeping track."

"Yes, yes, I am aware!" he interrupted, holding up a hand to dismiss her protest. "Who do you think built the device for them to observe this phenomenon?"

He waved his hand once more and the designs on the table began to shift and morph again. This time, it took on the unmistakable form of Earth. Tiny pockets of blue emerged on the flattened globe, each in strategic points around the world.

Lillia watched the table. "Those are the gate protectors, right?"

Boggle nodded, then waved his hand again, but not before Sam noticed that there were still blue dots nearest to where the White Pine gate was likely located. He was sure Emma noticed as well.

Those dots gave them the slightest bit of hope that the protectors in White Pine were still safe.

The pockets of blue remained as the map changed yet again. This time, small concentrations of green emerged in remote parts of the world.

"This is the Metim population in Creation a month ago," he said.

He waved his hand again. "And this is today."

Deep concentrations of green were splattered across all continents. Stunned, they watched as more and more joined the masses, as if they were growing by the minute.

"I shouldn't be showing you four this, but frankly, I am unsure what to do," he told them.

Sam stared at the map inked with large green stains, comparing it with the tiny blots of green he saw moments before.

"So they started appearing after I opened the Sha'ar Gate?"

Gus's eyes widened. "Or they could be using the gate to move from Lior into Creation."

"Now that I know what has happened in White Pine, yes, I tend to agree with Gus," Boggle said. "The Darkness is active once again in Creation, that is certain. Light save us!"

Emma paced around the table, refusing to take her eyes off the map. "The PO—and Daddy must know this. They use the Darkness maps in their offices."

Boggle shook his head. "No! They don't in Creation. When I built the detection system nearly forty years ago, the PO was all too eager to install them in Lior. But they refused to install one in Creation… said it was unnecessary! Can you believe that?"

He threw his arms up, nearly knocking Emma out, who was still pacing behind him. "*But* I suppose they were just the tiniest bit concerned the Watchers wouldn't approve…"

The Watchers. Beings that followed the Creator and used the Light to protect people of Creation. Evidence of them in Lior and Creation was everywhere. And yet Sam had only met one.

Emma, who was still looking intently at the map, pointed to a spot in South America where the concentration of green seemed to be growing the fastest. "They are moving here," she said. "Well, most of them are, anyway."

Boggle and the others peered at the map. "By Sarse-sapping-gobble-snatchers, she's right!" he hollered and dashed over to his workbench, tossing aside old dusty inventions to search for something. As he did, he knocked over his cup of coffee that had been teetering on the edge of the workbench.

He turned toward them, holding what looked like a giant ant with long tentacles. "You four! I must work in peace! You must leave and come back another day! I will call on you! I promise I will have more information for you then!"

The old inventor turned back to his ant tentacles, then swirled back to face them one last time. "Do you mind if I keep the Stars here for the time being?"

Sam nodded, and Boggle swirled back to his tentacles, paying the four young people no more mind.

Annoyed and a bit shocked they had just been thrown out so abruptly, Lillia unloaded on them as they walked back toward town. She had known Boggle before any of them, and now she felt a bit betrayed that he hadn't asked her to stay and help.

"At least he's back to normal," Emma said, hoping it would ease the ranting.

Sam laughed. "If he ever was to begin with."

It was nearly two o'clock by the time they made it back to the City Center, and they realized they hadn't eaten anything since breakfast. Smells from Thalo Street's many festival vendors greeted them the moment they arrived, so they ventured in for a hearty snack of chocolate Fuzer nuts and a powdered pastry puff before heading to the parade.

The week-long Light Festival was just about to kick off once more, with feasts, vendors, acrobatic shows, and even a dragon—Orono, whom they now knew personally.

They had been looking forward to the Light Festival all summer,

but this year's festivities would be very different without the others with them to enjoy it with.

The feeling of not knowing what was happening in White Pine was the worst part.

Then the discovery of the Watcher device and the tower. And now the Stars in Boggle's workshop. Strange things were piling up, it seemed.

Sam could tell that Emma's concern for her parents was growing again, and Sam couldn't blame her. He too wondered about the fate of White Pine, and of their families. That included Amos and Nuriel, for they had been there as well.

Nuriel may be a Watcher, but he was vulnerable, like any of them. He may even be more of a target. Oddly enough, Sam worried the least about Amos. He seemed to be one that had a knack for survival. That, and he was as tough as a bear.

But for now, they had to take their minds off of their concern for their families. The festival was here, and they needed to attempt to enjoy it. For all too soon, Mentorship would be upon them.

And from what Gus had told them about the training, it wasn't for the faint of heart.

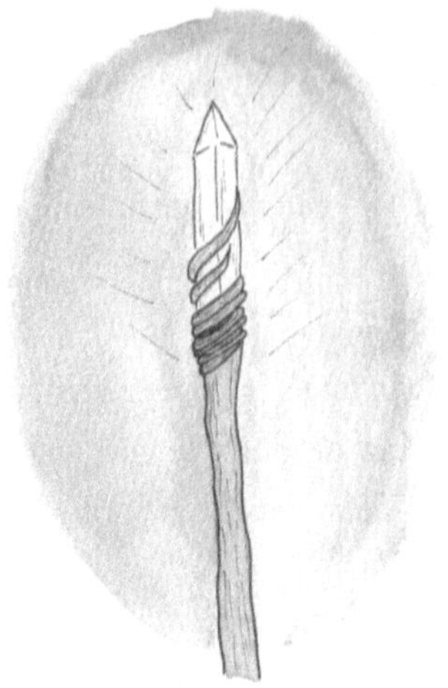

Chapter Fifteen
Lazuli Powered

Wake up, sleepy face."

A familiar face greeted Sam from the doorway of his and Gus's bedroom in the cabin.

Sam rubbed his eyes and squinted as the morning sun poured through the window. There in the doorway was Sayvon, her brown hair in a long, thick braid as always.

"Good morning," Sam yawned. "And it's sleepy*head*," he told her.

"Oh, sorry," she said, blushing.

Her warm rose skin glowed in the golden light. "I've been practicing, but still don't have all of them down."

Sam jumped out of bed and gave her a giant bear hug. He hadn't seen her since last festival. In his letters to Talister throughout the year, however, he had included a note or two to Sayvon.

Thankfully, before leaving Lior last year, he had a chance to tell her about his mother being raised with Sayvon's father. Now that there were no more awkward feelings between them, Sam could actually

look at her as his family. Maybe not a blood relation, but it was enough for him.

Sayvon hugged him back. "I missed you, Samuel!" she said, laughing. "I can't believe Mentorship is here already."

He tossed on a shirt. "Yeah, I know," he said, checking his breath to see if it was good enough for going to breakfast without brushing. "Are you ready?"

"Yes," she said sadly. "I love my parents, but I'm kinda ready to make my own way, you know?"

Sam understood what she was saying, but couldn't resonate with it. Unlike her, he never had parents around enough to be annoyed with. He wanted to experience the world, however, so he was still excited.

She grabbed his hand. "Let's go. Breakfast is waiting."

The other three were already downstairs, with Talister and his wife, Julena, as they had just sat down to stacks of pancakes and birch syrup.

Emma peered at Sayvon and Sam a bit strangely as they came down the stairs hand in hand, but promptly caught herself. They were family.

Sitting down to breakfast with the Talisters gave Sam, Lillia, Emma, and Gus a little taste of normalcy. They had missed the family atmosphere that the cabin circle provided, and it felt good to be with others they knew.

The four teens had spent the entire festival week going to the feast, acrobatic shows, and Light illusionist acts by themselves. Although they had enjoyed it, having eaten way more than they should, and staying up far too late telling stories next to the fire, they still missed having the others there with them.

Talister apologized profusely for having to leave them alone all week, though they took no offense to it. Judging from his tone, Sam could tell that whatever he had been dealing with was in the north was unavoidable.

"You know, you four should come with us to Telok someday," Julena told them. "Rolling hills, and a lake where you can see down fifty meters clearly."

"I like the Maripoth Forest," Sayvon added. "Huge ancient trees that seem to speak to you as you walk through them."

Talister sipped his coffee as the rest of them finished off the last of the pancakes. "Yes. Truly remarkable they are. It is said that there, the Watchers from long ago will tell you the secrets of Lior."

"Really?" Emma asked.

He nodded, smiling. "They have spoken to me a time or two when I was in a very dark place."

Gus was skeptical, but careful not to offend Talister. "I certainly do not fault those who visit the forest for those reasons, but there are quite a few in the scientific world that would agree that the voices are there simply because we want them to be."

Talister laughed and patted him on the back. "Always the pragmatist, Gus, my friend! I suppose one day you will have to find out for yourself."

Cleaning up the dishes, they said goodbye to the Calphers, who promised to retrieve them long before the start of the Kolar game and the sendoff of the student candidates to Mentorship.

They had no idea what to expect or what to bring. They only knew they were allowed a large backpack with whatever belongings they could fit inside. Trying to pack too many things would only get in the way, Talister had warned them, as Mentees were trained to make do with only the basic necessities.

Sam packed slowly, trying to make sure he wouldn't leave any of the essentials behind. Toothbrush, journal, shirts, pants and undergarments. His coffee mug, shoes, and a few other odds and ends he could think of.

The last thing he took from the closet was the new training robe he had purchased at Osan's shop the day before. Each of the Mentees were required to have one, and Emma thought it best to check on uncle Osan, anyway.

Mr. Sterling had also suggested that anything they might have forgotten could be purchased in the southern city of Cembra prior to arriving at the school.

"It is the closest place to the school, which isn't really close to much of anything," he had told them.

Sam joined the others in the living room about an hour before the games were to begin. It was an odd excitement that they carried for what was to come in the next months. Paired with it was the anticipation of what they would learn, and how well they would do learning the Light gifts.

Emma had come to accept the fact that their parents weren't going to be there to see them off. She and the others had visited the Protector's Office twice that week, hoping for some news, but no one offered them any information. Not that they had any to give.

Furthermore, they had not heard from Boggle since they saw him at his workshop and left the Stars with him. He had promised to give them updates about what he found, but even he let them down.

If it weren't for Talister and a few others in the circle, they would have been truly alone.

When Sayvon, Talister, and Julena arrived at the cabin, they locked up and walked together toward the stadium. Sam's pack was lighter than he thought, and he was thankful he had left much of it in the cabin.

Gus seemed to be struggling a bit with his pack. Judging from the looks of it, he had added a few more books than he normally carried.

Books, Sam thought. That was one thing he had forgotten. Hopefully, he could find one or two in Cembra City.

As they waded their way through the throngs of people entering the stadium, Sam caught a glimpse of Tarmin, the Son of Light that helped save them last year from Arazel in the forest. He nodded and smiled at Sam, then turned and disappeared through the crowd.

"Through this way, Mentees!" a large man with a short grey beard hollered, pointing behind him to a set of half-moon double wooden doors leading behind the stadium. "All Mentees going to Helel Malach this way!"

Talister led them to the doors, then gathered them around him. "This is where we must leave you, I am afraid," he told them, a tear forming in his eye. "I remember the day when I entered Mentorship, and now… so much time has passed."

Julena clung to his arm, tears welling up in her eyes as well.

Talister grabbed his daughter's hand and motioned for the others to take each other's hands as well. "I will leave you with the same prayer that my father left me with."

"May the Creator give you peace, and guide you toward truth. May he shelter you with his Light, so that you may see through the Darkness."

"You are never far from the Light, young people," Talister said, finishing the prayer. Then he opened his arms and embraced all of them at once. "Now, it's time you leave us old people to get some rest before we keel over."

They laughed and said their goodbyes to the Calphers. The last of the Mentees were making their way through the doors, so the five teens picked up their packs and followed the stragglers into the dark hallway.

The only light came from the wall of stained-glass windows lining the hallway, which cast the occasional red, blue, or green ray on the Mentees as they passed.

Their steps echoed on the stone as they made their way to another set of wooden double doors, where Mentees filed through into what looked like a large room built under the stadium.

"This way!" Another shorter man with curly dark hair and glasses shouted and pointed at the last of the students walking down the hallway. "Hurry up then!"

The room was large indeed, and just as dark. Torches lined the walls and gave off a cave-like appearance, but the only other source of light Sam could see was the glowing stone on the face of the man who stood on a small stage in front of them.

"Good evening, Mentees," thundered the voice of a tall, thin, hooded man in a white robe. Sam immediately recognized him as the one who led the ceremony last year with the Sons of Light.

He smiled largely, the light from his staff illuminating his face in blue Lazuli Light. "I am Mentor Aron of the School of the Shining

One! I would like to welcome you all here this evening, as I am sure you are all greatly anticipating your journey to Helel Malach!"

Cheers rang up from the hundreds of Mentees standing before Mentor Aron.

"Now, let me offer my sincerest gratitude for your willingness to serve the Descendants of Lior in Mentorship, and to warn you…" he paused for a moment as ripples of chatter flitted through the crowd. "You have all been given a great gift. One by the Creator—the Almighty himself."

Mentor Aron's staff exploded, illuminating the entire room so brightly that Sam and the others could not stand to look at it.

"Do not use this gift lightly," he said as the light retreated back into the staff. "For it is given with purpose, as you here have been called with purpose. The Light you hold within you is sacred, and only to be used for good, not evil. To dispel the Darkness, and to fight those who attempt to snuff out its life."

He paused as another hooded person whispered something in his ear. Nodding, he looked at the crowd of Mentees once again. "Remember, the gift that is within you is not yours to control. It is a part of you, as the Creator is a part of you. It will always be there, just as the Creator will be!"

More cheers came from the crowd. This time, Sam and the other four cheered.

Suddenly, the staff and Mentor Aron disappeared, and the only sounds came from the stadium above them as the ceremony and Kolar game commenced.

The Mentees waited in the darkened room throughout the ceremony and the entirety of both Kolar games, during which several of them became agitated with the ordeal. Why would they bring them here so early just to make them wait in the room? Some grumbled, but others stayed silent and listened to the roar of the crowd above them. Occasionally a bit of dust would unloose itself from the ceiling and make its way down to a Mentee's head when the cheering got exceptionally loud.

<h2 style="text-align:center">Chapter Fifteen</h2>

Gus, Sayvon, Sam, Lillia, and Emma stood patiently, waiting for the end of the games. Not only did they know that all of Mentorship training was essentially a test, but also that it was of a sacred order. Before they left, Miss Karpatch had warned them of that very thing.

Others did the same, having been warned by someone as well, no doubt. It soon became clear in the crowd who would have trouble while being mentored and who would not.

"Remember what she told us," Emma said quietly. "Mentorship is not about serving us, but learning to become the servant."

"It's true," Sayvon agreed. "It's going to be tough for all of us to learn that."

Sam nodded. He admitted that this was going to take some work, having been raised with a maid for quite some time. He was used to being waited on by Estella whether he wanted it or not.

Occasionally he would catch himself expecting things to be a certain way or would lash out just the slightest when something was not done for him on time.

But he also recalled the day he saw Estella scrubbing his socks by hand until they were gleaming white. He had gotten used to walking around the floor in his sock feet and often into the garage or patio, and his socks would become exceptionally dirty by the end of the day. He had always thought that the washing machine would take care of it, but now he knew the truth. Someone had to scrub his socks clean because he was too lazy to put on his slippers.

But Lior—and the Creator—had changed him in ways he could have never imagined. Those things he used to desire he did no longer, like becoming famous or rich, or taking revenge on those who abandoned him. His friends and family here meant more to him than anything he could have asked for or demanded. Perhaps servanthood wouldn't be so bad.

The cheers above raised to a fever pitch, then died as the voice of the Chancellor was heard throughout the stadium.

Sayvon spotted a friend of hers crying in the middle of the crowd.

"Hey guys, I'm going to stay with Yadris," she shouted over the cheering.

Sam watched her go, a bit saddened that he wouldn't get to spend the trip getting to know his only cousin. At least they would be together at Mentorship.

"Before we send our very own Mentees on their journey to training, I would like to offer a word of caution to all here this evening," The Chancellor's voice thundered above them. "The Protector's Office of Lior has alerted me that an increased number of Metim have been spotted in some of the more remote locations. While we are indeed safe under our warrior's protection, caution must be taken while traveling back to your regions."

The Chancellor paused as the crowd murmured above.

"Please take care to travel in the daytime and avoid remote paths or roads that could be potentially hazardous."

Below the murmuring crowd, two large metal doors opened swiftly before the students waiting in the darkened room.

Sam and the others shielded their eyes from the piercing lights of the stadium. Soon, they could see the form of the Chancellor standing in the mid-center of the field, arms held out in front of him.

"Descendants! Liorians of Themane, Nais, Thalo, and Telok, let us welcome together our newest Mentees. Chosen by the Creator, of the year four thousand four hundred and fifteen!"

The crowd stood and clapped noisily, waiting for the students to emerge from their cavern below.

Mentor Aron appeared in front of them, beckoning the Mentees out onto the Kolar field.

They followed him onto the soft grass, stopping in front of the Chancellor. The mentor then motioned for them to turn and face the crowd.

The stadium erupted in thunderous applause, the Kolar fans cheering and clapping as the Mentees stood gazing back at them.

For several minutes, the clapping and cheering continued, until finally the Chancellor and Mentor Aron had to send up flames of Lazuli into the air to get them to quiet down.

The Chancellor prayed a blessing over the group of hooded youths, his voice sincere as he recited the ancient words.

Sam had not gotten to see this part last year, for this was about the time they were sneaking away to ride the Lightway to the Old City.

The Chancellor finished, and the crowd resumed its cheers. Then, from somewhere in the dark expanse of the sea behind the field, the deep echo of a horn sounded four short blasts into the night air.

Mentor Aron and the Chancellor motioned for the group to circle behind them toward the back of the Kolar field, where a small door had opened in the wall leading out of the back of the stadium.

Single file, the snaking line of robed youths exited from the stadium, toward the dark sea. From the back of the line, Sam watched as they filed into the opening, their silhouettes disappearing against the moonlit horizon.

As they drew closer, Sam turned and glanced at the blurred crowd as the lights of the stadium *blinded him. They contin*ued to cheer as the Mentees made their way, some stomping in rhythm along with the clapping.

Emma snatched the sleeve of his robe and pulled him toward the dark opening where Gus and Lillia were already entering, scolding him to keep up with her or they could risk getting separated.

There were only a few others behind them, but none were paying much attention to Sam or Emma, as they, too, wore the same apprehension on their faces.

Through the doorway, their path ended abruptly, curving downward toward a thin stairway carved into the side of the cliff. Using the moonlight to guide them, they made their way downward, realizing that one wrong move could pitch them over a hundred-meter drop to the sea below.

Still holding his sleeve, Emma gathered her courage and started down the stone steps, lugging Sam behind her. He reached out to the

wall on his left, keeping his hands on the cold stone for support as they progressed downward toward the dark water.

The stairs seemed to go on forever. With each step, the noise of the waves crashing against the rock grew louder.

Soon, however, the stairs turned inward and entered the rock face, where the source of light shifted to the flame of a small torch fixed to the wall.

They continued their descent, following the line in front of them until they heard shouts echoing off the stairway walls below. The line slowed, then stopped, then inched along for several minutes. Emma let go of his robe and clasped his hand, her skin cold and clammy.

Sam and Emma stepped off the last step into the cool cavern, finally able to see the surly men that ordered students onto the ship. Gus and Lillia waited for them, clutching their large packs and watching the mass of students being directed toward one of four large wooden ships. Sam looked around for Sayvon, but concluded she must have already boarded.

The interior of the cavern was enormous, and nearly as tall as it was wide. Each of the ships stood five stories tall or more with their masts and were as long as they were high. They were sleek in design, though Sam could tell the ships were several hundred years old.

A shorter raffish man wearing a thick woolen sweater and sporting a long beard directed them to the ship on the far side of the docks. They clomped past the first three ships to the fourth vessel, where another man as short as the first whistled to them and pointed to the plank spanning the dock to the ship's deck.

They followed the remaining students of the line over the thin plank to the ship's bow, dropping their laden packs with the others on the sprawling deck.

Some were already being directed into the expansive cabin of the boat, while some stayed on the deck to watch the remaining luggage being loaded and the last-minute checks by the crew before the caravan would shove off.

"Rigging secure!" one of the small men yelled as he circled the hull from the docks.

"Aye," a hefty man in a green robe said gruffly from a balcony behind them. In front of the man was the ship's helm.

"Full to the gunwales, Captain!" another of the crew yelled from the belly of the ship.

The captain nodded to the first officer beside him, and immediately he began yelling commands to the crew on the deck below. They sprang into action, tightening ropes, securing various cargo items, and checking the ship from bow to stern once more before pulling up anchor.

Gus ran to the side of the ship, gesturing for the others to follow. "Here we go!"

Emma, still holding Sam's sweaty hand, now let go and hurried to where Gus stood at the ship's side. She waved for him to follow.

Lillia shrugged and shoved Sam toward the others playfully. "Here we go, wonderboy," she said.

A burst of blue Lazuli Light shot downward from the bow of the ship into the seawater below, lurching the magnificent vessel into motion. Slowly, it backed out from the cavern.

The churning surf of the Yarey sprayed a salty mist over the deck of the ship as it emerged from the safety of the cavern into the moonless night.

The three other ships backed out from their ports inside the cliff soon after, the Lazuli from their bows flooding the angry waves with powerful beams of Light.

Sam was fascinated. "They are Lazuli powered," He said aloud. "Do they even use the sails?"

Gus scowled. For once, he was stumped. "I'm not sure. I have never been on one of these ships before."

"It's enchanting and beautiful," Emma acknowledged, as the four ships pivoted away from the cliffs and accelerated toward the dark expanse of the sea.

Chapter Sixteen
Turning of the Dragons

Behind them was the city in all of its illuminated beauty, and its familiar spires rising high into the night sky.

The crowd from the stadium would either be headed home now, or they would be off to the festival streets for a nightcap. Or to catch the last of the acrobats from Themane Street.

Sam, Gus, Emma, and Lillia stood on the ship's deck for nearly an hour as the vessels fell into line and powered out into the night. Then, after a heavy fog sank in around them, they made their way inside the cabin where most of the others had already gone.

Just as they were about to open the sea-weathered doors to the cabin, however, a scurry of movement behind them and a series of shouts made them turn back around to see what was happening.

"Clear the jacks!" the officer at the helm yelled out as two short men pulled the pins from the main sail. "Hoist the main!" the first officer continued. "Get the seawater out of your trousers, men! We've got us a breeze!"

The men rushed around the deck working, until all three enormous sails billowed out willingly into the beckoning wind. Each of the sails took on the shape of the Irin, a Watcher's wing.

"We are at full sail, Captain!" one of the deck mates called up as the ship caught the steady wind and lurched forward.

The Lazuli Light behind the ships blinked out one by one as each deployed their sails in favor of the natural propulsion the air currents provided.

Steadying themselves, Sam, Emma, Lillia, and Gus followed a few other students who had remained on deck to the cabins below to await the two-day journey to the port closest to Cembra City. Then it was on to Mentorship.

"I just don't see how we have to get stuck with that shadow-sucker and his friends," said a voice from a crowd of students gathered in a cluster of chairs. Ignoring it, the four friends found an unused cluster of chairs on the other side of the cabin.

Immediately, Sam picked out the voice in the crowd of other faces. An average sized boy with brown hair and tan skin glared at Sam as he picked through the other clusters of chairs and tables.

Two other thin blond boys and a thicker, dark-haired girl laughed loudly at his rude comment. Their group was sitting around a large central fireplace in the middle of the room, feet propped up on chairs so others couldn't sit in them.

There seemed to be more than enough other places to sit, however, and none of the others seemed to mind giving them plenty of space.

"That's Yorin Moge, one of the High Council's grandsons," Lillia whispered. Then she tossed Yorin and his friends a nasty look that only she could produce.

"Biggest imbecile in Lior, by far," Emma agreed. "It's said he actually convinced his grandfather to replace one of the guards simply because they wouldn't let him into a restricted area of the city."

Sam turned and glanced at the bully once more. His look drew more laughs and jeers from the group.

Now that he had dealt with Bush back home, and Arazel here in Lior, the fact that someone was bullying him didn't seem that big of a

deal. They seemed harmless for the most part, anyway.

"Just ignore them," Emma said, just loud enough for the jeering group to hear, making them laugh all the more.

"I plan to," Sam said, flopping into a comfortable leather chair that faced the fire. The flames danced on the pile of wood inside the iron gating.

The others sat with him, pointing their chairs toward the fire. Judging from the draft behind them, the fire seemed to be the only source of heat in the ship's interior.

Sam glanced around the modest cabin, noticing the bunks lining the walls for the first time. Some students were already in them, making good use of the rest time on the way to Mentorship.

From what Sam could tell, the ship had everything they needed for the two-day trip. Lavatories just off to the right of the stairway up to the main deck, beds with bunk rolls already furnished, and a small kitchen that looked as though it could fit two cooks as long as they weren't too portly.

He sunk down in the chair, barely noticing the stares from around the cabin. By now, everyone had heard the rumors about his encounter with the Dark Lord Arazel—and no doubt Sam's potential connection with the Prophecy of Darkness.

Eventually, they would ignore it, just like every other rumor out there. It would just take time.

Emma leaned over in the chair and put her head on his shoulder, her hair draping over his chest.

The feeling made his skin tingle, as it had done so many times before when she had gotten close to him.

Emma was his rock, and the best friend he had ever had. She knew him better than anyone he had ever known in his lifetime, family included. She always had his back, regardless of the situation. For that, he was truly grateful.

At some point he must have drifted off, because when he lifted up his head from the chair, a line had formed near the kitchen and a wonderful smell was drifting past his nose.

Gus slipped his shoes on and stood. "Late snack. Anyone interested?"

Lillia stretched, apparently having napped with the rest of them as well. "I'm in."

Emma lifted her head up suddenly. "Are those cheese tibbs I smell?"

"I do believe so," Gus smiled. "It's been awhile since I've had those!"

Lillia rolled her eyes and sunk back down in her chair. "Cheese filled sour bread gives me heartburn this late at night."

Sam hopped off the chair and joined the others in line. Smelling the baking bread and melting cheese made his stomach growl.

"First, they sour the bread for nearly a week, then use barrel-aged cheese and cook it in with the dough," Gus narrated as they moved through the line. Sam was sure Gus smacked his lips a dozen times as he recounted the entire recipe.

Two short but hefty women plopped a heaping basket of what looked like hush puppies on his plate, then motioned for Sam to take one of the steel cups at the end of the window full of greenish liquid.

"What is it?" Sam asked as he sipped the sweet substance when they had returned to their chairs.

"Green tea and falshorn fruit." Emma's eyes lit up as she tasted it. "One of my favorites!"

Sam slipped one of the cheese tibbs into his mouth, allowing the melted goodness to ooze onto his tongue. The bread was sweet—but savory at the same time. It was delicious. More than delicious. It was divine.

Slinking into the chair, Sam then noticed the middle-aged bearded man sleeping in a bunk in the corner of the room.

"Whoshat?" he asked, mouth full of warm cheesy bread.

Gus turned from his own basket and pushed his glasses up on his nose. "Mentor Sauravin," he said quietly, as if his voice would suddenly wake the man. "One of the most powerful Mentors, many Descendants believe."

Emma peered at the man, noticing the black braided beard tucked neatly behind his chin. "Daddy says he's a bit unconventional in the way he does things."

"A rebel. I like that." Lillia smiled and nodded.

Gus slipped two more tibbs in his mouth. "I heardth—one thime he kill'th a Dark Lord by himthelf."

His eyes were wide, but it was tough to take him seriously with his mouth full of bread. It was too much for Emma, who burst out laughing so hard she ended up spilling her tea all over her pants.

Lillia rolled her eyes. "Think you could fit another four thousand of those in your—"

BOOM! She was cut short by a colossal explosion that rocked the ship.

BOOM! Another explosion on the main deck. This one threw all four of them out of their chairs. A good number of other Mentees were also dazed and scattered about the cabin. Cheese tibbs rolled everywhere.

Gus picked himself off the floor and helped a dazed Lillia to her feet. Sam too, after regaining his balance from the heavily listing ship, helped up Emma.

"What in the name of Light was that?!" Gus said.

"Let's go up and find out!" Lillia hollered, ripping her hand from Gus's grasp.

The four raced up the cabin steps and landed out on the deck to find a scene of chaos. There were multiple masts ablaze and one side of the ship's deck had a huge flaming hole in it near the edge.

Three of the short Themane deck mates were frantically trying to put out the fires while simultaneously firing bolts of Light up into the dark sky above them.

Sam looked up and suddenly saw what had just caused the fire to rain down upon them.

Two massive dragons circled high above the group of ships, their iridescent scales glowing green and blue against the blackness of night. A streak of blue and red fire erupted from one of the beast's mouths as it swooped down upon the ship in front of them, torching its deck fiercely with a spray of deadly flames.

"WE HAVE TO DO SOMETHING!" Lillia yelled at the stunned teens. Others had gathered on the deck to watch what was happening as well.

Lillia ran out onto the deck with the other men and began tossing bolts up toward the dragons. One of her more powerful bolts struck the side of the dragon closest to the ship. Feeling the blast, the dragon changed course and began flying back toward them.

Finally, driven out of shock, Emma ran out on the deck to join Lillia, who continued valiantly throwing bolts toward the oncoming dragon as quickly as she could. Emma held up her hands and waited for the imminent destruction to befall them, her eyes as red as the flames already consuming the deck.

"WAIT!" Lillia yelled. "NOT YET!"

Emma nodded, her eyes fixed on the beast above.

Closer it came, dodging nearly every bolt Lillia and the other men threw up at it.

Then it opened its massive mouth and bellowed a spray of piercing blue flames directly at the two teens.

The deck mates watched helplessly as the flames raced toward them. They scrambled to get to Emma and Lillia before it was too late, but were hindered by the raging fires surrounding them on the deck.

Sam was stuck where he was, watching the deadly firebolt descend from the mouth of the ancient beast toward two people he cared deeply about. Gus was no different, paralyzed in place next to him.

"NOW!" Lillia screamed at Emma, who was shaking as she held her arms fast.

At first, nothing happened. Lillia looked at Emma in horror.

But then, as if the Creator himself had thrust his own Light into her, an enormous shield burst from Emma's hands that surrounded the entirety of the ship, stern to hull.

The intensity of the Light was incredible, instantaneously dousing all the burning flames on the deck.

Then, the shield was besieged by the firestorm from the dragon's hail of flames, and Emma went to her knees.

Sam finally snapped out of his paralysis and ran out to help Emma keep her balance as the torturous heat rained upon them. Lillia was with him, each of them holding her arms up to support against the powerful flames.

Just about the time Sam thought they would all collapse, the deafening roar from the flames ended. The giant shield blinked out, and Emma fainted.

Sam caught her, and he and Gus carried her back toward the cabin. The crowd of students had disappeared, no doubt taking shelter below deck.

Behind them still raged a war against the dragons, with streaks of Light piercing the sky all around each of the ships as Themane men threw as many bolts above as they could.

Sam glanced back to see two bolts of Light seeming to dance among the dragons, each throwing bolts and producing shields as they fought the beasts.

Mentors, Sam thought. *Creator, be with them.*

Suddenly, the man with a braided black beard opened the door of the cabin and helped them carry Emma down the stairs to one of the chairs.

It was Mentor Sauravin. "If you have it from here, I believe my brothers need me up above."

Lillia nodded.

"By the way, you two ladies performed marvelously," he said, then dashed upstairs and out into the raging night.

On a whim, Sam raced upstairs behind him, only to see a brilliant flash as the Mentor transformed into Light and streaked off toward the battle high above.

Sam watched as the three Mentors fought bravely, but with each attack, the dragons only seemed to grow more irritated and spew more ferocious blasts of fire.

The two other ships behind them had managed to get the fires on the deck under control, thanks now to the Mentors who were drawing the attack from the fleet below.

Then, in one moment, all three Mentors gathered in the air and sent one immense blast of Light. It hit one of the dragons square in the side, sending it tumbling through the air.

At once, the chaos halted. Both dragons circled the group of three warriors, then broke off and disappeared into the night.

The sounds of battle ceased, leaving only the soft crash of the waves against the hull of the ship to fill the void. All four ships were smoking as their decks recovered from the flames.

The Themane deck mates wandered aimlessly about the deck, scanning the skies above for any trace of the dragons to return. Then three more brilliant flashes appeared near the bow of the ship.

"What in the name of Creation would cause them to attack us like that?" a hooded young Mentor asked, his voice harsh.

"It has not happened for thousands of years," the elder Mentor responded. "Is everyone safe?" he said, turning to one of the deck mates.

"Sir, yes, thanks to you. We got the signal flash from the other ships just a moment ago," the bewildered Themane man answered.

"We have to respond," the younger Mentor said.

The elder Mentor held up his hand. "First, we must send word that the dragons have turned—at least some of them. Then we can consider our responses to this action—"

Mentor Sauravin held a finger to his lips and pointed at Sam, who still stood at the door to the cabin. "We should discuss this later," he said. "Consequently, I believe the information should be given in person. Do you agree?"

The other Mentors nodded.

Then Sauravin pointed at the sails above, which were in shambles. "However, a message should be sent to the school that we will be arriving a bit later than usual."

The elder Mentor clasped his hands together and then held them open, a small ball of Light forming in his hand. With his other hand,

he scribbled a brief message into the Light and then tossed it into the air. Off it streaked into the night toward its recipient.

"Sauravin, would you be so kind to deliver the news to the Chancellor? I think I will pay a visit to Keeper Tanniym and find out what happened."

Sauravin nodded. "And what happens if the dragons return?"

The elder Mentor gestured toward Sam and the cabin door. "Well, make sure you recruit the young ladies who helped saved the ship. Creator knows we need more like them."

Then, in a burst of Light, two of the Mentors were gone, leaving only the younger one behind. He glanced briefly toward Sam, then disappeared over the railing toward the ship behind them.

Sam slipped back into the cabin and down the steps to where Lillia, Emma, and Gus were sitting. If they weren't before, the four of them were most certainly the center of attention now.

Emma was awake when he sat down, her eyes dim and tired. "Are you okay?"

Sam snorted. "I should be asking you that question."

She smiled. "I'm fine. Just glad it didn't fail."

Sam knew she was referring to the shield. "Biggest one I've ever seen. Even bigger than any of the Mentors'," he told her.

"So what now? Are the dragons against us now, too?" Lillia said, clearly irritated. She directed her question toward Gus, who could only shrug.

"I don't know. I-I mean, once long ago the dragons fell to the Darkness, but that was during the great war of the Fallen Ones, when the Dark One led the war against the Creator."

"So we are looking at another war with the Dark One, now that he is awake," Lillia responded.

Gus didn't answer. Instead, he stared off into the corner where Mentor Sauravin had been sleeping. "I suppose that is the responsibility of the Chancellor and PO now."

Lillia grunted. "Would have been nice to see the PO around—no offense, Emma."

Emma nodded wearily, but didn't respond. Her body was still weak from producing the shield, and she needed rest, not an argument.

Soon, the ship lurched forward again as the Light propellers substituted for the scorched sails. They heard the muted crash of sea waves against the side of the ship as the fleet got underway.

The gentle swaying motion was enough to put most of the Mentees in the cabin to sleep. They still had a full day and night left in their journey on the Yarey to reach Cembra City, and eventually Mentorship.

Chapter Seventeen
Helel Malach

Sam awoke to the sounds of a marina—ship's crews yelling out orders, cargo being transferred from ship to dock, and the sounds of vendors calling out their wares for sale to the fresh visitors.

Glancing around the cabin, he noticed everyone had gone. Except for Emma, who had spent the previous day and night still recovering from the ordeal with the dragons.

He slipped out of his bunk and sat beside her, causing her to stir.

"Hey shield guru, I think we made it to port."

Her eyes fluttered open. "Call me shield *master*," she toyed. "Is it still night?"

Sam shrugged. "No idea. You'd think they would have a few windows down here in the dungeon."

"It *is* a very old ship."

Once out on the deck, the full sight of Cembra City's port came into view. The deck mates were already lashing their ship snugly to the dock, with the other two ships coasting into port just behind them.

The port was larger than most, with buildings scattered on both banks of the river. Several other ships were being loaded and unloaded of their cargo.

They hadn't been awake when the fleet left the Yarey and headed up the river to the interior of Themane where the region's city lay, but Gus had already given them the complete guided tour before even leaving for Mentorship. Still, as they embarked and met the throngs of people in the central market, Sam was in awe of what he saw.

Being from the forest, Themane people were master wood craftsmen. Each of the city's buildings was expertly constructed into ornate works of art. They were so impressive that the group felt as though they were walking through a living museum.

The city's residents were bustling about the streets, in and out of shops. They carried baskets of all sorts of fruits and vegetables, fish, and fragrant breads. They were all shorter in stature, like the deck mates, and caused Sam and the others to feel like adolescent giants as they waded through them.

"Welcome to Cembra City!" Gus announced. "Where should we go first?"

Emma shook her head. "I don't think we have the time to explore, Gus—look, everyone is already gathering over there by the statue."

She was right. All ships had docked in record time, and students were spilling out of the port and making their way toward the growing crowd.

"Mentees, follow me this way!" The younger Mentor said, motioning beyond the narrow park where the wood statue of a well-dressed man stood proudly among the delicate yellow and orange flowers.

Pines enveloped the little park in a sea of green, where another mentor stood beside a shadowy path leading into the forest. "Make sure you have all of your belongings!" He called.

None of the Cembra inhabitants seemed to pay mind to the group of students as they disappeared into the trees like a stream of people exiting a stadium after a Kolar game. No doubt they were used to it, however, since Mentorship occurred every year.

They followed the throng of students through the park and into the trees, where a tower spiraled high into the sky.

Sam could tell this tower was different from the other Lightway towers they had come across. It was constructed of wood, and spacious, no doubt meant for larger groups to travel more efficiently.

The line moved swiftly up the winding stairwell. Even before reaching the entrance to the tower, Sam heard the familiar hum of the Lightway as it dialed in its destination and produced the wave of Light.

It was difficult to see with the canopy of foliage above, but they still could recognize the burst of Light from the tower as the wave made a connection.

"They must be keeping the Lightwave constant so that large groups can get through quickly," Gus suggested.

They huffed up the stairs with their packs, following a group of girls that were nervously chatting about the ride on the Lightwave. One of the girls was attempting to stifle her sobs.

Emma inserted herself into the conversation, comforting the sobbing girl and reassuring the rest that it was as easy as riding a bike.

****

The ride on the Lightwave was just as wondrous as the others.

Sam loved the warmth of the Light, and the exhilaration of careening across the sky with nothing holding him up but the wave. He soared over mountains, then a collection of lakes, then more mountains, until arriving on a rocky ledge high atop one of the peaks.

Blinking as he stepped out of the tube, a wiry-framed luggage porter greeted him coldly. Then he snatched his pack from him and pointed to the stairwell below, where Gus and the others were already waiting for him.

Sam was stunned by the view just outside the tower. The school, which had been built at the mountain's pinnacle, stood prominently in front of them, overlooking a grand vista of a hundred other snow-capped peaks. Nestled around the school were located several other commercial-looking structures, where a few wind-worn inhabitants were closing up shop for the day.

An ancient central domed building made of stone stood amid other similarly aged structures. Snaking up the sides of the mountain were tiny dwellings clinging like bats to the walls of a cavern.

As the last of the Mentees came through the Lightway, the travelers were herded through the main arched gates of the mountain city and down the cobbled street toward the domed structure.

As they approached the building, the four friends noticed an extensive cadre of staff lining the steps, remaining utterly still as the stream of students passed through them.

Sam knew it wasn't polite to stare, but he couldn't help but steal a glimpse at the robed men and women he and the others proceeded through. They were all shapes and sizes, and most were aged. Many of the men were bearded, and each showed the years they had contributed to the school and to Lior. Sam had no doubt each of them had stories to tell.

As they climbed the steps, they realized they were once again the last ones, bringing up the rear of the other students. Once they passed, the hooded staff behind them broke rank and followed them through the entrance and into the building.

As they entered through the enormous wooden doors, Sam noticed the words HELEL MALACH carved into their exterior. Behind the phrase were two large watcher wings etched into the worn wood on either door.

Mentees were led through a grand lit foyer, down a long torch lit hallway and past a large amphitheater, where they were separated into the boys' and girls' dormitories.

The boys' dorm rooms were up another set of stairs to the left, where each boy was assigned a roommate and sent to a room down one of the narrow hallways branching from another main hall. Fortunately, Gus and Sam were assigned a room together. Not because they were afraid to meet others, but because it was one familiar thing they could count on in a very unfamiliar place.

The room was small, but comfortable. There were two small bunks with bedsheets and a pillow, two armchairs, and a small fireplace with a stack of wood next to the hearth.

Immediately, Sam and Gus laid down on the bed to catch their breath. Sam's stomach growled loudly, echoing off the room's stone interior. Gus laughed, then patted his belly, indicating that he was hungry as well.

They were relieved when the younger Mentor who had accompanied them called down the hallway, "Mentees are to report to the dining hall at the fourth chime!"

Sam looked at Gus, who shrugged. Neither of them knew what the fourth chime was, but they hoped it was soon.

A few moments after the announcement, the first chime rang out somewhere beyond the halls of the center. As the second chime rang about thirty minutes from the first, their packs were delivered to their rooms, giving them some time to unpack and freshen up for the evening's meal.

When the fourth chime rang, Sam and Gus were already among those gathered outside the dining hall, which had been rather difficult to find throughout the vast corridors. Emma, Lillia, and Sayvon were there waiting for them when they arrived.

After a few moments, the doors opened to the spacious hall, where simple ceramic dishes and cups lined several long tables. Like the rest of the building, the hall, too, had soaring ceilings held up by magnificent stone archways. On each of the walls, banners hung from each of the regions of Lior.

"Students are encouraged to sit with someone they do not already know this evening," the booming voice of Mentor Aron called from a table in the front of the room.

Emma threw a sour look toward Sam at the Mentor's advice, then snatched his arm and sat down at one of the tables near the back. Gus, Lillia, and Sayvon found seats next to them.

When all in the hall were seated, the Mentor spoke once again. "Welcome Mentees to Helel Malach, the School of the Shining One!"

A cheer erupted from the dining hall. Then, the staff that had welcomed the students through the entrance of the building filtered through the door in the back, seating themselves among the Mentees at various tables. Prior to sitting down, they introduced themselves.

Sam and the others had already taken a section of table to themselves, but that didn't stop a stout older woman from pulling up her own chair and squeezing in with them.

"Are you all settled in, then?" she asked with a jovial grin.

Yes, ma'am, we—" Emma began, but was interrupted.

"Oh my Creator, I forgot my glasses—" she exclaimed, then bowed her head shamefully. "Oh my, I promised I would stop saying that phrase!"

She stood abruptly and wrapped her robe around her waist (though it didn't quite cover the whole thing) and hurried off toward the door. "I shan't be eating unless I can see what it is I am putting in my mouth!"

And just like that, she ran into the dining hall door.

Emma leaped from her chair to help the woman.

"Oh, my, Creator me, that was incredibly silly of me," the woman said, laughing while she rubbed her head. "Can I really be going that blind?"

"I would like to help you find your glasses, Ms.—" Emma began.

"Oh dear, the one thing I was supposed to do my first meeting with you all and I forgot—" she laughed again, shaking her head. "My name is Mentor Wenthrow. And what is yours, my dear?"

"Emma, ma'am."

"Ah, Emma, such a pretty name. Well, you'll do just splendidly here."

Then the two disappeared through the dining hall doors to find the old woman's glasses.

Sam couldn't help himself, thinking about how the woman could possibly move quick enough to fight off Metim. "She's a Mentor? I think the librarian, Miss Nance, could move faster than her."

Gus held back a laugh. "I'm just wondering if she hasn't lost more than just her glasses."

Sayvon grabbed Sam and Gus's arms and shushed them. "Boys, don't. We shouldn't be talking about Mentors like that. Especially not here."

Gus hung his head, and Lillia chuckled. "She's right, turd-brain. We gotta watch what we say."

Sam knew she was right but couldn't help but wonder what the Council was thinking by appointing this woman as a Mentor.

It was only a few moments before trays of food began pouring out of the doors of the kitchen. A young blonde server brought a large basket of broiled chicken, while another young woman with very blue eyes brought them root vegetables and seared greens. Finally, a shorter young tan-skinned boy brought rolls and glasses of Jurana for everyone.

Sam was just about to ask why the servers were so young when Mentor Aron once again stood at his table, holding his arms wide to bring the hall to silence.

"Let us pray for our blessing," he said loudly. "I ask that you join me in thanking our Creator for all that he has provided."

Sayvon took Sam's hand, and he took Gus's. But no one prayed. There was only silence.

He began praying silently, out of habit. And like many times before, the words slipped past him on repeat, automatically.

"Mentees, I want you all to understand that this school is a very special and unique place," the mentor continued. "Your time here will be very deliberate and influential."

He gazed around the room. "More will be taught to you in the coming months, but there is one particular item I would like to leave with you all here tonight, and that is the idea of servanthood."

He held his arms outstretched, as if embracing them. "Everyone in this place who has gone through Mentorship already understands the power of serving others, remaining humble, and being called to a higher purpose. This school runs only on service, nothing more. Your attendants tonight are former Mentees, like you, serving because there is a need. Your Mentors, whom you will come to know, serve from their souls, not from the surface."

He exhaled. "This places value above all for others, for it is born out of love. Love for Lior, love for your fellow man in Creation, and love for the Creator. I pray you all—from whatever backgrounds that led you here—will come to desire this value, and to cherish it."

He paused before continuing. "Now, let us not toil longer before the food gets cold."

Chairs moved about and silverware clinked as Mentees enjoyed their dinner.

Sam sat with the others but didn't reach for the food right away. His mind was on the Mentor's words—particularly the one about serving from the soul. What did that mean?

He knew what he had to do. Hopping up from the table, he raced out of the dining hall doors and searched around for Emma and Mentor Wenthrow, who were nowhere to be seen.

This is stupid, Sam, he thought. They've probably found the glasses already.

He would help them search for them, anyway.

He sprinted out the huge wooden doors of the building and into the courtyard of the school, half expecting to see Emma and the Mentor walking back from her cabin, glasses in hand.

Instead, he saw something very different.

There, in the middle of the courtyard, was Orono the dragon, towering over three figures. The dragon's iridescent blue scales reflected magnificently in the waning sunlight of the day.

Mentor Wenthrow and Emma were there with him, and another man Sam didn't recognize.

Sam raced to the group to see the dragon. Recognizing him, the great beast lowered its enormous head in anticipation.

"Orono! What are you doing here?" he said breathlessly, as if expecting a response from the creature.

Orono's piercing gaze met Sam's eyes. Instantly, the connection between man and beast returned, the same as before.

"He's here because the Council doesn't trust him anymore," the

man said. Sam recognized his voice as the man he heard in the tower that night on the beach outside of Old Lior City. The dragon keeper, Jonathan.

"And of course, if Talister's behind it, then it's bound to happen," he said harshly, the sun showing the aged features on his tanned skin.

Emma gave him a harsh look, but it didn't seem to faze him.

Jonathan wore a plaid shirt and stained linen pants. His dirty grey robe fluttered in the wind. "I know who you are, girl. Doesn't change the fact that your uncle wants to see the end of all dragons in Lior."

"That's not true. Talister would never do that," Emma said, scowling.

The dragon keeper shrugged, but Sam could tell for Emma the conversation wasn't over. No doubt she would want to get to the bottom of it when she saw Talister next.

"Well, my dear students, we are missing dinner. We best let Jonathan here tend to his dragon," Mentor Wenthrow told them. "Follow me, please."

Sam and Emma obeyed, but right away, they could tell there was more that wasn't being said. Whatever Mentor Wenthrow knew, however, it wasn't going to be said out loud. Especially to two Mentees on their first day of Mentorship.

After dinner, Mentor Aron instructed the new Mentees to go to their rooms and spend the rest of the evening getting settled. Tomorrow would be the first day of training, and the day they would be assigned to their Mentors.

"I'm hoping for Mentor Aron," Gus said back in the room. Sam had already arranged his clothes in the small dresser next to his bunk and was now trying to get a fire started. The cold seeped through the walls, chilling the little room quickly.

They kept information on the Mentors confidential, but Sam had to agree with Gus about Mentor Aron. He was the leader of the Mentors, no doubt for good reason. He had the appearance of a wise warrior, calm under pressure but willing to unleash hell if necessary.

But then there was that Mentor from the ship—Mentor Sauravin, the one who had been asleep in the bunk when the dragons attacked. Sam remembered hearing his name from one of the other Mentors. There was something different about him he couldn't put his finger on.

"What about Mentor Sauravin?" Sam offered. "He seems to know what he is doing."

Gus whistled. "That would be an interesting Mentorship, I would say."

It annoyed him, but he wasn't sure why. "What's wrong with him? Is it just because he's different from the other Mentors?"

Gus turned on his bunk and studied him with concern. "Oh, please don't misunderstand me. I think he's great. I didn't mean to offend you."

Sam shook his head. Why did that irritate him so much?

"Don't worry about it. I think I'm just tired."

Gus groaned as he sat up. "Hey, I know what we need to do. Is it still light outside?"

Sam peeked out the tiny window. It was nearing dark, but some spatters of light still shone on the courtyard.

Gus threw his shoes on, a big grin on his face. "Get dressed. Let's do some exploring."

Sam complied, but was struck by Gus's sudden spontaneity and disregard for the rules. Though, technically, they hadn't been specifically told yet not to roam the grounds.

Sam tied his shoes and followed Gus out the door.

"This way. I think I saw an exit out the back," Gus said.

The dormitory hallway was dead, and nearly as dark. The boys tiptoed down the hall until they reached the door Gus believed led to the outside. Lifting the handle and giving it a slight shove, they slipped out.

The air was biting cold, and Sam was glad he grabbed his thick fleece. There was a bit more light in the rear of the courtyard, so getting to the path Gus was hoping to find wasn't that much of a chore.

"A former Mentee told me to check out this place a while ago," he whispered to Sam as they stole over the stone wall that encased the

school's courtyard. Beyond the wall lay a path up the mountain, but Gus chose instead to pick his way through the sunken boulders that protruded through the lichen as they headed toward the mountain's edge.

A sharp turn to the left brought them down a steep, unused pathway, ending abruptly at the top of the mountain face. Two large flat boulders had embedded themselves perfectly into the cliff's edge, making a splendid overlook to a sheer drop of several thousand feet to a valley below.

The view was breathtaking. The sun had just sunk below the mountains, leaving an orange and red imprint on the horizon that couldn't be equaled anywhere else. The moon had crested just above the mountain range and was making its way up into the awaiting sky.

They watched the mesmerizing colors for several minutes in silence, huddled against the boulders to block the icy mountain winds.

Sam knew Gus brought him out here to get away for a few minutes. Sure, Mentorship hadn't started yet, but he had felt the familiar head throbbing anxiety beginning to take over.

Gus didn't talk to him about Mentorship, or Emma, or Nuriel, or even the rumors of the Dark One waking. He was a true friend—one who knew him well enough to know what he needed, even when Sam himself did not. *And this*, he thought, gazing out over the view before him, *was exactly what I needed.*

Before the light had faded entirely, the two boys headed in for the night, hopping the wall and slipping back in through the door they had propped open with a stone they dug up from the courtyard.

After a quick stop at the lavatory and a good stir of the coals, Sam sunk down into his covers, feeling the last of the heat from the dying fire on his face. He sent up a quick prayer, making sure he thanked the Creator for Gus's friendship.

Chapter Eighteen
A Test

Sam and Gus were up at the first chime in the morning. Having not quite figured out the chime patterns, they needed to be ready for whatever schedule-related activity that may occur.

Today was orientation, and aside from getting some questions answered about Mentorship, they would also be assigned their Mentors.

Sam found the bath in the lavatory to be quite invigorating, for not only was it water drawn from a natural hot spring somewhere deep below the mountain, but it also contained Lazuli similar to the ones in Warm Springs.

By the third chime, both boys were dressed and sitting on their beds, stomachs growling for breakfast.

When the fourth chime rang, they were first in line. Lillia, Emma, and Sayvon weren't far back, so they let those behind go ahead so they could be near them.

Once they were let in the hall, the mentor again encouraged them to sit with someone they did not know. But still, the five chose to stick together.

"I'm nervous," Emma said in a low tone once the prayer was over and the eggs, biscuits, and root hash were served. "I can't eat when I'm nervous."

And just like that, her stomach growled painfully loud.

Lillia poked at her midsection. "Your stomach says otherwise."

Emma swatted her hand away. "It could be—other things," she trailed off.

Lillia poked her again, smiling. "Like gas? Come on Emma, even princesses fart once in a while."

Emma rolled her eyes and swatted Lillia's hand away once again. "Thanks for reminding everyone of that."

"You're welcome," Lillia said with a giant grin on her face.

They finished their breakfast in silence, all of them contemplating what the start of Mentorship training would look like. And who their mentors would be.

They didn't have to wait long, for as soon as the servers cleared the tables, Mentor Aron stood and addressed the dining hall. "Mentees will have four chimes to report to the amphitheater, dressed and ready for Mentorship training."

Chairs scooted and tables cleared as Mentees rushed to get back to their dorms and prepare. On the way out of the dining hall, Sam caught a glimpse of Yorin and the small crowd that followed him everywhere. Since that night on the ship, he hadn't had much trouble with him. Perhaps he didn't think Sam was worth messing with anymore.

At Gus's request, the group sat near the front in the amphitheater to get a better view of the middle, where a grand podium stood unclaimed.

Nervous faces waited anxiously as the last of the students found seats and quieted down. Emma pulled out her journal and a pen and searched around the room for someone to address them. No one came.

At first, only pockets of students would mumble quietly, wondering what was happening. After several more minutes, however, the entire amphitheater was talking.

Only when the lanterns were snuffed out and darkness overtook the room did the silence return.

But then, with a brilliant flash, creatures of all types made of Lazuli Light filled the room. Oxen, lions, bears, and various dinosaurs pranced the aisles, stomping about and roaring so loudly that some students dove under the benches for protection.

But as quick as they came, however, they disappeared.

From the rear of the amphitheater, the doors opened, and the Mentors entered. The hooded members walked down the aisles in silence before taking their seats on benches on either side of the podium.

Suddenly, as if appearing from nowhere, Mentor Aron stood at the podium. The lanterns dimmed once again, and Lazuli Light began softly snaking up the arched columns of the interior of the amphitheater. Unnerved, students returned to their seats.

"Students of the Light, Mentees, please stand as we thank our Creator for giving us breath."

As Mentor Aron prayed, Sam felt his heart beating faster in his chest. It wasn't so much the prayer that excited him, but that he was a part of something so powerful, and so real. The Creator, wherever he was, felt real in this place.

"Students, Mentors, please be seated," Mentor Aron said.

They took their seats, the distraction from the Light animals finally abating. As the residual Lazuli drifted up toward the ceiling, it added a calmness to the room.

"Long ago, the School Helel Malach was established by a Watcher. Second to the Creator Himself," he began.

Right away, Sam knew who Mentor Aron was talking about.

"This Watcher, brilliant in mind, beautifully created, was a symbol of Light for all other Watchers to see. He was given vast, sweeping territory to manage, with thousands under his command. He was loved deeply, absolutely. He was provided with as much trust that could possibly be given to a celestial being."

"It was the Dark One." Gus whispered to Lillia seated next to him. But students three rows back heard him as well.

Lillia shushed him, giving him a dirty look. "I know *who*. Now shut it."

"He was called the Prince of Light, for he was the sole being that had power over Light and Darkness, other than the Creator. It is unknown how the Darkness entered the worlds—but the Prince was given the power to vanquish it from existence. He was the most powerful of the beings, and his ability to manipulate the Light was unmatched."

The tall Mentor paused. "He set out with his most trusted warriors to seek out and destroy the Darkness, searching the farthest reaches to discover its most hidden places. When he found it, he immediately discovered the power the Darkness held. He battled it for days, and in the end, it overcame him. Or, perhaps I should say, the Darkness beguiled him."

Gus leaned over once again toward Lillia, but immediately she stuck a finger in his face to shut him up again.

"The Prince seduced half of the legion of Watchers, who trusted him and swore their allegiance to the Darkness as he had."

Then Mentor Aron threw his arms up into the air, and immediately a globe of pure Light appeared before them, filling nearly the entire amphitheater. Details began to come into focus. It was Earth.

"When the Creator made man, the Prince was intrigued—and jealous. Man was a simple creature, and yet—he was more. He had a soul and could choose his own fate. The Prince thought the Creator had made the greatest mistake by creating man. Not only was man weak, he was considered the most treasured by the Creator. Now, the Prince had a new goal—to turn man against his Creator."

Mankind really is weak, Sam thought, remembering his own flaws.

"But there was something that the Prince did not consider in his quest to darken the souls of man," Mentor Aron continued, but then paused. "Man, with all of his weaknesses, retains something more incredible than any celestial being ever made. He can love more profoundly and more absolutely than any other created being. Because of this love—man was extremely difficult to turn to the Darkness."

All in the amphitheater were still, their focus directed at Mentor Aron.

"Regardless of what you may believe about man, and Creation, your job as a Descendant is to defend that which the Creator loves so deeply. Here at Helel Malach, you will be taught not only to fight as a warrior but also as a servant. Those you serve, man, the Descendants, the Watchers—and ultimately the Creator, are what you swear to protect, to love, and to die for if necessary."

Sam glanced over at Yorin, who seemed quite amused by the words of Mentor Aron. If he was being honest, however, Sam was a bit uncertain himself.

"Each Descendant that has succeeded through Mentorship has followed the path of a Mentor. In turn, Mentors decide which Descendants proceed through Mentorship. Consequently, an equal amount of consideration has been given for each of your Mentor assignments as well."

Just then, all other Mentors rose to their feet in unison.

He motioned for Mentor Wenthrow, who stepped forward and removed her hood. "Mentorship is a test, above all else. Each of you will face numerous challenges, some large, some small. One of you has been tested already."

Sam heard Emma gasp.

"Miss Sterling, your actions yesterday are the essence of what becoming a Descendant is all about. Mentor Wenthrow informs me that you have passed your first test," Mentor Aron said.

Emma nodded, her face beet red.

"Others will be tested as their Mentors see fit. If you pass them all, you will graduate a *Shomer*, or Guardian. Then you will receive your Eben stone."

There was murmuring throughout the amphitheater. Every Descendant child had been waiting for the day they would receive their Eben stone.

A Test

Mentor Aron waited for the whispering to end before continuing. "As you are tested, some of you will discover that one of your gifts may be more powerful than the others. It is not to be discouraged, but encouraged in your training, as each gift is diverse. Embrace the gift that has been given to you."

Again, he motioned behind him, and a short dark-skinned Mentor stepped forward. He held up his hands, and abruptly, the creatures made of pure Lazuli Light returned to the aisles. Some students were nearly as startled as they were the first time they showed up, a few scrambling to get away from the glowing beasts.

Mentor Aron smiled. "Mentor Kablu has been given the gift of *magen*, which means he is able to produce these marvelous creatures out of pure Light. Which, of course, will not harm you as long as you don't provoke them."

Then Mentor Sauravin stepped forward and held out his hands, Light leaping from his palms into the aisles where the creatures still roamed. The Light formed into multiple shields, almost net-like as they trapped the creatures underneath.

Then both Mentors lowered their hands, and the shields and the creatures disappeared.

Sam watched in awe as the two Mentors returned to their spots. A quick glance around the room told him that the other Mentees were just as impressed with what they had just seen.

"Mentor Sauravin, too, has been given the *magen* gift. Both the shield and the beasts of Light are the greatest protection a Descendant could have. As you can see, our talented Mentors are able to use their gifts in unison."

Another Themane man holding a staff nearly twice his height stepped forward at the end of the line of robed teachers. He lifted his hands, and out hurled a bolt of incredible force directly at Mentor Aron. Students gasped at the sight, but before they could react further, a shield ejected from Sauravin's hands and blocked the deadly blast.

Another chill went up Sam's spine as a hand reached out and grabbed his arm.

"Oh, sorry," Lillia said when she realized what she had done, quickly removing her hand from his arm. "I really thought he was a goner on that one."

"Yeah, same here."

The room was hushed when Mentor Aron opened his mouth to speak once again. "My friend and fellow Mentor Darnow has been gifted as a *bolt*, a gift all Descendants have, but not quite to this level. Bolts are warriors and must be fearless in battle."

He paused, then let out a chuckle. "It is a good thing that we planned this ahead of time or I might be smoked sausage about now."

Pockets of nervous laughter filled the amphitheater at the Mentor's words. Some cringed as another taller Mentor with dark shoulder-length hair stepped forward.

From the back of the amphitheater, an inky mass began to pour from the entrances, making its way down the aisles. When those closest to it realized what it was, panic began to overtake the room. Mentees scrambled over one another to keep away from the growing cloud, which was spreading more by the second.

Sam caught a glimpse of the Mentor who had stepped forward, and his eyes glowed a strange Lazuli blue as he held up his palms toward the Darkness.

"It's him!" Sam said, pointing at the Mentor. He's calling the Darkness in!" He looked around, but no one was paying attention.

Then Mentor Wenthrow stood and hobbled forward, holding her palms high above her head. An arc of incredibly blinding Light erupted from her hands and filled the room instantly. It surged through the cloud of Darkness, causing it to wrench and writhe as though it were in pain.

The battle continued until the massive arc of Light overcame the cloud and forced it back through the doors of the amphitheater. And then it was over.

A hush fell throughout the Mentees, who struggled to make sense of what just happened. All eyes turned to Mentor Aron and the other two Mentors that were obviously the source of all the commotion.

"From the most ancient of days, the Darkness has been our enemy. It is a powerful foe, seducing and destroying even the most capable of Descendants, Watchers, and men. The greatest Watcher of all, the Prince of Light, could not himself deny its allure."

He gestured toward the Mentors at his side. "Fortunately, the Darkness this evening has been a trick by our own Mentor Korin, a Seer from Telok."

Mentor Korin nodded.

"Aside from being able to see events as they occur, Seers have a unique ability that allows them to imitate almost anything using Light. Even Darkness. It is a gift that is still not fully understood, shrouded in mystery. It is a rare gift, but that does not mean there are not some in this room right now…"

Students glanced around the room as though a Seer could just pop out of the crowd.

Then Mentor Aron gestured toward Mentor Wenthrow. "Finally, and perhaps the rarest of all gifts, is the *Arc.*"

Whispering commenced throughout the room. "Mentor Wenthrow not only has the ability to manipulate an incredibly powerful source of Light that can pierce the Darkness, but she is also able to use the other gifts as well."

They were awestruck. The most unlikely of Mentors, Mentor Wenthrow, was perhaps the most powerful of all of them.

"Now, Mentees, stand and receive your assignments."

Chapter Nineteen
Vanished Village

Sam rolled over in his bunk, hearing the first chime. "Are you serious? It can't be time already."

Gus blinked and sat up slowly. "I feel as though I just shut my eyes a minute ago."

Today was more bolt training. It was something Sam and Gus had looked forward to at the beginning of Mentorship, but after two full weeks of agility courses and duels from dawn till dusk, it was beginning to wear on them.

Mentor Wenthrow was chosen as Sam's Mentor, and as it turned out, she was neither forgetful nor hard of seeing. She was, in fact, the toughest of the Mentors, and from what Sam could tell, even tougher on him.

Gus was assigned to Mentor Korin, which had been a perfect fit because Gus was showing signs of having the gift of Seeing. He would come back from his specialized sessions with Mentor Korin talking nonstop about how he was an intellectual who had memorized many of the ancient texts. And how he had taught him that Seeing was much

more than simply getting "visions."

Lillia was elated to have Mentor Sauravin as her Mentor, not only because of his ability to use all the gifts quite well, but because he seemed to enjoy challenging the status quo.

Emma was chosen to follow under Mentor Aron, with only two other students. Emma loved having him as a Mentor, but, like many other students, could not figure out why she was chosen among so many others. Some would start rumors about why she was, such as having special privileges because she was the daughter of the head of the PO. Others would just simply speculate that she was "special" for some reason or another.

Whatever the case, she didn't say much about her training with Mentor Aron. She only told them that he was a "remarkable teacher."

Sam had learned a lot about Light manipulation since he had arrived. He could produce an intense shield, throw a remarkably accurate bolt almost twenty meters, and even See bits and pieces of events that were happening somewhere in Lior.

Mentor Wenthrow seemed particularly interested in Sam's abilities with the gifts and often spent more time working with him to hone his skills. Surprisingly, she didn't focus too much on what Sam thought he was best at—throwing a bolt—but more on the "inner gifts" training. Some of it frustrated Sam, but he remembered to always respect his Mentor, regardless of what she asked him to do.

One of the stranger tasks she had him do every day was to repeat the Mentorship creed by memory. Since he had done it every day for six weeks now, he had the entire thing memorized so well he could recite it in his sleep. The minute he was released from group training to train individually, she would hold out her hand for him to place his own into hers, and recite with his eyes closed,

In daily breath and Light within,
I cast my pride upon the wind.
It is my purpose to serve the land,
and those made by the Creator's hand.

Chapter Nineteen

Whether in pain or joy, I strive to live,
a creed to Him that I will give.
Be faithful, be true, be a servant in all,
until my name, one day He shall call.

There were a few other Mentors that required the creed to be said by their Mentees, but Mentor Wenthrow seemed to be particularly interested in making sure Sam knew it. Perhaps it was because he hadn't grown up in Lior, or known anything about the Descendants until he was older. He promised himself he would ask her one day.

It was the last day of the week for training, which meant that tomorrow they could do as they wish. That usually consisted of relaxing and reading, or exploring the little mountain village surrounding the school.

The village was a fascinating place, a self-contained city with a farm, bakery, and small shops, all on top of the mountain. Supplies arrived through the Lightway daily, including wood from Themane and fresh fish and dairy. Still, the village was self-sufficient on its own.

The population of Descendants that were residents year round in the village were there solely to support the school or the development of the gifts. There was a research facility on site that was frequently the source of regular interruptions, as curious sounds and odd Light formations would arise from its halls.

Sam looked forward to the days off, since Light training was draining. The past two weeks had been especially difficult, since producing bolts was more taxing than the other gifts, save for Seeing.

He and Gus brushed their teeth and slipped on some clothes for the early morning session. All Mentees met for the general sessions out in the courtyard, where targets had been placed in various stations for students to practice throwing bolts.

The first week had been difficult for Gus. He had still not produced a solid bolt to date, and students gossiped regularly how he would most certainly fail if he could not. By the second week, however, something his Mentor taught him stuck.

His first bolt trickled out of his palms and singed the grass below. A few days later, he was throwing bolts with the best of them.

"I hope they don't make us run again today," Gus said as the two boys hurried down the hall past the kitchen to snag a few cinnamon rolls before training.

"I agree." Sam responded, filling a mug of coffee. "I think they know that some of us will never blend, so we will have to run to get away."

Blending was the last training they would do before they graduated, and was considered one of the most difficult maneuvers to accomplish. Since blending involved turning oneself into pure Light and traveling without need of a Lightway, it required a lot of concentration. It was similar to the Ruasch, but used more in battle situations.

The boys left the dining hall and hustled to make it to the courtyard on time. As they passed the amphitheater, however, Sam heard voices speaking in a low tones from inside. He slowed his pace, listening to the voices as they passed. Then he stopped.

Gus turned to look at him. "We are already pushing our time to get to the courtyard, Sam." He told him. "Mentor Darnow will make sure we run more target rounds if we are late."

Sam ignored him and inched his ear as close to the cracked door as he dared.

"… attack on the Shimshon Outsider village was most certainly Arazel acting on Kachash's orders," a hushed voice spoke. "We've been tracking the original Dark Lords for some time, and he seems to be the likely candidate."

"Are you certain the three originals are in Creation? Could this be the beginnings of their main attack?" another voice whispered.

Sam strained to listen, but could not make out either of their identities.

"We know they are gathering in the South, and there have been reports of them being sighted, yes. What we don't know, however, is why they are gathering there. And why would Arazel would attack one of the villages…"

"Then who attacked the other village in Clear Lake? Who is capable of that much destruction?"

Silence.

"It was strange. Both villages were destroyed beyond recognition, but we can only find bodies at Shimshon. There were none at Clear Lake—almost as if everyone just vanished."

"That's odd. So where are the villagers?"

"Unknown."

"Sam!" Gus whispered harshly. "We have to go!"

Sam held up a finger as if asking for another moment.

"—scribe from the Council asking Mentors to keep watch either way. We can't know for sure what prompted the attacks."

"Agreed, Korin. I wish Jack were here to give some guidance—"

The creak of the door being ever so slightly moved caused both men to cease talking, looking in Sam's direction. Once Gus had figured out what Sam was doing, he too had leaned in to listen. Ultimately, it was Gus's shoe that bumped the door.

Sam never ran so fast in all of his life, doing his best to make his feet light on the stone floor of the hallway. He and Gus sprinted toward the dormitory areas, out the back door, and into the courtyard in record time.

Panting, they joined the other Mentees already stretching before their bolt training.

"Where have you guys been?" Emma whispered angrily.

"Tell you later," were the only words Sam could get out.

They thought they had gotten away with their tardiness, but when duels began, both Sam and Gus were chosen first.

"For our duels today, we are going to add a little different element to make it more interesting," Mentor Darnow barked. "I need two more volunteers willing to duel our tardy students here."

Yorin Moge was the first to raise his hand. Immediately after, four more hands shot up, as each wanted the chance to duel next to Yorin.

"Yorin, Madria, join me in the middle," Mentor Darnow said, smiling.

Sam shuddered when they made their way up front. Yorin was excellent with a shield, and his bolts were stunningly powerful. Madria still could not produce a shield, but she had made up for it by being able to throw bolts at blinding speeds.

Gus had worked hard to get to where he could produce a solid bolt, but he was slow at it. Sam was proficient at both bolts and shields, but he was not quite as fast as Yorin and Madria. The one thing he and Gus had going for them, however, was that Sam had learned to throw his bolts with deadly accuracy. Yorin nor Madria had not.

Mentor Darnow motioned for the four duelers to take their positions across from each other. "Remember, in the courtyard, all gifts have been reduced in their potency to protect duelers and other students. Outside of this area, you could risk serious injury or death should you attempt it."

"Are you ready for this, Gus?" Sam mumbled, shooting him a glance. Gus had already taken his stance, palms raised.

Without warning, bolts began whizzing by them from the other side. Yorin had not even waited for the signal from Mentor Darnow.

Sam produced a large shield over himself and Gus, and it was a good thing too, because the barrage of bolts that Yorin and Madria were throwing would have allowed no way for them to escape otherwise.

Bolts bounced off the shield harmlessly, but Sam couldn't hold it forever. He watched Gus, who was still working on producing his own bolt. Sam waited until the blue glow of the Lazuli grew large enough in Gus's hands before dropping the shield.

"Now, Gus!" Sam hollered and dropped the shield. Both he and Gus threw a bolt at that moment, aimed directly at their opponents. But Yorin and Madria were too fast, and at the last moment they ducked out of the way, leaving Madria with only a singed shirt sleeve.

Sam threw two more in the time that it took for Gus to ready his next one. Sam would have hit Yorin square in the chest with one of the bolts if Madria hadn't tossed a quick shield in his direction.

But the near miss only angered Yorin. "You think you are a real Descendant now that you are not living with the gullas?" he hollered.

"Come on now, show us your real side, dark sucker!"

And with that, he threw two quick bolts that just about clipped Sam's ear.

Sam shook it off and threw two more in return, both near misses. Somehow, the duel had turned into just him and Yorin. Throwing bolt after bolt, both boys dodging each one swiftly, as though they had been training for years.

He glanced over at Gus, and his hopes of winning were suddenly dashed. Gus lay on his back, out cold. Madria had stepped back triumphantly and was watching the duel with a smile on her face.

It startled Sam so badly that he didn't see the bolt screaming directly at him.

****

"Samuel, your time has come. The Dark One is waiting."

It was Arazel's voice echoing in front of him, but Sam couldn't see him.

He was in a fog, and his hands were shaking. He couldn't speak.

"Come forward. He awaits."

His feet began to move on their own. Walking toward the voice of Arazel. Toward the Dark One.

Suddenly the fog cleared, and Arazel stood before him, robes billowing in the wind. His eyes glowed green. From behind Arazel, a figure approached.

Fear gripped him. Choking, piercing fear.

The figure drew closer, its body draped in fluid blackness, moving, shifting. The eyes were voids of hollow green light, flaming, but soulless. When they rested upon Sam, he felt as though something was being ripped from his chest.

The figure moved toward him—he felt the fear throbbing inside his head.

Then everything went dark.

Vanished Village

****

"Mr. Forrester, are you well?"

The smiling face of Mentor Darnow was looking down at him. "You took a wicked one to the face, my boy."

Sam sat up and rubbed his eyes. Forty other students surrounded him, watching the spectacle. It reminded him of the time Bush beat him up in the hallway.

He looked around for his friends and found them standing next to Mentor Darnow.

Lillia rolled her eyes. "You two really are pathetic."

"We tried, Sam," Gus said, shrugging.

Sam glanced around and looked for Yorin and Madria. Both were standing outside of the circle of onlookers with the others in their little group, talking and laughing at what had just happened.

It hadn't mattered to Sam who said what or what anyone thought of him until now. But this—whatever just happened—seemed to stir up something else inside.

"I'm fine, thanks," he said angrily, ignoring the extended hands to help him stand.

"What was that about?" Emma asked him later while they were standing in line for the evening meal.

Sam pretended he didn't understand her. "You mean me getting a royal beating today?"

"You know what I mean. You were *angry* because you got beat."

"Well, could you blame me? If Gus hadn't—" he stopped. "Never mind."

"You said you didn't care about Yorin."

"I don't."

She turned away, flustered. "Sure doesn't seem like it."

Obviously, Sam's confusion tactic had worked to some level.

But the truth was, he was angry. He was tired of being the one that was picked on, for whatever reason. Sure, today they were beat fair and square, but did they have to rub it in so much?

Chapter Nineteen

The next few weeks were some of the toughest of Mentorship. Students were tested on a variety of things—from physical endurance to learning to control yourself under pressure. Lillia and Sayvon quickly mastered each task, and surprisingly, Gus was able to show real improvement as well. Sam trained harder than ever, learning to focus while manipulating, and even learned how to produce a very faint Light creature.

Emma, however, had become incredible with producing large numbers of creatures with astonishing Light intensity. So much so that the Mentors were taking notice.

"She's a prodigy, and I am certain they know it," Gus said over eggs and cinnamon toast one morning. "Just like Mentor Sauravin was—or is—"

Sam picked at a stray piece of egg on his plate. "What happened to Sauravin anyway? He seems to be kind of a loner around here. Always eats alone, doesn't talk much with the other Mentors…"

Gus leaned forward across the table. "It was the Council's decision to make him a Mentor, and I believe I know why. He had a run-in with Kachash, and he nearly killed him. It was kept on the low-down for a long time, but Achiam let it slip to me one day that he was being kept under close watch so that Kachash didn't attempt revenge."

Sam was speechless. "He almost killed a Dark Lord? Incredible."

Emma, who had been lost in thought, turned to center her gaze on a table with only two students quietly eating their breakfast.

"What are you looking at, Em?" Sam asked her.

"I'm going to sit with them."

"Who, Yadris and that other kid? Why?"

She didn't respond, only picked up her tray and hurried to the other table.

"We should have done this long ago." Sayvon said, picking up her tray guiltily and following Emma.

Suddenly, it was quiet at the table. Gus shrugged and Lillia went back to eating. Sam glanced over at Yorin and his group, who immediately laughed when Sam looked at them.

A flare of anger welled up inside of him. Why did he care so much about a stupid bully?

Lillia stood up, grabbing her tray. "I'm going too."

Gus and Sam said nothing more. They finished eating and went back to the dorm. Since it wasn't a training day, they had decided to nap for a bit before Observation. Days off were valued at Mentorship, and so was sleep.

At lunch and evening meal, the same thing happened. Mentor Aron made the same announcement that mentees should sit with someone they don't know, and off Emma and Lillia went to sit with Yadris and the other Themane kid.

They ate in silence again. Sam sipped his coffee, glancing around the room for Yorin, but he wasn't there. What he did see, however, was that much of the dining hall had changed in the last few weeks. With regards to where students were sitting, anyhow.

Many of them had taken the advice of Mentor Aron, finding people they didn't know and sitting with them. Emma's group had also attracted some new people as well. So much so that they had pushed three tables together to fit the new people.

She had invited Gus and Sam multiple times, but each time Sam waved her off and Gus ignored her.

On the week before they were to graduate Mentorship, Sam found the courage to accept Emma's invitation.

"Gus, I'm going," he said finally.

Gus looked up from his mashed root vegetables. "Please stay," he begged.

It was then that Sam realized what Gus's greatest fear was. He was brilliant and brave, but meeting someone new was like torture.

"Let's go together."

"No, thanks."

Sam grabbed his tray and walked it over to Emma's new group. Then he circled back and grabbed Gus's tray from under him. "If you aren't going to come with me, you aren't going to eat, either."

Gus turned a shade of red that Sam had only ever seen once before when he was angry at Lillia. When he realized what Sam was doing, however, he steadied himself.

"You will walk with me?" he squeaked.

"Of course."

He stood reluctantly, face still red.

They walked to the table, where the group had found two more seats for them. Emma immediately began making introductions. "Hey all, this is Sam and Gus." She said, working her way around the table.

"This is Yadris. She's pretty wicked with a bolt. And this is Murray. He's from Themane. And Pestril loves dragons—he is from Telok. Cestray is the goofy one of the bunch—he is from Telok, too. And this is Julia. She is from Lior City. Apparently, she is an incredible baker."

There were a few more that smiled and waved to them, but other than that they didn't pay much mind to Sam and Gus.

"That's Parray, Cogan, and Sambon," Emma whispered as Sam and Gus took their seats. "We aren't sure why they eat with us—they kinda just keep to themselves."

The next few days were even tougher training than they had the days before. Mentally, it was a day-to-day struggle not to lash out at the Mentors, who did their best to break down their resolve.

Sam struggled not to let his anger get the best of him, and most of the time, he was successful. The Mentors would do their best to get a reaction from him, but he discovered he could hold up well under pressure when he was prepared for it.

Only Yorin seemed to bother him, and he did his best not to think of him while in training. Doing so seemed to make him momentarily lose control of himself.

The day before Mentorship training was to end, Mentees were finally given details of the *Shomerin*, which is where they would be given their Eben stones—if they had earned them.

"Students that have passed all tests and are given the recommendation from their Mentor will have the opportunity to choose their Ebens," came the announcement from Mentor Aron.

Murmuring erupted throughout the dining hall.

"If a Mentor believes their Mentee is ready, they will travel to Mount Tannin to participate in their final test. If the dragon Halsoph believes you are worthy, you will be able to retrieve an Eben stone from his lair."

Students were talking louder this time, and some even clapped.

Mentor Aron held up his hands. "Those of you who are not recommended will travel home, where you will be invited to attempt Mentorship once more at some point in the future."

The clapping and talking stopped, and the hall quieted.

"Students, I assure you this is no easy decision for a Mentor. But you who are not selected will certainly be able to attempt Mentorship once again. Now, your toughest days of training will be these next few. You will want to take advantage of your precious sleep, so I advise you to make your way to your dormitories."

Students took the last few bites of dessert and began filing out of the dining hall. Sam, Emma, Gus, Lillia, and Sayvon too headed out the door. Before they were to split into their respective dorms, however, Emma bolted down another hallway and motioned for the others to follow her.

She led them down several corridors until they reached a door that led them to the courtyard outside.

"I have news you all should hear." She said, flopping down in the grass. The sun had long since slipped behind the mountains, and the air was cool.

"You have news from White Pine," Gus said quickly.

She nodded. "The town has been overrun. Daddy says that the Metim have come out of hiding. He says there's a Dark Lord there."

"Wait, you mean people can see what's going on?" Sam asked, feeling a bit stupid.

Gus shook his head. "No, but they will certainly feel what is going on. I wouldn't doubt some crazy things have been happening there with the residents."

"Like demonic stuff?" Sam offered.

"Very much so like that," Sayvon said. "The Darkness can affect people differently—make them do things they wouldn't normally do. Especially if they are not very strong. That's what my dad says, anyway."

Gus nodded. "No doubt it's a bit of a nightmare there right now."

"Daddy says they had to evacuate the gate."

"How do you know all this, Em'?" Gus asked. "Wait, have you been scribing him this whole time? How?"

Emma looked sheepish, studying Sam. "Oh Sam, I'm sorry, I didn't tell you!"

"Tell me what?"

Lillia snorted. "Hey, are you all too dumb to figure it out? He's asked her to keep an eye on Sam for him."

Sam stared at her. "Is it true?"

She didn't answer.

"I suppose if Mr. Sterling was able to rig up some sort of device—"

"Gus. Shut up," Lillia interrupted.

"He wanted me to take the radio with me, not really for spying, but just to make sure Sam was okay," Emma said.

"I get it. It's fine," Sam blurted.

The truth was, it was fine. He accepted the fact that he was going to be of a freak show for everyone. There was a couple-thousand-year-old Dark legend that said he would turncoat and go mad, anyhow. Maybe it was just as well he was being watched.

"So, where are they now?" Sam changed the subject.

Emma shrugged. "I don't know. He won't tell me. He only said they were safe."

Lillia sounded flustered. "What should we do? Is this what they've been talking about? The start of the Dark One's final attack?"

"I'm sure the PO and Council know," Gus added.

Emma couldn't answer either of them. "Dad did say that they were looking into Henry Bostwick's research on the artifact found in the Amazon. They aren't sure if the reason the Dark forces are gathering there is related or not, but they're checking into every possibility."

Sayvon turned and watched the remnants of the light as it faded

into the night sky. "My father told me this would happen. It's just the beginning."

"That reminds me, uncle Talister is coming to address the students at the closing ceremony," Emma added. "I just thought you should know first."

They sat in silence, watching the last bit of pink get swallowed up by the night. Oddly, it reminded Sam of the strange vision he had when Yorin hit him with the bolt. Could they be seeing the last bit of Light before the Darkness begins to take over?

He knew it wasn't real, but he couldn't shake the image since it happened. The eyes of the Dark One—they burned in his mind so heavily...

Chapter Twenty
Shomerin

A very tired Talister Calpher arrived the next night in a brilliant Ruasch cloud. Sayvon and the four others waited for him just outside the courtyard. Oddly, Boggle stepped off the Ruasch with Talister.

"I am assuming Emma has told you all the details," he said quickly as they headed toward the school. "I need to speak with the Mentors before I can chat with you all—I have not yet informed them of my reasoning for being here."

"Father, is everything okay?" Sayvon asked as he mounted the steps toward the domed building. Talister's robes billowed slightly in the mountain breeze.

"Oh, my dear daughter, yes. The Creator will ensure it is so. You—and the rest of you included—concentrate on getting your Eben stone. You let us worry about this."

Then he turned and disappeared into the entrance of the school.

Lillia threw her arms around Boggle, who was startled at first, then laughed out loud.

"Boggle! You never came to see us before we left!"

Lillia was genuinely upset with the old inventor.

"Ah! Well, I—um see it was just too—oh dear, I am sorry."

The smile faded from his lips. "You guys just can't keep your nose outta things, can you! I tell you, if I were in charge of ya's, I'd probably go looney! Crazy, for certain."

Emma grabbed hold of Boggle and hugged him once Lillia had let go.

"Seriously, Boggle, we just missed you."

He laughed again, a tear welling up in his eye. "Oh, you all are so young and… carefree, yes! Those were the days I tell ya."

Sam was suspicious. "Why did you come now?"

Emma smacked his arm. "That was rude!" she said, then turned back to Boggle. "Yeah, Boggle. Why *are* you here?"

Boggle threw his hands up. "Oh, you all are going to get me fired, you know that? I shouldn't be telling you *anything*!"

Lillia raised an eyebrow. "But?"

"Oh, show me to the courtyard and I will tell you what I know. I'm not going to be talking about all this on the steps of the Helel Malach! Oh dear, you all are going to make me lose my job!"

When they had made it safely to the middle of the expansive courtyard, Lillia started in on him once again. "Wait, Boggle, what job are you talking about?"

"Oh, the PO hired me for a project or two—which I absolutely cannot talk about, so don't even try!"

"We wouldn't dare." Lillia said, winking at the other four. "Now, what do you know?"

Boggle repositioned his glasses and cinched up his coat tighter. Then he looked around to see if anyone was in earshot and hunkered down among the group. "Do you remember the conversation we had in the lab before you left?"

The four of them nodded, but Sayvon was quiet.

"Wait, who's she?" he said, pointing a bony finger at Sayvon.

"I'm Sayvon, Talister's daughter," she answered sheepishly. "I can leave if you'd rather—"

He patted her on the head. "Nonsense. I remember you, dear. And if these four shoe-nobbers trust you, I suppose I can too."

"What's going on, Boggle?" Lillia persisted impatiently.

"Well, after you four left, I couldn't hold on to the information any longer, so I went to the PO—but of course, Jack wasn't there. So they directed me to your father, Sayvon, and I told him everything."

"About the Metim in Creation?" Emma asked.

"About the Metim *and* the tower," Boggle responded.

They were quiet at this news. Up to this point, there was still doubt about the tower's existence and its purpose. And while its function was still unknown, the fact that Mr. Sterling and now Talister were taking it seriously caused them to think differently.

The tower could indeed be a weapon, and one of the Stars could be the key that activated it. But what did the weapon do? And which of the Stars would do it? Sam assumed it was the one that glowed, but he couldn't be sure.

Sam had been trying to put the pieces together for quite some time now, but still nothing was making sense. He knew there was far too much evidence that proved the tower existed, but why was Arazel destroying Outsider villages? Was he looking for the Stars already? If that was the case, the one holding the Stars would become a primary target.

And then the Shadow. Who was he? And why would he give Ansher Salus the drawings for his book on Watcher devices?

"Boggle, what about the Stars?" Sam prodded.

Boggle looked suddenly shocked, then produced a small leather bag from under his coat. "Actually, that is precisely why I am here."

"You didn't tell them about them?" Emma said loudly, drawing a hush from everyone in the group.

"No, I didn't."

Emma scowled. "Boggle, I thought we determined those things could be dangerous."

He blinked. "I want you to hide them here, at the school."

"What? Why here?"

The rest of them shushed Emma again.

Gus smiled. "Because Helel Malach is one of the safest places in Lior."

Boggle nodded. "I know it could put you all at a bit of risk, but I thought it would be best if as few people knew of it as possible…"

Gus stretched out his hand bravely to take the satchel from Boggle. "We will do it, Boggle."

Emma protested at first, but then dropped it, knowing full well that Boggle was right. "We will hide it tomorrow first thing after breakfast," she said finally. "We have to get it done before Shomerin."

Boggle patted her head. "Thank you, dear Emma. And—I would like to say that I am so proud of each of you for passing your requirements."

"Oh, we don't know if we have passed yet. We find out tonight," Gus corrected him.

"Ah, well, may the Light and Creator be with you all then!" he chuckled awkwardly. "Now, I must be joining Talister with the Mentors. He will be expecting me to join the conversation! Glad they finally figured out I wasn't their enemy—for Light's sake!"

Immediately after Boggle had left them, Gus and Sam went to put the Stars in their room to hide until morning. They all knew that at some point, the chimes would sound and they would be summoned to the amphitheater for the closing ceremony. They would then know whether or not they passed Mentorship to receive their Ebens.

It was an agonizing hour and a half before the first chime rang. Since they didn't really have much to do to get ready except put on their robes and comb their hair, all they could do was wait.

Gus did his best to make small talk, but the whooping and hollering down the dormitory hallways was enough to distract anyone. After a few minutes of listening to the chorus of Helel Malach's patronal anthem, *The Light Impetus*, they finally went out and joined them, singing to the top of their lungs as they raced up and down the hallway, bumping into one another.

By the third chime, Murray, Pestril, and Cestray had convinced them to form a huge chorus line all the way down the hallway, kicking their feet in rhythm to the singing. Even Yorin and his group joined in.

It was the best moment of Mentorship that Sam could remember. Though Mentorship had been short, he had made some lasting friendships.

When Sam and Gus sat down with Emma, Lillia, and Sayvon in the amphitheater, the soft snaking Light of the Lazuli was already wandering toward the ceiling. The Mentees were buzzing with excitement and nerves of their impending results.

Emma was whispering nonstop with Sayvon about Murray, who Sayvon apparently had developed a crush on, while Gus began relaying the history of the Shomerin and the Eben stones.

"No Descendant really understands how they are made. They just know the dragon has always been a sort of 'gatekeeper' for a Mentee to receive a stone."

"I just think it's strange that the Council has such an issue with dragons and yet they let kids walk into a *lair* with one," Lillia said.

Gus thought for a moment, the noise of the amphitheater growing louder. "I will agree it's strange, but the Descendants's relationship with dragons has been strange too. Some Descendants have even had a sort of connection with them, meaning they could communicate with them and such."

"Yes, but they attacked us," Lillia argued. "They have to be somewhat freaked out by them now."

Gus thought again, even amid the growing fever pitch in the room. "The only time throughout history dragons have attacked Descendants has been when they have fallen away from the Light—or they have been overcome by the Darkness."

The amphitheater darkened, and the room grew quiet as Mentor Aron strode down the center aisle.

"Students, Mentees, Descendants, I call to you now to stand with me and give thanks to our Creator."

The room hushed as Mentor Aron prayed for several minutes. His words were genuine and filled with concern. Sam could only guess it was because he had been updated with new information from Talister.

When he finished and students opened their eyes, floating in front of them were four giant glowing banners representing the four halls of Lior, waving as though a soft breeze had crept into the room.

"When you arrived at Mentorship, you were simply Descendants from four areas of Lior. Themane, Telok, Nais, and Thalo. Each region, different in its own way, as is each of our students."

Lillia jabbed Sam in the ribs. "Yeah, especially fancy-pants boy here."

"Now, as graduates of Helel Malach, the School of the Shining One, you will *all* be recognized as one region, the region of Lior!" he shouted.

All at once, the four banners collided into one massive banner of Lior.

The students cheered, standing and clapping as the banner waved proudly before them.

Mentor Aron held his hands up for quiet. "No one here should not be commended for the incredible resolve they have shown going through the training of becoming a Shomer, and therefore, all of you should be recognized for the accomplishments you have already achieved.

Orbs of glowing Light filled the amphitheater, each one seeking out a student in the room. Sam, Lillia, Gus, Emma, and Sayvon watched as an orb descended and hovered in front of each of them.

"Reach out and take your orb," Mentor Aron instructed.

Sam reached in front of him and took the ball of Light into his hands. It was warm, and it pulsed softly in his grasp. Then, the Light disappeared, and in his hand was a dark brown cuff bracelet. In the center was a spot for an Eben stone.

When the admiring of the bracelets began to die down, Mentor Aron held up his hands once again.

"Before we have our closing instructions, I would like for each of you to take your seats and welcome our own High Councilmember Talister Calpher to the podium. He has some very important information that concerns our safety here in Lior."

Whispering began again as Talister stood and walked to the podium. While it wasn't unheard of for a High Councilmember to visit during Mentorship, it wasn't common practice to address the students on safety issues.

Talister smiled widely as he looked over the crowd of young people. "My friends of Lior, I congratulate you on your accomplishments here at Helel Malach. Do not forget these days, as they are some of the best of your lives."

His voice boomed in the amphitheater. No one spoke as they waited for his announcement.

"I would like to bring to your attention some news that has surfaced here in Lior that concerns you all." He said, clearing his throat. "I am certain that each and every one of you have heard the rumors surrounding the arising of the former Watcher Nasikh—otherwise known as the Dark One."

All eyes were on the High Councilmember.

"Students, I am here to tell you that those rumors have now been confirmed. The Dark One has indeed awakened."

He paused to allow the whispering to cease. "As you travel to obtain your Eben stones—and eventually back home to your regions, please remember to take the most diligent of cautions. The Dark One is not only extremely powerful, but he is also very cunning. It does not matter how proficient you are with your Light gifts; he is more so with the Darkness."

Sam glanced at Emma, who seemed to be handling the news better than he thought she would. Lillia, who was next to him, however, shivered slightly.

"The Dark One has been the greatest of all foes throughout

history—both for the celestial and for humankind. But I assure you, students, that the Light is greater than the Darkness. And when hope is lost, and it seems the darkest, know the Light is always there to guide you. Always, students, seek the Light."

Talister left the podium and sat down to a silent room. Mentor Aron had not been ready to take his place, so awkwardly, as Mentor Aron hurried to the podium, the silence grew even more deafening.

"Students, this evening you will all receive your Shomerin results in your dormitories. As the Shomerin will begin early tomorrow morning, please remain in your rooms for the rest of the evening. You are dismissed."

Students filed out of the amphitheater with mixed emotions. Some were still admiring their bracelets and talking excitedly about whether they would receive their Ebens, while others talked solemnly about the news from Talister.

Sam hadn't really felt nervous about the results, but just as Mentor Aron dismissed them, he felt the butterflies take over his insides. It didn't help when Talister approached him just before exiting the amphitheater.

"Sam, may I have a word with you?" he said, tugging gently on his robe.

Sam followed him through the crowd of students and out through the rear of the amphitheater. Talister led him down a series of old stone hallways and into what looked like a Mentor's office. Mentor Aron was already there, along with Boggle, Mentor Korin, and Mentor Sauravin.

Sam was silent as they motioned for him to sit in a chair opposite Mentor Aron, who was seated at his desk. The butterflies turned slowly to a lump in his stomach.

"Sam, we brought you in here because there is something you should know," Mentor Aron began.

The lump grew larger inside.

Mentor Aron looked to Talister, who seemed reluctant to speak. But as he saw he wasn't going to escape it, his eyes grew sad as he turned to Sam. "We have been tracking two attacks on Outsider villages in Shimshon and Clear Lake. Mentor Korin saw it occur in a vision recently…"

Sam fought the urge to say, "I know," as he and Gus had eavesdropped on the Mentors discussing it only a few weeks earlier.

"Okay. What does that have to do with me?" Sam said, confused. "I already know I'm a target. Does that make me next or something?"

Talister's eyes shifted to the Mentors, who said nothing. Then he sighed and focused back on Sam. "We don't know what their next target is, but we know *who* attacked the two villages."

"Arazel," Sam said automatically, drawing strange looks from all in the room.

Mentor Aron nodded. "Yes, Arazel attacked the village at Shimshon."

"The other one too, right?"

"No, we are certain it wasn't him who attacked the village at Clear Lake."

"Then who?"

Talister sighed sadly. "Sam, it was Nuriel."

"No. You're wrong."

Silence.

Sam felt the anger rising quickly. "Why? Just because he is here in Lior while the other original Dark Lords are in Creation? Where's your proof? Is it just because he is powerful enough to?"

Talister reached out to touch his shoulder, but then withdrew. "I knew Nuriel. I would have trusted him with my life. If I didn't know for sure, I wouldn't be telling you this."

The lump in his stomach moved to his throat, and his face was hot. "Impossible! You can't be sure a Seer's vision is always true!"

"This one is."

"How? Impossible! Prove it!"

His anger was reaching rage, so much so that Mentors Korin and Sauravin stood to ready themselves for a possible intervention.

Talister waved them back. "I was there when it happened, Sam."

"What? Why?"

"I was—checking up on a report of—*someone*."

Sam didn't care, but in his anger the words left his lips, anyway. "Who?"

"Your *mother*, Sam."

****

Sam laid on his bunk, the anger still flowing through him. But now, it was mixed with hurt and confusion. He didn't remember leaving Mentor Aron's office, but the string of questions he fired at Talister didn't clear any of it up. The only thing he could take away was that he didn't trust any of it.

Gus was in his bunk as well, as was everyone in their rooms, all waiting for their results to be delivered. The dormitory hadn't been this quiet since the first night of Mentorship.

He hadn't told Gus anything yet, and he wasn't sure he wanted to. Instead, he told him he wasn't feeling well to avoid any suspicion something was wrong.

But now, in the quiet, with Gus reading silently, Sam stewed on the details.

A report that his mother was possibly alive. Talister said it came from an Outsider who lived in the same village with the woman. But that's all that Talister would tell him. Could it be true? Where had she been his whole life? Why didn't she come looking for him? If she even knew *he* was alive…

Still, any mother would have gone looking for their child they abandoned. If it were true, why would she ignore him?

Then Nuriel. Was he really the attacker of the Outsider village? What would cause him to do it? Talister had said he had personally seen Nuriel attack the village, and strangely, Sam believed him. Unless he was simply just trying to discredit the Watchers for some reason…

He had a fleeting thought to run to Emma, spill everything, and then have her hold him and tell him it was okay. But it would be impossible now. Boys were not allowed in girls' dormitories, and with how quiet it was with everyone waiting for their results, sneaking in would be unfeasible. Not to mention he wasn't the type to run crying to someone. It was just not how he did things.

"Is something wrong?" Gus asked suddenly. Apparently, Sam hadn't hidden it well enough.

He considered telling him. Gus was easy to talk to, and reasonable. Perhaps it would be for the best. If anything, Gus would be more of a help than to add to the emotions churning inside.

"I—" he started to say, but was interrupted by a flurry of excitement rolling down the dormitory hallway.

Gus sat up suddenly. "I think it's time."

A light began to glow softly in the hallway, then grew brighter as it moved from room to room.

Past the doorway floated a cluster of orbs, flowing in unison but each with a different intended recipient.

Two of the orbs paused, then made their way into the room, one in front of Gus's bed, and one in front of Sam's.

Whooping and yells began to fill the hallway as students received their recommendations for Shomerin. Sam looked over at Gus, who seemed perfectly terrified of the orb floating contently in front of him. He finally tore his eyes from it and met Sam's eyes.

"You first," Gus said with a squeak.

Sam shook his head. There was no way he was going to get a recommendation first and then have to console Gus if he didn't get one.

Gus had done remarkably well with all the training, but when rumors were circulating about who was the weakest of the group, Gus's name always popped up.

"No Gus, you deserve this."

Gus reached out in front of him and took the orb with his eyes closed. "Be faithful, be true, be a servant in all, until my name one day he shall call..." he recited.

Then he opened his eyes and let out a yelp.

"I made it!" he shouted, then leapt out of bed and danced around the room. "I did it! Can you believe it? Me!"

Hearing the ruckus, some others pulled him into the hallway to join their celebration. It seemed most of the Mentees had made it.

Suddenly, Sam wanted to join them. Forget everything that he had heard today. Ignore the storm of emotions inside and just go back to having fun with his friends and fellow students.

Sam reached out and took his orb, which unfurled itself into a small piece of parchment, which he unrolled.

Samuel Forrester has not been recommended to take part in Shomerin, it read.

Chapter Twenty-One
Clear Lake

It was past midnight when Sam silently grabbed his boots and his backpack. Gus was snoring contently, so Sam carefully reached in his pack and pulled out his journal.

Then he tiptoed to the corner and removed the loosened stone in the wall Gus had found the other day. He reached in and pulled out the small leather satchel hidden behind the stone. Opening it, he peeked inside. The two Stars laid side by side, one glowing, and the other not.

He stuffed them into his pack and slipped out the door of the room that had been his and Gus's for the past few months. Pausing, he put a hand on the door, wondering if what he was doing was the right thing.

He padded down the hallway and out the dormitory doors into the cool air. Fog had settled deep into the courtyard of the school. He pulled on his boots and waded into the fog toward the gate, which opened easily when he pushed.

Heart thumping, he walked down the street with the fog as cover, making it easy to stay out of sight. Not that anyone was awake, anyway.

Lucky for him, the moon gave just enough light for him to spot the path that led to the tower that housed the Lightway.

He was out of breath by the time he reached the top of the tower's stairway, but he wasted no time firing up the Lightway. It hummed as he worked the dials, setting the coordinates for the Shimshon tower. According to Gus's map in his journal, it was closest to Clear Lake, making it only a half-day's walk to the Outsider village.

He kept his pack near him as the machine hummed, hoping he had remembered everything. It was a hasty packing job, and most likely he would be short of food and proper bedding. It was no matter, however. He would be there and back to Lior City in only a couple of days.

Sam glanced at the glass on top of the machine, but it remained a murky brown color. Not even a hint of blue.

He checked the coordinates again, but still had no luck. He leafed through Gus's journal to find the coordinates for Mount Halpa. Setting them, he waited.

The glass indicator remained brown.

Was there a security device engaged? He looked around for a key, or a switch, or something. But nothing presented itself.

Trying three more coordinates produced nothing.

Angry, he kicked the machine, which only hummed. Sam, on the other hand, had stubbed his toe quite badly.

He mumbled angrily to himself as he limped back down the stairway. It was possible that the Lightway was locked during the night hours to prevent unwanted travel. Of course, with his temperament upon hearing the news this evening, he hadn't thought about whether he would run into problems like this.

He took the path that led to his and Gus's spot overlooking the mountains and found a spot out of the wind. He would wait it out until first light. The Lightway may be unlocked by then.

Even in the stillness of the fog, the air was chilly as he pulled his robe out of his pack. It wasn't meant for cold weather, but it would help regardless.

If only there were another way to get to the village. Walking would take weeks, possibly a month, with the mountains as high as they were. He would have to cross several mountain passes and a massive forest to reach the south side of Clear Lake. He certainly didn't have the proper clothing or equipment to do it alone. Not to mention he would run out of food, eventually.

An insane idea popped into his head. *Orono.*

Gus had talked about Descendants throughout history having connections to dragons. Last year, Orono seemed to understand him, almost sensing his needs before he needed them.

It was a crazy thought, but he closed his eyes, anyway. *Orono, if you can hear me, I need your help. I need to get somewhere, and I can't get there without you,* he said over and over in his mind.

****

Sam must have dozed off, because when he heard it, the fog was just beginning to lift at the first signs of daylight. There it was, a steady beat of air, rhythmic, almost unreal sounding.

He hopped off the rock and peered over the edge of the cliff. Nothing.

Then he felt it. Behind him, the heavy warm breath of a dragon, only feet from where he stood. Turning, he scrambled up the rock and over to where the silhouette of the great beast stood softly in the grass, wings outstretched.

"Orono!" he said hoarsely, reaching out to touch the dragon's snout. "I can't believe you heard me!"

The dragon's enchanting eyes motioned behind him, signaling for Sam to climb aboard. Sam slung his pack up onto Orono's lowered wing, then hoisted himself up and shimmied up to his great neck. There was no basket this time, so Sam cinched up his pack as tightly as possible and grabbed the massive iridescent scales as best as he could.

With a great leap, Orono lifted into the air and aimed straight for the edge of the mountain. Down the face of the cliff they rocketed, causing Sam's stomach to lurch. Just before meeting their end at the

bottom of the mountain, Orono leveled out abruptly, soaring only feet above the tops of the trees in the valley.

When Sam was able to breathe again, he repositioned himself and regained his grip. Orono continued to hug close to the ground, weaving his way through the jagged mountains on either side.

When Orono's flight path smoothed out past the mountains, Sam ventured into his pack and pulled out Gus's journal. He flipped to the page with the map and attempted to determine where they were. He knew Orono was flying North, but anything beyond that was just a guess. Most likely, the dragon knew Lior much better than any map did, and if he truly had understood Sam, he knew right where to go.

Either way, Sam wanted to follow along on the map. From his best judgement, they were over the Ayori Forest, and would be for quite some time. If they drifted at all to the east, they would be near the Old City of Lior. If not, he should be able to catch a glimpse of the crescent white beaches of the Lazuli pools.

He folded the map and stuck it back in the journal. He felt bad taking it—Gus held onto his journal like it was a part of him. If Sam were to lose it, Gus would be devastated. It wasn't something that could be replaced.

Daylight had crept up on them, and Sam figured that's why Orono stayed close to the treetops. The trees grew larger the further north they flew, and the great dragon had to keep changing his altitude in order to stay above them.

A few hours later, Orono swooped low in between the towering trees and landed in a small clearing next to a bubbling stream. Lowering his wing, he let Sam clamber down and fill his canteen with the clear mountain water.

Before climbing back onto Orono, Sam stretched his muscles and then kneeled down on the bank to sip the water straight from the ice-cold stream.

With Orono at his side, Sam's fear and confusion seemed to melt away like the warming caps of the mountains. The brisk air bit at his face, but it was welcome as it kept him awake, alert.

He wasn't running from something, but rather to something. It was time to stop questioning everything, and instead venture out and do something. He hated waiting for things to just happen. He wanted answers now.

Back in the sky, the hours passed quickly. Nearing evening, Sam caught glimpses of the pools, sparkling like crystal blue gems below. He thought about requesting a stop, but then changed his mind. There wouldn't be much time before the night would be upon them.

They reached the lake at sunset, and Orono seemed to understand Sam's thoughts about finding a place to stop for the night, because he spotted a small island just off the coast and headed directly for it.

Finding a small grassy area between two large boulders, Sam hunkered down for the night, using his robe as a blanket. Soon the sound of heavy breathing was heard from both man and dragon.

The next morning, with his stomach growling fiercely, he woke to the smell of a fire and breakfast cooking. Startled, he sat up and peeked around the boulder.

There, next to a fire, was hunched an old man, paying no mind to the great dragon that lay peacefully next to him.

"Ah, you're awake. 'Bout time," the man said, his voice raspy and weak.

"Who are you?" Sam asked, his hand clutching the knife in his pocket he had slipped into his pack before leaving the school.

"You don't need that wee knife, boy," he said as he ladled rootcake batter into the sizzling pan, not bothering to even look in Sam's direction. "What you need is breakfast. You look like you haven't eaten a proper meal in days."

Sam stepped closer to the fire, examining the man in front of him. He was shorter, with a thin frame and thick silver hair. The robe and shoes he wore looked as though they had long outlived their purpose, and judging from his hardened skin and chapped lips, he hadn't left the mountains in quite a while.

"Orono said you needed to eat."

He turned to look at Sam. His eyes were a perfect and soft blue, contrasting every other feature about him.

"What? Can you talk to him?"

The old man laughed. "And you can't?"

"Well—I don't know for sure…" he stumbled. "I think… he hears me."

Again he laughed. "So you aren't listening then, is that it?"

Sam was stunned. "You can hear what dragons are saying?"

He nodded, then scooped some smoked fish and wild blueberry rootcake onto a plate and handed it to him. "Birch syrup is right there at your feet—which you are about to kick over."

Sam sat and dug into the food he was given. Either it was delicious, or he was just incredibly hungry. Whatever the case, he hoped there was plenty more.

"You are a *levah tannin*. You've been given the gift of dragon speak," the man said, placing a coffee pot on the coals of the fire.

"A what?"

It was a term he hadn't heard before.

"*Levah tannin*. It means 'fire beast' in the old tongue."

Sam finished the fish and pancake, and the old man refilled his plate. Then he handed him a cup of coffee. "Who are you?"

The old man peered at him, as if searching his intentions. "Romael Jorgin, my young traveler. Rom for short, or RJ if you must."

"Orono called you here?"

"Are you hard of hearing, boy? He certainly did. Said you were needing tending to. Not that I don't find waking early to make you breakfast one of my most enjoyable tasks."

Sam chuckled. "I bet not."

Then Rom reached into his robe and withdrew a short sword still sheathed in its leather scabbard and tossed it at him.

Sam caught it, then drew the sword so that the blade peeked out. The blade and handle were older but well-made and adorned with symbols on the metal he didn't recognize. He stood and wrapped the leather belt around his waist, cinching the clasp so that the sword held fast against his leg. It seemed to fit perfectly.

Rom smiled, sipping his coffee. "Orono also told me you needed that."

Sam looked at Orono, who was yawning large puffs of smoke as he stood and stretched, paying him no mind.

Rom gestured to the dragon. "Ya best be gettin' on. I'm thinking you have somewhere to be."

Sam set his coffee cup at the old man's feet. "Thank you for the sword," he told him. "And the breakfast."

Sam grabbed his pack and headed to Orono, who had already dipped his wing for Sam to climb aboard. Finding his spot on the dragon's neck, he cinched up his pack and waited for liftoff.

Then the man called up to him. "Sam, not all Descendants appreciate the gift you've been given. Be wary of those who despise the dragon's might. Fear is not part of the Creator's design."

As they left the tiny island on the lake behind, Sam watched as the man snuffed out the fire and then disappeared with a flash of blue light.

Could he really talk with Orono as Rom did? If so, what do you say to a dragon? Either way, his warning was clear. Dragon speakers aren't always welcome. He supposed he should just add it to the list of reasons he was already disliked.

The dragon flew another two hours before the north side of the lake became visible. As they soared closer, Sam could make out the outline of a settlement among the trees.

Orono turned left before reaching shore and glided toward a grassy hillside just outside of the village. With a soft thud, they landed, the torrent of wings coming to a stop.

Sam swung down onto the soft knee-length grass and paused, admiring the view of the lake behind him. The northern shore was nestled between two ranges. To the right, the jagged outline of the Agam mountains, and to the left were the towering peaks of the Shimshon.

Sam found a path near the lake that led toward the village. It was only a few hundred meters of easy hiking before he emerged through the trees to find himself in the center of what used to be the main square.

Sam stood, mouth open, taking it all in. Clear Lake was now a shell of what it used to be. What was obviously once a thriving epicenter of commerce was now charred remains. Skeletons of buildings stood among the wreckage, the occasional chair or cast-iron pot tossed into the street, somehow escaping the destruction. It was jarring to observe.

Sam picked his way through the piles of coals and blackened beams of one of the former structures, looking for something—anything that would confirm that what Talister said was true.

He spent the better part of the day going from building to building, looking for evidence of what had happened to the former residents of Clear Lake. But by late afternoon, he had found nothing. No clues of escape, or forced removal, or even the remains of a person.

What happened to them? It was as though they had vanished into nothing. Just disappeared.

It was possible his mother had lived in one of these former buildings. Waiting, perhaps, for her son to come find her.

Seeing enough, he walked down to the shoreline, wiping the sweat and ash from his forehead. He paused at the bank and splashed water on his face, disturbing the glassy surface in front of him.

He wanted to scream. Why was all of this happening to him? All of his life, he had only wanted a mom and dad who loved him. It didn't matter if they were from Creation or Lior, he just wanted parents who cared. Really cared.

He reached down and unsheathed the sword Rom had given him. Poised, he swiped at the air in front of him, wishing suddenly the individual who had been responsible for destroying his family was in the path of the blade.

Nuriel. Where was he?

"COME FIGHT ME YOU COWARD!" he screamed into the stillness of the lake.

Chapter Twenty-One

The only response he received was from the soft breeze filtering down from the mountains.

∗∗∗∗∗∗∗∗∗∗∗∗∗∗∗∗∗∗∗∗∗∗∗∗∗∗∗∗∗∗

Sam awoke in the evening to the thump of Orono's tail on the ground next to him. He threw an angry glance at the iridescent blue beast, who only responded with another thump of his tail, closer this time.

"What do you want?" he grumbled back.

Then abruptly in his mind exploded an image of the tower—the same image as the one from the Watcher device by the cabin.

You want me to go here? He looked into the deep eyes of the dragon. *Why? What will I find there? Except maybe my own death?*

In his mind rushed more images. A burning village, flashes of blue setting buildings aflame. And then a figure—cloaked in the shadows. He was alone. There was no screaming, no villagers running for their lives...

He peered at Orono. *Do you know where the tower is?*

Orono dipped his wing.

Chapter Twenty-Two
The Keeper

Wings swept back, Orono sped over the mountain peaks toward the sea. Sam held on tight, unable to see the scenery because of the speed they were traveling.

Sam thought about his friends, who were no doubt in a panic trying to find him by now. Not to mention everyone else at the school. It wasn't fair that he left without telling them, but he wasn't sure they would have let him go.

And where would he have gone, anyway? Remain in the dorms until the students traveled back to the city? He didn't pass Mentorship, so he would have had to travel back with everyone else who had received their Eben stones. How delightful of a journey that would have been.

He even considered not returning at all after this. Live in the mountains like Rom, away from everyone—and their dumb legends.

Before long, the sun was setting once again behind them. Sam felt the last rays of warmth slip from his back and the cold air of the mountains take their place. He was glad he had his robe on, but it

didn't offer much protection, with the wind whipping around him as Orono raced ahead.

Soon he could make out the coastline and the eerie white splash of moonlight on the sea. He carefully unfolded the map and squinted to see where they might be. Judging from the way the coast jutted to the North, they would be over the Sea of Yaum in only a short while. Then into the Sadak Mountains, and the unknown.

Sam fought to stay awake as the dragon flew on, but at some point he dozed off, holding tightly to Orono's neck. He only hoped that if he started to slip off, Orono would alert him.

****

Sam awoke to the steady beating of dragon wings as Orono prepared for a landing in the darkness below. Wearily, he opened his eyes and shot a glance downward into the faint outline of the trees. There, a tiny spot of blue appeared like a weak beacon in a sea of black. As they landed, Sam thought he caught a glimpse of a small structure immersed in the blue light.

He descended carefully onto the mossy ground, keeping his eyes on the light ahead. Turning, he looked for guidance from Orono, but the dragon merely collapsed on the ground from exhaustion.

He gripped his sword and stepped carefully toward the light, realizing as he drew closer that it turned out to be inside the window of a small stone cabin.

Mounting the weathered steps, he pulled the doorknob and kicked the door open with his toe, hand still on the sword.

The cabin was dimly lit from the Lazuli lamp in the window, casting a glow on the meager contents inside. A fireplace, cot, table and chairs, and a small makeshift kitchen made up the interior—and judging from the inch of dust on the furniture and cobwebs in the corners, it had not seen an inhabitant for a long time.

After cleaning up a bit, Sam locked the door and stretched out on the cot. The bed linens had an old musty smell to them, but he

didn't care. He just needed sleep. Tomorrow, he would do some more exploring.

****

"Samael. You were born with a purpose," the dark figure with the shifting eyes echoed inside his head.

"Come fulfill your purpose with me," he said, his body morphing suddenly into that of a dragon, ablaze with incredible fire. Then the beast's mouth opened, the Darkness spewing out…

****

The next morning, Sam dug through the dusty kitchen to find a coffee pot and poured in some of his canteen water to rinse it out. Grabbing some of the coffee he had stashed in his pack before leaving, he tossed in some grounds and poured the rest of the canteen water into the pot. Then he lit a fire in the small stove in the kitchen.

Last night had been tough sleeping, as strange dreams of all sorts ran through his head, including the one with the dragon. There was no doubt that the nerves mixed with exhaustion from the trip were partly to blame. Where the rest came from was still a mystery.

The smell of coffee wafted through the old cabin, which perked him up enough to have a look around. The cabin was minimal and had no luxuries to speak of. There was a washbasin and a few cupboards, and a tiny table set with two old, but sturdy, chairs.

He hadn't started a fire last night out of tiredness, but did notice the large hearth that extended well into the room. This morning, however, he considered tossing in a few logs to chase away the chill, but then thought better of it. Smoke could be seen from miles around, and he couldn't be certain of who might be around to see it.

In the corner was a bookshelf with a few old books and a leather journal, which he pulled off the shelf and flipped through. It was

written in the old language, which he did not know—even after the countless hours of Gus trying to teach him.

One word he did recognize was "name," which in the old tongue was *Beshema*. Next to that was the word *Naryea*. Searching through Gus's journal proved successful once again. *Keeper?* He studied the words to make sure they were a match.

"Keeper of what?" he said aloud as the coffee pot let out a sputter, letting him know it was ready.

He closed the journal and returned it to the shelf. It may have been an interesting find, but he had no room in his small pack to carry anything else.

Venturing outside with his coffee, he caught a first glimpse of his surroundings.

The cabin was hidden by a rock outcropping overlooking a vast expanse of tundra on all sides. In the distance beyond, stood some of the most majestic mountains Sam had ever seen.

Strolling some distance from the cabin, Sam turned to take in the scene behind him. He was stunned at the sight.

Behind the cabin, large as life, was one of the largest mountains he had ever encountered. It rose up like a giant before him, dwarfing the tiny cabin.

The peaks he had first seen paled in comparison to the behemoth rock rising out of the valley behind the cabin. Its top was completely engulfed in a cloud, leaving the mountain's true summit a mystery to the observer. It was breathtaking, to say the least.

Stop sightseeing and get moving. You have a tower to find. A voice in his head prompted.

He hurried back to the cabin and packed his things. Seeing a rope hanging on the wall near the door, he borrowed it, securing it to his pack. Then, without another glance, he latched the door behind him and stepped onto the porch.

He walked briskly back to where Orono had left him. When he arrived, however, the dragon wasn't there.

"Orono!" he called out, then waited for the thunderous flapping

of wings. After several minutes of hearing only the wind, he called again. There was no response.

Orono. I need you to take me to the tower, he called from his thoughts. *Where are you?*

Nothing.

After an hour of lingering, he headed out on his own, hoping Orono would catch up with him and take him the rest of the way.

He figured he would start toward the great mountain behind the cabin, since that seemed like a landmark worth remembering. He could end up in the complete opposite direction of the tower, but he needed to begin somewhere. He couldn't wait for Orono forever.

Cinching up his pack, he had a thought. The holomap.

He cleared his mind, hoping the images would appear as they had so many times before. They hadn't guided him in a specific direction thus far, but he hoped it would give him an idea if he was on the right trail or not.

Right away, the images emerged. Though they weren't as clear as before, he could still identify the gigantic mountain looming overtop the mysterious tower.

His mind searched the scene, looking for clues. It didn't take long for him to find one. A spot on the mountain where the peak split in two. It had to be the same mountain.

He set off, circling the cabin, where a long, gradual hill spilled into a valley in front of the mountain. Speckles of grey poked out of the tundra where the tips of rocks were exposed. Seeing one of the larger rock formations, he veered toward it, careful not to twist an ankle on one of the smaller stones.

Then, as he drew closer to the formation, he noticed something peculiar about it.

It can't be. He thought, shaking his head.

He yanked his pack from his shoulders and pulled out his journal. Inside, he removed the folded-up sketch that Henry Bostwick had given him of the tower. The carved tower symbol on the rock in front of him was a match to the sketch he held in his hands.

Henry had found this one in the Amazon region of Creation, and now, here was another.

Stepping up to the carving, he traced its outline, which was no doubt thousands of years old. The surface of the rock had worn away over the years, but its intricate features told Sam it had been expertly crafted.

The rocks provided just enough room to enter the center of the outcropping, so Sam cautiously walked around to inspect the rear of the formation that held the carving. Inside, there was ample space for several people to walk around, as well as a tiny spring that bubbled up and then quickly disappeared somewhere beneath the ground.

He bent down and filled his canteen with the water in the spring, then cupped his hands to drink as much as he could. Traveling with the others to the Old City had taught him to take advantage of water sources while you have access to them, because you may not later.

As he sipped the cool water, something in front of him caught his eye. An opening in the rock beyond the spring. Was it large enough for a person to fit through?

Holding out his palm, he closed his eyes and allowed the Light to enter his body, down his arm, and into his hand. Opening his eyes, he saw the bright blue Lazuli Light pulse in his open palm, contained in a tiny orb. Extending his arm, he let the orb fall from his hand and into the dark opening.

The opening illuminated, revealing that it was much larger than he had anticipated. Curiously, it reminded him of the opening for the cave where they had discovered the holomap.

The Watchers sure loved making people work to find things, he thought, retrieving his pack.

He didn't particularly like the idea of descending down into a dark opening, especially alone. But with the carving and the curiously placed outcropping, there was likely no other choice. Taking a deep breath, he stepped over the spring and slipped into the opening of the rock.

His orb had faded, so he held out his palm and produced another,

keeping it in his hand as he ventured down the rocky incline toward the unknown below.

He stumbled along, the Light from his palm casting eerie shadows all around. He kept a hand on his sword as he inched forward, but then found it necessary to steady himself on the tunnel walls instead. Deeper and deeper he went—the air growing strangely warmer the farther he descended.

He stopped for a moment, listening to a rushing noise that grew louder the further he went. *Water.*

It meant that he might be near the bottom.

If I were to slip and fall in here, no one would ever know where I went, he thought, holding the orb of light lower to the ground to miss some of the larger rocks that had fallen from the ceiling. Again, he regretted coming here alone. He truly missed having his friends with him.

Nearing the bottom, a dim light appeared from below, emitting a soft blue hue. Dousing his own orb, he used the faint light the rest of the way down.

He had been right about the water. As his feet felt bottom, the tunnel opened up into a larger cavern, where a gushing stream wound its way through the middle.

The Lazuli in the stream made it possible to see the inside of the cavern in its entirety, so he took a few moments to explore.

The cavern wasn't exceptionally large, nor were there any identifying features about it. Other than where the stream entered and exited, there wasn't an obvious way out.

That didn't mean it wasn't there. Previous experiences with the ancient sites in Lior had proven that entry points weren't always visible right away. That they might take some searching to find.

He made his way around the cavern, inspecting the dull grey rock for clues. He was so intent on finding a way out that he didn't even notice the skeleton beneath him until he had stepped on its arm and snapped it in half.

He jumped back and gripped his sword, heart racing. When he

figured out what happened, he gathered himself and returned to examine the remains.

The bones were from an individual who was rather small, though he suspected that from the shape of the skull, it could be that of an adult. Lying a few meters from the body was a staff, its top hollowed out but missing its talisman.

He was about to turn away and continue looking for the exit, but then stopped, his heart suddenly in his throat. Turning back, he picked up the staff.

Reaching into his pack, he pulled the glowing star from the leather satchel and inserted it into the staff. It fit perfectly, like it was meant to be there. Leaning it up against the rock wall, Sam stared at it for several moments, bewildered.

Was it possible the Star had been in the staff before? If so, then the person—well—*former* person at his feet knew about the Star. Could this have been the Keeper from the journal in the cabin?

He had to keep going. He kept the Star in the staff, taking them both with him. If this was the remains of the Keeper beside him, he wouldn't mind. Besides, he could use something to help keep his balance in the mountainous terrain.

After a bit more searching, Sam finally spotted the elusive exit hidden within the wall and shimmied his way through the opening. When he emerged out of the cavern, the landscape had changed drastically.

****

In front of him lay a dark forest of old, sprawling trees. Canyon walls reached hundreds of feet up on both sides of the forest, strangling out the little light from above.

The crooked stream disappearing into the cavern wall behind him wound its way past and through the canyon, where the gnarled canopy of branches engulfed it.

The Keeper

It was eerily calm and balmy inside the canyon, like the weather just before a terrible storm blows in.

Staff in hand, he convinced himself to press forward, and followed the stream through the gnarled trees. Each step he took on the rock echoed off the canyon walls, so he did his best to walk as lightly as possible.

He noticed the canyon widen as he kept walking. The forest widened as well, carrying some of the echos of his footsteps with it. Warily, he gripped his sword, keeping the staff and the Star at his side. At any moment, he could make a break for the deeper part of the forest if need be, zipping down one of the thin paths leading away from the stream.

After a while, he noticed it was getting darker. Had the day passed already?

Stopping to look around him, he realized that there was no way he could tell what the time of day was. The sun didn't reach far into the canyon, so any light that did make it down to the surface would fade quickly as night drew closer.

His heart beat faster, knowing he had potentially made a serious mistake by not keeping track of the time. He would need to find a safe place to stay for the night if it was this late in the day.

He considered hiking back to the cavern to try the following day, but didn't care to spend the night with a dead Keeper. He wasn't afraid of his remains, but of what had killed the man.

Deciding that where he was now was as best as any, he chose a spot under a tree near the water, with a good view upstream and down. Digging in his pack, he found his Lazuli firestarter, then picked up a few of the dead branches from the edge of the forest for his fire. The flame would be a welcome friend in the dark, even if it were too warm to need it.

Just then, he heard a snap from the trees to his right. His eyes searched for the source of the sound, but there was no movement. Then again, this time from the left.

Snap.

He unsheathed his sword partway as quietly as he could, still searching for the movement's origins.

Snap. SNAP.

He leapt to his feet, palm outstretched in the noise's direction. His other hand gripped the sword.

Something, or *someone,* was there. And he was alone to face it.

He waited, heart banging in his chest.

Peering into the darkness, Sam thought he caught a glimpse of something—were those eyes staring back at him?

More movement. Then the sound of raspy breathing behind him.

Sam spun to meet the hollow eyes of a faceless Metim only meters from him. Suddenly, it lunged, reaching out with its haunting claws right at Sam's neck.

Sam tried to bring the sword up, but it was too late. The Metim was on top of him, pinning him to the ground. A thick black liquid oozed from the gruesome mouth of the Dark creature as it prepared to spew venomous Darkness from its lungs.

Sam fought to remove the beast, but the incredible strength of the Metim was too much for him to push it off of him. He struggled against the force of its unnatural weight, crying out in anger at the foul monster.

Just as the Metim began expelling the vile goo from its mouth, Sam managed to get a palm up between it and him.

Closing his eyes, he felt the warm Lazuli come to the surface of his body, then down his arm and to his palm in an instant. With a bright flash, the Metim was rocketing into the air away from him with a massive hole through its middle.

Instantly on his feet, Sam's training took hold, and he began firing bolts at anything that moved. Metim after Metim emerged from the cover of night to meet a blast of Lazuli Light from Sam's palm.

He spun as he fired, the lethal bolts taking the beasts down. Still, more came to replace the others, determined to extinguish Sam and his Light. As they poured from the trees, he quickly realized that he wouldn't be able to keep up with the advancing horde. Grabbing his

sword, he waited wearily for them to come closer.

They surrounded him, eager to consume their prey. Their hollow faces rippled with the soulless Darkness, each one stepping toward him in unison as though an unearthly force were controlling their movements.

He would not win this fight.

Instead of fighting, Sam dropped to his knees and prepared to be overtaken by them. Exhausted, he released the sword, which clattered to the stone beside him. He closed his eyes and folded his hands above his head, waiting for the first of them to strike.

The putrid taste of Darkness entered through his nose and mouth, instantly entering his lungs. He struggled to keep upright, but all he could taste was death.

Then, the feeling changed. The Darkness left him, and he felt the warm feeling of Lazuli flowing through his body again. It was strangely invigorating, almost *familiar*. But where did it come from?

His eyes shot open, seeing nothing but blue. It was a shield, fitting perfectly around him where he kneeled.

Emma.

Just beyond the shield stood three figures. One of them was the source of the shield. The Metim were nowhere in sight.

"Here!" he called weakly, struggling to get to his feet.

The three of them rushed to help him, but before he knew it, the ground was crashing toward him. His eyes closed, and his body went limp.

****

"You stupid, pathetic idiot."

The words echoed in Sam's head as he opened his eyes to meet Emma's. "How could you think you were doing the right thing by running off on your own?"

Sam blinked and tried to sit up.

Lillia pushed him back down to rest on Emma's lap. "Lay back down, you big fool. You were nearly Metim dinner."

"We were almost too late to help you," Gus nodded.

Lillia snorted. "I told 'Em we could finish you off ourselves if she didn't have such a bleeding heart."

Sam attempted a laugh, but it wouldn't escape his lungs.

"Just rest, Newb."

Sam complied.

When he awoke again, Gus had a fire going and was roasting something that smelled delicious. His stomach growled, protesting the fact he hadn't eaten much all day.

Emma was asleep next to him, as was Lillia. Gus must have agreed to stay up as watch.

"Nice staff you got there," he said, gesturing to the staff Sam had taken from the cave. The Star was still in the top.

"Yeah, I found it with the skeleton. The Star fit right in."

"I believe it was meant to," he whispered, trying not to wake the others. "The Keeper's diary said that it was his duty to protect it."

"You found the cabin."

Gus nodded. "It wasn't easy…"

"Gus, I'm—" Sam started, but Gus held up his hand.

"I know why you left. It's okay."

"No, I should have told you guys I was leaving. It was dumb to think I could do this alone."

Gus nodded. "I was angry at first, but then I thought about it more," he said. "I can't imagine being where you are right now… I think none of us can. We haven't given that enough consideration in the past."

"Thanks."

Gus smiled, his glasses fogging up from the humidity. "For the record, you are family to us. Where you go, we go."

"Even when I run off and nearly get killed, right?" Sam said, coughing.

"Yep. It was pretty shortsighted, admittedly. Rash, unintelligent, ill-advised, ludicrous…"

Sam laughed. "I get the point. How did you guys find me, anyway?"

Gus pointed to his head. "I have a map of Lior, remember?"

"Right. But how did you get here?"

Gus motioned toward Emma, who was sleeping soundly. "Emma called a Ruasch. Her gifts are becoming quite extraordinary."

"Were you able to get your Eben stones?"

Gus reached down and pulled the sizzling meat off the stone. Taking one himself, he handed one to Sam. "No. We left to find you before the Shomerin began."

Sam shifted nervously. "I'm sorry Gus."

Gus turned and looked deep into Sam's eyes, unlike he had ever done before. "If there's one thing Mentorship has taught me, it isn't about earning anything. The Light isn't earned, it's given to a Descendant. The Eben stone would have been nice to have about now, but it's not about obtaining it. I would rather have you as a friend than some stone."

Tears welled in Sam's eyes. He was normally good at hiding it, but under the weight of sheer exhaustion, it was impossible.

They talked some more and nibbled on their meager dinner, waiting for the girls to awake. They both looked so peaceful as they slept, as if there wasn't a care in the world.

The next morning, they made a game plan to continue forward. It was likely that they had just scared the Metim off, so they had to be prepared for anything. It was Lillia who finally brought up the question of why the Metim were there.

"Could be they were trapped here. Fell down the tunnel and forgot their way out of the cavern," she suggested, taking the lead as they started off once again.

Gus disagreed. "Metim aren't that dimwitted. They have capacity for formulating plans—attacking strategically."

Sam took up the rear of the group as they walked, sword in hand. "Could there be another entrance?"

No one had an answer for this. Although they didn't know what lay before them, the canyon didn't seem to have any other way of accessing it. But it was possible.

"Okay, maybe they are trapped. Maybe they killed the Keeper in the cave?" Emma said.

Lillia glanced at her. "Or maybe someone brought them here."

Emma raised an eyebrow as Gus and Sam hopped over a bend in the stream. "Whatever happened with the Metim, I'm sure they are others around. It makes me nervous about what's still waiting ahead."

It didn't take them long to find out. For as they turned the corner where the stream curved right, the silhouette of a tower rose above the trees, its darkened spires reaching high into the gloomy night.

Chapter Twenty-Three
The Watcher Tower

Far ahead, a Lazuli-fed waterfall glowed a steady blue as it tumbled down the rocks into the stream. Above it was the soaring black tower, looking both majestic and chilling at the same time.

They fought the urge to stop for lunch, continuing on toward the ominous falls. By late afternoon, they had found a way to its top, and paused for a few moments to catch their breath. Perched on a dull grey rock overlooking the valley, they nibbled on some provisions Emma had brought.

"Do you feel the Lazuli?" Emma asked Sam.

Sam looked at her. "It's weak here, but of course I do. Why do you ask?"

She turned away from him. "I don't know. I—just wanted to hear it from you, that's all."

"You don't trust me."

She sighed, turning back to face him. "I do. It's just—the Darkness is really strong. And I know you feel that, too."

She was right. He did feel the Darkness. It was like an aching pain that felt good when you rubbed it. It had always been there, but he had been able to push it back in his mind, so much so that he often forgot about it.

"You don't feel the Darkness?" he asked her.

She dug her hands inside her robe pockets. "Yes, I do. I think every Descendant does to some point. But I think it affects some more than others."

"So you know I failed Mentorship."

"Yes."

He pulled her close to him, burying his face in the hair on top of her head. It smelled unwashed, but like her.

"Em,' nothing is going to happen to me. No, the news that I didn't pass wasn't fun. Sure, it bothers me. But people have been screwing me over for years. I'm used to it."

She smiled at him, but he could tell it wasn't genuine. She was holding back.

They packed up and set off for the tower once again. Judging from how far they had already traveled, they would reach it well before nightfall—plenty of time to get some exploring in before they would have to find a place for the night. Hopefully, the tower provided that, but one couldn't be sure.

Late afternoon brought them within a few hundred meters of the tower. From this vantage point, it was obvious that the structure had taken many years to construct. Whoever did, they had built it with precision and elegance.

Sweeping arches and elegant buttresses adorned the exterior of the tower, and upon the ledges of each of the peaks were detailed likenesses of creatures of all types. Embossed in the center of the tower was a giant Irin—the Watcher's wing—expertly carved into the stone.

The structure showed no signs of life, or Metim, so they advanced with caution, weaving through the many boulders that had dislodged themselves from the cavern walls and rolled to a stop in front of it.

"Do you really think it's a weapon?" Lillia asked Gus nervously as

they mounted the fanned stone steps of the haunting building.

Gus tip-toed up the steps gingerly. "I—really couldn't be sure unless we get inside." He said, his voice cracking heavily. "Which I'm not certain I'm quite ready for just yet."

Emma grabbed Sam's hand. "Are we really doing this tonight? I mean—shouldn't we wait for first light?"

They turned and looked at her, not out of judgement, but out of consideration for her suggestion.

"We are still a bit overtired from the trip here," Lillia reminded them. "And I could go for some deliciously overcooked meat strips and stale bread about now."

Emma started back down the steps. "I agree."

Sam and Lillia retreated down the steps after her. Gus, however, paused behind them.

He stood resolute on the top step. "No," he told them.

The three others turned around to look at him. "But you just said—"

"I know what I said. I was wrong. We have to do this now."

They stared blankly at him. A moment ago, he wasn't ready, but now something sounded urgent in his voice.

"What is it Gus?" Emma whispered.

Gus lifted his head and searched the tree canopy all around them. It was deathly still.

"I don't know. I just *feel* something," he whispered. "Something *wrong*."

Sam's stomach lurched. He had never heard Gus speak like that before.

"Gus don't do this to us—" Lillia started to say, but Sam hushed her.

"I feel it too."

Gus was right. Sam couldn't quite understand it, but the urgency to finish what they started and get out seemed all the more pressing suddenly.

"The Metim. We know they've been following us," Emma said.

"No," Gus warned. "It's not the Metim."

Lillia mounted the steps back toward the tower quicker than Sam had ever seen anyone move. "Then let's get inside this stupid thing and get this done!"

She proceeded to search the giant metal door for a way to open it.

The rest of them rushed to help her, searching the door, steps, and walls to either side to find a way in. Not surprisingly, they found nothing.

Frustrated, they took a quick water break, gathering their packs near them in case they needed a quick escape. Emma was put on alert to call a Ruasch if necessary.

Sam leaned up against the door, the staff next to him. Suddenly, from behind the door came a soft clicking noise, then a low rumble. The door parted in the middle and rumbled open behind him.

The staff clattered to the floor inside the tower's open door. Sam scooted quickly away, joining the others, who were peering through the opening at the top of the stairway.

Gus took a step forward, then another, palms outstretched in front of him. He disappeared inside the dark interior for a few moments, then returned and motioned for the others to follow him.

"It's clear," he said quietly. "Grab your packs and come on in."

They obeyed, following him inside the tower. Immediately behind them, the door closed, leaving out the little light they had with it. The only source of light was now the staff that lay on the onyx-colored stone floor. Sam picked it up and stared at the Star in the hilt. It seemed to glow more prominently.

"You think it was the Star that opened it?" Lillia asked him.

"It only makes sense," Sam responded.

Gus held out his hand, and Sam handed him the staff. Examining it, he said, "Well, we can try it again on the next door. Sam, do you mind?"

Sam shook his head, and Gus walked the staff to the next door, which seemed to be the interior entrance to what lay inside. He held the staff up to the door. The Star brightened.

A click, then a rumble within. The door began to open, creaking loudly on its hinges.

Blue Lazuli Light flooded out of the entrance and spilled into the outer room, blinding them. They covered their eyes, but again Gus moved forward right away, wielding the staff in front of him. Sam and the others followed, their eyes adjusting to the light.

Columns of pure Lazuli Light laced the walls throughout the inside of the tower, soaring to the ceiling, where the Lazuli pooled like a cloud at the top. Each of the columns was laden with hundreds of ancient symbols, their outlines projecting luminous shapes on the interior walls.

In the center of the room, they noticed one small pedestal rising from the smooth stone floor. It was identical to the one they discovered in the cave next to the holomap, with one small exception. In the center of the pedestal was a small hole, about the size of the Star that was in the staff Gus was holding.

They gazed at the podium, watching it come to rest about a meter off the floor. The room pulsed silently with Lazuli, as if it were waiting for them to insert the Star and complete their purpose there.

"Unbelievable," Lillia said, her whisper leaping from wall to wall. "I can't believe this exists."

"What do we do?" Gus asked.

They peered at him. He usually had an answer for everything.

"It's a weapon, is it not?" Emma mused, her eyes moving about the room.

It seemed to remind them even more of the gravity of the situation. Here they were, standing in an ancient tower with unknown secrets beheld within. The podium in the center of the room seemed to beckon to them, as if knowing they had the Star. It was chilling to think of what would happen if they used to activate the tower. Who knew what it did? And what consequences would they provoke by activating it?

Still, the possibility existed for them to use it. There were Metim out there, who would love nothing more than to kill them. Perhaps they could use it to kill them first. Wield the tower for their purposes. Rid Lior of a few more bad guys.

The intoxicating thought flitted about, tempting them.

No. Sam thought. We don't know what could happen.

Gus turned to face them, eyes wide with guilt. He must have come to the same conclusion as Sam had. That it was too dangerous to attempt.

"Sam, I know you were hoping to find your mother, but I think we have served our purpose here. And we need to get this Star in the right hands before we do something foolish," Gus said.

Lillia cringed. "Maybe if we get on our knees and beg forgiveness, they will still let us complete the Shomerin when we get back."

Suddenly Sam realized just how naïve he had been for bringing the Stars with him. He just put them all in incredible danger. This had not been one of his better plans.

He snatched up his pack. "Let's get out of here. Emma, you said you can call a Ruasch?"

"I can."

He turned and headed for the interior door, which had closed them in the room as they entered.

Gus followed, handing Sam the staff.

Sam held the staff to the door. It opened, once again allowing for the Lazuli Light to spill into the room. They hurried across the room to the door that would lead them outside. Sam held up the staff a second time. Again, the door clicked and rumbled open. They squeezed through before the door opened fully, ready to be rid of the place.

Outside, they paused, but only for a moment. Sam glanced out over the canyon, the waterfall roaring softly in the distance. The same feeling he had before entering the tower was back.

Gus must have felt it too, because he gazed over the scene next to him, a scowl on his face.

"Okay Emma, do your thing," Lillia prodded her.

Emma closed her eyes, lifting her hands up to the sky above her. She stood motionless, whispering into the air.

"What's the problem?" Lillia asked after only a moment.

Emma shushed her. "Give me a minute. I'm trying to focus."

A few more moments passed, and Lillia tapped her on the shoulder. "Today, Ginger."

A bead of sweat formed on Emma's forehead. "I'm trying, okay? I think I'm just—stressed."

Out of the corner of his eye, Sam caught movement just inside the tree line. Squinting, he strained to see where it had come from. Was that a person? Or an animal?

Suddenly Gus grabbed his arm, pointing to a figure in a dark robe standing off in the distance directly in front of them. It was Arazel.

"Too late. He's already here," Gus whispered.

****

Sam's heart sunk, a sick feeling rushing over him. There was Arazel, the same Dark Lord that had attempted to steal the Watcher Key from him and nearly killed his friends.

"Get back inside," he said to the others, turning and placing the staff on the door once more.

"WAIT! I CAN—" Emma cried, her hands still aloft.

Lillia didn't let her finish, picking her up and dragging her through the opening door mid-sentence. Gus helped her to move Emma, then helped Sam kick their packs inside.

As soon as they were back in the tower, Sam let the staff clatter to the floor, which instantly released the Star from its hilt. It rolled across the floor toward him, landing at Gus's shoe.

Give the Star to me. A voice spoke from the darkness of the tower.

Wait. Sam thought, confusion wreaking havoc in his mind. Why would I give the Star to Arazel?

His thoughts were suddenly a blur. What was the purpose of Sam coming here? Was it to find his mother? Or the source of his visions? Perhaps Arazel willed it—spoke the images into his mind. Perhaps a connection to the Darkness meant a connection to Arazel. Perhaps he was right, it was inevitable. He was destined for the Darkness.

What would possess him to think this way suddenly? Was he losing his mind?

Bring me the Star.

The image of Clear Lake flooded back. They had no doubt it had been Nuriel who caused the destruction. The fraud of a Watcher had lied to him. Then he destroyed the village his mother had lived in. Arazel had destroyed the other.

Arazel wanted the Star. He could feel it. And if it was what Arazel wanted, then he could have it. Then, when he got what he wanted, Sam would kill him.

Sam snatched up the Star and the staff and slipped back through the closing door to the outside before anyone could stop him.

Ignoring the shouts and pounding on the door behind him, he stuffed the Star in his pocket and began walking toward the figure in the distance.

As he walked, he brought to his mind his last encounter with Arazel—the fear, the confusion, and even the hatred that all overwhelmed him in those moments.

The Mentors at Helel Malach did their best to train him for moments like these. To control your emotions, not let them control you. To search for peaceful resolutions before violence. To be a servant, even to your enemy.

But Sam did not feel peace now. He didn't want a peaceful resolution. There was no servant heart in his chest this moment.

He wanted Arazel dead.

"WHERE IS MY MOTHER!?" he yelled at the cloaked figure, the green glow in his eyes now visible.

Arazel didn't respond.

Sam walked faster. "TELL ME!"

The Dark Lord's eyes blazed, but he still did not respond.

Sam broke into a run, his palms outstretched before him. In a few moments, he would be in range of throwing a bolt.

Then Arazel lifted up his hands, a cloud of Darkness forming above him. Suddenly, the cloud fell to the ground, where twenty hollow-eyed Metim warriors appeared next to him.

Sam skidded to a halt, palms still outstretched. "ARE YOU AFRAID TO FIGHT ME?!" Sam yelled, his voice cracking.

The panting Metim turned and looked at their master, like dogs waiting for the word to attack. Arazel stared at the fearless boy standing in front of him, alone and vulnerable. He held up a hand to his warriors, motioning for them to stand down.

Then he walked forward a few paces, facing Sam.

"You have come to accept my offer," he said, his voice booming darkly.

Sam stared at the haunting green eyes, his focus thrown off momentarily. He fought to get it back. "NO! I told you, I will NEVER be what you want!"

Arazel held his gaze. "Samuel Forrester, you are destined for the Darkness—"

But Arazel didn't finish his sentence, because a perfectly thrown bolt had left Sam's hands and was heading directly for the Dark Lord's midsection.

Arazel blocked the bolt with the swipe of a hand, his eyes wide.

Sam sent another bolt, and then another, but Arazel blocked them easily without so much as moving his body.

"You cannot kill me, Samuel. You are not yet strong enough."

The anger escalated. Sam pointed a finger at the fallen Watcher in front of him. "YOU DON'T GET TO TELL ME ANYTHING!" he screamed, his body burning with rage.

Then something strange began taking him over, as if feeding the anger. Deep, powerful electricity crawled up within, fighting its way to the surface. It was raw, untamed power, and it felt good.

A potent arc of mixed blue and green electricity left his palms and rocketed toward the Dark Lord. Arazel attempted to avoid the blast, but was unable to escape it. The brunt of the blow scored his shoulder before ricocheting into the trees.

Arazel went down to his knees, a stunned expression of fear on his face. Returning to his feet, he retaliated, sending a cloud of Dark electricity toward Sam, who in the last moment blocked it with a shield.

He sent cloud after cloud, each hastily blocked by Sam.

Fury on his face, he stood once again and looked skyward. Instantly, a vortex of Darkness descended between them, a violent torrent of lightning exploding throughout its exterior.

It raced toward Sam at incredible speed. He attempted a shield to halt it in its path, but the tornado roared right through it. He sent bolt after bolt into the swirling mass, but nothing seemed to stop it. Just as it was about to engulf him, the vortex ripped apart violently, disbanding into the air.

Shocked, Sam looked around for his savior, but there was no one. Then he realized it was Arazel who stopped it.

Angry, he pummeled bolts at the Dark Lord, each with blinding speed. Each was blocked with no retaliation.

"FIGHT ME!" Sam screamed weakly. "WHY WON'T YOU KILL ME?!"

Straining, he attempted to form another arc like the first, but he was too weak. Pulling his sword from the sheath, Sam lunged at Arazel, swinging wildly. The hungry Metim poised for attack once again, but still no word came to defend the Dark Lord.

Every swing of the blade was met with an invisible force that stopped it before it could hit its target. Exhausted, Sam collapsed to the ground in front of Arazel.

"I will kill all of your friends if it will make you understand," he echoed softly. Then he spread his arms and motioned to the Metim, who still waited in the tree line.

In the same moment, a flash of Light crashed through the trees behind Sam, and then he was being dragged away by arms that held him fast. He struggled to get free, but his muscles wouldn't cooperate. Turning, all he could see were hoods on the strangers that carried him. At one point, one of them slipped a hand in his pocket and took the Star from him.

The next thing he heard were the doors of the tower being opened. They carried him inside and set him on the floor next to one of the columns of Lazuli Light.

Emma was crying, but he couldn't focus on her. Dazed, he stared into the light that pulsed its way up the column on the other side of the room.

Arazel had been right in front of him, and he had nearly killed him. If only his arc would have been slightly to the left, he thought.

Lillia slapped him, snapping him out of the daze.

"Where's my Star?" he muttered.

Five figures came and stood next to Sam, Lillia, and Gus. That made eight total in the room with him.

"You mean the glowing thing in this girly-looking bag? Right here, champ," the familiar voice said to Sam. He couldn't place its owner until he looked up at the tall boy with blond hair.

"Cestray," Sam recalled.

"The one and only," he said as he dropped Sam's satchel in his lap.

Sam looked at the others beside him. "Pestril, Yadris, Murray, Sayvon—how did you all get here?"

They looked at Sayvon, who shrugged in return. "When I found out what happened, I called a Ruasch and asked the Light to take me to you."

She smiled. "And it did."

Pestril pulled his hair back behind his robe, his Eben stone glowing prominently on his wrist. "Right timing too. You'd be dead by now."

"You all got your Eben stones." Sam said, glancing at the other's wrists.

They pulled back their sleeves and held them up for the others to see. Each was either white or grey, rippled with Lazuli blue. Each contained a vein of color, indicating the gift they had been chosen for.

Pestril's and Yadris's were yellow for a Bolt, Cestray's was white for a Magen, and Murray's red for a Seer.

Sam sat up slightly, watching them admire the Eben stones. Emma, Gus, and Lillia didn't have theirs. And it was Sam's fault.

Suddenly, Murray straightened and peered at the door. "They are closing in on the tower," he said.

Cestray and Lillia pressed their ears to the door, straining to listen. They watched Murray for Seer updates, but he could only shake his head. "They're blocking me somehow. I can't see anything now."

Sam attempted to open his own ability to see what Murray was seeing, but his head was swimming from the encounter with Arazel. Something had happened out there—something that shot fear through him when he thought about it.

It wasn't that he could produce an arc, but rather that it was the Darkness inside him that had produced it.

The potential to produce Darkness was inside of every Descendant, buried somewhere, always tempting its host to be used. It had called to him more than once. But being a Descendant was about learning how to suppress the Darkness, disciplining themselves to keep it under control.

He didn't want the Darkness. He thought he had done everything he could to avoid it. And the last thing he wanted was for it to affect him. But now it had.

He stood to his feet. *I have to get it together,* he thought. *This is not me. I am not that person.*

While the others waited by the door, Emma wiped her eyes and put her arms around him. "I am so sorry I didn't talk to you sooner," she began, forcing back the tears. "I knew you were going through something... It was obvious—and I chose to let it be."

He flinched at her touch, then allowed her to embrace him, his nerves easing from the warmth in her arms. "It's not your fault, 'Em. I'm just working through some stuff."

She hugged him tighter. "It's the anger, Sam. You can't let it control you. That's how the Darkness wins."

He turned away, watching the light dance across the symbols on the wall. "I can't help it. It just happens."

Then Gus turned and faced everyone. His face was white as a ghost.

Lillia saw it and rushed to his side. She grabbed his face in her hands. "What's wrong with you?"

Gus pulled away from her, staring at the satchel on the floor that contained the Stars. "I saw him," he stuttered, suddenly having difficulty breathing.

Lillia looked into his eyes. "Who? Gus—who?"

"The Dark One," he said, shaking. "I think he is coming."

Chapter Twenty-Four
The Shadow

When? Gus, are you sure?" Lillia said, holding Gus's face in her hands.

Gus didn't reply.

Yadris's expression tightened into a grimace. "We have to do something."

Sayvon turned away from the door, scribbling a Light scribe and tossing it into the air.

"Not going to work," Pestril told her. "We are too far. It'll just bounce off the canyons and disappear."

Gus nodded. "He's right."

Cestray ran his hands through his hair nervously. "Then what do we do? Isn't this thing supposed to be a weapon? Why can't we use it?"

They all looked at Sam.

Lillia snatched up the satchel. "Well, can we? We came all this way, didn't we? Maybe that's what we are supposed to do!"

Emma scowled. "No, we don't know what it does—"

Emma was interrupted by a massive explosion that rocked the tower, sending all of them to the ground.

BOOM! Another came.

Sam crawled over to Emma, yelling to her above the crashing sounds around them. "We can't stay here!"

Lillia called out behind them. "Sam! The weapon! Use the weapon!"

Sam's thoughts were still muddied from the interaction with Arazel. A small voice inside, however, became audible above the noise. It was faint, but clear.

You must fight. It told him.

Sam gazed into Emma's eyes. "We have to fight them," he told her.

She shook her head, mirroring his gaze. "We can hide in the trees!"

"It won't work. They will just hunt us down," he said.

"I can't do this," she said pleadingly. "I'm not ready."

He reached out and ran his palm across the side of her face.

"Trust me," he told her.

They stood, palms out, and motioned for the rest of them to stand up and join them. "We have to fight them!" Sam yelled to the others.

BOOM! Another explosion hit the tower.

Lillia stood, expression determined. "Use the weapon!"

Sam faced her, then reached out and took hold of her arm. "No. We can't," he told her firmly.

Lillia relaxed, her demeanor steadying. "Are you sure?"

He squeezed her arm. "No, but I think someone else is."

She looked at him, understanding the meaning. She gestured to his head. "That better be the good side talking to you," she said.

He nodded.

The others understood too, acknowledging Sam's decision not to use the tower.

"Get ready to fight!" Sayvon yelled to the group, who were gathering alongside Sam and Emma, their Eben stones glowing steadily.

Yadris looked at the tower shaking around them. "Creator help us."

Lillia held the satchel up to the inner door, which opened painfully slow. Pieces of the ceiling were falling around them now, some larger chunks landing dangerously close. Finally, they were able to slip through the door to the outer room, which was collapsing even quicker than the inner chamber.

"When I open the door, spread out and fight for your lives!" Lillia yelled.

As if in slow motion, Lillia held the satchel containing the Stars up to the door. It clicked and rumbled slowly inward, revealing the scene outside.

"Now!" she yelled.

The nine Descendant teens rushed out of the tower's entrance and down the stairs, running in all directions.

Arazel and the Metim warriors were still some distance off, the Dark Lord continuing to hold them back. But now, seeing the teens flee the tower, he gave the word for them to attack.

Then he concentrated back on the front of the tower, casting cloud bursts of Darkness toward the structure like mammoth cannonballs of electricity.

Sam fought the urge to charge Arazel again and chose instead to stay with Emma, Gus, and Lillia as they waited for the Metim warriors to come within range.

They readied themselves in the formation that their Mentors had taught them. Lillia and Sam stood out front to prepare the first bolts, and Emma readied her shield. Gus stood behind them, attempting to See and relay events as they happened.

The Metim nearest Sayvon's team came into range first. Pestril and Yadris commenced throwing bolts at the gruesome creatures as they ran, the streaks of Light zipping across the clearing.

"Bolts ready!" Lillia called when the next wave of Metim reached the one-hundred-meter mark, charging at the second team.

"Shield ready!" Emma called shakily from behind them.

"Seer ready!" Gus called.

At the fifty-meter mark, Lillia and Sam opened up on the six

creatures advancing first, throwing brilliant bolts of deadly Light at their targets.

Two of the hollow-eyed creatures were hit directly by a bolt, their bodies crumpling immediately to the ground. Four more continued their attack, evading every strike hurtling at them.

Suddenly, two beams of Light struck the ground directly in front of the four remaining Metim, momentarily throwing them off their focus. Disoriented, the Dark beasts stumbled and blinked as though they had been blinded. This gave Sam and Lillia a chance to send bolts through two more of them.

The last two charged in unison, bearing their foul teeth in rage for what happened to their fallen comrades.

Sam drew his sword, ready for the last two. Lillia continued throwing bolts, neither of them noticing the four Metim to their left bearing down on them from the trees.

"Left!" Gus called, beginning his assault on the sneak attackers who were less than fifty meters away.

Emma closed her eyes, lifting her hands above her head. Light poured from her palms onto the ground, morphing into great predators that attacked the Metim as soon as they became visible. The Metim warriors held up their own deformed hands, meeting the Light creatures with their own wall of Darkness and enveloping them in the thick fog. But Emma's Light manipulation had become extremely adept, and the creatures punched right through the wall, ripping the surprised Metim warriors to pieces.

The two other warriors, both injured from Sam and Lillia's bolts, bore down on them, hurling their bodies forward at full speed. Sword ready, Sam stepped forward and sliced at one of them, taking off an arm. It spun and lunged at him but fell to the ground instantly, as Lillia had thrown a bolt through his neck.

Seeing the fallen warrior next to him, the panting Metim turned on his heels and ran away, aiming for the trees. Lillia lifted her palm to fire a bolt at him, but Emma stopped her.

"Stop! Let it go!" she hollered.

Sayvon's group rejoined theirs, having stopped the Metim warriors that had attacked them as well. But no one cheered from their victory.

Arazel was still there. And he was laughing.

"If we work together, we could take him," Cestray said, dusting off his pants.

Yadris pointed off into the trees above Arazel. "No, we can't."

A Dark cloud had silently begun to make its way through the canyon behind the Dark Lord. Electricity sparked dangerously throughout the evil front, the whole of the Dark mass spanning as wide as the canyon itself.

They stood and watched in terror as the front settled over Arazel, dropping tendrils of murky Darkness to the ground, where hundreds more Metim warriors melted from out of them.

Then, mid-center of the front, a haunting pillar of green light descended to the ground beside Arazel.

The eight Descendant teens fearfully gaped at the figure within the beam as the cloud receded. He appeared to be young and had a strikingly perfect physique. He wore a sheer white robe and carried a gleaming golden sword.

"Kachash," Gus said quietly.

The others turned to him in alarm.

Lillia's eyes widened. "Like as in, the Lord of Deception?"

He nodded. "The one and only."

"I think it's time we make our exit," Murray stuttered, looking to Sayvon to call another Ruasch.

The others agreed, quickly crowding into a tight group to make ready for the cloud of Light to appear. But once again, as Emma had trouble calling in a Ruasch, Sayvon did too.

"The Darkness must be blocking me," she announced in horror.

Emma threw her own hands up, closing her eyes. After several moments, she put her hands back down, shaking her head. "It's still not working for me, either."

"We're trapped," Sayvon said.

The Shadow

****

They stared at the army of Dark warriors before them, knowing there was no escape. Sheer rock walls flanked both sides of them, which meant climbing out of the canyon was almost impossible. And, if another exit out of the valley existed somewhere, they hadn't found it. The only other option, hiding in the forest, meant they would be hunted down like animals, one by one.

They would have to fight.

Sam glanced at the sky above him. *Nuriel, where are you?*

Anger burned within him at the name. This had been part Nuriel's doing. None of them would be out here if he hadn't destroyed that village. Now he would be responsible for their deaths, as well.

Mentorship school had taught them to control their emotions, especially on the battlefield. But none of them expected that something like this would happen so soon after. Still, everyone in the group held their composure the best they could. They may be but a few inexperienced Descendants of Light against an army of Darkness, but none of them were going to go down without a fight.

Without a word, they stepped forward, together, hand in hand, toward the Dark army. As they walked, Sam began digging deep within, searching for the power he had summoned once before. The one that had nearly killed Arazel. Could it be that since he was the son of a Watcher, he could summon incredible power? Enough to save them all?

There were so many. There was no way.

Then there was the anger. He could use that. It had been easy to access, even easier to use. It felt almost a part of him now.

No. Not who I am.

He fixed his gaze on Arazel, ignoring Kachash. Arazel stared back at him, not with contempt, but amazingly, with respect. His green eyes gleamed, and he seemed to be almost nodding his head in approval.

Hatred stirred within Sam. *Does he really believe I am coming to join him? To join the Darkness? No one is that ignorant.*

Chapter Twenty-Four

But if Arazel wanted war, he was going to get it.

They stopped fifty meters short of the two Dark Lords and the army of Metim. Lillia's hand was sweating profusely, so he let go and stepped forward in front of the group. He didn't care who this Kachash guy was. He wanted to talk to Arazel.

"You are brave, walking up to a Lord," Kachash said giddily, his robe flowing as he spoke animatedly. "Such fortitude. Did you learn that from your father?"

Sam refused to acknowledge him, his eyes still on Arazel. "Where is my mother, Arazel?!" Sam called across the stillness of the battlefield.

Arazel didn't answer, but Kachash seemed to enjoy the question immensely. "Is that what this is about, dear boy?" he laughed loudly, his voice echoing off the canyon walls. "You are angry because you think he has your mother? What a pathetic existence you have! I am sorry to inform you that she is dead, along with the other peasants of that miserable village!"

Sam broke the gaze and looked at Kachash. His face was pure white, almost too perfect. And his eyes glistened as though they had glitter on them.

"How do you know?" Sam yelled, the rage surging inside him.

Kachash laughed wickedly. Then he lowered his voice. "Because, dear Samuel, I sent Nuriel to kill her."

Sam's blood burned hot, his face flush and deep red. The anger was just beneath the surface. "MY FATHER WOULD NEVER DO THAT!" he screamed at Kachash, astounding even him.

He drew back, snatching the sides of his robe and pulling them together, as though he attempted to cover himself. Controlling his own anger, he forced a smile back to his face.

"Oh, then, you don't truly know your father, do you?" The Dark Lord said, glancing at Arazel. "You haven't told him yet, have you?"

Arazel lowered his gaze, refusing to speak.

Sam was irritated. He was tired of listening to this half-naked man.

Sam glared at Kachash. "Why should I care what you say?"

"YOU DARE TALK TO ME LIKE THAT?!" Kachash's fury

suddenly got the best of him, electricity surging throughout his body. But again he forced it down, taking a deep breath. "It's expected, such a young child so naïve…"

"Sam," a voice said softly from behind.

It was Emma.

Sam ignored it, his attention now focused on Kachash, the Lord dominating the confrontation.

"ANSWER ME!" Kachash yelled at Sam. "How well do you *know* him?"

Sam didn't respond.

Kachash laughed again, rubbing his hands together in glee. Then he turned to Arazel. "You really do have a fondness for these Descendants, do you not?"

Arazel was quiet.

Sam broke his silence. "Arazel, what's he talking about?"

"Sam, please," Emma whispered behind him.

Thunder rumbled long and low from behind the Dark Lords, resounding throughout the canyon.

Kachash let his robe flow freely in the breeze that accompanied the ominous front, his skin glistening with each flash of lightning.

"You cannot deny the irony is fascinating," he hissed, peering at Arazel, "that your only child is a follower of the Light?"

The thought shot through Sam like a bullet. What did he mean?

"Samael, the destined one to become second to the Dark One, is the son of Arazel, the Shadow Lord of Lior?"

Arazel nodded. He looked upward, centered his gaze upon Sam.

"I cannot deny he is my child."

"LIES!" Sam yelled at Kachash, who simply laughed as the thunder grumbled above them.

Sam felt the anger swell further. His eyes began to blur as thoughts rushed through his mind. There was no way this foul creature was his father. Nuriel had told him just last year he was his father… and Sam had *felt* the connection. The Shadow Lord… Was Arazel the Shadow that would call to him?

"SAM!" Emma called again, but he couldn't hear her. His body coursed with anger, the green light flooding his vision.

"I will kill you," he growled at Kachash.

The Dark Lord raised his hands, Darkness flowing through his fingers. "You are smitten with rage, follower of the Light. You must learn to control it before you can hope to kill a Lord."

He hissed again. "There are many dead at my feet that have spoken to me with more respect than you."

Sam raised his palms to the Dark Lord, tendrils of Darkness sprouting from his fingertips. The rage was intoxicating.

"I may not have the authority to kill you, follower, but I do, however, have permission to destroy your friends," Kachash spat.

As the bolt of green electricity left Sam's palms, so too did a piercing spear of Darkness leave Kachash's.

In that same moment, Emma produced a powerful shield that covered the entire group. But the shield was a second too late, for the spear had already met its intended target.

Yadris lay dead on the ground, a darkened hole through her midsection.

Chapter Twenty-Five
Dark Forces

There was screaming, and then they ran, Sayvon and Pestril carrying Yadris away from the army of Metim. Away from Arazel and Kachash.

Emma held the shield behind them as they ran back toward the tower. There was no plan, only to get away.

One of them was dead.

A shout ripped through the air behind them, and then the Metim were released. They had one order—kill all, but save one.

The sky darkened further as they ran, the lightning strobing a sinister green on the tower's exterior.

They slowed as the adrenaline gave way to exhaustion, and the Metim gained on them. Carrying a limp body was difficult, even after switching carriers. They would not make it to the tower before being overtaken.

The ground shook as the army closed in on them, drowning out the thunder from the storm overhead. Sam frantically looked for something that could save them but couldn't think straight. His head throbbed, and his eyes burned in their sockets. He was about to turn and face the army alone, knowing that he could kill off quite a few of them before they would get to his friends, but something up ahead stopped him—and the rest of the group—in their tracks.

Brilliant beams of blue began streaking across the sky, coring holes through the storm front and striking the ground with incredible force. From each of the beams of light flowed hundreds of Light creatures of all kinds and sizes. In a few great leaps, they were tearing into the first of the Metim army, ripping into their bodies and rendering them lifeless on the ground.

Then four great Light clouds punched their way through the storm and hovered over the battlefield. Light warriors dropped from the clouds, separating the group of teens from the Metim army.

Two of the warriors rushed to the young Descendants, throwing blasts of Light that blended into one brilliant shield over the retreating group.

Five more Light warriors banded together in a circle, palms outstretched toward one another. Light pulsed in a circular motion between their hands, moving faster and growing brighter until its intensity was too strong to watch. With one motion, the warriors sent the ring of Light through the oncoming army of Metim, where it plowed through the soulless bodies, slicing them in half.

Behind them, a mix of putrid green and thick Darkness prevailed in the sky, allowing only a small window of moonlight to pour onto the battlefield. Out of the corner of his eye, Sam watched two large-winged bodies making their way through the opening toward them. The dragons swooped down quickly on the warriors of Light, scattering them. Torrents of fire ripped through them as they fought to throw up shields against the creatures.

The army of Metim, momentarily slowed from the warriors' arrival and fierce onslaught, now advanced once again. The warriors fought bravely on two fronts, casting powerful arcs and countless Light creatures on the Dark forces.

Sam and Lillia attempted to veer from the group and join the battle, but the warriors quickly reined them back under the shield.

"LET US HELP THEM!" Sam screamed at the stout warrior with the short, dark hair and searing eyes.

The Light forces were losing ground, the toll of the dragons taking effect. The warriors protecting them never acknowledged Sam or Lillia's request, only held fast to the powerful shield over them.

"HELP THEM!" Lillia joined him in pleading with the warriors.

The taller warrior with the blond eyebrows glanced at his partner questioningly. The dragons were getting dangerously close.

Suddenly, another powerful blast of Light burst through the Dark-filled sky. Seven dragons erupted from out of the murky front, led by Orono. Each deposited something on the battlefield, then roared after the two attacking dragons above.

From each of the deposits sprung a machine of strange design, each a tank-like vehicle with what looked like an enormous cannon on the front.

More Ruasches arrived, each filled with more warriors joining the fight. Included in them were most of the Mentors from Helel Malach and Talister Calpher.

From another of the Light clouds, Amos, the Sterlings, Farmers, Sarah Karpatch, and Henry Bostwick descended to the dusty ground. Immediately they rushed to the teens, Mrs. Sterling and Mrs. Farmer joining in the aid of protecting of the young Descendants. Sarah, Henry, Mr. Sterling, and Mr. Farmer scattered to help the Light forces.

The strange machines roared ahead, their cannons belching powerful rounds of Lazuli into the middle of the Metim, exploding upon impact and scattering their ranks. Lillia, who watched the machines, pointed at one of them.

"Boggle! I knew he would finish those things!" she shouted above the sounds of war. And certain enough, the machines had Boggle's handiwork all over them.

As the battle raged on below, the clash with the dragons intensified. The two dragons who had turned Dark refused to give up without a fight. Fire spewed everywhere, the two Dark dragons managing to take down two of their enemies before plunging in a fiery heap into the trees.

Once they were defeated, Orono led the fight to the remaining Metim. With the dragons out of the way, the warriors of Light closed in on the dwindling ranks of the Metim, until at last the call went up for the Dark forces to make a hasty retreat.

A few moments later, the battlefield grew strangely still. The Light forces used the opportunity to regroup and wait for their enemy's next move.

The warriors guarding the youths let their shields fade. Sayvon ran to Yadris's side. "YOU HAVE TO SAVE HER!" she screamed.

Two healers rushed to tend to the girl's body. One of them lifted his arms up in the air, where a small but steady stream of Light made its way down from the exposed Light high above. It drifted down through his hands and into Yadris's body. The other healer held his palms over her chest and head, whispering softly in the ancient tongue.

The others gathered around Sayvon as she stood to let the healers work. Emma pulled her close as she wept uncontrollably.

Several more moments passed. Finally, the healer who tended to Yadris stood, a look of sadness on his face. "I'm sorry," He said sadly. "We are too late."

Sayvon sobbed and clung to Emma. The other teens surrounded them, each of them trying to hold back the tears.

****

"Children, I am so sorry for your loss." Mr. Sterling addressed them as they watched some warriors carry Yadris's body away.

"Thank you, sir." Sayvon replied, attempting to wipe the constant flow of tears from her eyes. "I know she is with the Creator now."

Mr. Sterling drew Sayvon and his daughter in for a hug. "You don't know just how wonderful of a place that is."

He smiled, then wiped a tear from his own cheek. "She is part of the remembered now, and forever she will be in our hearts."

Others gathered around as Mr. Sterling led them in a short prayer. He prayed loudly, as though he was unapologetic if the Dark forces were to hear him.

"Fear not, Follower of the Light, you are now beside the Creator, as He continues to watch over us as we fight the Darkness," Mr. Sterling prayed.

"For as we remain, we continue the battle that you have so bravely fought, and are now victorious. Yadris, Descendant, Follower of the Creator, we release you into His presence."

When he finished, Sam looked up to see all the warriors of Light on their knees, heads bowed.

****

"We were unsure of the tower's existence until now." Mr. Sterling patted Henry on the back as the warriors began to regroup. "Thanks to Henry, we finally came around to see the truth."

"We still don't know what it does," Gus told them. "I haven't had time to read any of the symbols inside."

Mr. Sterling looked at Henry, who merely shrugged. "I wish I had more to tell you, but the tower's purpose has been incredibly speculative in nature."

"That's step two," Mrs. Sterling said forcefully. "Step one is getting these kids back to safety."

"Agreed," Mr. Farmer said, nodding. "Once the Dark forces exit the canyon, we can begin removal of the Darkness. That'll allow us to call the Ruasches back."

He glanced toward Gus, who was obviously showing great concern that his parents were not present. "Oh, Gus, not to worry, chap. Your parents were able to get out of town before any of this ever happened. They went to see your aunt Mildred in Yorkshire for a spell."

"A good thing they did, too. But they send their greetings and will get here as soon as they can," Mr. Sterling added.

"Dad, how did you all get here?" Emma asked.

He smiled at his daughter. "By the skin of our teeth, I believe. We managed to make it up to the Vestrahorn gate in Iceland."

A young Light warrior stepped up to Mr. Sterling. "Sir, the Metim are regrouping. Would you like to advance on them?"

He shook his head. "Not yet. I am uncertain their plan involves any more fighting today. Best let them tend their wounded and crawl back to the swamps."

The young warrior nodded. "And ours, sir?"

"How many?" Mr. Sterling asked solemnly.

"Fourteen dead, forty injured."

"Take them to the tower. Set up camp just outside the trees. We will have to get them out when we can reestablish the Light in the canyon."

The warrior left to spread the word, passing Talister as he joined the Sterlings and Farmers around the teens.

"I am glad to see all of you well," Talister said.

He glanced at his daughter, who was still crying. "What happened?"

They filled him in, his eyes empathizing with their pain as they told the story.

"Kachash, you say?" He said, gathering Sayvon in his arms.

Gus nodded. "He was here."

He whistled low. "Better not count them out just yet. Kachash isn't one to give up easily."

"Then what are they doing?" Sam said, struggling to control the anger.

Mr. Sterling peered at him, looking him up and down. Then he turned back to Talister. "I'm not sure. They may not have the forces to attack directly, but—"

"What about the Dark One?" Lillia interrupted, instantly drawing the entire group's attention onto her.

"What do you mean, the Dark One?" Mrs. Sterling whispered, her voice hushed.

Lillia turned away. "Gus saw him. Said he was coming."

Mr. Sterling grabbed Gus's shoulder. "Son, are you sure you saw him and not Kachash?"

Gus shook his head, the blood draining from his face. "I'm sure. I had a vision. It was him."

"I don't think you would be able to See him unless…" Talister began.

"… he was in Lior," Amos added gravely.

A great thunderclap pounded the canyon walls, the lightning that followed tearing through the cloud and striking the ground repeatedly.

The battle was far from over.

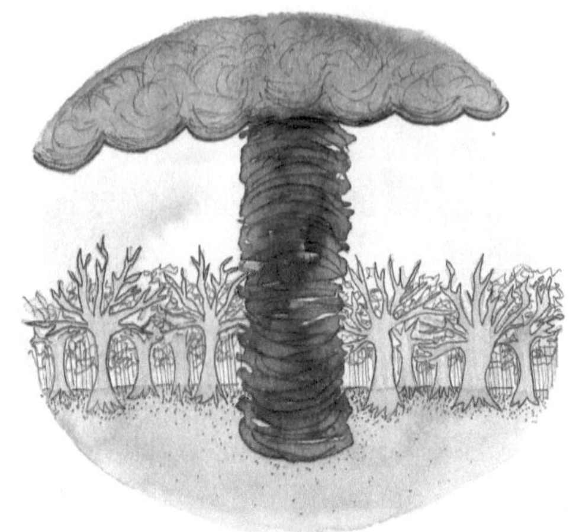

Chapter Twenty-Six
The Star

Jack, we need to get these kids—and everyone—out of here. We are not equipped for that confrontation yet," Mrs. Sterling said with urgency.

Mr. Sterling looked stricken. He still wasn't sure he believed Gus, but he would not take any chances, either. Lior had been ready for the return of the Dark One, but not this soon. Not here.

Finally, he regained his composure, though he was unable to hide the alarm from his voice. "All of us need to fall back to the tower. As soon as we can clear the area, we will work on getting everyone out of here."

The withdrawal went quickly. Warriors, dragons, and Boggle's vehicles all retreated toward the dark tower, converging near its base. Orono landed close to Sam and the others, so he, Gus, Emma, and Lillia took the chance to go over to him. He was easily the largest of the dragons there, and perhaps the most beautiful.

And now they knew he was one of the fiercest. It had been Orono

who had retrieved the other dragons to help fight for them, and he had also been instrumental in turning the tide of the battle.

When all the Light forces were finally stationed near the tower, Sam gathered his pack from where he left it near the tower's entrance. His head pounding, he noticed the satchel containing the Stars and retrieved them as well. Reaching inside, he picked up both Stars, examining them. The one still glowed faintly while the other remained lifeless.

As he studied them, a curious thing happened, startling him. The fake one began to glow, even as he held it in his hand. It began softly, then brightened, quickly outpacing the glow of the other Star. Soon it illuminated the interior of the satchel.

Another crack of thunder sounded through the canyon. A chill ran up Sam's spine. Something inside of him aroused once again.

Turning, he peered onto the battlefield where the hundreds of dead Metim still lay. Something was stirring among them.

One rock lifted from the ground, then another, and still another. More joined them, gathering into a whirlwind of dust and rock. It moved among the dead, throwing bodies from its path. As it reached the middle of the battlefield, the whirlwind stopped.

Unable to move, Sam watched the whirlwind grow into a swirling mass of Darkness as it sucked more energy into itself. Then, faces began to emerge from the spinning mass.

Samael, the hollow faces whispered.

It was like they were calling to him from inside his head. The feeling was overwhelming. He let them in, basking in their euphoria.

Then the mass evolved. It grew wider, spilling Darkness across the ground like a fog in an early morning swamp. At its head, the thick smoke billowed away from itself, and then morphed into something—a shape.

Samael, it whispered again. It was almost inaudible but sounded like glass breaking in his head.

It called to him, beckoning. *Come.*

# Chapter Twenty-Six

Something inside was fighting for control of him. Like two caged animals in a death match for survival. One side was winning.

Come.

Automatically, Sam withdrew the Star that once had shown no sign of life, now blazing vigorously in his hand.

He began walking toward the morphing cloud of Darkness, which began to take the shape of a monstrous horned dragon.

Sam continued forward, watching the dragon's eyes turn blood red as it faced him.

Hearing voices shouting behind him, he broke into a run. No one was going to stop him. Everything inside told him that the dragon had the answers.

Light speared the ground at his feet as the Descendants threw bolts near him, attempting to get his attention. Senses heightened, he watched them leave the warrior's palms behind him, and saw the bolts before they struck. He evaded them easily, his focused trained on the Dark beast in front of him.

He skidded to a halt in front of the dragon. Sam watched it transform once again, back into a massive cloud of Darkness, then into the figure of a man.

The lightning above revealed the details of the figure for only a split second. His eyes were like dark red rubies laced with charcoal veins, his skin a deathly tone of grey and black, which crawled like liquid over his body. He wore a tattered grey robe that flapped in the wind around his legs.

The man held out his arms, as though he were expecting an embrace.

Sam stood in front of him, his heart thudding loudly. The inescapable intoxicating feeling seemed to emanate from him, like the origins of an inconceivable force, draped in a celestial form. The power resonated through Sam, and he immersed himself in the feeling, letting it creep into every corner of his being. It was cold and empty, void of any Light. But it was vigorous and raw power. He desired for it to consume him fully.

The Star

The man reached out, his skin rippling like water on a drum. Sam gazed into his eyes, knowing exactly what he wanted. Reaching into his pocket, he drew out the Star, holding it out to him.

Off his palm it floated, shining brighter than Sam had ever seen. When it reached him, he withdrew a sword from the Darkness that encompassed him and placed the Star in its hilt.

****

The man turned to face the remains of the Metim army before him, and Arazel and Kachash. He lifted his arms up, Darkness springing from his fingertips in all directions, each drilling into the body of a Metim laying on the battlefield. Slowly, the dead Metim began to convulse violently, their bodies twisting on the ground. Then, all at once, they rose to their feet, fully restored.

With a voice that sounded like whispering thunder, he called out something in the ancient tongue, and the ground began to rumble at Sam's feet. In front of him, more Dark creatures emerged from the surface as though they had crawled their way through the dirt from deep below.

The creatures were not unlike the Metim, yet carried some of the same features as their master. Their skin rippled like fluid, and their eyes bore the same deep red color, laced with an aura of pure evil. Standing at full height, they were nearly twice as tall as the other Metim warriors, and each carried a sword half the length of their body.

Sam felt a presence behind him, indicating he wasn't alone on the battlefield with the Dark warriors any longer.

Stealing a glance, he found the entire Descendant army standing to his rear, ready to engage the new enemy. All of his friends were there, including the Sterlings, Farmers, Sarah Karpatch, and Talister. Emma, Gus, and Lillia stood among them.

They screamed to him, but their words were lost in the Darkness. What were they saying?

It was as though a great wall of distorted glass stood between them, like a veil separating two worlds.

BEHOLD YOUR LORD.

The thunderous whisper ripped through his mind. The dragon-man faced his new army, arms still outstretched.

Stillness filled the air as thousands of resurrected Dark creatures knelt before him, bowing their faces into the dirt. For several moments, they lay prostrate in deathly silence.

He removed his robe, letting it fall to the dirt, his gaze centering on Kachash. "Your god requires clothing."

Kachash hesitated, terrified. Then he removed his own robe and hurried to his master. Shuddering, he placed it on the man's shoulders.

"Kachash, Lord of Deception," the man thundered.

"My Lord."

"You have done well for yourself. Who is your disciple?"

Before Kachash could answer, Arazel stepped up beside him, his head still bowed in respect. "Lord, I am Arazel, Shadow Lord of Lior."

His eyes flickered to Arazel. "And have you proven yourself, Arazel, Shadow Lord of Lior?"

Arazel glanced at Sam, sending a chill up his spine as he spoke. "I have, my Lord. An entire Outsiders village."

The man nodded approvingly. "A necessary sacrifice for the preservation of the light."

He returned his gaze to Kachash. "You have done well, servant, leading the Descendants to the tower where they can be slaughtered like sheep in the canyon. A just reward awaits you."

Sam could hear the voices behind him, but he still couldn't make out the words. Behind the invisible veil, they called his name.

His mind raged with thoughts he couldn't control. Images he couldn't shake. A world led with power rather than freedom. A rigid system where all followed the same lord, whether they chose to or not. Order, not chaos. Where those who were pious were rewarded, and those who rebelled would suffer until they complied.

Freedom only paved the way for rebellion. It was borne out of

weakness and tolerance. Allowing mankind and Descendant to choose would only lead to destruction.

My heir. My son. Come.

Arazel called to him in the fog of his mind. His father, the Shadow, was calling to him.

Samael, come.

He blocked out the shouts from the other side of the veil behind him. He took a step forward, then another.

A tiny surge of warmth crept up through his finger and into his hand as he brushed against the satchel. The jarring warmth broke his concentration suddenly. Glancing down, he peered at the Star Boggle gave to them. It was glowing brighter than before.

He stopped, puzzled. Opening the satchel, he reached in to touch the Star. It smoldered with Light, and another surge of warmth crept through his hand. Why did it glow so brightly now when it hadn't before?

The Darkness beckoned to him, reminding him of his purpose.

The Star was now blinding, but he kept his gaze upon it, ignoring the Darkness enveloping him. He could see inside of the Star's interior, now, through the metallic shell. There was a figure, a woman, and she was saying something to him. What was it?

He grasped the Star, holding it before him, feeling the full force of the warmth enter his body. He looked closer at the woman—was it his mother? No—she was much younger.

"You can still choose," the woman mouthed from inside the Star.

Sam felt the Darkness fighting for control over him. It clawed at his insides, desperate to destroy the Light. The Light, steady and persistent, held its own against the compelling evil.

You can still choose.

He let the warm Light in further. The anger receded.

"I can still choose," he whispered.

The anger lashed out vengefully, attempting another grip on his mind. But he forced it back down, allowing the Light to aid him.

"I choose Light," he breathed. Then louder, he yelled, "I CHOOSE LIGHT!"

Noises began to flutter past his eardrums. Shouting, screaming, like people in immense pain. They swelled louder suddenly, then faded away...

****

"Sam."

It was Lillia's voice, calling to him through the noise. Turning, he watched her through the shroud of Darkness stretching across the battlefield. A thin tunnel had burrowed its way through, allowing him to see her. Emma, Gus, and Sayvon were there too, calling his name, but he couldn't hear them. He could only hear Lillia.

Intuitively, he ran toward her. Through the tunnel of Darkness connecting them.

Dark faces shrieked at him from the tunnel walls as he ran, but he ignored them, keeping his eyes on Lillia. He was almost through.

Reaching out, he grasped for her hand, and she took hold of his, pulling him through the tunnel the rest of the way. With a thunderous roar, the shroud broke loose of him, and he fell to the ground on the other side. Then he closed his eyes.

When he opened them again, Emma was holding him tightly. His friends surrounded him protectively. Lillia was touching his head, whispering something inaudibly.

He sat up, taking in the scene. Sounds of battle preparations filled his ears. To his right and left were hundreds of Light warriors, taking up defensive positions against the thick black cloud of Darkness that separated the two armies. Mentor Wenthrow stood in front of him, worry on her face.

"How do you feel, Samuel?" she asked.

"Help me stand up," he asked Cestray and Gus, who stood on either side of him.

As they helped him, his head began to spin. Closing his eyes, he

waited for the spinning to subside, then opened them again. "I'm okay, Mentor."

Looking down, he noticed the satchel was gone. Opening his hand, however, he saw that the Star still remained in his grasp.

There were hushed awes from everyone around him.

Gus, who had been holding him steady, now let go to get a closer look. "It's incredibly lambent!" he exclaimed.

Lillia shook her head. "Gus—what?"

"Sorry. It means really bright," he said sheepishly.

Henry, who was among the others, now pushed his way through the crowd surrounding Sam. "May I see that, Samuel?" he asked excitedly.

Sam handed him the Star, the warmth going along with it. The veil of Darkness behind him now began tugging at him once again. Fortunately, it was but a fraction of what it had been.

"Astounding!" Henry exclaimed, turning the brilliant object over in his hands. "This is a *Merkoh*, I believe…"

"What is that?" Cestray asked.

"It's believed that it's the source of power of the celestial, the origin of all Light, contained in a tiny orb."

Mr. Sterling and Talister had joined the conversation upon hearing Henry's description. Talister pointed at the Star. "You mean the power to control the Light, inside of there?"

"It's believed so, *yes*," Henry nodded. "But we must understand that these are celestial objects, and what is known about them is very limited. The Watchers have always been very secretive with their information—and with their ancient artifacts."

"Boggle said they were a sort of activation device to the towers." Sam said, his voice cracking.

Henry nodded. "Yes, and much more. But very little was known about them, and that was before we lost the records at the Old City."

"He has one." Sam said, remembering the account with the Dark One. "He put it in his sword."

Solemn looks filtered around the group.

Talister held his hand out, taking the Star from Henry. "Best to keep this one safe. Once the Darkness is lifted and we can call a Ruasch, I'll make sure it gets to the archives."

Just then, a young Light warrior ran up to Jack Sterling, worry on his face. "Sir, the wall of Darkness is fading."

Jack looked at the warriors lined up along the wall of Darkness. "Alert the Sons and prepare the Protectors. We don't know what to expect on the other side when it drops," he told him. Immediately, the warrior was off, barking orders to the forces of Light.

Sam and the others watched the wall of Darkness intently. It was hard to tell, but it did appear to be shrinking.

"Stand your ground when it drops!" Jack Sterling called along the lines of warriors.

For the first time, Sam got a good look at who had been fighting next to him. Men and women warriors from all four regions of Lior, wearing robes of their respective hall colors. Some carried swords, some staffs, and others carried nothing. They stood ready, palms outstretched. Staffs and swords were in defensive positions.

Mrs. Sterling and the Farmers wanted to hurry the teens to safety, but to their dismay, none of them would have it. They had gone through Mentorship, and now they were warriors. No one was going to pry them away from helping to defeat the Darkness.

Emma stood beside Sam, gazing at him thoughtfully as the veil of Darkness receded. "I always knew you were fighting harder than all of us," she said quietly. "You shouldn't be ashamed of what happened."

He glanced at her, blinking. He didn't know how to respond. Truthfully, he was ashamed. Ashamed of a lot of things. Leaving the school alone, not tell them where he was going…

And the anger. Giving into the Darkness…

But he had been given a choice, and he had chosen. Someone had called to him within the Star, and he had heard her. Now it was time to stand against the Darkness with the rest of them.

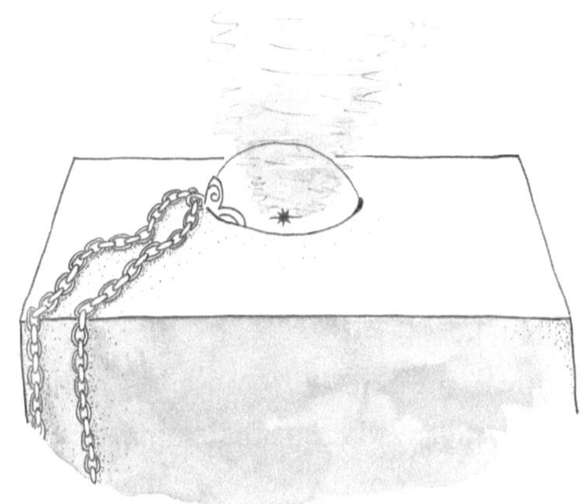

Chapter Twenty-Seven
Confrontation

They waited in apprehension as the wall of Darkness faded away, displaying the vast forces stretched out across the canyon. Kachash and Arazel stood beside the Dark One in the center of the revived army.

The Light forces stood resolute, their numbers dwarfed in comparison to the immense threat poised before them. The dragons had taken to the air and were circling the battlefield, waiting for Orono to bid them to fight.

Jack Sterling stood next to Talister, in front, waiting for someone to make the first move.

Sword at his side, the Dark One stepped forward, his rippling form changing once again. His body took on that of a man, with shoulder-length sandy hair and golden skin. The only thing that remained of his previous form was the charcoal-veined glowing red eyes.

The Dark One spoke in the ancient tongue. Mr. Farmer translated for them.

"Descendants, I was once of the Light as you were," he began, his voice sizzling like electricity throughout the canyon. "Bound by the confines of the Light, forced to walk in the shadows of the Creator like you do now."

Lightning ripped across the sky behind him. "But the Light cannot offer what I propose to you today—and that is the freedom to live. To exit this canyon unharmed and return to your homes and families, whole, and unscathed."

He extended his arms out in front of him. "You will not receive another invitation such as this."

Sam looked down the line of hundreds of Light warriors, who hadn't budged following the Dark One's ominous offer. After a few tense moments, Talister responded to him, again in the ancient tongue.

"You have no authority here, Nasikh, Lord of Darkness! Your banishment may have been lifted, but the powers of the Light remain intact!"

Then he paused, adding a final grim warning. "If bloodshed is what is required to remove you from Lior, then bloodshed is what you will receive!"

The Dark One stared contemptuously at Talister. Then he drew the gleaming sword from under his robe. The Star glowed brightly in its hilt.

He brought the sword up, pointed directly at Talister. "Then the ancient war has been rekindled."

Deathly silence filled the air as the forces of Light waited for the first strike.

Instead, from the air above them, a powerful beam of Lazuli Light illuminated the middle of the confrontation, and fourteen figures surfaced between the two armies. Among the figures stood Nuriel, his staff gripped in his hands.

Kachash, surprised at Nuriel's appearance, stepped forward, pointing a glimmering finger at Nuriel. "You have violated your agreement to submit yourself to me!" he roared. "You submitted yourself to the Darkness! To *me*! By ancient law, you are to be killed!"

With incredible speed, a whip of pure Light flashed from Nuriel's

palm, wrapping around Kachash's neck and pinning him to the dusty ground.

Then Nuriel faced Nasikh. He spoke forcefully in a strange language, like a combination of wind and thunder that swirled about the canyon. Surprised, the Dark One peered at him, clearly disturbed at his words.

"You were dead!" he hissed. "By my hand, you were slain!"

"The Light is very forgiving. You of all should know that," Nuriel said quietly, a sadness on his face. Then, out of the corner of his eye, he glanced at Sam. As their eyes met, Nuriel nodded toward the Star, which was still in Talister's possession.

Nasikh responded angrily in the unknown language, his golden skin rippling in phases of Darkness as he spoke. Sam was sure he saw the dragon's form bursting through a time or two. Nuriel listened quietly, refusing to take his eyes off of him.

Sam knew what Nuriel wanted him to do. Strangely, even after being lied to, he trusted Nuriel, recognizing that his intentions were true.

Moving silently from his spot, Sam maneuvered himself through the warriors to where he could be directly behind Talister. Reaching into his robe pocket, he took out the Star in his hand, covering its glow so it couldn't be seen.

Emma, who had just noticed what he was doing, grabbed his arm as he retreated back within the crowd of Light warriors. "What are you doing?" she whispered.

"Come on. We need to get to the tower," he whispered back, grabbing her hand and dragging her through the crowded battlefield.

When they reached the rear of the army, they sprinted to the tree line that ran alongside of the open field near the tower. Behind, they could still hear the thunderous wind of the two Watchers speaking heatedly in the strange language.

At the tower's entrance, Sam held the Star up to the door, which clicked and grumbled open. They slipped past the door and proceeded to the second entrance. Once inside the tower's interior, the pedestal lifted up from the floor and came to rest, the hole at the top opening, ready to receive the Star.

"Are you sure?" she whispered, her words echoing off the tower's walls.

"No. I'm not sure," he said, shrugging. "I have no idea, in fact. I'm just guessing at this point." Sam placed the glowing orb into the orifice and then stood back to await the result.

At first, nothing happened, then the Star changed color. Deep red engulfed the entire Star, which expanded into a hazy cloud up into the air from the pedestal. Quickly, the cloud rose to the tower's ceiling, where it mixed with the Lazuli blue to create a red hue. Then it sprung out from the tower above, the inside ceiling of the tower rumbling suddenly in a deep humming rhythmic pattern.

Sam and Emma ran through the now open doors back to the field outside, where an unbelievable sight beheld them. A mighty shield of Lazuli hung over the entire army of Light warriors. Outside of it stood Nuriel, palms outstretched, the intense Light where the shield originated emanating from his fingertips.

They watched the haze radiating from the tower's spire spread across the canyon sky. When it reached the cloud, the Darkness recoiled, as if bitten by a great serpent.

Then, with a magnificent blast, the tower belched haze through the battlefield, accompanied by a resounding explosion. The blast arced over the great shield, cascading into the unprepared Metim army. Instantaneously, the Dark warriors were leveled, their soulless bodies reduced to ash on the ground.

Just before the blast, Sam caught sight of three figures disappearing into a vortex of Darkness, escaping the tower's eruption a moment before it struck.

****

Sam and Emma sprinted across the field to where the army of Light lay unharmed.

Confrontation

The shield that had covered them had vanished. Warriors looked around, blinking their eyes, confused. Sam searched the scene for the Watchers, and for Nuriel, and found them in a circle. A body laid at their feet.

Before he could run to them, however, the Watchers lifted the body up into their arms and disappeared into a beam of Light that materialized from above.

Sam ran to the beam, missing it by only seconds before it faded away. He dropped to his knees, gazing at the spot where Nuriel had been.

Tears flowed freely, even though he tried to control them. He was confused, his mind a blur. Nuriel had sacrificed himself in order to save others, not to destroy them. Why would he destroy a village and then sacrifice himself for the Descendants? Now that he might be dead, there would be no way of knowing.

With the anger receded, something inside of Sam told him there was more to the story. That Nuriel had a deeper purpose—that he was not deceiving him, or anyone.

He stood and turned, noticing Emma, Gus, and Lillia behind him. Next to them were Pestril, Cestray, Sayvon, and Murray.

He wiped his eyes, scanning the silent battlefield. Light warriors were now spreading across the canyon, casting blankets of Light in all directions to dispel any remains of the Darkness that lingered. Though, from what Sam could tell, the tower had already cleared most of it.

Mrs. Sterling rushed over to the group, gathering Sam and Emma up into her arms. Amos and Sarah Karpatch were right behind her, as were the Farmers and Henry Bostwick.

"Oh you dear things, I am so sorry you had to go through this!" she sobbed, kissing them both on the top of the head. "Let's get you all out of here."

"Mom, we are fine," Emma said, chiding her mother. But she still submitted to the embrace.

"I know, it's just you are all growing up so fast, and it's such a dangerous time—"

Emma hugged her mother tighter, fighting the tears. "Yes, I know—you don't need to worry so much. We are all in the Creator's hand."

Henry clasped his hand on Sam's shoulders. "Really something, isn't it? The tower did exist! And did you see what it did to those Metim warriors? Amazing! To think we are standing in the middle of something the Creator had the Watchers build…"

He continued to talk, but Sam had turned his attention to the conversation Mr. Sterling was having with one of the Sons of Light.

"—there's not a chance we can let them just roam Lior without keeping tabs on them. We need to pursue them with everything we have got. Perhaps we still have a chance of capture if…"

"Excuse me, Mr. Sterling?"

Sam left Henry and hurried over to where the two were talking. "Did Boggle tell you about the Metim gathering in South America? Near the Peru gate?"

Mr. Sterling peered at him. "No, he didn't. What are you talking about, son?"

He relayed the account from Boggle, and the map he showed them of the Metim. When he was finished, Mr. Sterling frowned, then glanced at the young Son of Light warrior next to him. "Would you mind fetching Mr. Bogglenose for me?" he requested.

The young warrior nodded, disappearing into the crowd of Light warriors, who were returning from their task of clearing the canyon.

Mr. Sterling pulled Sam aside, away from anyone who could hear them. "I want you to keep the Star hidden. Pretend as though it is lost— or destroyed. Just don't let anyone know you have it," he whispered.

Sam blinked. "Mr. Sterling, why do you want me to keep it?"

He shrugged. "I'm not sure. There's a lot I don't understand about the Watchers and their artifacts. But something tells me you have some sort of connection to this one."

Then he excused himself to go find Bogglenose and give orders to the warriors.

Back with the others, Sam chatted with Sayvon and Pestril until

they were called over to the group that readied the Ruasch that would lead them safely out of the canyon.

It was determined that all but the Light warriors would travel back to the school since it was the closest to where they were. There, the young Descendants would gather their things before going back to the city.

As they grouped together, Sam stole a glance at Lillia, who was locked in an embrace with her parents. She glanced back at him, rolling her eyes at Sam as her mother clung to her.

Suddenly, the image of the woman inside the Star flashed through his mind, and Sam realized who the woman in the Star had been all along. It was Lillia. The similarities between them were unmistakable.

Two Ruasches came soaring overhead, summoned by Talister and Amos. In two groups, the adults and teens stepped into them, ascending into the cloud. Soon, they were soaring back over the peaks toward the mountaintop where the school rested.

Chapter Twenty-Eight
Restoration

Sam awoke to the sounds of birds fluttering outside their dormitory window. Gus was still asleep, his snoring snuffed out by the blanket that had wrapped around his face. From the looks of it, he had spent the night wrestling with his bedsheets.

Sam sat up, keeping the cool air at bay by pulling the top blanket up over his shoulders. Listening to the birds for a few moments, he allowed himself the chance to breathe.

For the first time, the Dark One's face wasn't at the forefront of his mind. Neither was Arazel's or Nuriel's. He inhaled, taking in the cool air into his lungs. Then he exhaled, feeling suddenly comfortable in his bed.

The anger was gone. No longer was it just below the surface, ready to overtake him. It was a freeing feeling, and he allowed his body to bask in the moment. It was though he had just been released from a great weight.

Since returning the day before yesterday, however, some events still lingered with them—especially Yadris's death. The mentors had held a

small memorial in the courtyard of the school before sending her body back to Lior City through the Lightway. Along with the other warriors who had given their lives that night.

It had hit Sayvon the hardest, and following the service, they had seen little of her. Emma had tried to talk to her, but she requested to be alone.

Sam understood that request. Had Emma, Gus, or Lillia died, he wouldn't know what to do with himself. He would want to be alone, too.

But now, even with the loss of Yadris and other Light warriors at the tower, most of the others still kept their spirits up.

"To be asleep with the body means we are awake with the Creator," Mr. Sterling had said at the memorial service. Sam hadn't been raised to believe that, but now, being a follower, he could see why they had such hope. If it were true, what did it matter to be killed for such a worthy cause as protecting the Light? To be across the divide, to meet the Creator. Those were amazing things to hope for.

The smells of breakfast wafted down the hallway. Padding over to Gus's bunk, Sam reached down and plugged his nose. With a great snort, Gus sat up and began mumbling incoherently. Then, as his eyes opened, Sam smacked him in the face with a pillow.

Gus leaped to his feet, bleary-eyed and pillow in hand. When he discovered what had happened, he chucked a pillow back at where he thought Sam to be. Sam laughed hysterically from outside the room.

At breakfast with the others, Sam and Gus both ate more than their fair share of berry pancakes and sausage. To their surprise, all the Mentors joined them as well. It was kind of nice to be the only ones there, since the rest of the Mentees had been sent home after graduation.

Tomorrow, Sam and the others would head back to the city, where all of them would settle in full time in the cabin circle. The White Pine gate had been deemed too dangerous since its takeover, so it would become a recovery mission when the Light forces regrouped. Mr.

Sterling couldn't say much more than that, other than that it would happen soon.

Near the end of breakfast, Mentor Aron stood to speak, his long white hair braided behind his head. For the first time since Sam first saw him, he wore a sword at his hip and leather cuffs around his arms. A quick look around the room told Sam the other Mentors wore similar items. No doubt they needed to be ready for anything.

"It has come to my attention that a few of our student Mentees could not complete the Shomerin due to their valiant efforts to assist another," he said. "And while we as Mentors do not condone their reckless actions to leave the school and travel to a very dangerous place…"

He paused and peered toward the young Descendants, "we as Mentors have decided that the gravity of the situation far outweighs the consequences of not acting. There are rules in place so that we may follow them, therefore I request that three months from now the violators spend twenty days in the service of Tanniym, the dragon keeper. There, they will spend their days helping to relocate the more stubborn masses of the reptile's excrement."

Lillia glanced over to Sam, mouthing the words "thanks Newb" to him. He smiled and winked back at her.

"With that being said, I would like to ask for a vote to determine whether these Mentees will indeed still receive their Eben stones and join the rest of the graduates in their Shomerin." Mentor Aron said, looking around the table at the adults seated. "I would invite all to take part, not only our Mentors here today."

Slowly, each one of the Mentors and adults stood, leaving none sitting. It was unanimous.

"Mentees, please stand."

Gus, Lillia, and Emma stood facing Mentor Aron. He peered at them, then turned to Sam, who was still seated.

Mentor Wenthrow stood abruptly, bumping the table on her way up and leaving coffees sloshing in cups. "I'd like to add something to your most—generous offering to our young Mentees here."

Mentor Aron nodded. "When I chose to mentor young Samuel here, I wasn't sure what I was going to get. He was determined and talented, but quite confused. I saw a deep anger had taken up residence within him, capable of inflicting tremendous harm on himself and to others. Throughout our training, the anger spread into enmity, and I could see it had consumed him."

Mentor Wenthrow turned to Sam, who could feel the blood rising in his cheeks. "But equally as compelling was the fight this young man led to resist that anger. I saw daily his resolve to stand for peace and goodness, especially with those he cares about."

Sam looked at the floor, kicking a crust of bread around that had fallen from the table. Being in the spotlight was not his cup of tea.

"I, Mentor Wenthrow, hereby withdraw my recommendation of 'no,' and replace it with a resounding 'yes,' effective immediately. Do I have any objections?"

There was silence around the table, but only for a moment. One by one, they stood again. This time, they added to it a hearty round of clapping and cheering.

****

When they had changed and put on their robes, the four young Descendants followed Mentor Aron down a long series of corridors they had never seen during their time at Mentorship. At last, they reached a thick wooden door that looked as though it had been there long before the school was built. On the door was carved a Watcher wing.

Mentor Aron spoke to the door in the ancient language. "*Bara ora,*" he muttered.

Sam struggled to translate, but before he could, he heard Gus whisper the words, "The Creator's Light."

Lazuli appeared around the frame of the door, illuminating the elegant but tiny carvings in the ancient wood. Through the door it spread until it reached the iron pulls near the latch. When it stopped, the tall Mentor pushed on the door, opening it.

Inside, in the center of a large cavern room, stood an illuminated arch. Mentors Korin, Wenthrow, and Sauravin were already inside. Mentor Korin stood nearest the arch, where he held out his hand to Gus.

Gus took it, following him through the arch portal, where their forms were swallowed up by the blinding Light. It was several minutes later when they returned, a gleaming Eben stone on Gus's wrist. On his face was a mixed look of awe and reverence.

Before Sam could ask him how it went, however, Mentor Wenthrow was reaching out her hand to him for his turn through the arch. Sam took her hand and walked through the arch, the warm radiance enveloping his body. He let the Light reign through him, feeling its embrace as they continued forward.

Closing his eyes, he remembered the feeling of the Darkness through him, and the incredible power. And then he remembered how it left a cold emptiness when gone. Feeling the Light was different. It was a fulfilling, lasting warmth. A subtle, but enduring type of power.

The Light disappeared, and suddenly they were standing on a ledge of an immense mountain range made of only rock and stone. Below the ledge was what seemed like a boundless drop into the valley, where one could fall for an eternity before hitting the surface of the raging river below. Above them, the mountain continued for several hundred meters to its peak, where the distinct shapes of dragons hid on the ledges beneath it.

"Welcome to the Tannin region," Mentor Wenthrow said quietly. "We want to be extremely careful not to disturb the inhabitants here."

"Dragons?" Sam whispered back.

She nodded. "They are curious creatures, and exceedingly mysterious. Completely dedicated to the preservation of the Light, but they can often be perilous for Descendants."

"Like how they attacked the ships on the way to Mentorship?"

She scowled. "Dragons are loyal to the Light, so we were surprised

when that happened. Something had to have caused them to believe there would be a danger to the Light aboard those ships."

"Or someone," Sam interjected.

She leveled her eyes, pondering his words. Her pause only gave Sam the proof he needed.

"Samuel, you are a follower of the Light. Because two dragons were deceived into believing you were a threat does not make it so. Orono knew that, and he was willing to attack his own species to defend you."

"I suppose," Sam agreed reluctantly.

Mentor Wenthrow led him to the back of the ledge, where a small opening radiating Lazuli Light beckoned them inside of the mountain. Through the narrow passageway they ducked, following the tunnel until it opened up into an enormous cavern. Inside, Sam was stunned to see a Lazuli waterfall in its center, dropping hundreds of meters into a broad pool below.

Rising from the pool was a glimmering blue mist, blanketing the cavern's interior with gleaming Lazuli Light.

"You must jump," Mentor Wenthrow said firmly.

Sam looked into the abyss, barely able to see the pool far below. It was a long way down.

"Are you serious? Into the pool?" He looked at her.

She nodded. "I should think this would require little effort, given all that you've already been through."

Sam looked down again. She was right. This was a piece of cake, considering all they'd done. And she would not have brought him here just to have him jump to his death. This was part of the test. And if Gus could do it…

With a running start, he jumped headlong into the mist. Down he fell at breakneck speed, but slowed as he neared the bottom. The mist lowered him gently toward the pool below until he was hovering just above its glistening surface. In front of him, on the other side of the pool, was a large ledge, and upon the ledge sat a great dragon.

Iridescent red scales adorned its exterior. Its captivating red and charcoal eyes watched Sam as he hovered above the Lazuli-infused water.

Taken aback, Sam thought of the Dark One and his piercing, dragon-like eyes. For a moment, Sam looked around the cavern for a viable escape. But there was none. Only up.

The dragon continued to watch him as he struggled to move himself through the mist toward the edge of the pool. Then, the mist let him go, and into the water he plunged.

Coughing as he surfaced, he swam for the side opposite the ledge away from the dragon. When he reached it, he hoisted himself up and stood soaking wet on the bank—the dragon watching his every move.

You chose the Light. The words echoed in his mind. The dragon seemed to be the one speaking. Gathering his courage, he walked around the edge of the pool toward the ledge. When he reached it, the great dragon closed his eyes.

A brilliant light materialized from the center of the pool, and a small orb rose from its surface. Over to Sam it drifted, until it was within arm's reach.

Behold, a gift from the Creator, the dragon spoke.

Sam reached out and took it, holding the smooth stone in his palm. It was dark grey, containing not one vein of color, but four. Red, white, yellow, and black colors rippled through the stone in equal amounts.

He placed the stone into the empty spot on his bracelet, securing it beneath the latches. It fit perfectly. Immediately the stone glowed, and Sam felt the familiar pulse of the Lazuli flowing through his body.

It came eagerly. Much more so than before.

He was admiring the stone when he realized he was floating upwards. Soon, he was face to face with Mentor Wenthrow once again.

"You have to allow yourself to move through the Light—oh dear boy, no one taught you to blend, now did they?"

She looked cross-eyed at him, watching him squirm through the Light to reach the edge. Finally, she removed her robe, tossing the end for him to grab onto.

"Pull yourself in, that's it."

When he reached the side, she pulled him onto the ledge, slipping her robe over him. "Well, you weren't supposed to fall *in* the water, you know. Oh, but I suppose if you had *known*—oh, never mind. Let's just figure this thing out right now. The others won't mind. Now, extended your arms."

Shivering, Sam stood next to his Mentor, arms outstretched.

"Palms out, eyes closed, that's right," she whispered. "Now, breathe. Yes—in deeply, and out."

Sam breathed in and out, feeling the Light with him.

"Do you see the source of the Light? It's that little glowing thing inside you—now reach out with your mind toward it. You should be able to see the cavern around you. Yes—keep your eyes closed. But look from *within*. You can see everything."

Sam reached out toward the little orb that moved within him. The source of the Light. *Inside* of him.

"Now go to the other side of the cavern."

Eyes still closed, Sam saw the other side of the cavern. Swiftly, he could see his hands dissolving before him, morphing into pure Light. Then his arms, feet and legs, and his middle. His chest and head were last.

"Remember, the Light carries you to your destination," the Mentor said, her voice far-away.

But Sam had already understood. The Light was all around him, and he was simply a part of it.

He moved about the cavern, over the ledge, by the waterfall, zipping with incredible speed. Spinning, he obeyed Mentor Wenthrow and zipped over to where she had told him to go.

Reappearing was even easier. As he let go of the source, and all of his members became visible once again.

"Impressive. It takes most Mentee graduates a few days to catch on."

He walked back over to where she was standing, the chill from the water gone. Blending was incredible, and his whole body surged with excitement as she led them back out of the cavern.

Before they walked through the arch back to the school, however, Sam paused, looking over the vast landscape. "Mentor Wenthrow, why did the Darkness draw me so much?"

She turned to face him, her expression concerned. "Sometimes, it is the greater gift of Light that one is given that makes them more vulnerable to the Darkness."

"I don't understand."

"Samuel, you have been given a power unlike any of your fellow Mentees—and I fear to say greater than most other Descendants. I saw it from the beginning, which is why I chose you as my student. Your gift is truly extraordinary, and thus it will also be your burden. The greater the power, the more the responsibility one has to control it."

"What if I can't? *Control* it, I mean. What if the Darkness controls *me* instead?"

She put her arm around him. "Unfortunately, it is something you will have to fight for the rest of your life. You cannot rid yourself of the Darkness. It will always be there, waiting until you are weakest. Which is why you must yearn to seek the Light whenever possible."

Sam pondered her words, his mind shifting to Arazel. "Ara—uh—my father, is he really the Shadow from the prophecy?"

The Mentor gazed up at the morning sun, which was disappearing behind a cloud. "Perhaps you have misunderstood the prophecy, Samuel. From the little I know of it, I believe the correct phrase was that the last prophet would call unto *himself* the Shadow."

She patted him on the back, urging him to follow her back through the arch to rejoin his friends inside the cave at the school.

****

When all four had received their Eben stones, it was lunchtime. On their way to the dining hall, they passed Sayvon, who nodded casually to them as she headed off toward Sam and Gus's favorite spot on the side of the mountain. Emma immediately turned to go after her, but Sam stopped her.

"Let me try," he told her, then hurried after Sayvon.

He found her on the same rock Gus had brought him to, gazing emotionlessly over the valley in front of her.

"I see you found my favorite spot," he said as he sat down on the cold stone next to her. She didn't respond to him.

"I remember the day I found out my parents died in a car wreck," he continued, gazing into the valley with her. "And even though I know now, that wasn't true—when it happened, it was like the life was ripped right out from me. Even that young, it was like it left a huge hole inside, like I could never be happy again. And now—even knowing the truth—or at least most of it, I still feel the hurt from that day. From parents that never really existed. To me, they are still there, on the side of the road. Waiting for me to come rescue them."

A tear made its way down Sayvon's cheek. Turning to him, she threw her arms around his neck, burying her face in his chest. "She was just a girl! I barely even spent any time with her! I was her only friend!" she cried.

Sam let her cry for a few moments, fighting back the tears in his own eyes. He hadn't even really known Yadris either. He had been content to stay with his tiny group of friends, ignoring the rest of the world around him.

"You cared enough about Yadris to be her friend. She may have been alone otherwise, and you gave her something no one else could have. The time you gave her was enough."

"But it's not fair. She didn't have to die," she said bitterly.

It was strange to hear her speak like this. To Sam, Sayvon was one of the nicest people he had ever met, but now she was letting the anger win. He wanted to tell her this, but didn't quite know how. She was strong, however. No doubt she would be just fine in time.

She sobbed for several minutes, and then they sat in silence.

After a while, Sam convinced her to go to lunch, for which they were already late. When they came into the dining hall, Emma, Lillia, Gus, Cestray, Pestril, and Murray were still there, waiting for Sayvon and Sam to join them.

 Chapter Twenty-Eight

That evening, while Gus and Sam laid in bed waiting to fall asleep, Sam pulled the covers over himself. He was holding the Star, which still glowed dimly in the darkened room. His mind shifted to Lillia, the one who had called him from inside the Star. She had been the one he was able to hear through the Darkness. The *only* one.

Waiting until Gus's breathing became rhythmic, he slipped out of his covers and threw on his robe, inching the door open until the space was large enough to let him through.

He padded down the hallway, making his way to the girls' dormitories. During Mentorship, he could have gotten in quite a bit of trouble for being there, but since there were only a few of them sleeping there, he took the chance.

Tiptoeing to Lillia and Emma's room, he tried the door. It opened effortlessly. Tiptoeing inside, he saw the forms of the two girls in their beds and went to the one that showed a few wisps of dark hair poking out from under the covers.

He tapped her softly, and Lillia sat up, blinking. He covered her mouth with his hand, putting a finger to his lips. Then he motioned for her to come out the door with him.

Scowling, she followed him down the hallway to a common room near the amphitheater entrances. There, he led her to a small bench in a corner of the room.

"This had better be good, Newb. I don't do well without sleep," she growled, some of her hair standing up on end.

He hadn't prepared for what he wanted to say to her. He only knew he wanted to talk to her about what had happened.

Softening, she sat down next to him. "You want to know how I could talk to you and no one else could."

Sam nodded, seeing the moonlight cast a delicate ray on her face.

"Well, I suppose you could say we are the same—you and me. Call it a connection—or whatever, but it is what it is."

"I just don't understand why… you? Why wouldn't I be connected to—"

"Princess Emma, you mean?" she snorted. "Yeah, good question."

"Maybe I just needed *someone* that night, and you were just *there*," he said, regretting the words as they left his lips.

She rolled her eyes at him. "I have a theory," she said, sighing. "I think we've been 'connected' for a while, actually. Because of, well, the *Darkness.*"

His heart skipped a beat. "What are you talking about? You've given into the Darkness?"

She stood suddenly, facing him. A tear glimmered in her eye. "You think you are the only one that struggles with the Darkness? It's so hard to say no to it! I fight it every day, Sam. *Every day!*"

He looked down at her bare feet, feeling the cold emptiness that once took hold of him. Still holding the Star, he let the warmth of the Lazuli overpower the feeling.

"I understand."

"*You* think you understand, but you don't see what others go through around you, since everyone pays *you* attention when you cough even the slightest. They're immediately at your side—Sam, are you okay? Sam, is it the Darkness taking over your body? How can I help?" she said angrily. "No one sees I have been fighting it for years! There's no one that rushes to me and tries to help! I just—want to hurt people sometimes! It takes everything I have to just shove it back in, to ignore it!"

"I didn't know," he told her.

"That's because you aren't looking! You're so caught up in your stupid prophecy thing that you don't notice!"

Sam stood, reaching out to her. She turned and started away, but he caught her. Pulling her close, he hugged her tightly. "Lillia, I am here for you. I understand now. You can talk to me about it."

She resisted, then let herself go into his arms. Then she pulled away again, looking into his eyes. "I don't think you *do* get it. The reason I could call you from the Darkness is because I understand it very well. It's there, every day."

"Like a wolf waiting in the shadows for you to turn your back."

She squinted at him. "Yes. A little on the dramatic side, but yes."

Sam laughed at her, earning him a five-star eye roll. "If you weren't my friend, I'd smack you right in the face."

He smiled, then felt the Star pulse in his hand. "But you were in the Star, too. That's not of the Darkness."

She paused, not knowing how to answer. Then her frown changed back into a grin only she could produce. "I guess that means we are stuck trying to figure it out together, right?"

He chuckled, and she play-punched him in the shoulder. Then she latched onto him once more, holding him steadily for several minutes. "Thank you," she whispered into his ear. Then she hurried off back to her dorm, leaving him alone in the common room.

Sam strolled back off to his room, feeling uplifted by the talk with Lillia. It hadn't been romantic, but he felt like there was a connection they had that no one else could claim. A connection they would have to keep secret, perhaps. And it was nice to know she was there if he ever needed her.

✳✳✳✳✳✳✳✳✳✳✳✳✳✳✳✳✳✳✳✳✳✳✳✳✳✳✳✳✳✳✳✳

The next morning, they packed early and then headed to the dining hall to have breakfast before departing back to the city. At breakfast, Gus told them what he had learned from translating the Keeper's journal Sam found at the cabin.

The Keeper had been tasked with protecting the Star, and spoke about someone who had been following him, looking for it.

"Who was after him?" Emma asked.

"You're never going to believe it, but he said it was someone called the 'Shadow.' Said he believed it was a Dark Lord in training, looking to prove himself upon his master's request."

Lillia whistled. "You think it was Arazel's first act in the Darkness?"

Gus peered at Sam, suddenly aware of the fact that they were talking about his father in this manner. "Perhaps," he said gingerly.

Sam waved it off. "Guys, it's okay. I know who he is. It changes nothing."

Lillia glanced at him, a tiny smile crossing her lips.

"Supposedly, he found this out and left to go hide the Star. He said he knew of the perfect person who could make things 'disappear unknowingly.'"

"Boggle," all of them said at once, followed by a round of laughter.

Chapter Twenty-Nine
Aftermath

Packs in hand, Sam, Gus, Emma, and Lillia stood at the edge of the mountaintop village of Helel Malach, waiting for their ride on the Ruasch back to Lior City. Talister had arranged for a few of the Sons of Light to accompany them back to the city, since the Lightway to and from the school might put them at risk.

The four of them stood among the group of adults, watching the gloomy clouds gather far in the northern horizon. They weren't the normal clouds one might see before a front moved in, no, but something much more ominous.

Gus had found out from Mr. Sterling that they had originated over Sheba Haloth, where the White Palace stood at the edge of Dark Lake, and where the kingdom of the Dark One had laid dormant for thousands of years.

The clouds had appeared just after Gus, Lillia, and Emma had gone after Sam.

"It's been pretty much silent until now," Gus told them.

Just then, another image appeared on the horizon, that of a dragon,

flying high in the distance in the direction of the city. Judging from its considerable size compared to the sky behind it, Sam guessed it had to be Orono.

Emma, who had been watching it soar past, turned to finish the conversation she had begun with Talister about the fate of the dragons in Lior. Sam, Gus, and Lillia inched up as close as they could, doing their best to not look like eavesdroppers.

"Don't you think that having a positive relationship with the dragons is important now, given that they too sacrificed themselves for the cause of the Light?" she said, negotiating with her uncle.

Talister seemed quite impressed with her growing debate skills.

"Yes, well, I… yes, I do see what you are saying."

"So then you will speak to the Council regarding the lifting of the ban on them?"

"Darling, it's not quite that simple."

"It was simple when they were banned, so *un-ban* them," she retorted. "Please."

Talister sighed, watching the dragon as it disappeared out of view. "You must understand, I am not against them in Lior, but I must answer for their actions—especially those that involve them attacking our children. What I will promise is that I will attempt to open their minds about how and why dragons do what they do. If you must know, I have already sent for Orono to return to the city."

This seemed to satisfy Emma, who hugged her uncle and returned to her friends.

"Wow, that was something," Gus said approvingly. Lillia and Sam nodded in agreement.

It seemed to add to Emma's energy. "It's just time people stop thinking one way just because they don't understand," she said. "Dragons are misunderstood."

When the Ruasch arrived, two Sons of Light appeared in the cloud at the ground. Another watched cautiously from high above.

Stepping onto the Ruasch, Sam glanced back one more time at the school behind him. The entire staff of Mentors were standing in the courtyard, waving to them. As the Light carried him to the cloud, he waved back. He would truly miss the school, and the Mentors.

Moments later, they were flying over mountain ranges, lakes, and vast forests, until at last the sight of the city came into view. The Sons aimed the cloud directly over their cabins, and before they knew it, they were standing next to their old hangout—the pavilion in the center of the circle.

Two shorter PO members greeted them immediately upon landing, escorting Amos, Mr. Sterling, and Talister back to the office for briefings, while Mrs. Sterling hurried Emma, Gus, and Sam inside to get resettled in the cabin.

Lillia moved her stuff over to stay with her parents in their cabin, and Gus took up residence in the Sterling cabin until the Ablesworth's could make it back to Lior.

The rest of the day was spent cleaning, organizing, and making up for lost sleep. That evening at dinner, as they were putting a good dent in the apple pie Mrs. Sterling had baked, a Lightscribe flitted into the window, stopping in the center of the table where Emma was seated. As Emma touched it, the Scribe unfurled into a note for the four of them. It read:

Friends, the four of you are invited to join Mr. Sterling and me in the PO Briefing Room this evening at the seventh chime.

Truly, Mr. Calpher

Only moments after the Lightscribe had opened in Emma's hands, a gonging noise rang from the orb. Then it floated up into the air above the door.

Mrs. Sterling stood and brushed herself off, her apron still around her waist. "Well, that's the first chime, I believe. The Farmers and I can handle taking care of dinner. Why don't you four get a head start to the City?"

"Mom, we can help—" Emma began, but was shooed away by her mother.

"Not necessary. Somehow, I think what my husband and Talister have cooked up is more important than cleaning up dinner. Go! Yes,

get a move on! You're going to run out of chimes quickly!" And she was right, for the next chime sounded as she finished her words.

The four friends scooted upstairs to get their robes and shoes on, making it out the door before the third chime sounded. The orb followed them, pulsing happily as they hurried down the walkway toward the City Center.

With just seconds to spare before the seventh chime, they huffed through the center doors and up the stairs to the hallway where the PO office was.

Outside the massive brass door, two PO officers stood resolutely, eyes fixed forward. Each held a staff that flared blue as the youths approached. One turned and placed his hand on the doorframe, sending Lazuli Light shooting throughout the exterior of the door. Much like the one that had opened the door to retrieve their Eben stones.

The door groaned, creaking painfully as it opened ever so slowly. On the other side stood Amos, Talister, and Mr. Sterling. They had huge grins on their faces.

"Welcome! Glad you could join us!" Talister greeted them warmly, as though they hadn't just parted ways only hours before.

Sheepishly, they walked through the opening, only to find an incredible sight on the other side. The PO office was much more than a briefing room. It was like the central command for all of Lior.

"Welcome to the Keep, you four," Mr. Sterling nodded. "Right this way." He led them through a series of Lighted arches, each one pulsing slightly as they passed through. "Don't mind those. They are simply an extra measure of security should you be up to no good."

"Guess you better stay behind then," Lillia said, winking as she passed Sam. Sam stuck his tongue out at her.

Through the arches, the room opened up into a frenzy of activity, where PO officers were busy peering at one of the many holomaps in the room. Others stood in front of large walls of hundreds of holographic moving images, analyzing them carefully. Still others were sending and receiving Lightscribes quicker than Sam could keep up, funneling them up into the spire above.

"Everything that falls under the jurisdiction of the Protectors is monitored in this room," he told them, leading them to one of the holomaps. "Sam, I'm sure you are familiar with one of these." He reached up and turned the globe with his palms. "Although, the one you discovered somehow escaped us."

"And right near the cabin, too," Amos said, shaking his head in wonder.

Sam looked for the tower on the globe, but it wasn't there. "So you've been using Watcher devices this whole time?"

Mr. Sterling nodded. "Anytime we find one, we have it brought here to help us do our job. We've scoured Lior for them and thought we had found them all. It was truly a surprise when you four discovered this one."

"What do you use them for?" Gus asked, feeling very much in his element.

Mr. Sterling pointed to a black blot on the globe. "Mainly to track pockets of Darkness—monitoring to see if they are growing or contracting. If we see one growing, or getting more concentrated, we send out PO officers to attempt to eradicate it."

"Couldn't that be dangerous?" Lillia asked.

"Yes, very," Talister answered her. "Which is why we must always be vigilant."

Lillia seemed fascinated by the dreamy Light-enhanced moving streams of unknown people and places on the wall. "What about those images?"

It was as though someone had attached a holographic projector to a century-old video screen.

"Seer images. They are converted to holoimages that we can use for detection of Darkness in Lior and in Creation, on occasion. Let's just say their necessity has increased exponentially over the past year."

Emma pointed to the handful of Protectors that were slinging Lightscribes up into the spire.

"Communications throughout the regions, and with our teams. The spire masks the scribes upon exit, in case you're wondering why you don't see them ever come from the Center while outside," he told them.

Then Mr. Sterling led them over to a holomap on an old wooden table, which looked a bit different from the others in the room. Sam recognized it immediately as Earth. The large blot of green on the map near South America was even larger than before. A few more weeks and it could nearly cover the entire continent. "This was just installed a few weeks ago—"

"By Boggle," Lillia interrupted.

"Yes—how'd you know?" Mr. Sterling said, glancing at her.

She shrugged, a smile on her face. "Just a guess."

He peered at her suspiciously. "Yes, well, this has become one of our greatest assets here at the Keep. Dark forces have been quiet in Creation for nearly a thousand years. Now, this map dominates much of our time here. In fact, it is about to become the center of our operation."

The youths listened intently, certain they were some of the only Descendants their age that were able to witness any of this.

He pointed to another area of the map that showed a tiny concentration of Light. "The Keep is gearing up for a strike in Creation," he told them as he pointed to a tiny town that glowed a very prominent green, "You know that the White Pine gate has been compromised, and now gates around the world are falling to the Dark forces. Without these gates, Protectors cannot enter Creation to stop them. We have evacuated the remaining gates as a precaution. We simply weren't ready for this to happen."

"If the Council would have listened to our recommendations, it wouldn't have occurred at all," Talister grumbled.

"I agree. This could have been prevented," Amos added.

Mr. Sterling nodded. "Unfortunately. We have repeatedly asked for more protection at the gates, but Descendants in the regions have been reluctant to admit that there is a Darkness problem."

"And now it's too late," Lillia said with a smirk. "Ah, politics. Gotta love it."

Talister smiled slyly. "A girl after my own heart."

"But there is one gate that we believe has not yet been discovered by the Dark forces—oddly, the one that we thought would have been discovered first."

"The Sha'ar Gate," Gus said, wide eyed.

"Exactly the one," Mr. Sterling acknowledged. "For some reason, we were under the impression that when the gate was opened, there would be an influx of Dark forces that would be attracted to it. However, that has not been the case. It has been silent to this day, as far as we know."

"You are going to sneak through the Sha'ar gate and attack from the other side," Sam said, guessing. "But I thought we didn't know where the Lior side of the gate was."

Talister nodded. "We didn't, until you led us there, my boy."

"The tower?"

Again, Talister nodded, smiling. "Seems there was more than one important Watcher artifact in that canyon."

"And fortunately for us, its location is still hidden from the Dark forces," Amos said.

Gus scratched the back of his head. "So if the Watchers hadn't shown up that night, the Darkness might have taken control of the tower and discovered the other side of the Sha'ar Gate."

"Right again. Nuriel came through at the last moment," Mr. Sterling confirmed.

Sam recalled the red haze exploding suddenly across the canyon, killing the entire Metim army. He turned to Mr. Sterling.

"Sir, I still don't really understand the tower. Why was it built?"

Mr. Sterling backed away from Boggle's map to make room for the Protectors who were gearing up for the mission.

"A question I have asked myself, and I'm afraid I can only speculate based on what I've seen and information I have been able to scrape together," he told them. "I believe that the tower was built as a failsafe

in case the Darkness got out of hand in Lior. Should it, the tower would destroy it."

"But it didn't—destroy all the Darkness in Lior that night, did it?" Lillia said.

"No, it didn't. We believe Nuriel stopped it before it could," Mr. Sterling answered. "The shield did more than protect us, it—"

"Contained the haze to the canyon," Gus added.

An older Protector with a peppered beard who looked as though he spent most of his time in the Keep approached Mr. Sterling and Talister. "Gentlemen, the teams are in position, and we are ready. The Keep is at your command."

Mr. Sterling nodded, then whispered to the four, "You'll find seats over there on the observation deck." He pointed toward where the holomaps and Boggle's map stood in the center of the gathering crowd. "We have sent in two teams. One will strike the White Pine Gate, and the other will gather intelligence on the large gathering in South America. It will be the largest mission in Descendant history. We have most of our Protectors out there—including the Sons of Light."

Emma looked at her dad with a scowl. "Are you sure we should be here?"

He squeezed his daughter's shoulder lovingly. "You kids deserve to see this. I wouldn't have it any other way."

****

Mr. Sterling took his place in front of the map, where an exploded view from two holomaps concentrated on each of the strike areas of Creation. Talister led them all in a quick prayer, asking for the Creator's guidance and protection for the mission.

When he was finished, the Chancellor and four other Council members emerged from the Lighted entrance arches and were led to special observation seats near the front of the room.

The room had grown quiet, with all Protectors taking their places in front of their stations. Holomaps were in position. Lightscribers had ceased sending scribes for the moment. Images from the Seers still flashed across the wall.

"All stations, report," Mr. Sterling called.

"Scribes ready, sir," one called from the Lightscribe station.

"Watchmen ready," another said from the holomaps.

"Ready Seeing," said another from the wall of moving images.

Mr. Sterling turned to the Lightscribers. "All strike teams, standing by?"

A scribe shot up into the spire, returning only moments later with a response. "Yes, sir. At the gate in the canyon."

"Send them through," he said authoritatively.

Another scribe went up into the spire at breakneck speed. The room grew quiet again as they waited for the first reports back from the teams.

After several minutes with no response, they could tell some of the Protectors were beginning to grow nervous. Even Mr. Sterling showed signs of concern.

"Send through the reserve Sons," he directed one of the Lightscribers.

Again, several minutes ticked by. Emma shifted in her seat, so Sam grabbed her hand. "I don't like this," she admitted.

Suddenly, a glowing orb came careening down the spire and into an awaiting scriber's hands. At the same moment, something strange began happening to Boggle's map. From all around the world, deep red spread swiftly from multiple points, converging upon each other until the entirety of the map was covered in the color. Then the map blinked out completely, leaving nothing but a wooden table underneath.

"Sir, you need to see this." The scribe cradled the Lightscribe in his hands, as though it were the last one in existence.

Mr. Sterling and the older Protector next to him hurried to his side, and upon reading the message, a grave look crossed their faces.

"Sir?" a flush faced young Protector called from one of the holomaps. Turning, Mr. Sterling looked at the Protector, then at the globe. It, too, had turned red, as well as the others.

Aftermath

The images from the Seers too, began to blink out, one by one. Exclamations of bewilderment were heard throughout the room.

"Jack, Amos, Talister, a word." The Chancellor said, standing and walking toward the back of the room. Mr. Sterling and Talister followed.

"What just happened?" Lillia whispered loudly to the other three.

Gus leaned forward to try to get a glimpse of the map. "I don't know," he told them.

Returning, Mr. Sterling addressed the Keep suddenly. "I need everyone working on obtaining as much information as possible, as quickly as possible. Meir, I need Henry Bostwick, *now*. Leib, Moshe, get to the gate, but do not go through. Dov, Eitan, Seer's chamber. Find out what they are Seeing—if anything."

The five Protectors blended there on the spot, their Light traces zipping up the spire. Then Mr. Sterling and Talister turned back toward the table, speaking in hushed but heated voices.

Emma, who could take no more, stood and hurried to her father, throwing her arms around him. He held her tightly, then walked over to the other three still seated. "It looks like they knew we were coming," he said soberly. "I'm afraid I'm going to have to ask you to go until we know anything more."

"Sir, what happened? Why is Boggle's map red and there are no more Seer images or communication from the teams?" Gus asked.

"Are they—dead? The red haze… I saw it on the map. They are dead, aren't they?" Lillia said, wide-eyed.

Mr. Sterling sighed, his eyes replete with apprehension. "Please, you must go now." He said, pointing toward the Keep door. "I promise I will share more when I am able."

Gus stood, an overwhelming look of despair on his face. His parents were still in Creation, though they were a thousand miles from any gate.

"I'm sure they are fine," Lillia said as they made their way toward the Keep door. As they did, a young blond-haired guard came rushing past them. He was headed straight for Mr. Sterling.

"Sir, stop the mission!" he shouted, struggling to catch his breath. "Don't—send them through the gate!"

"What are you talking about, son?" Talister rushed over from his conversation with the Chancellor.

"We—were briefing some of the refugees coming into the city—and one of them said she knew of a trap! Towers—in Creation, hundreds of them! Built by the Dark One! They are waiting for the attack so they can activate them while our forces are in there!"

Mr. Sterling spun the young guard around, looking at him dead in the eyes. "Who told you this? How do you know?" Then, seeing Sam and the others still watching the scene, he pointed toward the door and mouthed the words, "Out, now," to them.

They hurried through the arches and through the open door, where the guards still faced forward, as though nothing had just happened. They jogged down the corridors toward the Center's exit, hearts still thumping from the commotion behind them. What was happening?

They slowed finally when they met the long line of weary refugees coming through the Center doors. They appeared unkempt and thin as they made their way into a room off the main hallway where makeshift beds and living quarters were hastily being set up.

"Who are they?" Sam asked the other three, but they looked just as confused as he was. Two older ladies shuffled the refugees through the doors, where two more wearing healer robes directed them to their temporary spaces.

"I don't know. Maybe refugees from one of the villages?" Gus said.

The realization struck Sam immediately. Could these be the missing villagers from Clear Lake? He rushed over to the line and began searching their faces as they droned past.

No one stood out to him as someone that could be his mother. *I'm looking for someone that isn't even alive,* he thought, attempting to push all hope out of his mind. But he continued to search the tired faces, looking for a tiny glimmer of something he could recognize from any of the women passing by.

When the last refugee filed past, he turned back toward the others.

Sadness filled Emma's eyes as they walked out into the night, but she refrained from attempting to console him.

Sam could feel the hurt she had for him, and it touched him. He took her hand, gripping it tightly as they walked back to the cabin.

The night air was cool, and it felt good on his face. The city was quiet as they walked in silence, the moon overhead giving them enough light to follow the pathway through the trees.

As they breeched the crest of the hill, however, a figure came rushing out to them in the darkness. Mrs. Sterling's face appeared in the moonlight, her eyes filled with wonder.

"You have to go back, Samuel. Jack just sent word he needs to see you immediately," she puffed.

"Mom, can we go with him?" Emma blurted.

She glanced quickly at her daughter. "Of course, of course, get going," she told her.

Turning, the four sprinted down the pathway back toward town, through the trees, past the red hall street, until they had reached the Center entrance once more. Talister, Amos, and Mr. Sterling met them just inside.

"Come with me, Samuel," Mr. Sterling said quickly. "This way."

He led them down the hallway and into a smaller room that was connected to the large one housing the refugees. "Through here."

He then pointed them to a set of comfortable looking chairs in an office where extraordinary paintings of the Lior mountains were mounted on the wall.

A woman sat in one of the chairs. Her back was to Sam, but immediately he could tell she was the perfect age. Turning, she stood and faced him, tears streaming down her cheeks. She had long amber hair, soft skin that retained the slightest bit of weathered toughness, and blue eyes, almost identical to Sam's. She was truly beautiful.

Something within him burst, and a well of tears poured out uncontrollably. His mother was standing right in front of him. Of this, he had no doubt.

She ran to him, clutching her son in her arms. He buried his head in her chest, sobbing. She, too, wept as she held her son.

Amos, who had been weeping openly, joined them finally, and all three held each other tightly.

What seemed like hours ticked by, but no one cared as they watched the miraculous scene unfold before them. Three generations reunited after fifteen long years.

When they did finally separate, Mr. Sterling took the moment to brief them all of what had occurred during the attack by the Light forces in Creation. Sam's mother stood near Mr. Sterling, as to give him support as he relayed the story.

He, too, fought back the tears. "We have lost all the forces we sent through the gate. The Dark One had it planned all along, and knew exactly where to strike," he told them. "A precision plan, put in place centuries before any of us were ever born."

"More towers?" Gus asked hesitantly.

Mr. Sterling nodded. There was an edge to his tone now. "Hundreds, built all over the world, and designed for one thing only—to destroy all celestial Light followers within Creation."

"They're dead?" Emma shouted. "All of them?"

He nodded, looking at the floor. "At my command, yes."

Emma hugged her father's arm. "Dad, you can't blame yourself for this."

He smiled sadly, his eyes filling with tears as his daughter's concern washed over him. "I wish I could rid that from my mind, darling. But I'm afraid it's something I will always have to live with."

Sam shook his head. "I can't believe this happened. *How?* I mean."

"One of our Sons of Light made it back through before they took the gate. The gathering in South America was the central tower, the one the Dark One used to activate all the others. Using the second Star."

"When activated, it caused a chain reaction throughout Creation. It couldn't have been anticipated," Amos said gruffly as he wiped the

tears from his eyes. Sam could see he was fighting back the anger as well.

Suddenly Sam thought of the Star he had found in Warm Springs—how it had been lifeless until the Dark One's arrival. Then he thought of the one Boggle gave him, and how its Light grew to incredible intensity during the battle, then faded back to what it had been before. To his knowledge, it still glowed softly in his pack in the cabin.

"Both Stars were real," he said.

"Yes," Mr. Sterling acknowledged.

Gus curled his eyebrows up in confusion. "The Dark One's Star didn't glow until he showed up in the battle," he said, working through his thoughts out loud. "But the Star Sam has now—the Creator's Star—was glowing all the time."

"Dimly," Lillia added.

"Until—" Gus began.

Until... Sam thought. It was Star that had called him back from the Darkness. The Creator's Star. The one that Lillia had spoken to him through. The one that had saved him from submitting to the Dark One. It had shone the brightest when the Watchers arrived. When *Nuriel* arrived.

It couldn't be.

"Is Nuriel..." Lillia began, pausing suddenly in awe, "the Creator?"

****

At that moment, a full faced Protector burst through the door of the office, a look of bewilderment on his face. "Sir, you are never going to believe this."

Jack faced the Protector, wiping the remaining tears from his eyes. "What is it now, Leib?"

"Sir, there's another one claiming refugee status outside the gate."

He looked at his subordinate, perplexed that he would even be reporting this news to him. "Well, debrief him and bring him in to get settled."

# Chapter Twenty-Nine

"Sir, you better handle the debriefing."

"Why?"

The Protector's eyes grew wide. "Because, sir, it is the Shadow Lord, Arazel. He is surrendering himself. He claims he knows how to stop the Dark One."

* * *

ABOUT THE AUTHOR

Troy Hooker is the author of the fiction series Descendants of Light, The Watcher Key and The Watcher Tower.

Troy lives in a snowy part of Michigan with his wife Stacy and a cat that stops by every now and again. He taught high school History and Spanish for nearly ten years before authoring his first book.

Wanderers at heart, he and Stacy make it a point as often as possible to get outdoors and travel in their second home, a twenty-five foot remodeled school bus that serves as a perfect place to make coffee and write.

If you would like to know when Troy's next book will be available to purchase, visit www.troyhooker.com to sign up to receive an email about the next release.

When I cried out for mercy, You gave it to me abundantly. When
I called for your guidance upon my wandering mind, You sent me
peace. When I turned away from You in anger, You reached out Your
hand gently and directed me back.

DESCENDANTS OF LIGHT

"A LITTLE LEWIS. A LITTLE TOLKIEN."

— JOSHUA DAVID —

"ONE OF THE FIRST BOOKS I'VE READ IN A LONG TIME THAT DOES JUSTICE TO THE GENRE OF CHRISTIAN FICTION.."

— ETHAN BAUMGARTNER —

News & Discounts

www.troyhooker.com